continued . . .

"Rich historical and cultural details mix with distinctive magics to create a charming tale, and an excellent first novel."
—*Locus*

"The mix of exotic setting and unique magic paints an incredible landscape. . . . A unique and whimsical novel that nonetheless has some serious things to say about the journey of self-discovery that occupies everybody. This novel ends all too soon."
—*The Davis Enterprise*

"Leah R. Cutter's debut novel soars like the magic creatures that fill its pages."
—*The Historical Novels Review*

"Leah R. Cutter has written a cutting-edge historical fantasy balanced between plenty of action, strong visualization of ancient China, and deep introspective pondering on the part of a delightful protagonist."
—BookBrowser

"This is a beautiful, delicate, intricate book, the words origami-folded into one of those flowers that just keeps opening and opening and revealing more of itself with each new day. . . . *Paper Mage* is the sort of book I can recommend to any fantasy lover without hesitation. . . . Leah Cutter's debut novel proves that she has what it takes to become a great new talent."
—The Green Man Review

THE
CAVES OF BUDA

LEAH R. CUTTER

A ROC BOOK

ROC
Published by New American Library, a division of
Penguin Group (USA) Inc., 375 Hudson Street,
New York, New York 10014, U.S.A.
Penguin Books Ltd, 80 Strand,
London WC2R 0RL, England
Penguin Books Australia Ltd, 250 Camberwell Road,
Camberwell, Victoria 3124, Australia
Penguin Books Canada Ltd, 10 Alcorn Avenue,
Toronto, Ontario, Canada M4V 3B2
Penguin Books (N.Z.) Ltd, Cnr Rosedale and Airborne Roads,
Albany, Auckland 1310, New Zealand

Penguin Books Ltd, Registered Offices:
80 Strand, London WC2R 0RL, England

First published by Roc, an imprint of New American Library,
a division of Penguin Group (USA) Inc.

First Printing, April 2004
10 9 8 7 6 5 4 3 2 1

To Maria, Janka, and Luca—
for showing me the true heart of the city

Acknowledgments

Many people helped with the specialized research I needed to create this book. Any mistakes that remain are despite their excellent help.

Sarah Fowler, for the Latin translation.

Jonathan Drnjevic, for information about Roman curse tablets, Budapest bridges, and good places to eat in Phoenix.

Weston Cutter Sr., for information about the game of bridge.

Diane Lockhart, for information about hospital procedure.

Chad Munn, for one of the best character critiques I've ever received.

Jessica "Ildiko" Castellanos, for all things Hungarian.

Cliff Winnig, for information about Hebrew and growing up Jewish.

Julie Michels, for love, support, and for being a fan.

Michael Brotherton, for encouragement and listening to "sound bites" ten thousand times.

Author's Notes

There is no Szarvas-hegy in Budapest. If it did exist, it would be near Látó-hegy, between Kecske-hegy and Nyéki-hegy.

While archaeologists have found Roman curse tablets in Óbuda, they have not found curse tablets in the Labyrinth.

Guide to Name Pronunciations

Name	Pronunciation
Laci	LAH-tsee
Bélusz	BAY-lus
Csoda szarvas	CHOH-dah SAR-vash
Zita	ZEE-tah
Judit	YU-deet
Ephraim	eh-FRY-eem
Ferenc	FAIR-ents
Margit	MAR-geet
János	YAH-nosh
Turul	TOO-rul
Lewy	LU-ee
Erzsébet	AIR-zjay-bet

Part I

Top Level, High Ground

Laci struggled to get away, but the thing holding him only squeezed his shoulder tighter. The creature brought up its other hand—mainly composed of yellowing bone—and clamped down on Laci's other shoulder. It shoved the boy against the wall of the cave, bruising his back, pinning him with unbreakable strength. He froze as the creature brought its head toward him. The scent of moldering cloth and spoiled earth, a graveyard smell, washed over him.

The small corner of Laci's mind still able to think noted that the thing in front of him used to be a man. The flesh of its face had rotted off. What skin persisted across its cheeks and forehead flapped loosely as it moved. Its nose had been eaten away, as had its lips. A decaying purple velvet cap covered its ears. Only its eyes remained alive, burning with a blue fanatical light, studying Laci with hunger.

"I used to be like you, once," it hissed through broken teeth.

Laci bit his tongue to hold back his scream. Screaming would only bring the Nazi soldiers, soldiers who would kill the Jewish families he'd stumbled across hiding down here in the caves. Or it might bring János—his best friend, also lost—who he fervently hoped had found his way out of the caves by now. Instead, Laci swung his head wildly from side to side, seeking a way to escape. The light from his dropped kerosene lantern only illuminated his feet. To his left lay sinister blackness. A firelike light spilled into the darkness to his right, flickering and reddish. Something waited for him there, sitting in that familiar light. He could feel its draw, like a relentless undercurrent. He pushed away from it, whatever that unknown was, pushing himself farther into the grasp of the thing holding him.

Surprisingly, the hand holding his left shoulder released its grip. Laci looked up. The thing was slowly reaching for him, hand outstretched. The boy hit his head on the rock, straining to get away. He flinched when gentle, cool fingers stroked his cheek. Fear of this unexpected kindness froze him in place.

"Magician."

The word buzzed through Laci's bones, branding him. Fervent denials ran through his head. He only played at being a magician, pretending with his friend János. It wasn't real. *Magic* wasn't real.

The existence of the creature holding him proclaimed that it might be.

"Let me go," Laci whispered. If only he could get away. He would stop pretending to have power. He would never do another ritual, no matter how much János pleaded with him. He would forget all of Grandma Zita's stories. He would . . .

Flaring blue eyes caught Laci's attention. The creature grew unnaturally still. Laci wondered what the thing struggled against.

"I cannot." The light from the creature's eyes died down and it shook its head slowly. It brushed the back of its hand down Laci's arm to his wrist, which it then caught in a crushing grip. It forced the boy's arm up behind his back and pushed him down the passage, toward the unsteady light. The skeletal magician was stronger than the mere bones Laci saw. The cold of its hands ate into Laci's shoulder and arm.

Stumbling words accompanied their halting progress. "Must take you to see . . . Bélusz."

Laci remembered stories from Grandmother Zita about a five-eyed demon by that name, whose gaze turned people to stone. The boy struggled to get away, kicking up and rocking from side to side. The thing yanked on Laci's arm, pulling it higher, as if to break it. It pushed him forward, as relentless as fate.

The passage on Laci's right opened up to a large chamber. Three huge bonfires lit the space, as well as candles held up by their own wax on leveled-off stalagmites. Half whispers mingled with the crackling sounds, as if water surged nearby. The intense heat caused sweat to trickle down Laci's face. Green, not black, smoke rose to the ceiling and dissipated. Broken pieces of stone statues—heads, legs, torsos—lay scattered across the floor. Above the cavern was a long open space—a dry gallery. A large eagle with ill-kept feathers roosted there.

Movement drew Laci's gaze. There were—things— in the chamber. Only his special sight, the one Grandmother Zita had taught him to use, allowed him see them. More corrupted men, like the one that kept him moving forward, blended into the shadows, pressing against jutting rock walls. Others, gliding in and out of the flickering light, seemed to be combinations of men, beast, and plant; the beak of a raven implanted on a mottled green face, a frog man with a dripping tongue and webbed fingers, bilious sap dripping out of a treelike knot mouth. Rank body odor mingled with the scent of wet fur and sweet rotting vegetation.

Laci took shallow breaths, fighting to keep his fear from choking him. One of the creatures sidled up to them, a wolf with a man's body. Laci found himself instinctively pushing back against the thing that held him, as if it would protect him. Bared fangs drew closer. A snarl from the lupine face made the hairs on the back of Laci's neck stand up. The thing kept pace with them for a few steps, licking its elongated lips, gray feral eyes riveted on Laci's neck. Then it abruptly stalked off, melting into the darkness between the lights. Laci forced his eyes away, keeping himself from searching for it. Death could come from any of the half-seen creatures in the chamber.

With a shudder, he told himself that he would not die here. Grandmother Zita would be ashamed of him if they met in heaven because he'd died in this place. He closed his eyes in denial, then opened them again.

His breath caught at the huge stone carving of a stag now before him. Its beauty made Laci falter. The statue caused Laci to forget his situation, and for a moment, it gave him hope. Its neck curved with more grace than a hawk's flight. The twists of its antlers caught and held on to the light. Sightless eyes adorned its elongated head, and nostrils flared for unneeded breath far above Laci's head. Powerful hind muscles outlined in cool stone bulged, making it seem as if it were about to leap. Delicate front hooves stood amid the broken statuary and garbage of the cave floor, as if disdaining to touch the filth.

Laci continued to stare at the stag until he realized they'd stopped. Only then did Laci look up.

Corrupt, stained, and pitted stone made up the creature—Bélusz, Laci assumed. It was the antithesis of the unblemished stag. Bulges, like horns, poked out between the three craters spaced across the demon's forehead. Its eyes sat below this cliff, like dark pools of marsh water with slimy tops and hidden snakes. Its nose had been broken off, so just a concave impression was left. Craters pocked its cheeks. It smelled of guano, sulfur, and things long buried. The arms of the rock throne that held the demon had grooves in them, worn smooth by the creature running its fingers along them. The demon's feet and legs looked like they'd grown from the earth.

"Another?" Bélusz asked in a voice that rolled effortlessly through the chamber, velvet soft and compelling. It leaned forward toward Laci, the mobile stone of its lips twisted in a sneer.

Laci's mouth dried with fright. The pit of his stomach dropped. Had this demon captured János as well?

"My great bringer," Bélusz said, its voice like silk caressing stone. "You broke the first of the five Roman plaques holding me. Then you brought me the miraculous stag, the guardian angel of your nation, just so I could turn it to stone. The bird followed, but it couldn't resist my powers either."

A shiver ran down Laci's spine. The statue. It must be the *csoda szarvas*, the mythical stag who'd led the seven tribes into Hungary. His country's protector. And the eagle in the dry gallery above the cavern must be Turul.

"You've brought me two of the remaining plaques. Now you've brought me this sweet boy who stinks so strongly of magic." It shook its head, as if in denial. "Two magicians. In one night. My freedom must be near! Ah, to feel the sun and be truly warm again!" Bélusz held up its arms as if receiving blessings from heaven. Laci winced as the other creatures in the chamber howled together. He looked around the room fearfully, searching for his friend János. All he saw were demons and gathering shadows disrupted by the bright bonfires.

Bélusz was staring at Laci when he brought his gaze back. The kindness the boy saw on the demon's face froze his soul. Threats and anger suited that face. Benevolence somehow made it more ugly, unnatural, and frightening.

"Now *you* will be my servant. You have the sight. You will find the last two plaques that bind me. You will be greatly rewarded."

Laci knew the only reward he'd receive at Bélusz' hands would be death. "No," he said, surprised he could speak at all through his choking fear.

"You see what happens to those who disobey me," Bélusz said, indicating the floor of the cave, the broken statuary. "They spilled dust like blood, their cracking bones the only screams they could make. Can make."

Laci shivered at the implication. Had all the ruined figures been men, turned to stone, and smashed? Were they still alive? He shook his head.

"You will help me," Bélusz continued. "You will free me from the dark, help me destroy the land that has held me prisoner, pound the mountains into sand, turn the rivers red."

Laci tried to swallow past the sudden lump in his throat. The war—the Great War, as the Americans called it, or the Great Catastrophe, as he personally knew it—had been raging for the last four years, a lifetime for a fourteen-year-old boy. He'd seen bodies in the streets, torn apart by shrapnel, buildings crumbling from the bombs. He knew the hunger of not enough food, no place to play, no room for dreams. The horror of greater destruction than what he'd already experienced made him nauseous.

"I'll kill myself first," Laci heard himself say. And he'd spoken the truth. He had so little to live for. The war had destroyed or ruined everything he'd known. His father had been killed in the first weeks of battle; his carefree mother had disappeared under the worry and strain of moving in with their relatives; his books, toys, clothes—even his favorite foods—all unavailable, either sold or stolen by his uncle, or denied them because of their poverty.

Something in Laci's tone must have convinced the demon that the boy didn't spin tales. Its animation gave way to stillness. Laci could almost believe it was a statue.

Bélusz nodded its head after a moment and said, "A sightless magician still has its uses." It beckoned for the creature holding Laci to bring him closer.

Laci struggled to break free. The ancient magician behind him had too tight a grip on his arms. When Laci dug in his heels, the thing merely picked him up and presented him, legs dangling, to the demon.

Bélusz put its finger on its lips. Its tongue rasped across its finger as it licked it. Then, with the very tip, it touched the center of Laci's forehead.

The acid spittle burned Laci's skin and sent waves of pain through his head, worse than anything he'd ever felt. Laci screamed and shut his eyes. The thing holding him dumped him on the floor. Laci slumped, crying. He brought his hands up to cover his wound, as if hiding it might ease the ache.

Bélusz waited until Laci only whimpered, then

spoke the words of its intended curse. "Your death belongs to me."

Laci didn't pass out, though the agony impaled him, causing the world to spin around him. He opened his eyes only when he believed the throbbing wouldn't push them out of their sockets.

Gloom filled the cavern.

The demon had burned out Laci's special sight. He could no longer see the other creatures in the cave clearly. Only dancing silhouettes remained, suggestions of shapes, things that tugged at the corners of Laci's eyes.

That wasn't the worst of it though. Just as darkness threw its cloak around everything Laci looked at, it had reached inside him as well. Shadows lurked and bloomed there now. His soul felt heavier, as if Bélusz had wrapped it, too, with a layer of rock.

Bélusz had tied Laci to itself. Only it could kill him. And it would—it would turn him to stone and shatter him—even if he obeyed the demon's every wish.

Bélusz laughed. A spark of anger shot through Laci's consuming fear and he struggled to his feet. He wanted to hurt the demon, but could he, without his special sight? Bélusz didn't seem to think so. It sneered at Laci, then raised its arms, like a conductor, encouraging the creatures around it to convolutions and undulations. Even the thing that had caught him joined in the frenetic dance.

Grandmother Zita's spirit guided Laci then, almost as if he heard her words directing him what to do. He put his finger in his mouth, like a two-year old with a tough decision, touched his forehead where the skin still burned, then ran it under his eye, mixing his spit with blood and tears, a holy trinity.

Laci crept closer to the throne. The demon had turned its head away from the boy. Balancing on his toes, Laci reached up a steady hand and touched Bélusz in the center of its forehead, in the same place where the demon had marked him. Then Laci used the same words. "Your death belongs to me."

All the things in the cave roared. The howling and cacophony rang in Laci's ears, louder than any bombing.

It's difficult to tell when the frightful are frightened, but Laci saw it. The demon's eyes widened and its head pulled back, like a dog that had caught an unfamiliar, threatening scent. When Bélusz' eyes grew hard and glittery, Laci ran.

Laci thought perhaps that the ancient magician, the former man that had caught him earlier, helped Laci escape by blocking the others after the boy slid into a small tunnel just past where he'd been caught. Maybe it saw that its eternal mistake was ending.

Laci didn't know for sure. He just ran.

Chapter 1

Zita

"Grandpa?" Zita called as she pushed the door open. "Hello? Anyone home?" She stood at the threshold, listening. The constant wash of traffic from Sixth Street pushed at her, urging her forward. The silence and the smell emanating from the house held her back.

Zita took a deep breath. She told herself that the unlocked door didn't necessarily mean someone had broken into her grandfather's house. He usually didn't lock his door when he was home. They'd argued about it more than once, but her grandfather wouldn't believe any danger existed. Not here in America, he'd insisted. Not in Tucson, Arizona.

The stench worried Zita. The air smelled burnt and metallic; a hint of rotten-egg sulfur rolled under the odor, as well as things Zita couldn't identify. The scent seemed old, well-congealed, baked together. Pieces of it had been around for weeks. How could Grandpa have lived with it? Zita hadn't been in her grandfather's house for at least four months. Every time she'd suggested meeting there, he'd arranged that they meet somewhere else, as if he didn't want her in his home anymore. She'd assumed it was his way of showing disappointment at her continued involvement with Peter, her boyfriend.

Zita forced herself to walk into the house, breaking through the unseen barrier formed by the silence and the smell as easily as a child bursting a soap bubble. A yellow Post-it note on the closet to her left caught her attention. It listed words in Hungarian, her grandfather's mother tongue. She closed the door and locked it. A mass of Post-it notes hovered at eye level, written in English as well as Hungarian, listing things such as "shoes," "jacket," and "keys." What was Grandpa doing?

Zita walked into the living room. The clutter astounded her. The "Messy One" had always been *her* title. She'd never been able to clean to her family's satisfaction. Zita wished briefly for a camera to record the momentous event, to prove that even her perfect grandfather could trash a room.

The couch provided the only place to sit in the living room. Magazines lay strewn across the floor, along with unopened mail. Stacks of cans—fruit, soup, and vegetables—stood on the low table in front of the couch. Thick dust lay on the tops of half the cans. Piles of clothes and linens took up the rest of the available space. Post-it notes adorned every surface— on the lampshades of the two remaining lamps, on the magazines, on the wall next to the light switch.

Zita grew uneasy as the importance of what she saw sank in.

She made her way to the kitchen. A scorched black area covered the wall behind the stove. Had there been a fire? Why hadn't Grandpa told her about it? All the knobs from the stove were missing.

Zita's unease turned to fear. Slowly, she turned to the note-covered refrigerator. She didn't want to open it. She didn't want further confirmation of her grandfather's condition. She had the urge to go through the house like the proverbial "white tornado," cleaning everything in her path, removing the evidence of her grandfather's downfall. But she couldn't stop now.

Zita wrenched open the refrigerator door, searching for the strawberries. Her grandfather always had fresh ones on hand, in season and out, not because he liked them, but because they were Zita's favorite.

The berries had white beards around their edges.

Disappointment and resignation landed hard on

Zita's shoulders. Black fungus covered the peppers, mushrooms, and other vegetables. She didn't have to pick up the milk container to know it was rotten: she could smell it. Bright green algae floated in the glass orange juice container.

Zita closed the refrigerator door and leaned her forehead against it. She understood now. She'd thought her grandfather had become a little forgetful, not remembering to meet her and Peter for breakfast that day. She'd ignored the times when he'd ask the same question over and over again, not wanting to fight with him. Or she'd laughed with him when he'd accidentally swapped English and Hungarian words.

The condition of his house told her the real state of his mind. He was barely surviving.

And she hadn't seen it. She'd failed him, again, like she'd always feared she would. Like he'd told her she would when she'd flunked that semester of college. She had disappointed him again.

She *had* noticed little things, like the time he'd forgotten to wear socks with his shoes, or when he'd shaved only half his face. She hadn't linked them together though. Her grandfather had made a joke once about getting lost going to her apartment. Zita had been alarmed, but she'd allowed her mother, her grandfather's only child, to talk her into believing she'd overreacted.

Zita hoped her grandfather wasn't lost and wandering somewhere right now. No, he had to be here, in his house. She had to find him. She pressed her palms against her eyes, forcing the tears out and wiping them away.

"*Nagyapa*?" she called, using one of the few Hungarian words she knew, the word for grandfather. Maybe he'd respond to that. She tugged on her hair, smoothing it over her cheek, letting its softness soothe her. He had to be here.

Resolutely she pushed her hair behind her ear and rushed to the bathroom. There, she found blackened towels rotting in the corner, rows of unopened shampoo bottles, and a razor with two inches of duct tape wrapped around the handle.

She found more cans of food in his bedroom, clothes lying in heaps, no sheets on the bed, and the blankets, soiled.

"Grandpa?" she called again. She poked one of the piles of clothes with her toe, afraid he might be hiding under it. Momentarily relieved that it didn't move, she turned to leave the room. The sight of the top of the dresser stopped her.

No clutter existed there.

Taped to the wall above the dresser was a page torn from a magazine—a stylized graphic of a reindeer, white and silver on a dark blue background. Spiraling streaks shot out from the reindeer's antlers, around its body; then the tight lines fanned out, as if spreading magic. A single candle stood in the dust-free space underneath the picture, burnt down to a nub.

The disparity frightened Zita. Was Grandpa not only unable to care for himself, but delusional as well? She vaguely remembered something about a deer that was special to Hungarians. The stories had come from her namesake, her grandfather's maternal grandmother. He'd described her as a gypsy. Had she taught him to worship pagan things? Maybe the only clear memories he had now were from his childhood.

Zita walked back to the living room. Where was her grandfather?

Maybe he was out in the garden. Zita walked quickly through the kitchen, averting her eyes from the disarray, then out the back door.

"Grandpa?" she called, standing still for a moment as the warmth soaked into her skin. She didn't see him among the cactus and potted plants. "Grandpa?" she called again as she made her way along the winding path to the shed. She couldn't see any of the ruin in the backyard that she'd seen in the house. Then again, it would be hard to tell. Cactus wouldn't show much damage just through neglect. The native grasses looked a little brown, but that could have been because there hadn't been much rain that spring.

The smell of rotten eggs grew stronger outside, along with a coppery smell that seemed familiar. Zita stood still for a moment, trying to figure it out.

The red stains on the door to the garden shed told her what the scent was: blood.

Zita ran to the shed, not caring when a barrel cactus leaning toward the path scratched her leg. She wrenched open the door, ignoring the stickiness of the blood-covered handle.

The chaos inside stunned her. Everything in the shack had been broken or smashed. Rakes and shovels, their handles splintered, were scattered across the floor. Spades and trowels lay bent at odd angles. Shards of red clay flowerpots spread across the top of the workbench.

Her grandfather sat against the back wall, partially hidden by tree stakes and his wheelbarrow. Long gouges ran across his forehead and blood covered his face. His arms looked as scratched as if he'd embraced a cactus. A large gash in his neck bled slowly. Zita lowered the wheelbarrow and knocked away the stakes. Her grandfather didn't move at the clattering sound. She forced herself to reach out and touch his wrist, to feel for a pulse.

He was alive.

Zita shook her grandfather, called his name. She untied the silk scarf she wore around her neck and pressed it to his, staunching the flow of blood. She needed to call for help. But how? She didn't have a cell phone, and the phone in her grandfather's house didn't work. He'd told her he'd been fighting with the phone company about something and they'd cut his service off. She wondered now if in fact he'd forgotten to pay his bill.

Her grandfather moaned. His eyelids fluttered. She had to get help.

"*Nagyapa*. Grandpa. I'm going to call an ambulance. I'll be right back." Zita stroked her grandfather's white hair, the only part of his body she could reach without touching blood. She turned to go.

Her grandfather shot out his hand and gripped her arm, hard.

"Bélusz. *Ördögök. Támadás*—"

"Grandpa. In English. Please."

He blinked. He looked around the room, as if checking that they sat alone, then pulled Zita closer.

Zita tried not to recoil from his bloody face. The color of her grandfather's eyes was so black Zita couldn't distinguish the pupils from the irises. To Zita, his eyes had always seemed full of light. The light still dwelt there, even in that dusky garden shed, but it had changed from a springlike sunshine to a terrible, compelling glow.

"Bélusz. The demon. Its minions. Attacked me."

He had to be raving. Or maybe he wasn't fully conscious.

"I'd hoped Bélusz would just die when I died, Zita. But demons don't die. They have to be killed. I have to go kill it. Back to the caves, back to the dark. *Segíts meg Istenem.*" He sighed heavily and shook his head.

Her grandfather couldn't be sane anymore. What was she going to do? She didn't want to agitate him; he looked so weak and otherworldly with the blood dripping down his face, covering his pale skin.

"It's okay, Grandpa. It's going to be okay." Zita stroked his hand, forcing herself to ignore the stickiness. Maybe now her mother would believe that something was wrong.

Zita's grandfather closed his eyes and collapsed, like a balloon with all the air let out. Zita held his hand for a moment longer. She had to leave him, go call an ambulance.

She glanced down at the hand she held. A curled ball of something gray clung to one of her grandfather's nails.

Zita dropped his hand when she realized it was skin.

*   *   *

"Good afternoon," said a large, well-fed Indian man as he stepped into the hospital room. "I'm Dr. Shankar." Under his white doctor's coat he wore a wide tie with an abstract design done in black, brown and blue, like a bib that would hide any food he spilled.

Zita stood up and shook his proffered hand. "I'm Zita Gárdos." She paused and looked back at her grandfather sitting in his hospital bed. He crossed his arms over his chest and scowled. Awkwardly, Zita continued. "This is my grandfather, László Gárdos. Laci."

"I need to go home," Laci announced, not addressing the doctor, but staring straight ahead.

"Ah, Mr. Gardose," the doctor started, reading the name off the chart. He pronounced it the American way, with an "s" sound, instead of an "sh" sound, stressing the last syllable instead of the first.

"GAR-dosh," Zita said, correcting the doctor before Laci could.

"I'd like to ask you some questions," the doctor continued.

"I fell. I cut myself. I need to go home."

When the EMTs had arrived, Zita's grandfather had stopped his wild talk about demons attacking him and needing to go back to dark caves. Instead, he'd insisted he'd fallen in his gardening shack, that a hoe had cut his neck and a plank had knocked him unconscious.

"I see," Dr. Shankar said, looking back at his chart.

Zita walked over to the doctor. "Could I talk with you for a moment, privately?" she asked.

The doctor looked up, blinking. "Of course," he said, backing out into the hallway.

Zita didn't know how to start, how to tell the doctor of the horrible condition of her grandfather's house. That would mean admitting her own failure, how much she'd missed, how she hadn't paid close enough attention to his health. She needed confirmation before calling her mother though, or talking with Peter. Neither of them had believed her worries about her grandfather. Now . . .

Best to say the worst first, to get it over with, like ripping a bandage off a wound. Zita took a deep breath, then said rapidly, pushing the words out of her mouth. "I think my grandfather has Alzheimer's."

"Why do you think that?" Dr. Shankar asked, skeptical.

Zita fell quiet for a moment, still in shock from saying the word aloud. "Alzheimer's." It was worse than any of the creatures her grandfather had told her about as a child. Neither the village priest, nor the proper incantation, could drive it away. You couldn't trick it into hiding in the oven so you could burn it alive. Alzheimer's didn't go away. It only got worse. Zita didn't want to say anything more, to give the word more life.

However, she'd started down this path. She had to stay on it. She described how forgetful her grandfather had become, the notes in his house, how he'd gotten lost going to their apartment at least once, the times he'd forgotten the English words for "beef" and "table."

"We'll do some tests," the doctor said when Zita finished. "But I'm not convinced. You do know that the wounds across his forehead are self-inflicted, yes?"

Zita gulped. The edges of her vision grew dark. She didn't want to hear affirmation of that horror. She shuddered, remembering the small piece of skin under her grandfather's fingernail. It didn't make sense. Why would her grandfather hurt himself?

"When I first got there, Grandpa told me he'd been attacked. . . ." She didn't continue. She'd already betrayed him by talking about the conditions of his house. If he'd forgotten about the demons, so would she.

"Well, his neck wound probably isn't self-inflicted. He may have fallen on a hoe. Nevertheless, he gave himself those scratches on his forehead. I've never heard of an Alzheimer's patient deliberately hurting themselves."

"It might be something else?" Zita sagged against the wall. Alzheimer's threatened horrible years ahead, but at least she could learn about it. It flourished as a solid specter she could prepare for, fight against.

"I can't say for certain until we do more tests. Because some of his wounds are self-inflicted, we're required by law to hold him for at least seventy-two hours, possibly longer, and put him on a suicide watch. In addition, he's very dehydrated. Some of his recent confusion may be caused by that.

"Shall we?" Dr. Shankar continued, gesturing toward the door.

Zita nodded and walked in. She kept her head down, like a chastened schoolgirl, back from a talk with the principal. She positioned herself on one side of her grandfather's bed and took his hand. The doctor returned to the foot of the bed.

"Let's move on to those questions, okay?" the doctor said.

Her grandfather stared straight ahead, his lips tightened. Zita squeezed his hand, hard.

Laci sighed, then nodded, indicating he'd cooperate.

"What's your name?" Dr. Shankar asked.

"Gárdos László," Laci replied, in the Hungarian fashion, listing his last name first.

"What year were you born?" the doctor continued, taking no notice.

"1930."

"And that would make you . . . ?" Dr. Shankar paused.

"Seventy-four," Laci answered proudly.

"When did you come to this country?"

"In 1956." Now Laci looked down, away from the doctor, as if ashamed. Zita had seen her grandfather do this before. He considered the ones who had stayed and fought the Communists from the inside heroes, while he had run away, escaped to America.

"And how old is, ah, Zira?" the doctor asked, gesturing toward Zita.

Laci looked confused.

"Zita," Zita said.

"*Édes*?" Laci looked at Zita, asking for help.

Dr. Shankar shook his head, warning Zita not to say anything.

She shrugged, gritting her teeth together. She wanted to help, but she couldn't.

Laci laughed. "Even she doesn't know."

"What's today's date?" the doctor asked.

"*Péntek*," Laci said with certainty.

The doctor looked at Zita for confirmation.

Péntek meant Friday. She remembered the Hungarian word through association, because it sounded like "payday."

"*Szombat*," she said, Saturday. She remembered the funny sleeping bat her grandfather had drawn for her, a mnemonic to help her.

Her grandfather didn't acknowledge her correction.

"Can you start at twenty and count backward for me, by twos?" the doctor asked.

"Twenty," Laci started off, confident. He paused.

Zita willed her grandfather to say eighteen.

"Twenty-two." Laci paused again. "Nineteen. *Tizennégy*," he said, switching to Hungarian. "Two," he said, finishing.

Dr. Shankar's face didn't change expression.

Zita's stomach hollowed out.

"Can you tell me the names of the last four presidents?"

"Bush. That idiot. He doesn't understand what war is." Laci shook his head.

"And?" the doctor prompted.

Laci shivered, as if waking from a dream. He looked up at Zita. "Judit?" he asked. He patted her hand and said something in Hungarian.

Zita tried to pull away from her grandfather. He held on tightly, whispering. The husky, rough quality of his voice conveyed bleak despair, even though Zita couldn't understand a word he said.

"Grandfather. Grandpa. *Nagyapa!*"

Laci blinked several times. "You're not Judit," he said. "Where's Judit?"

Zita took a deep breath. She squeezed her grandfather's hand with one of hers, and with the other, wiped at the tears that her grandfather's plaintive tone had wrung from her. He sounded like a little boy lost in a frightening place. She'd never heard him like this before.

"Who's Judit?" Dr. Shankar asked.

"That's the name of my grandmother, his first wife," Zita answered. Her grandfather sat motionless now, looking down at his lap. Zita couldn't see his face, but she knew he cried. "The one killed by the Communists in fifty-six."

"Has your grandfather had many episodes like this? When he confuses the past with the present?"

Zita shook her head. She didn't trust her own voice.

Her grandfather looked up. "I need to go home."

Zita reached out and brushed his hair back. It was still wiry, full of life. "You've been sick, Grandpa. You need to stay here for a few days."

Laci opened his mouth, about to argue. Then he turned to the doctor and said, "Okay."

After a moment of silence, Dr. Shankar said, "I'll see you later this afternoon, Mr. Gárdos."

Laci didn't acknowledge the doctor's departure. He grabbed Zita's hand and pulled her down toward him. His breath had an old man's smell of sour medicine and coffee mixed with unbrushed teeth.

"I don't mean back to my house," he whispered urgently. "Budapest. I need to go home to Budapest. Back to the caves."

"Maybe this fall," Zita said. Would her grandfather still be alive by this fall? Or even know his own name? The horror of it astounded her. She pushed the thoughts down as quickly as they had risen. There had to be something she could do. She had to be able to make him better. Somehow.

"No. Now. I have to go to Budapest now."

"Why?"

"Demons don't die. They must be killed."

"Please, come in. Sit down," Dr. Shankar replied to Zita's knock. Early-morning sunlight streamed through the windows. Books lined all the walls. A batik print of a dancing man wearing an elephant's head hung next to the door.

The doctor sat behind a huge desk, wearing yet another in his vast array of abstract biblike ties. He'd worn a different one every day Zita had seen him as seventy-two hours stretched to five days. Two blood-red leather chairs with brass tacks along the edges awaited before the desk. Zita sat in the one closest to Dr. Shankar. A part of her ached, exhausted from the continual fighting dialogue she had with the doctor, discussing the complications of her grandfather's illness and arguing over possible treatments.

Zita had spent every minute of her spare time surfing the Internet, educating herself. She felt responsible. She was the only family member who lived in Tucson, so it fell to her to oversee his care.

She wished someone sat in the other chair, someone on her side. Maybe her mother, who'd finally acquiesced to come. But she wouldn't be there until Saturday, and it was only Thursday. Or maybe Peter. The audition he'd gone to might be important to him, but *this* took precedence with her.

"Ms. Gárdos." The doctor hesitated. Was his news so bad he couldn't say it?

"Your grandfather presents with inconsistent symptoms. We can't make a diagnosis that accounts for his behavior. All we can say for certain is that he has dementia of unknown causes."

"You have to give me more than that," Zita said.

"We really don't know," Dr. Shankar said.

"What might it be? Can't you tell me that? If you

don't know for certain, at least give me some possibilities. I promise, I won't sue. I just need to know what it could be."

The doctor sighed.

"You know I won't leave here until you give me some options," Zita warned.

Dr. Shankar nodded. Zita felt momentarily ashamed of how late she had kept the doctor two nights before, haranguing him about her grandfather.

The doctor looked at his hands for a moment, clasped together on his desk, before he spoke. "We've considered Dementia with Lewy bodies, but again, we don't know for sure. And we wouldn't know, not without an autopsy."

"Doesn't that usually manifest with Parkinson's?" Zita asked. She'd dismissed it as a possibility because of that.

"That's only one of the three main symptoms," Dr. Shankar said, smiling smugly.

"Okay," Zita said. Score one point for the doctor. "If I remember correctly," Zita continued, determined, "Dementia with Lewy bodies would account for the Alzheimerlike symptoms my grandfather shows, like his memory loss and his living in the past. And don't the Lewy bodies produce hallucinations as well?"

"We don't know the exact mechanism behind the hallucinations," Dr. Shankar said.

Zita only scored him half a point for the clarification.

"But essentially, you're correct," the doctor said. "Dementia with Lewy bodies might be the cause of your grandfather's demons."

"There are other things that might have caused his delusions, right?"

"Yes, however, another reason we considered Dementia with Lewy Bodies, or DLB, is because of the striking fluctuations in cognitive performance your grandfather displays. I'm sure you've noticed he has good days as well as bad days."

Zita nodded. The changing symptoms had made her attempts at diagnosing her grandfather difficult. As well as making it almost impossible to convince her mother of his predicament. Her grandfather talked coherently at times. They could discuss the unusual spring heat that year, how incompetent and disorganized her boss was, or the cactus blooming in the garden. Bad times came too, when he kept repeating conversations as if his short-term memory had shorted out, saying over and over again that he had to go kill the demon living in his childhood home of Budapest. Worse times came as well, when her grandfather sat as if in a stupor, dazed and inattentive.

Zita hadn't finished fighting with the doctor yet. "What about his attack?"

Dr. Shankar sighed. "That's another problem with declaring DLB as the only cause of your grandfather's illness. It doesn't explain his attack. Alzheimer's patients, as well as patients with DLB, don't hurt themselves. So we don't feel we can make a definitive diagnosis."

"What kind of medication can he take to reduce his symptoms?" Zita asked.

"We can treat the dementia, using something like haloperidol. The problem with these types of drugs is that they sometimes induce Parkinson's in patients with DLB. Something like sertindole may be safer. However, I must caution you, Ms. Gárdos. If your grandfather has DLB, there is no magic pill. Nothing is going to cure him."

"I can't accept that," Zita said. She looked up, startled. Had she really said that aloud?

"You must accept it. You won't be doing him any good if you won't recognize that he's ill. He can't live alone anymore. You do understand that, don't you?"

"Yes, but he'll be better once he's in a structured environment, won't he?"

"Structure may help lessen the bad times. It probably won't stop them. He needs help."

"I've arranged for a full-time caregiver," Zita said,

giving in. Of course, her grandfather's health insurance didn't cover it.

"Have you talked with your grandfather about giving you power of attorney, or legal guardianship?"

"He brought it up, actually." It had startled Zita. As much as she'd wanted to deny her grandfather's illness, at some level, they both knew he had diminished capabilities.

If only she could convince Peter, her mother, and herself, of how sick he really was.

"The doctor was just being melodramatic," Peter told Zita that afternoon when he heard the news of her grandfather's diagnosis.

Zita sat on their couch with her mouth open, shocked and hurt. "Haven't you been listening? Didn't you hear me talk about my grandfather's house? The rotten food, the stacks of unopened bills? He can't live on his own anymore."

"He isn't coming here to live with us," Peter said.

"Not if we stay in this dinky one bedroom apartment, no. But we've saved enough for a house. We could just get a bigger one, with an extra bedroom."

"That's not what we planned," Peter said. "We don't want to buy a house here. What about L.A.?"

Zita willed herself to ignore the petulant tone in Peter's voice. Sometimes Peter's intractability reminded her of a two-year-old, adamant about his way, his schemes.

At one point in her life, she'd needed his planning, like a young tree needs stakes to help it survive a winter storm.

Winter had passed some time before.

"And I suppose you expect me to take care of him?" Peter added.

"You could help out when you're between parts. Besides, Grandpa won't need that much taking care of. He *has* been living on his own. It's not like he's an invalid."

"Now, you mean. What happens when he gets worse? The doctor said he'd probably get worse."

Zita refrained from pointing out to Peter that he believed the doctor only when it was convenient for him.

"When he gets worse, we'll deal with it," she said. She got up off the couch and stalked into the kitchen. She wasn't hungry or thirsty, but she didn't want to continue this confrontation with Peter.

"*You* can deal with it. He's your grandfather. Besides, aren't you the one who always handles everything?" Peter said from behind her.

"What if I'm tired of being responsible for everything? Maybe you need to start dealing with things, be a grown-up for a change," Zita said. With a start, she realized what she'd said. Zita turned around, her hand over her mouth.

"You didn't mean that. You're just tired and stressed," Peter said, using his "father knows best" voice, his face a mask of sympathy.

"Don't 'act' with me, Peter," Zita said, her anger coming to the forefront, any apology she might have said forgotten. "Maybe I *am* stressed, but I still know when you're not being real. Don't play this 'understanding' role with me. If you're angry, say so."

Peter grinned at her. "See? You're so good for me. You keep me in touch with my real feelings. I'm so lucky I can depend on you. So is your grandfather."

Zita's spirits sagged. How do you "fix" something that the doctors wouldn't even diagnose? She turned back into the kitchen.

"I'm sure you'll have everything arranged by the time we move to L.A. You won't disappoint me," Peter continued.

Zita put her hands out on the counter and let her shoulders sag. Peter's words hit her like physical blows. He relied on her so much. Couldn't he see that she needed a little support in return? Why was it always up to her to make their relationship a success? As much as she'd hate to fail at anything, there were times when she felt it would be easier to be on her own than to stay with Peter.

Before she could stop them, the words popped out of her mouth. "Or maybe when the Big Break comes you could move to L.A. on your own."

The silence behind her grew long and brittle. She'd spoken the words. Zita's back grew stiff and rage flooded her sight, blocking out everything else. She shouldn't have said them—those hateful words that expressed what both of them had been thinking for a while now.

Not even her grandfather's demons could make her take them back.

"Whatever you decide," Peter said.

Zita heard Peter get up off the couch and leave the apartment, quietly closing and locking the door behind him.

Freedom. Zita tried to turn away from the forbidden thought. She closed her eyes and hugged herself. She should have argued with Peter, pointed out that when he was between parts he had time to look after her grandfather, and could do it now instead of that caretaker she'd hired. So they could keep saving money, or she could, for when they moved to L.A.

The little golden thread of freedom wove around her sense of imminent catastrophe, trying to squeeze the life out of it. She remembered the sense of liberation she'd felt when she'd first gone to college, away from her controlling mother, on her own for the first time. How she'd reveled in it.

How she'd gone crazy with it, and flunked out.

This time though, it could be different. Maybe she could make her own structures, live her own life. Maybe she could be free.

Later that evening, Zita sat with her grandfather in the hospital, stroking his hand with one of hers. With her other hand, she pulled her hair from behind her ear and rubbed it on her cheek. The softness comforted her. She wished she could bring it across her nose, like a veil, to block out the medicinal hospital smells. Or across her eyes. Or maybe her ears. To hide from her grandfather and his demands and crazy talk.

"The demon. Bélusz. It has to be killed. I have to kill it. Whether I want to or not."

"Shhh," Zita said, trying to calm her grandfather.

Jack, the patient in the other bed, spoke up. "Sounds like it's a good time to die," he said, rather jovially.

Zita controlled her urge to shudder. She knew Jack didn't mean anything by what he said. He seemed to be stuck with that one phrase. How other people said, "Oh," or "I see," Jack said, "Sounds like it's a good time to die."

It seemed ominous that the hospital had transferred him to her grandfather's room. The nurses had assured Zita of Jack's harmlessness. Still, he unnerved her. At least the doctors would release her grandfather on Friday, the next day.

Laci laughed at Jack's pronouncement. "Yes, Jack, it *is* a good time to die. But only if your death means something, eh? Only if the demon dies with you." Laci balled up his right hand into a fist, then hit his left palm with it, like a child planning the "big fight" in a Saturday morning cartoon.

Zita hated the times like this, when her grandfather obsessed over killing this Bélusz. She wanted her old grandfather back, the one who made clever word puns, who always had the appropriate Hungarian saying, who gave wonderful dinner parties out on his porch, evenings overflowing with good wine and witty conversation. Not this delusional, argumentative old man who insisted that demons had attacked him—and would soon find her. Or who cried like a baby, saying he didn't want to die.

"It will start another war. *Hazám.* My poor country. I have to stop it! I must go back to Budapest. I must kill Bélusz."

Zita sighed. She'd insisted on reading all the literature Dr. Shankar had given her about the various drug

treatments before she would allow the doctor to pre-
scribe anything. She refused to make a rushed, and
possibly dangerously incorrect, decision. But it meant
that her grandfather wouldn't receive anything for his
delusions until the next day. As he hadn't had an attack similar to the first, the doctor had agreed to
delay treatment.

Her grandfather hadn't been paying attention to
Zita all evening. Zita didn't think he knew she existed.
Instead, he'd kept up a running monologue about
going back to Budapest to the caves to kill this Bélusz.
Now he turned to Zita, eyes blazing.

He saw her again.

"You must promise me to stay here, in America.
You can't go to Budapest. You can't go to the caves.
Bélusz will find you. Or János. You have to keep away
from János. Even Peter would be better than János.
You must remain in this country. You'll be safer here.
Not safe. But safer."

"Okay, *Nagyapa*. I won't go to Budapest. Or the
caves," Zita said. Since finding her grandfather in the
shed, she'd had nightmares about cold, damp caves,
and being trapped in dark places with clawed things
scrabbling behind her. They kept getting closer.

Her assurance that she wouldn't go seemed to calm
her grandfather. He lay back on his pillows, a slight
smile on his face.

"Though Budapest is beautiful at this time of year,"
he said. "The air, coming from the Duna—Danube as
you call it in English—has a special glow to it in the
spring. It makes all the women prettier."

Zita smiled and sat back as well. Her old grandfather had come to the surface again. Age had never
diminished his vigor. The day nurse had told her he'd
been caught in a female patient's room earlier. The
nurse had thought her grandfather had been disori-
ented, wandering, and had threatened to put him in
restraints.

Zita knew that her grandfather might have been
confused, but another explanation could be offered as

well. Laci loved women. Though he'd never remarried after his second wife had died in the late eighties, there had always been one or more women around. Laci dated a lot.

The door to the hospital room opened. A nurse and an aide entered, rolling a cart between them. Zita tried not to show the relief she felt. She could leave after Grandpa finished dinner. Though Zita loved spending time with her grandfather, it was hard to see him this way. But she considered it her duty to visit him every day after work. Sometimes though, it felt like she'd taken on a second full-time job.

"This nurse. Nurse Flying Owl. She's evil, you know," Laci said in a whisper loud enough for everyone in the room to hear.

Zita looked away from her grandfather. She knew she shouldn't feel embarrassed. On bad days, like today, her grandfather couldn't be held responsible for what he said. Shame still burned across her cheeks.

The aide placed Laci's dinner tray on his lap stand and poured him a glass of water. Nurse Flying Owl put a small paper cup holding pills on Laci's tray.

"Make sure he takes them," the nurse said, her voice breathless and deep, like Lauren Bacall with a cold.

Zita forced herself to look up. Nurse Flying Owl stared back with a flat glare. Her eyes reminded Zita of a stuffed rattlesnake she'd seen at the International Wildlife Museum, with inanimate glass eyes that had followed her as she'd walked past the case.

The nurse turned away and went to the other bed in the room. Laci took a sip of water and continued in his loud whisper.

"Owls are evil. They attack the Tree of Life and steal the unborn souls who nest there. They also steal the souls of children. Turul the great eagle used to protect them. . . ."

Laci's voice faded as Nurse Flying Owl walked past, going toward the door, staring at Laci. Her face was round and smooth, like a honeydew melon. Her nose

looked as though it had melted across her cheeks.
Only her eyes broke the solid plane, sunk deep in
their sockets, glittering like chunks of black ice.

Goose pimples broke out along Zita's forearms. She
shivered, blaming it on the air-conditioning.

"She's been sent here to watch me. She's not
human, you know. None of them are," Laci told Zita
after the door closed.

Zita couldn't stay silent any longer. "Grandpa, you
know better. Native Americans are just as human as
you and I."

Her grandfather looked at her, his dark brown eyes
open wide. Then he chuckled. "I'm not prejudiced.
My grandmother, your namesake, had gypsy blood. I
visited her farm, near Lake Balaton, every summer.
She taught me about herbs and told me about Turul
and the *csoda szarvas*. But the parents of the boy two
farmhouses away wouldn't let him come over because
everyone 'knew' gypsies stole children and sold them
into slavery."

He fell quiet while Zita thought for a moment. He
was right. She'd never heard him use a racial slur. A
diverse mix of people had attended all the parties at
his house.

The last time she'd seen them all together had been
at her grandmother's funeral. They'd tried to cheer
Zita up. They'd failed, not for lack of trying, but because losing her grandmother had been only half her
problem. The other half had been seeing her grandfather as old for the first time. His wife's death had aged
him. His skin had suddenly sagged from his neck, his
arms had melted away to mere bone, and his hands
had metamorphosed into claws. It seemed like his hair
had gone white overnight.

Brushing aside her sad thoughts, Zita forced herself
back to the present. She should enjoy her grandfather's company while she could, even if he lived in a
delusional world.

"When I came to this country in 1956," her grandfather continued, "people told me blacks were lazy,

Mexicans stole, and Indians drank. I knew they lied. People are people.

"But that nurse." Laci paused as he picked up his fork. "She's not human. She's sold her soul. A demon sits on her shoulder and directs her. I can see it." He pointed to the scar between his eyes with his other hand.

Zita sighed and leaned back, away from her grandfather, pressing herself against the cold plastic of her chair. Bright red lines ran parallel to the wrinkles across his broad forehead. He'd even broken the skin of the teardrop scar sitting between his bushy eyebrows.

"I've never told you how I got this, have I?" Laci asked Zita, his tone challenging as he pointed to his scar.

"It was an accident, remember? You walked into a door gate that had been pulled down halfway," Zita said, trying to keep her grandfather in the real world. She didn't want to hear about the demon that had burned his "eye" shut with acid. She didn't want to hear about the caves again.

"That's not what really happened." Laci speared some of the green beans on his plate, put them into his mouth, chewed, then puckered his mouth as if he'd tasted something sour. "Americans have a machine for everything. Even taking the taste out of food."

Zita couldn't keep herself from smiling, leaning forward, and patting Laci's arm. She also bit the inside of her lower lip to keep herself from crying. Every once in a while her grandfather sounded like his old self. It made her hurt as much as if demons had crawled inside of her and torn chunks out of her soul.

"Bélusz closed my eye so I couldn't see, or follow its minions. The demon cursed my death, you know. Only it can kill me," Laci added in a conversational tone.

Zita wished she could shut her ears as easily as she shut her eyes. She'd thought her grandfather had cycled into a good phase. She'd been wrong.

"I cursed it too," Laci continued. "Our deaths are tied together." He paused and sighed. "*Édes*, I don't want to die." He looked down at his lap.

Her grandfather's words rained down on Zita's heart, stinging like ice pellets. The conflict in her grandfather paralleled his confusion.

Before Zita could think of anything to say to console him, her grandfather said, "This is why I have to go to Budapest," harping back to an earlier portion of his monologue. "I *must* go back. Demons don't die," he said, looking at her as if he wanted her to complete the litany.

"I know Grandpa. I know. They have to be killed."

Her grandfather beamed at her, like a teacher with his star pupil. "Exactly! So I must go to Budapest. Back to the caves. That's where it lives, you know."

Zita had heard bits and pieces of the story all week: how her grandfather and his best friend, János, had found the cave, then dared each other to explore it. How this horrible creature, an ancient alchemist, had captured her grandfather and brought him to its master, Bélusz. How János had been corrupted. Her grandfather had repeated these parts of the story in different order all week.

One night, he'd told a different version of the story, starting with him finding a Jewish family hiding in the cave. Zita wondered if her grandfather had made up the whole story about the demons to cover his guilt of leading soldiers to these families and accidentally killing them.

"Maybe we'll go in the fall," Zita said, trying not to disagree with her grandfather, like Dr. Shankar had advised.

"I'll be dead by fall, *édes*."

"No, you won't," Zita said fiercely.

He gently continued. "I have to go back to Budapest now. To make my death count for something."

"You're not going to die," Zita proclaimed.

"Everything dies. It isn't natural to go on century after century. Like I will, with this curse."

"Not yet. You don't have to die yet." Zita knew she sounded like a two-year-old proclaiming that she didn't feel tired when everyone knew she needed a nap. She didn't care. She wasn't ready to lose her grandfather. Not now. Not ever. She was willing to believe his outlandish claim that he'd live forever.

"*Édes*. You don't have to worry about me. I won't fail when I die. I'll get it right. I promise."

Zita flinched. She reminded herself that according to the Alzheimer's literature she'd read, her grandfather couldn't be manipulative. He said what came to his mind. He didn't mean to taunt her about her failures.

He'd never understood why she'd dropped out of college for a while. Zita had come down with mononucleosis. Her friend Susan had given it to her. Zita had kissed her as part of a dare, after a night of too much partying. It hadn't been that long—or even that good—of a kiss. But it had been enough.

She'd flunked out that semester. The administration had been understanding, more so than her grandfather, and had let her apply again in the fall. She'd spent the rest of her life proving she'd changed, that she'd gone from being a pampered, self-centered party girl to almost an ascetic. But a rift had been driven between her and her grandfather, an unbreachable chasm of failure and disappointment.

"Everything's going to be okay," Zita said, picking up her grandfather's tray and placing it at the foot of his bed. "You have to rest now, Grandpa."

"*Jó éjszakát*," he said, beginning their evening ritual.

"*Szép álmokat*," Zita replied. Good night. Sweet dreams.

"*Nékid is*." You too.

Zita patted her grandfather's hand one last time. She told herself she didn't need to worry about the future. She should just enjoy the time she had with her grandfather now, before he died.

Because he'd die if he went back to Budapest. She didn't know how she knew, but she did.

Chapter 2

Ephraim

Ephraim circled through the parking lot in disbelief. Not only did a large white van squat in *his* spot, a second van had pulled up perpendicular to the first, blocking the next three spaces.

Ephraim had parked in the exact same location every day for the last three and a half years. What was he supposed to do today? He had a compelling desire to ram the offending vehicle, push it out of his spot, through the fence, and into the dry wash behind it, where water ran the few times a year that it rained in Tucson.

To be fair, TransWare Group didn't assign spaces in the parking lot. Ephraim just always used the same one. He'd also complained enough, and had "accidentally" sent enough company-wide e-mails that no one except Ephraim ever parked there.

Ephraim's parking place sat in the last row. Nothing marked the area as desirable: it required a long walk to the building; the wash ran behind it, and in case of a flood, it would be the first to be filled with water; the trees growing in the wash gave no shade in the morning.

Yet starting in the heat of the day and going on toward evening, shade did reach that section of the lot, and that made it desirable for Ephraim. The shade couldn't cool off his car: the overpowering Tucson sun ensured that only parking in an air-conditioned garage would do that. For Ephraim, he merely required that his steering wheel and gearshift weren't too hot to touch. In addition, parking in the shade meant his upholstery wouldn't fade. It stayed the same—how Ephraim liked things to be.

Ephraim drove past his rightful spot again. A small shield marked the doors of one of the vans, a security company. Maybe some bigwigs had stopped by for a tour. He sighed heavily. More disruptions. Ephraim parked in the next to the last row, in the same place he usually parked, just one row up. He knew the shade wouldn't touch his car, that by the afternoon, it would be steaming. He couldn't do anything about it. Spring had been unseasonably warm that year.

As Ephraim locked his door, a prickly feeling ran down his spine. He shivered, trying to throw off the bad feeling. There wasn't anything wrong. It was just a security company, just a change in his routine. He fought down the urge to bring his hands together in a circling gesture, a protection ritual. He refused to make such obvious motions where someone might see him. Besides, nothing existed here that he really needed protection from, right?

He still felt unsettled. Ephraim looked toward his office building, then back toward the white van. He wanted his spot. Maybe, maybe, if he walked back to where he usually parked, *then* went to his office, it would be as if he'd parked there. . . .

He turned and walked toward the van, moving slowly, like a sleepwalker. He got halfway between the rows of parked cars before he stopped himself. He stood motionless for a moment, teeth and fists clenched.

Ephraim would admit to being obsessive about certain things, like his routine, his rituals. He was *not* going to be crazy about them though. Walking to the parking place he considered "his," then back to the office, wasn't just eccentric. It was nuts. Shame flooded through him, as well as revulsion. How could he have let himself get this bad? No wonder Janet was no longer his wife, but his ex-wife.

"You're going insane," Ephraim told himself as he

forced himself to turn around and walk to his building, his gut churning.

"Good morning, Linda," Ephraim said as he walked in the door.

The cute receptionist smiled at him. "Good morning. How are you?"

Ephraim stopped at her desk. "Someone's parked in my spot," he said, the disgust making his voice sound harsh even to his ears.

"Oh, Ephraim, I'm sorry." She hesitated.

"What is it?" he asked. She obviously wanted to say something.

She smiled brightly at him. "Nothing. Did you have a good night last night? Do anything exciting?"

Ephraim chuckled. Everything had been working last night. In one hand, three passes had been made to him, and he'd had eleven and bid. He'd made three no trump with the five, six, and seven of hearts as his final tricks. It had been awesome. But he knew Linda wasn't a bridge player and wouldn't understand. Instead, he told her, "Nothing exciting. I hung out with some friends, played some bridge, drank, talked."

"Sounds like fun. Hey, maybe we could hang out sometime," she said.

Ephraim shrugged his shoulders, embarrassed. Linda had suggested such a thing before. He still didn't believe that a beautiful woman like her would be interested in a geeky guy like him, that she wasn't just being nice.

"Sure, sometime," he replied. An awkward pause came between them. "See you later," Ephraim finally said, tapping her desk with his right hand twice for luck—a hidden ritual that no one would question.

"See you," she said.

Ephraim walked away from her desk toward the bank of elevators. He looked around. No one else waited for a ride. He slowed as he passed the fire extinguisher hanging on the wall, snapped the fingers of his left hand, then pushed down with his palm.

The ritual worked. The far left elevator, the one Ephraim liked best, opened its doors for him. He breathed a sigh of relief. Maybe things would be okay.

Upstairs, Ephraim didn't hear the usual hallway chatter. He reminded himself that people were on their best behavior because of the visiting bigwigs. He didn't believe it though.

His fears were confirmed when he turned the corner and found Stu, his former boss, waiting for him in his cubicle. Though Stu had transferred recently to another department, he was supposedly still Ephraim's boss, as upper management hadn't found a replacement. However, Ephraim hadn't met with Stu once since the transfer.

"Mandatory department meeting. Conference room G-13. Do you always come in this late?"

Ephraim bristled. He bit down on his reply and merely nodded, afraid of what he might say. Ephraim prided himself on his schedule. He always came in at the same time, or within five minutes of the same time, depending on traffic. It was Stu who'd never bothered to learn Ephraim's routine. Ephraim wasn't a nine-to-five kind of guy. He would have preferred eleven to seven, but had compromised on nine thirty to five thirty, and generally stayed much later than that.

Ephraim stepped into his cubicle and picked up his coffee mug. He didn't care how important this meeting was. He was damned if he was going to it without coffee.

Stu stood arms akimbo, as if to physically block Ephraim's way.

Ephraim looked at his empty mug, then looked at Stu. He didn't know any ritual to bend another's will to his. He reached down with his right hand and tapped the top of his desk twice, for luck, as he had Linda's desk.

Stu hesitated a moment, then backed up one step.

Ephraim didn't allow himself a smirk. Though he would have a different boss eventually, his former manager could still make trouble for him at some unknown future date. To appease Stu, Ephraim told him as he passed, "I'll be there in a second."

Ephraim hurried down the hall toward the little kitchen. No one sat in their cubes. Management had already scooped up everyone in the R&D department. This relieved Ephraim. It was probably just a reorganization announcement. Ephraim didn't hurry, but he didn't dawdle either, after he poured his drink.

The air in the conference room was solid with tension and turned the coffee taste in Ephraim's mouth from comforting to sour. If he could have turned around and walked back out, he would have. He should be at his desk, checking his e-mail, preparing for the status meeting that afternoon, finishing his response to the strategy guy about the latest release of the software. What was everyone so nervous about? The room was set up lecture style, with all the chairs facing a podium. Ephraim took a seat by himself and looked around.

Only about half the people from his department were there, the half that did "pure" research, not the ones who specialized in applying that research to products. Before Ephraim could puzzle that out, he saw the Human Resources people sitting behind the podium. In his experience, all HR people were evil, trying to minimize salaries, pensions, and benefits, in order to save the company money. He stiffened his arms against the sudden desire to do a breaking-away ritual with his hands, a swinging motion up and down with one hand, then the other. Whatever news HR had, it wouldn't be good.

He wasn't mistaken in his opinion.

"As you know, TransWare Group has had some bad luck recently, between the downturn of the economy and losing our latest government contract. We've all had to tighten our belts. I'm afraid, though, we're going to have to do some more tightening. After long and hard deliberation, management has decided to focus on the revenue-generating portion of the R&D team, which means a reduction in force for the rest of it."

Slowly the information filtered in. Management would never use the word "layoff." It was up to them, the pure researchers, whose worth to the company could not be automatically added to the bottom line, to interpret the doublespeak. They'd all just lost their jobs.

Ephraim felt his heart jump into his throat. The shock literally astounded him. It was as bad as the time when, during a tournament, his partner had bid one, two, three, and four spades and he'd had none. Ephraim forced himself to lean back. This was what Linda had wanted to tell him about, but couldn't. This was what she'd been sorry about. If only she'd said something.

Ephraim felt his "game face" slip over his features. He couldn't think about the shock, how he was going to live, where he'd find another job. Not now. He had to be clever, live through the bidding and the play. He'd never be able to win, but he didn't have to be the dummy either, with no control over his hand. He folded his arms across his stomach and rubbed the long scar on the inside of his left forearm with his thumb.

Ephraim tuned the HR people out and looked around the room. Stu stood against the far wall, obviously monitoring the tensions in the room, preparing himself for fight or flight. Ephraim waited until Stu had turned his way, then raised his coffee mug in a toast.

Stu looked puzzled, then looked away, embarrassed. Ephraim smiled.

His former manager had left their group *before* the layoffs. Of course, Ephraim hadn't seen what it meant at the time. Janet had always told him he'd miss the nose on his face if someone else didn't point it out to him.

Ephraim tuned the HR people back in, not be-

lieving a word of their platitudes about what a good
severance package they were offering. Then they got
down to the gritty details. The HR people would meet
with each employee, calling them in alphabetical
order. After that, security would escort them back to
their desks, where they could pick up their personal
belongings.

Of course, they'd be watched to make sure they
didn't steal any office supplies or mess with the computers. Now, at least, he knew why that van had been
in his spot, far away from the building. Most people
hadn't seen them, and so weren't expecting anything.

A group of angry employees gathered in the center
of the conference room, discussing everything that was
wrong with TransWare, management, and the world.
Ephraim stayed where he was, on the sidelines. This
wasn't the time for general recriminations. None of
them had paid attention to the writing on the wall.
They should be angry with themselves, not management.

Ephraim rose when he heard his name called, his
heart pounding. This was it. The hand had been dealt.
Now came the bidding. He didn't know how many
tricks he could count. He had no trump. He still didn't
know how to give himself an advantage. He gave a
sad smile to poor Earl Zambrowski, sure to be the
last person in the room. Earl shrugged his shoulders
and smiled back, as if to show his fate didn't bother
him.

Julie, the HR person Ephraim mistrusted the most,
along with Stu, waited for him. Ephraim wrinkled his
nose when he walked in. Though only two meetings
had been held in the room before his, the air stank
of nervous sweat and stale promises. The urge to do
a protection ritual was so strong he had to pause for a
moment at the threshold, holding himself still, before
forcing himself to go into the room and sit at the table.

Julie started. "You're going to like the package we
have for you. With the kinds of offers I'm seeing, I'm
thinking of joining the reduction in force." She turned

and smiled at Stu, showing all her teeth, like a carnivore. Stu smiled back at Julie the same way.

Ephraim stayed silent. He wondered if Julie and Stu were seeing each other, if this was how Stu had had enough warning to leave their department before it sank.

"We're offering everyone one month's base salary, plus an additional week for every year the employee has been at TransWare Group. Of course, you'll be able to continue your medical benefits through COBRA."

Ephraim cleared his throat. This was happening too quickly. There had to be something he could say to slow the process down.

"How many people are you laying off?" Ephraim asked.

"We're not at liberty to say how large the reduction in force is," Julie said.

"Is it more than a hundred?" Ephraim asked, an idea tugging at the back of his brain. "I mean, aren't you supposed to give two weeks' notice if you're laying off more than fifty people?" Ephraim vaguely remembered that one of his college friends had sued her company because they hadn't given proper notice before their layoffs.

Julie and Stu exchanged a quick glance.

Maybe Ephraim had something.

Julie shuffled through the papers in front of her, then continued, "For those employees who have made significant contributions to the department, I'm authorized to increase the initial base from one month's salary to three months'. Stu has always spoken highly of you. You've been with the company for three and a half years—we'll round that up to four—which brings you to four months of compensation. What do you say?"

Ephraim had the feeling that if he pushed, he could get half a year's salary, maybe more. Was it worth it? Making threats about investigating the real law? Julie maintained her smile, trying to keep the bidding friendly. The hard points in Stu's eyes made Ephraim realize that to get anything more, he'd have to hire a lawyer.

Julie pushed the papers over to Ephraim's side of the desk. He started reading them carefully, just to piss off Stu and Julie, who obviously wanted the whole thing over with quickly. Besides, if he just scanned it, he'd only remember pieces of it, not the whole. Ephraim didn't have a photographic memory, but something akin to it: once he'd read through something slowly, he'd remember it.

Julie started talking about Ephraim's COBRA benefits, continuing his life insurance policy, and rolling over his 401K. Ephraim kept reading, listening with half an ear, until he heard her say, "Work will make you free."

Ephraim jerked out of the legalese in the papers he was reading. "What did you say?" he asked. His grandfather's voice, repeating that infamous phrase from Auschwitz, suddenly rang in his head.

"You can use the work referral program without any fee," Julie said.

"But you don't have to get another job right away," Stu countered. "Why don't you take some time off? Go travel. I just got back from this fabulous trip to Europe."

"Or go see some of the local sights," Julie chimed in. "Like the new caves, Kartchner Caverns."

"Or maybe go see some European caves," Ephraim added, trying to joke a little. An idea tugged at the back of his brain, something he couldn't quite articulate. Something about his grandfather.

"Exactly!" Julie said. "Now sign here."

"Hey, Ephraim," Linda said as Ephraim walked into the reception area, escorted by a slight but wiry security guard.

"Hey, Linda," Ephraim said. He stopped at her desk, the single box containing his belongings in his arms. He remembered that she'd asked about getting together sometime. Though that conversation had happened only a couple of hours ago, it could have been a few years.

"You have to keep moving, sir," said the security guard. He tugged on Ephraim's arm.

"I'm sorry," she said.

"Yeah, well, it happens," Ephraim said. "You, ah—"

"You must leave the premises," Ephraim's escort said, placing both hands on Ephraim's shoulders and pulling him back.

Ephraim tried to duck and twist away. He wanted to ask Linda for her phone number.

The guard reacted more quickly than Ephraim. He put one leg behind Ephraim's, then pushed slightly as Ephraim sank, effectively tripping him.

Ephraim stumbled and fell against the two large rent-a-cops that had come up behind him. They each grabbed one of his arms and hustled him toward the door.

As the men forced him to leave, Ephraim called over his shoulder to Linda, "See you around!"

Three of Ephraim's coworkers—David, Ty, and Janine—stood to one side of the door with several security guards standing shoulder to shoulder on the other, glaring at them. The men holding Ephraim walked him past the group to the first row of cars before they let him go. "You must leave the premises, sir," one said, indicating that Ephraim should keep walking. Ephraim looked back at his coworkers.

"Meet us at the Lazy B," David called.

"Maybe," Ephraim replied. Getting drunk might be a good thing to do, but privately, not in public. Besides, if he started drinking, he had no one to come pick him up. He didn't want to call his bridge buddies and face their derision and joking, or Janet and deal with either her pity or scorn.

He walked to his car. The white security vans still sat in *his* parking place. Though, strictly speaking, it wasn't his anymore. Ephraim could easily imagine a smug face in the wide-spaced headlights and extra bars on the grill of the van mocking him.

Ephraim had no spot, no place, nothing.

During the drive home, Ephraim pushed at the dark mood descending on him. He couldn't deflect it. Here he was, thirtysomething, divorced, no job, and few prospects. He already had three months of salary saved, and now he had his severance pay. His mortgage payments were low. He didn't pay alimony—he and Janet had never had any kids and she had her own income. His biggest expense was food. He didn't like to cook, so he ate out a lot.

What was he going to do? He was completely outside of his workday schedule now. He had no rituals, no patterns to follow. He couldn't even fall back on his weekend routine, because that usually involved going into the office. The only things waiting for him were an empty house, some video games, and a collection of porn movies. He hadn't dated since Janet left. He thought briefly of Linda, but knew he'd never be able to call her. Not after that debacle in the reception area with the security guards.

What was he going to do for the day? He could go grocery shopping. Maybe do some laundry. It was Thursday, close enough to the weekend. Then what was he going to do tomorrow, and the next day, and the day after that? Emptiness loomed ahead of Ephraim, as daunting as Sisyphus' boulder.

Maybe if he didn't have so much time on his hands, things would be better. Maybe he could kill this time with one blow. Maybe he didn't have to live without a routine, if he didn't have to, well, live. Maybe if he sped up, then swerved into the oncoming traffic. . . .

The honking horn of the car next to Ephraim startled him enough to make him jerk the steering wheel to the right, back into his own lane.

What had he been thinking? Was losing his job enough to make him kill himself? Did he despise himself that much? Could he not exist outside his daily drill? What kind of craziness was that? Ephraim might be obsessive about his habits, but he wasn't compulsive about them. He could give them up at anytime. *He* controlled *them*. They did not control him.

Yeah, and the first one is always free.

Ephraim slowed down and drove carefully, one lane at a time, to the shoulder. He pulled off and rested his forehead against the hard plastic of the steering wheel. He turned up the air-conditioning all the way and set the jets to blast cool air into his face. He gripped the steering wheel hard, wishing he had the strength to break it, grind it to dust in his palms.

Janet had always claimed he lived in a rut. She'd also told him that the only difference between it and a grave was that with a rut the ends were a bit farther out.

At least this was the first time he'd thought about killing himself.

As vivid as a movie, Ephraim suddenly remembered the previous Friday, when, along this exact same stretch of road, he'd also thought about driving into the oncoming traffic. He'd passed it off then as a strange fancy, something that everyone experienced, then had forgotten about it.

Ephraim let go of the steering wheel and slumped. Tears ran down his face. Other memories rose up, undeniable, like when he'd considered leaping off a cliff while on a hike, or jumping from the roof of his office building, or even bungling a bank robbery and being shot.

More suicide fantasies swarmed up. Ephraim looked at each, circled it clockwise like a round of bridge, then let it go, like a lost trick, a stack of cards he no longer needed. He wasn't going to hold on to any of them, or what they implied. He hadn't realized the depths of his self-loathing, his sense of worthlessness.

Ephraim sat back in his seat, staring up at the ceiling of his car. Shock made his breath come fast, like he'd been running. Ephraim consciously started breathing harder, pulling the air in through his mouth, then blowing it out his nose, like a bull.

He was damned if he was just going to roll over and take it.

He hadn't actively been trying to commit suicide. Now, there was no way in hell he'd do it passively. If he did, somehow, that would mean Janet had won. He still loved his ex, but he hated her as well. He was not going to let her be right.

Ephraim pulled back out into traffic and drove home, paying close attention to every car that passed him, every intersection, every potential danger. He was determined to break out of his routines. He wasn't sure how. The idea about the caves, and Europe, tugged at him again, but he couldn't afford to think about that now. He had to get home, safe, in one piece. He wasn't going to let his rut become his grave.

"Do you think she was just being nice," Ephraim said, concluding the tale of his conversation with Linda that morning, "or do you think she was actually interested?" He sat in front of his couch on the floor, resting his arms on his knees, holding his drink before him.

Toni, the only woman in Ephraim's bridge group, reached over and slapped his arm lightly. "You idiot. Of course she likes you. Sitting where she sits, she sees many men, no? She wouldn't say anything unless she was interested. Why wouldn't she like you? If I wasn't married, *I'd* probably like you."

Ephraim shot Toni a look of bemused confusion.

"You know what I mean," she said, waving her hand as if cleaning up her sentence. Though Toni had grown up in Italy, she spoke excellent English. However, when she drank even a little, mistakes crept into her conversation.

Ephraim chuckled, then took another drink from his rum and coke. He felt warm from head to toe. He couldn't believe his night. The whole gang had shown up without calling around five o'clock, explaining that information about the layoffs had made the news. They'd come bearing gifts of ribs, buffalo wings, pizza, and an assortment of alcohol, complete with mixers. They hadn't teased him about getting laid off. Instead, they'd just made themselves at home, serving Ephraim food, alcohol, and lots of laughs.

After they'd eaten, instead of playing bridge, they'd played silly card games, like Go Fish and Spike and Alice. It had been a great evening, full of easy banter and lighthearted competition. Ephraim's head was spinning, not just because of how much he'd had to drink, but because everything felt new and different. Most of his friends had left around ten because for them the next day was a workday. Just Toni had remained—she worked nights doing system maintenance on her company's computers—and didn't have to report in for another hour or so.

"What will you do now?" Toni asked.

"I don't know. I, uh, don't want to get another job, not right away." Ephraim wasn't going to tell anyone about his brush with suicide.

"Good. It's good you relax. Take a vacation. Go to Italy," Toni said, smiling broadly and gesturing with both hands.

"Maybe. I've never been to Europe." An idea niggled the back of Ephraim's brain again.

"See? It's all set. I'll call Mama. You stay with my brother. I have a cousin you might like."

Ephraim shook his head. "No thanks," he said. He didn't want to get embroiled in Toni's family. He'd been over to her house more than once while Toni had been on the phone with her mother. Even sitting outside in the backyard with her husband, he'd heard the shouting.

Toni pouted. "What's wrong with Italy? You speak good Spanish. You read Latin. Italian will be easy."

"Maybe I don't want easy," Ephraim said. He needed a change, something different. A half-remembered memory pulled at him. Something that Julie had said. Ephraim rubbed the scar on the inside of his left forearm, a mark he'd borne since he was twelve, when he'd lied to his grandfather and played hooky to go out bike riding, missing Hebrew lessons.

His grandfather. "Ferenc," Ephraim said. He stood up.

"What is a Ferenc?" Toni asked.

"That's the name of my grandfather—the one who taught me to play bridge."

"I remember now. The infamous Ferenc defense, right?" Toni said.

"He was born in Budapest, Hungary." Ephraim started pacing. "He emigrated from there—escaped—in 1944, when the fascists came to power and started enforcing the Nazi laws concerning the Jews."

"You've never told anyone this part of the story," Toni said.

"Hmmm," Ephraim said. He wasn't going to be distracted just then. He almost had it. He peered around the room, willing something there to inspire him. He turned away from Toni so she wouldn't see him ritualistically open and close his hands three times, as if drawing the idea to him.

When he looked up, he saw the darkened doorway to his den. An entrance to someplace else. The light on his computer monitor flashed once, twice.

That was it.

The words came slowly. "My grandfather. He told me stories. Stories of Nazis hunting Jews in Budapest. Stories of hiding in a cave—of gold left behind in the cave."

Toni asked, "What about these stories?"

Ephraim didn't reply. Instead, he walked from the living room to his study, flipped on the light, and sat down in front of his computer. He opened a browser and began an Internet search on "caves," "gold," and "Budapest."

Toni came up behind him and placed her hands on his shoulders. "What are you looking for?"

Ephraim half-turned in his seat. "My grandfather told me that some Jewish families, as they escaped from Budapest, hid in caves on the Buda side of the city. However, they didn't all make it. They left their gold behind. But they'd hidden it so well in the caves that the Nazis never found it."

"And what do you want to do?"

"Go find it," Ephraim said. The words sent a chill down his spine. It was like when he'd thought he'd overbid himself, then saw the dummy cards and knew that he'd won. The clarity rang through him, echoing like a silver bell.

Toni stared at him for a moment.

"What?" Ephraim said. He couldn't read her expression. Was that amusement? Wonder? Fear that he'd really lost it this time?

"You always"—Toni paused, as if searching for the perfect words—"follow the same path. Make the same bids. Your patterns are stronger than seasons. I could make a calendar based on what you do. This"—she paused again, waving one hand toward his computer—"is different. This is good." She placed her hands on either side of his face and kissed his forehead. "Keep going," she said. "I'll see myself out."

Ephraim sat for a moment. Toni was right. This was good. He had said he needed to break out of his routine. He was going to change. He was going to go to Budapest.

Ephraim surfed over to his favorite discount ticket broker. He wouldn't leave tomorrow, but the next day, Saturday.

He nearly got up and walked away when he discovered that a ticket would cost him two weeks' salary. Though he had four months of severance pay coming, as well as money saved, he couldn't spend it like that.

He forced himself to go to a different Web site and do something he'd never done before. He bid on a ticket. The anxiousness he felt nearly stopped him. He couldn't control the times he'd fly, the number of stops he'd make, what airlines he'd use, nothing. It scared him. After several deep breaths, he made himself go through with it.

They accepted his bid at once. Even with the taxes, the final price was about the same as a flight from Tucson to New York.

Ephraim sat back in his chair and gazed at his confirmation.

He'd just rocketed out of his rut.

He was going to Budapest, Hungary, for two weeks. He'd never done anything so rash. He found he was grinning so hard his cheeks hurt.

Ephraim's mother had always said, "*A Yiddish ashires iz vi a bintl shtrog*"—Jewish wealth is like a bundle of straw—meaning that it was easily broken apart and blown away. Ephraim didn't doubt it. Look what he'd just done.

She'd said it when she heard the stories her father told about the gold in the caves of Buda. He'd been so insistent that the gold was still there.

Which cave though? Ephraim dredged his memory, trying to remember the foreign Hungarian words. There was Látó-hegy—Lookout Hill. It wasn't the exact translation, but close enough. His grandfather's house had been in Pest, but they'd had picnics on Lookout Hill, which, as its name implied, overlooked all of Budapest.

Ephraim stopped himself, his fingers posed over the keyboard. Did doing research on the caves of Buda constitute too much planning?

He didn't think so. The task itself was improbable. He wasn't so much researching the caves themselves, as trying to figure out which one might have gold in it. Gold that no one had found for over fifty years. Ephraim grinned to himself, imagining a conversation with his ex-wife, telling her that no, he wasn't going to Budapest to visit family, but instead, to search for gold in the caves of Buda. It sounded impossible, crazy. It was out of character for him to do such a thing. Completely removed from his routine.

And that was the point, wasn't it?

Ephraim shook his head and sighed. He remembered reading somewhere that people didn't fight and die because of who they were, but rather because of who they defined themselves to be. A soldier threw himself on a live grenade because that's what brave men did. Ephraim had let his rut define him as a well-ordered, habit-driven guy, with ritualistic movements that brought only comfort.

No more.

After spending an hour hunched in front of his system, Ephraim rubbed his eyes, yawned, then stood up and stretched. He'd found many interesting facts that would be useful, later, if he remembered them. Right now, he needed sleep. He had things to do for his trip, like pack, change money, put his mail on hold, and so on. He refrained from making a list. Until the next morning, at any rate.

Ephraim forced himself to walk through the mess in his living room and not pick up a single thing. He wasn't going to spend the next hour cleaning. Everything didn't have to be put away, neat and tidy, as if he were expecting a surprise inspection. He made himself close his bedroom door and go straight to bed, head still spinning.

He dreamed of feeling parched as he ran an endless race in a dry wash, while riverbeds full of clear blue water lay on either side of him.

Chapter 3

Laci

L aci dreamed of demons.

The nightmare started as a simple dream, with Laci working in his garden, kneeling next to one of the big barrel cactuses, rounding out a hole for a new agave. The demons in his dream attacked him like they had the week before, starting as a swarm of gnats, brushing against his fingers, his neck, his bare legs, annoying him with their glancing contact. They buzzed his ears, distracting him. Then they started biting, one or two at first, then dozens. Laci couldn't brush them off; they crawled under his clothes, up his nose, into his eyes. He stood and did a crazed dance, waving his arms and legs, trying to shake off his unseen attackers.

The gnats withdrew for a moment. Laci's dream self knew without question that they were demons, and real. The previous week, when they'd actually attacked, he'd feared that he'd been hallucinating. He'd been so unsure of everything recently—what day of the week it was, how to get from his home to the store and back—that it didn't surprise him not to know the difference between reality and dreams.

The demons attacked again. Laci did, but did not, see them. They took the form of large transparent birds, as if made of plastic wrap, only with weight and sharp claws. Every once in a while he saw through to their real selves: the cracking leather wings; the sick, glowing yellow eyes; and the fanged teeth that grew beside their beaks. The creatures dove at Laci, scratching him as they flew past, smacking against his back, pushing him forward.

A cold dread filled Laci as he turned from one side to the other, unable to defend himself. What did the demons want? Were they minions of Bélusz? If so, then why was the monster attacking him now? What had changed?

Laci didn't know. He responded as he had the first time he'd met Bélusz. He tried to get away.

Laci threw his arms over his head and waved his hands to keep the birds from ripping out his hair or pecking at his skull as he raced to the garden shed. He spent a frantic moment trying to open the door, the handle made slippery from the blood on his palms. A demon rammed into him from behind, slamming him up against the door, forcing the air out of him. Laci got his left arm underneath himself and pushed back, fear lending him strength. When the creature flew off—claws scratching deeply into Laci's back—he wrenched the door open, then slammed it shut behind him.

As he locked it, something brushed up against him. Laci jumped and looked around.

Solid shadows stalked the room.

There was no other exit from the small shed.

The only weapon Laci could reach was a hoe. He grabbed it as the demons attacked. They came at him from all sides, pinching his arms, neck, thighs, whatever part they could reach. Nipping too, when they got a chance. The shadows melted away from his swinging hoe, pressing in on whatever side he wasn't defending. In desperation, Laci spun in a circle, his chosen weapon extended, driving the things back.

He couldn't spin forever.

Laci panted from his exertion. The demons hung back for a moment. Laci was puzzled at their behavior. Why hadn't the demons just killed him? Or did the curse still hold? Could he still die only at Bélusz' hand? It looked like these beings were just there to torture him. "What do you want?" Laci screamed at them.

The demons hissed in response as they surged forward.

A hand slapped Laci across his face. His head jerked to the side. A metal rake detached itself from the wall and threw itself against him while his head was turned, gashing his neck.

"Curse you!" Laci cried out. "I curse you. . . . Dissolve and dissipate . . . Powerless . . ." Laci desperately tried to remember the words Grandmother Zita had taught him as a child.

The demons laughed at him, a shifting sound, both deep and whispering.

Laci swung his hoe again. This time, an invisible force wrenched it from his hands. A loud crack marked its demise. The handles of the other shovels and hoes in the shack broke at the same time, a series of staccato bangs.

The demons continued to slap and prod and bite Laci.

How could he defend himself against things he couldn't see? He must see them to curse them, see them to battle with them. But Bélusz had burned out his special sight.

Laci reached one hand up to the teardrop scar in the center of his forehead. He jerked his hand away when he felt something move behind it. He forced his trembling fingers to return.

Something solid and hard lived behind the scar.

Something that wanted out.

Laci gently felt along the outside of the scar, noting the differences between the smooth wound and his wrinkled forehead. It occurred to him for the first time that it felt more like a patch than skin. Though he'd lived with his disfigurement for decades, he'd rarely touched it, afraid to reawaken the pain of the demon's influence, or sorrow over his lost abilities.

But the wound wasn't concave. Nothing had been taken out. It was convex, a lump. Maybe Bélusz hadn't removed Laci's special sight. Maybe he'd just closed Laci's eye, covered it over.

The attacking minions paused while Laci touched his forehead. As soon as he took his hand away, they came at him again.

Revulsion choked Laci. With perfect clarity, the kind that comes only in dreams, Laci knew exactly what the attacking demons—these minions of Bélusz—wanted. They wanted him to see again. *Bélusz* wanted him to see again.

The only way to do that would be to cut away the veil from his sight. With his own hands. Bile burned through his throat at the thought of purposefully injuring himself. The hand touching his forehead began to tremble. He didn't want to do this.

With a guttural cry, Laci flung out his fists, striking at the demons, failing to hit them. He continued punching the air, never connecting. He was panting, growing more tired. He had to do something to stop the attack, before the demons tried to open his eye for themselves.

With one fist still flailing, Laci reached up with his other hand and dug his nails into his temple, fighting his nausea. The pain halted his progress until a demon stomped on his foot. He had to go on. With a ragged scream, he dragged his hand across his forehead, tearing deep furrows and breaking the skin over his third eye. The pain, though severe, was less than the remembered pain of when Bélusz had touched him.

Laci pulled his hand away, shaken and sick to his stomach. The room slowly brightened, as if filled with the rising sun.

His special sight had returned. He *saw* his attackers. The demon in front of him was a toad man, with disjointed claws and a mouth large enough to swallow a head—whole. Next to him stood an owl woman, who was all eyes, beak, and silent killing.

Now Laci could attack. He felt like roaring his challenge to them. His fear and anger passed into cold deadliness. He struck out, his fist smashing into the toad man's nose. He followed it with an uppercut to the demon's jaw. Before he could kick out at the owl

woman, a rabbit man with flea-bitten ears and runny
eyes pushed Laci back and dumped the rest of the
equipment that had been hanging on the wall over
him. Then something hit Laci from behind, hard
enough for him to black out.

When Laci awoke, he was still in his dream. He
brushed away the hoes and gardening stakes, pushed
back the wheelbarrow, and stood up. His head felt
light, like it floated above his body, held on by just a
child's ribbon. In contrast, all his wounds stung. The
tips of his fingers on the hand he'd used to injure
himself burned, as if he'd dipped them in acid. He
stumbled out of the shed into his backyard.

The hole he'd been digging was now full. A
manikin-sized porcelain figure stood planted there,
buried up to midthigh.

Laci drew closer, fear pounding through him. This
was worse than the demons' attack. Worse than having
to tear his own skin. Worse, even, than knowing he
was going to die soon.

The figure was a replica of his granddaughter, Zita.

The artist who had created the sculpture had perfectly captured her flowing hair, full hips, and wom-
anly curves. Only one thing about the statue wasn't
identical to the original. An ocher eye burned the center of its forehead—the only thing moving in the entire garden.

Laci woke before the eye could catch him in its
terrible light.

He lay in bed, breathing fast, panic pulsing beneath
his skin, making his extremities tingle. He had to go.
Now. Why had he waited so long since the first attack?
Days had gone by. He was sure of it. And he'd sat in
the hospital, content to let doctors poke him and ask
him questions.

As Laci sat up, a hand touched his arm. He
jumped, startled.

"Going so soon?" asked a hushed voice.

The evening came flooding back to him. Laci had
asked Jack, his roommate, to sleep in his bed while

he came down to visit Edna. The night nurse on their floor was lazy and never came into the room to check both beds. Laci had thought about telling his granddaughter how poorly this hospital was run, but then decided against it. It was to his advantage that he had opportunities to slip away.

Like tonight.

"I have to get back," Laci said, leaning over and kissing Edna's forehead.

"It's only four in the morning," Edna said.

"I have to go." Laci pulled back the bedcovers with one hand and smoothed his hair with his other. He stretched as he stood, ignoring the creaks and pops his vertebrae made. He rolled his wrists, pushing strength into his body. Then he walked to the chair holding his clothes. He put on his shirt, the handmade white cotton button-down from the Jewish tailor down the street from his house. He was grateful to Zita for remembering it as his favorite and bringing it to him. He donned a pair of soft gray pants, black gentlemen's socks, loafers, and topped off his outfit with his herringbone tweed jacket.

"Aren't you afraid to go back to your room?" Edna asked.

"Why?" Laci asked, turning back slowly. Of course he was afraid to go back. Demons might be waiting for him.

"It's just that roommate of yours. He's so odd, always talking about wanting to die."

Laci chuckled, relieved that was all Edna was concerned about. "Jack's a good man. But he's in a lot of pain. He isn't afraid to die. By letting everyone know he's ready, he hopes he'll go sooner."

"Are you afraid to die?" Edna asked.

Laci came over and sat on her bed. "Yes. Yes I am." He paused. "I'm so scared, Edna." Scared to die. Scared to face Bélusz again. Scared to see János.

"It's impossible to swim against such a stream, yes?" Laci said, forcing a jovial tone into his voice. "*Falra hányt borsó*, like throwing peas against a wall."

"I suppose." Edna looked at Laci for a moment, then reached out and patted his shoulder.

"Good-bye Laci. Good luck," she said.

Laci covered her hand with his for a moment, pushing her warmth into him, letting himself rest for a moment. He longed to stay there, with her, to run away from the world, his responsibilities. But he had no choice. He picked her hand up, kissed the back of it, then went to the door and peeked through the glass. No one loitered outside the room. He quickly stepped into the hallway without looking back.

He had to leave. Fly back to Budapest that day.

Laci hesitated, then walked toward the stairwell. First he had to go back up to his room and get his credit card, his money, and his keys. He'd been worried about his money—had even accused the hospital of stealing it. He'd convinced one of the day nurses to let him see his wallet. She hadn't noticed when he'd removed a twenty-dollar bill and a credit card. He'd kept them hidden at the back of his closet. In addition, the staff had let him keep the keys to Zita's apartment, though they'd confiscated the ones to his own house.

The doctors would be releasing him soon. Zita had told him when, but he didn't remember. Margit, his daughter and only child, was coming as well, but again, he didn't know exactly when. Time had a fluidity now that made it difficult to grasp.

Laci couldn't risk waiting until he went home. Though it would be easier to leave from there, what if the demons attacked again? At least the first time he'd been alone. What if they assailed him while Margit or Zita were there? The demons would kill anyone who tried to help him. He shivered, remembering the vision from his dream of the corrupt statue of Zita. No. He had to leave now. He couldn't endanger them.

Rising terror made Laci pause for a moment. He forced himself to take a deep breath. It seemed that he felt panic, or something akin to it, at least once or twice a day. Maybe more often—he didn't remember.

Panic over not remembering a word, a face, a name. Panic when he got lost going from his room on the third floor of the hospital to the first. Panic, and a deep foreboding feeling, when he tried to think about his future. He couldn't remember as well as he once did. That's what happened when you got old. He hadn't expected the anxiety that went with it. After a few more deep breaths, Laci continued walking up the stairs.

Laci checked the hallway before he left the stairwell. The hallway stood empty, the lights lowered for the evening. Only the nurse's stand at the end of the hall still shone brightly.

He pushed the door to his room open just an inch, then stopped. Edna's salty scent, which had delighted him for most of the evening, was overpowered by the smell of singed hair, corrupt earth, and the coppery smell of blood. Laci looked up, suddenly aware of the bluish light spilling from the room.

Frozen, Laci stared for a moment. Then he pulled back and closed the door as slowly as he could, hoping the motion wouldn't catch the eye of the creatures surrounding his bed. He let go of the handle and peered through the window in the door.

Nurse Flying Owl stood at the head of the bed that Laci was supposed to be sleeping in. The demon who rode her had put its mask on her face, flattening her cheeks, making pits of her eyes, and lengthening her nose until it was beaklike and dripping. Her teeth shone, broken and sharp, in an overlarge mouth.

Other creatures paced at the edges of the bed, like wolves waiting for their turn to tear into fallen prey. In the dim light Laci could almost mistake them for doctors, their pale skin reminiscent of white coats. They laid hands on Jack, talked to each other in excited voices, then pressed two square irons on Jack's chest. Jack's body arched and jerked in response.

Laci saw through their disguises. They weren't helping Jack. The irons that hammered into his chest weren't for restarting his heart. They were killing him.

He recognized the toad man and the rabbit man from when they'd attacked him, but others had gathered there as well.

Laci couldn't just leave. He had to retrieve his credit card, his money. He couldn't go get any of the other nurses or doctors—they might be allied with the demons. Fear and indecision froze him in place. He hoped Jack was unconscious, knowing it was too much to ask that he be dead already. It was, indeed, a fine time to die.

The demons pounded the irons back onto Jack's chest, making his body wrench off the bed again. As they drew them up, the fount of Jack's life began to manifest. Again, they banged the irons down. The fountain grew, becoming distinct, until it rose a foot off of Jack's prone body.

Wonder at the fountain's beauty made Laci lean forward until his face pressed against the window. The carved white Italian marble surprised Laci. He'd thought of Jack as common—not coarse, but not re-fined either. The pure splashing water that flowed from Jack's life fountain didn't surprise Laci at all. He'd known his roommate was a good man.

The demons took turns sipping from the fountain, polluting the water with their filth, choking its flow until it slowed to a trickle, then stopped. Laci sagged back, away from the door, his forehead aching from being squashed so hard. Maybe now that Jack was dead, it was over. Laci whispered a prayer for him.

The demons didn't leave.

Nurse Flying Owl raised Jack's soul from his body until it floated above it, a warm golden figure, man shaped. Laci imagined he heard a soft sigh as Jack's soul shook itself free of its body. However, it couldn't escape. The demons flayed it with cruel curved knives and claws. They shred its fingers so it had nothing to hold on to as it moved from this life to the next. Then they disemboweled it and blinded it, desecrating its purity.

Laci realized his fists hurt from how tightly he

clenched them. He had to do something. He turned away from the door.

A dark shape flitted by. Laci turned back.

Turul the great eagle manifested, holding on to the rail at the foot of the bed and cawing loudly. Tears pooled at the corners of Laci's eyes at the sight of the magnificent animal in such poor health. What Bélusz had done to one of the symbols of his nation was ten thousand times worse than what the demons had done to Jack. Its wing feathers didn't lay in neat rows, but in the crooked lines of devils. Laci wondered how it was able to fly. Dirt and tidbits from its last meal clung to its breast. Two of the talons on its left foot had ragged edges.

The eagle cawed again and raised its foot. Loose and transparent, Jack's soul floated in front of Turul. It grasped the soul's chest with its talons. Jack's soul shrank to mouse size. For a horrible moment, Laci thought Turul would eat it. Instead, the eagle spread its wings and leapt into the air. It went around the room, counterclockwise, then flew into the far corner. Before it reached the walls, it disappeared.

Laci closed his eyes for a moment. He sent another prayer for Jack, hoping that maybe Turul would take his former roommate's soul to the Tree of Life where it could be reborn—afraid, instead, that the eagle would dutifully bring Jack to its current master, and he would dance forever in Bélusz' court.

The sound of soft chanting made Laci open his eyes. The demons had finished. He saw human forms more clearly now as they peeled gloves from their hands and surgical masks from their faces.

Laci backed up. They couldn't see him. They couldn't realize their mistake, that it hadn't been him in that bed. That they'd just killed his roommate, and not him. He had to run. Now.

But he still needed his credit card, his money, and Zita's keys. Or he wouldn't get very far. He had to get into his room. Laci looked up and down the hall. What could he do to distract the demons?

A red shape on the wall between his door and the next caught his eye. Laci ran to it and yanked down on the fire alarm with all his strength. He wished he could tear it from the wall. He should have found it sooner. Maybe he could have saved Jack.

Alarms sounded. Laci rushed into the stairwell. From there, he watched the doctors and nurses leave his room, wheeling the body between them. Patients came out from all their doors. Bright lights flooded the hallway.

Laci strode against the stream of people heading for the stairs as he walked to his room. The signs of the demons' work—rubber gloves, curled plastic tubing, empty hypodermic needles—littered the ground. Laci went over to the closet, reached into the back, and pulled his credit card and money from where it was wedged between the shelf and the rear wall. He also grabbed the keys.

Jack had died for him. Laci gulped hard, trying to swallow his guilt. Jack had been willing to die. Now it was Laci's turn.

He rushed out the door and joined the stragglers heading toward the stairwell.

As Laci walked out of the hospital, he thought he saw Nurse Flying Owl smiling at him. A terrifying idea came to him. Maybe she didn't think she'd killed Laci. Maybe that hadn't been the plan. Maybe she'd meant to kill Jack. To force Laci into action.

Laci slipped away from the milling group of patients as soon as he could. Since he was fully dressed, and they wore only hospital gowns, it was easy for him. He went around to the front of the hospital and got into one of the cabs waiting there.

"Where to?" the skinny taxi driver asked, adjusting the rearview mirror as Laci climbed in, slamming the door behind himself.

Laci felt like laughing. The answer was always the same. He had to go back to Budapest, whether he wanted to or not, to kill Bélusz.

Demons didn't die. They had to be killed.

                    *   *   *

Laci shifted the snapdragon bouquet from his right hand to his left as he dug for the keys in his pocket. He hoped they still worked, that Zita's *buta* boyfriend, Peter, hadn't made her change the locks. Again.

The dead bolt slid back easily. Zita had always been a good girl, giving him keys to every place she lived. She'd told Peter, in front of Laci, that it was in case she ever locked herself out. Laci knew better. It was her way of welcoming him into her home, even if Peter disapproved.

"*Halló*," Laci called as he walked through the door. "Anyone home?" Silence greeted him. Laci felt both relief and disappointment; relief that he wouldn't have to explain his presence, disappointment that he wouldn't get to see his granddaughter one last time.

A faint scent of cinnamon wove through the apartment. Laci walked to the dining room table and leaned over to smell Zita's expensive candles, enjoying their rich fragrance. Peter probably disapproved of these too, bewailing their cost, not appreciating how a simple smell transformed an apartment into a home.

Suddenly, Laci was transported.

Instead of standing next to a pale wood table in a white apartment, he was in his first apartment, the one he'd shared with his wife Judit. The scent of cinnamon-tinted wine filled the air. An aged oak table rested next to him. Chairs carved out of the same wood were drawn under it. Tiny Christmas candles burned everywhere. Shelves lined all the walls, full of old books, treasured books—what was left of his father's collection, augmented with Judit's family's books. The vision was so clear Laci could read the titles. He reached out and touched the dried leather spine of one of his favorites, "*Az ember tragédiája— The Tragedy of Man.*"

A sifting sound made him turn. Snow fell outside, leaving peace and clean whiteness in its wake. Laci took a deep breath, feeling tightness he hadn't known existed melt from his chest, like walking into a warm, moist house after being outside in the cold for days. It felt so good to be home. The dancing whiteness delighted him. It had been so long since he'd seen snow. He had an urge to go out sledding in it, as he had when he'd been a boy. He kept a wooden sled buried at the back of the hall closet, unused, but never forgotten. He could already imagine the sharp wind driving against his face.

A muffled explosion sounded to Laci's right, like a hurricane wind driven through a small baffle. He forced himself to turn and see what had happened. A huge hole gaped where the wall had been, and the small white bits fell inside. It took Laci a moment to realize that it wasn't snow, but millions of pieces of paper. They swirled around Laci and showed no signs of settling.

The scene had a surreal déjà vu feeling to it. It took Laci a moment to place it. *He* hadn't seen this destruction. Judit had, and she'd described it to him. When the Soviets had come back in 1956, with their tanks, they'd shot a round into Laci and Judit's apartment, destroying all the lovely ancient books.

The churning snow slowed and began to settle, melting the dark apartment, bringing back Zita's white one. Laci trembled, unable to move. He wanted to walk away from the table, but he couldn't do anything other than stand and breathe for a minute. His chest ached with his remembered losses: Judit, the fine books of vellum, his sister, the life he'd planned, his parents, the shining star that had been his beloved Budapest. He didn't want to go back and view the corpse left behind by the Communists. He'd run away rather than fight in 1956, run from that Jewish family in the caves in 1944, and now, in the present day, he'd run from Jack's death.

He wanted to keep running.

Laci forced himself to walk into the kitchen. He opened the cupboard above the stove, the one too high for Zita to reach without a stool. He found he'd guessed right. It contained all of Zita's vases and other extravagant items, things she wouldn't use every day. He brought down a handblown glass vase, fluted, with blue streaks running through it. After cutting the stems of the flowers he'd brought, he put them in the vase and set the bouquet in the center of the living room table. He took a moment arranging it, placing the candles around it.

Laci stepped back to look at the overall affect. Too symmetrical. He adjusted a flower.

A shadow in the corner of the room shifted.

Laci jerked around. Nothing was there. He was stalling.

Some part of him secretly hoped Zita, or even Peter, would come home and confront him, so he wouldn't have to go back to Budapest. So he wouldn't have to die. But he had to get going. His taxi would wait for only so long.

Laci walked over to Zita's desk in the corner. At first glance, it seemed completely utilitarian: papers and bills in neat piles; pens, pencils, and scissors in their holders; two neatly framed pictures in one corner, balanced with the box of tissue in the other. Laci saw the hidden luxury that Zita sought. The stamp holder, perfectly functional, was made of blue and green cloisonné. The bookends holding the cards to be answered were made of carved wood, as was the tissue box holder. Everywhere, the functional was given beauty. If only Zita could let herself revel in fine things, instead of sneaking them into her life.

If only she could forgive herself.

Laci had tried talking with her after their falling out. He'd forgiven her long ago for her failure. She'd never learn that now. He couldn't help her anymore. He could only help himself, stop the demons from killing another soul, or from corrupting those around him. Laci went through the desk drawers, looking for his passport. He was certain Zita had it, along with his other important papers.

She hadn't hidden his passport in her desk. Where else could she have put it? He looked around the living room. To one side stood the couch and the TV, clearly Peter's corner. Many drawers lined the kitchen, but she wouldn't have placed it there. Maybe there was another filing cabinet in her bedroom.

Kids shouting dares outside in the courtyard distracted Laci. He was halfway across the living room before he stopped himself. Let the kids yell. He had to stop procrastinating.

He approached the darkened bedroom with trepidation. It was a private room, part of Zita's inner sanctum. Piles of clothes lay along just one side of the bed. Laci guessed it was Zita's side, a subtle defiance of Peter, a throwback to her teenage days. Laci wrinkled his nose. Peter didn't smell too strongly during the day, but here the scent was concentrated. No candles stood on the dresser to take the smell away either. How did Zita stand it?

No matter. Not his business. He didn't want to check the nightstands on either side of the bed. It was likely other things would be there, things he didn't want to know about his granddaughter. He turned toward the closet.

There. On one side of the closet. A standing four-drawer filing cabinet. He found his passport in the top drawer, along with Peter's. Zita's passport wasn't there. Laci put his passport in his breast pocket, then took Peter's as well. He told himself that he was preventing Peter from coming after him. A cackling voice inside him spoke the truth: he only took the second passport to cause Peter inconvenience. Laci also picked up Zita's green backpack. It was small, just for day hikes, but that was fine, Laci didn't have much to take with him.

In the living room, he heard the kids outside again. He was certain he heard profanity. Useless punks. He went over to the window, intending to yell at them, tell them to go to school or something.

Palm and mesquite trees, as well as hop and jade bushes, brought a touch of green to the mostly concrete space between the two apartment buildings. A nonworking fountain also stood there. Three boys gathered at one end of the fountain, hacking away at the edge of it, trying to break the lip off.

The youths shimmered, and Laci saw them as they really were: demons. The toad man with his flicking tongue, the rabbit man, and a bug man with reflective eyes and moving mandibles. The toad man pounded not just on the side of the fountain, but also on the rabbit man's hand, forcing blood into the bowl of the fountain. When enough had gathered, he stepped back and lifted his arms. Red-stained water flowed from the center tower.

The three paused in their work and looked up at Laci. They pointed at him. Laci took a step back, afraid the demons would try something mundane, like shooting him. This made the trio laugh. As one, they made a sweeping motion with their hands, including the entire apartment building, then, with graceful movements, indicated the fountain.

Laci stood, blinking. They had made a threat, no matter how prettily they had presented it.

The three waved good-bye, and without another word, turned and walked away, undulating like prostitutes.

Laci caught a breath he didn't know he'd been holding. They'd corrupted a fountain. It was a clear warning. Leave soon, or they'd corrupt another. Zita's life fount.

Without another thought, Laci walked to the door. His plane left in three hours. Laci hoped that Nurse Flying Owl wouldn't notify Zita of his disappearance until after his plane had taken off. He didn't want to face his granddaughter again. Not now. Not when there was so much danger for her.

Laci left the apartment, then paused. The taxi waiting for him honked. He raised a hand in acknowledgment and went into the apartment again. He put Zita's keys on the table and walked out, closing the door behind him.

Deep breaths couldn't calm his clenching stomach,

or soothe away the tension spreading across his shoulders. He told himself he wasn't running away, no matter how much it seemed like it. He was going back. Not away. Back. Back to Budapest. He might be driven by demons, but he had made the decision to go.

He knew though, that he'd never return to this place again.

Chapter 4

Zita

"What do you mean he's missing?" Zita asked, struggling to keep her tone civil.

"He isn't in the hospital. His street clothes are gone too," said the nurse on the other end of the phone.

"When did he leave?"

"We're not sure. We assume it wasn't until after four A.M."

"Because . . . ?" Zita prompted when the nurse didn't continue.

"Your grandfather visited a female patient last night. He didn't leave her room until then."

Zita couldn't stop a smile from spreading across her face in response to the prudish tone in the nurse's voice. Of course, her grandfather had been with a woman. It was so like him. Tears threatened to spill out of her eyes. Oh, damn him. Anger, laughter, and fear fought to dominate Zita. The anger won.

"Why did you take so long to notify me? I mean, it's nearly"—Zita checked her watch—"ten o'clock!" They'd given her grandfather too much time. He could be anywhere.

"The other patient in the room with your grandfather suffered a massive coronary around four a.m."

"Jack's dead?" Zita asked, saddened, even though she knew it was what Jack had wanted.

"Yes."

"So why is it you didn't notify me sooner?"

"Generally, we move patients to another room before the doctors perform any kind of procedure. Due to the suddenness of Mr. Greenburg's heart attack, there wasn't time to move him. When this happens, we move the other patient to another room. Your grandfather wasn't in his room at the start of the procedure, so the nurse on duty assumed that someone had already moved him. It wasn't until it was time to return your grandfather to his room that we discovered he was missing."

Incompetence. Of course. That was what happened when you dealt with other people, when you didn't do things yourself. It was the same in every workplace, Zita thought.

"Have you notified the police?" Zita asked.

"He was due to be released today," the nurse responded.

"But he's a danger to himself."

"No, he was removed from the suicide watch, remember?"

Zita managed to say good-bye without any expletives. She held on to the phone handset resting in its cradle, her knuckles turning white as she gripped harder and harder. Damn him. *Damn* him. She had too much work to do today. The surgical glove suppliers from Mexico were threatening shortages, as usual, and needed to be convinced that her product was their highest priority. And she still needed to track down that shipment of glucose strips from Alabama.

With a sigh, Zita pushed away her thoughts of work. Where would Grandpa go? Back to his house? Given the shape in which Zita had found his abode, she doubted he'd go back there. It wasn't important to him anymore. To her place? She remembered how he'd whined, begging to keep the keys to her apartment when the staff wanted to take away all his belongings.

A cold dread filled Zita. Every time her grandfather had cycled into a bad phase, all he'd talked about was going back to Budapest. Would he actually try to go by himself? Or was he fighting demons in an alley somewhere?

Zita looked up the number for the police. She

wanted them to check the airport for her. There had
to be officers stationed there permanently, right?

The police seemed interested in helping Zita until
she made it clear that Laci wasn't a threat to himself
or anyone else. Then the man on the other end of the
phone assured her that the airport was secure and the
people there had enough on their hands without going
on some wild goose chase. He also suggested that she
go to the airport herself.

After Zita got off the phone with the police, she sat
and thought for a moment. Grandpa might have
known he was to be released today, or soon, at any
rate. She'd had to tell him the date every time she'd
seen him. But maybe he'd remembered this time.
Maybe he'd just left on his own. He might go to her
apartment, if he could find it.

Besides, Zita thought as she stood up, her grandfather needed his passport if he was going to travel over-
seas. And Zita had that.

She grabbed her keys and raced out, hoping to catch
her grandfather at her apartment. She told the receptionist she had a family emergency as she ran through
the lobby, knowing that her expression and the speed
at which she moved would forestall any questions.

Zita ignored the three youths hanging out in the
parking lot, grateful Peter wasn't with her. The punks
didn't do more than whistle at her as she passed. Her
boyfriend, if feeling heroic, would have tried to engage
them in conversation in his continual, insincere efforts
"to reach out to the youth of today." And been
mocked, spat on, or possibly beaten up, as he had
in the past. These were hard ones. Even Zita could
see that.

Zita put her key in the lock and turned. There was
no resistance. The door wasn't dead bolted. Zita froze.
Peter would never forget such an important detail.

Had she been robbed? Was there a burglar inside?
Should she go into the apartment by herself? Or
should she fetch the manager?

Or maybe it was her grandfather. He never locked the door. Of course that's who it was. Zita still couldn't move. She listened for a moment. She didn't hear anything over the frightened pounding of her own heart. It had to be him.

The warm metal doorknob turned easily in Zita's hand. She poked her head in, then took a deep breath. The apartment looked exactly the way she'd left it. No one had trashed it. She closed the door behind her and bolted it.

When she turned back around, she realized a vase of flowers stood on her table. She walked to them with trepidation. No note. Just snapdragons, one of her favorite flowers. A set of keys lay next to them.

Grandpa.

Hungarians traditionally give flowers on all occasions: birthdays, name days, weddings, funerals, saying hello—saying good-bye.

It confirmed her worst fears.

Zita still had a slim hope that her grandfather had left the apartment before he'd found his passport. She made herself go into the bedroom. The scent of Peter's sweat assaulted her. She stopped short of the closet, distracted and annoyed. At first, she'd loved how Peter smelled—reveled in it. Now it irritated her. If she was truthful, almost everything about Peter made her angry now. She turned on the ceiling fan, opened the window a crack, then went to the four-drawer filing cabinet she kept in the closet.

Laci's passport no longer resided in the top drawer. Peter's passport was missing as well. Luckily, she kept hers at the office, for her semifrequent trips to Mexico.

Zita debated calling the airport, or maybe one or two airlines, to figure out which plane her grandfather had gone on. It would be a waste of time though. There wasn't a direct flight from Tucson to Budapest. Her grandfather would have to pass through at least one other city, maybe more. Denver? L.A.? Chicago? She'd never figure out which hub he'd fly out of. Besides, the careful arrangement of the cut flowers, the keys, that he'd found his passport, all told her that today was one of her grandfather's good days. He'd be fully capable of buying his own ticket and getting on the plane. Would going to Budapest make him better? Or would being back in his childhood home trigger more—and possibly worse—hallucinations?

It didn't matter. She had to go after him, try to find him. That way she'd be there if he . . . Zita couldn't let herself think about Grandpa hurting himself again, driving his own fingernails into his forehead.

She heard the youths calling to each other in the courtyard. She walked back into the living room and looked out the window. For a moment, something seemed odd about the boys, as if they were fatter, more "bodied" than their bulky camo jackets made them look. Then she saw one of them pounding on the lip of the fountain. Another threw rocks at the center figure of concrete turtles piled one on top of another, each spouting water. How dare they?

The owner of her apartment complex had two properties, the Empress, about two blocks away, and this one, the Emperor. The Empress had more of a Western courtyard, complete with swimming pool, while this one was more Asian. Zita loved having a little green to soften the concrete. She especially loved the fountain. On hot nights, when Peter refused to run the air-conditioning—still saving for the move to L.A.—she sat next to it, listening to the dripping water, letting the spray splash her skin, smelling night jasmine in her imagination and pretending to smooth perfumed oils on her baking skin.

Something white caught her eye. One of the youths had undone his pants and sat on the lip of the fountain, letting his butt dangle over the water. Zita couldn't believe what she was seeing. How could he do something so foul? A long brown stream flowed from him. Zita didn't want to watch, but she couldn't turn away. When the youth finished, he walked away, doing up his pants. His companions followed him. The water pressure dropped as the excrement blocked the pipes.

Zita turned from the window, tears of frustration and rage blinding her. She needed to call the manager to let him know he had to clean the fountain. She had to call her mother and let her know about Grandpa. She had to go back to her office and make arrangements for being gone for the next couple of weeks. She needed to buy a ticket for Budapest. There were too many things to do and not enough time.

Peter was going to be pissed off. This was going to ruin his careful schedule.

Zita laughed for the first time that day. She'd been on his schedule for a long time. Maybe it was time for him to be on hers.

"Do you think he went back to atone?"

"Atone for what?" Zita asked. She'd decided to call her mother from her apartment, rather than from work, so if they fought, as they usually did, the argument couldn't be heard by half the office.

"Those Jewish families."

"How do you know about them?" Zita asked. She hadn't told her mother that part of her grandfather's story.

"Your grandfather gave a lot of parties when I was young. He sometimes drank too much. Like you do. I never wondered where you'd gotten it from."

Zita cringed, but didn't reply. She'd never be able to convince her mother that she'd changed.

"Anyway," her mother continued, "the deaths of those families always weighed on him."

"It's possible," Zita said. "Do you think I should check graveyards when I get to Budapest?"

"I still don't understand why you think you have to go. Grandpa's a grown man. He's perfectly capable of taking care of himself."

"No, Mom, he isn't."

"Well, I'm not going to argue with you. You've made up your mind, stubborn as always."

"Yeah, I got that from him too," Zita said wryly. To her surprise, her mother laughed.

"You were always more his heir than I was. It made me angry for a long time."

Zita sat back, blinking in surprise. She didn't know how to respond.

"I've thought a lot about my father dying," her mother said into the silence. "When you find him, be sure to tell him I'm not angry anymore. And tell him good-bye."

"Mom, I'll bring him back."

"Sweetie—" her mother said. She sighed. "Grandpa's sick. You know this. Wouldn't it be better for him to die where he wants to?"

"How can you be so callous?" Zita asked, standing up in anger. Her mother's attitude didn't surprise her. Zita took a deep breath and tried to calm down. This argument had a familiar feeling to it. As a teenager, Zita had spouted outrageous religious, political, and social beliefs, trying to force a reaction from her overly calm mother.

"I'm not being callous. I'm just being practical. Remember? I'm the one who always cleans up after everyone else. I just think it would be easier."

Zita swayed and sat back down. She closed her eyes and saw the regal dinner parties her grandfather had held, outside, in his backyard. A huge bouquet of snapdragons, tiger lilies, and other summer flowers overflowed its vase in the middle of the table. The scents of the cooling desert rock, the undertone of the cabernet they drank, the spicy salad and warm pita bread smells, all mingled together, going straight to Zita's head, more than the wine, the gentle night air, or her grandfather's charming company. The parties made up her favorite memories—from the summer before she'd gone to college. Before everything had changed.

She also remembered her mother and her step-grandmother in the kitchen, preparing the food, cleaning up afterward, her grandfather keeping Zita by his side instead of letting her help. Zita hadn't found out about her mother's resentment until her step-grandmother's funeral.

"Mom—" Zita started. She stopped.

"No, I'm sorry. I said I wasn't going to be angry anymore. And I'm not. I do want you to find Grandpa. And tell him I love him."

"He loves you too," Zita said.

"I know he does, dear. And I know you'll find him. You're too stubborn not to."

"Thanks for the vote of confidence," Zita said. She wasn't as sure about her abilities as her mother was. What would happen if she didn't find him? If he died, alone, among strangers? She remembered her premonition from the night before, that her grandfather would die if he went back to Budapest.

"Is Peter going with you?" her mother asked.

"No," Zita said. She hadn't even bothered asking him.

"Are you still on that silly diet he talked you into?"

"I gave it up." Zita knew she wasn't beautiful. Though her blond hair shone like gold in the sunlight, she'd inherited her namesake's body. She'd often joked with her friends about being "good peasant stock," with full hips, ample breasts, and lots of curves. She wasn't overweight—she just didn't have an anorexic supermodel body, the type Peter found most attractive.

"Good," Margit said. "Look, sweetie. I have to go. Give me a call from Budapest when you have a chance, okay?"

"Okay." Zita paused. "Love you," she said, keeping the statement casual.

"Love you too. Bye."

"Bye."

Zita gripped the handset for a minute, as if trying to push through the dead line all the things she couldn't say.

She couldn't deal with that now. She had other things to do. Some of her mother's practicality had rubbed off on her. She let go of the phone, grabbed her keys, and headed back to her office.

"It will be fine, Zita. Don't worry about it," Frank repeated.

Zita couldn't stop herself from apologizing to her boss again. "It's just that he's my grandfather, and I'm his legal guardian, well, almost, and I have to go after him. I'll be gone only a couple of weeks." Zita pushed away her other fears, namely, how she was going to find her grandfather. Would he still be alive when she got there? Where should she look once she arrived in Budapest? Hospitals? Morgues?

"Please. I understand about family. Don't worry. I'm sure you'll arrange everything before you leave. Any problems we have can wait until you return. Go with good conscience. I hope you find your grandfather."

Zita pulled on her hair and nodded. Her fears had overwhelmed her on her drive to work. What if her grandfather made it only halfway to Hungary? He was going to have a layover in at least one city, maybe more. What if his "demons" attacked him during a layover, so far from home?

Zita shook Frank's hand, then went back to her own office. Part of her felt relief at her boss' easygoing attitude. She should have known he'd be this unperturbed. He was relaxed about everything. His office meetings were always just this side of chaotic, with everyone talking at the same time. Still, things got done at Frank's meetings, more so than at Zita's, even though she ran hers according to Robert's Rule of Order.

Yet part of her was, well, scornful. Frank had just accepted her going without question. Of course he would. He could afford to. He didn't have the kind of job she did. She was always dealing with unpleasant surprises: suppliers having shortages, snowstorms on the East Coast delaying shipments, local salespeople not filling their quotas, and so on. She lusted after his job, just managing the office and the people there. If she had his job, she could afford to be as laid-back as he was.

"I can't believe you're just going. What about our plans this weekend?" Peter asked, following Zita from the kitchen back to the bedroom.

She put her tin box of tea bags in one of the side pockets of her roll-on suitcase and zipped it shut.

"What about my grandfather?" Zita asked as she picked up a pair of pants. She looked at the other clothes on the bed. She wasn't worried about fitting everything she'd chosen into her suitcase. She traveled often enough to know how to pack. This wasn't a business trip though. Did she really need to take these dress pants? She didn't like them much—they were scratchy—but they were practical. Both her mother and Peter approved of them.

"You don't even know he's gone to Budapest," Peter said, interrupting her stream of thought.

"Where else would he go?" Zita asked, folding the pants and packing them. "He took his passport. I checked the latest purchases on his credit card. He bought a plane ticket, an expensive one. He's gone to Budapest."

"He'll be fine. There's no reason for you to go."

"You sound like my mother," Zita said, exasperated. She picked up another blouse and rolled it, packing it tightly. Why was she taking it? She didn't like it much either.

"If I sound like your mother, you sound like the spoiled, self-centered girl you were when I first met you."

Zita turned to face Peter. Every other time when he'd thrown her past behavior into her face, she'd backed down.

Not this time. Maybe it was her overwhelming worry. Maybe it was because since she'd already failed her grandfather, she could afford to fail her relationship as well, disappoint her lover. Or maybe it was a residual behavior pattern from her continual arguments with the doctor.

"Explain to me how I'm being selfish, Peter. Did I decide to go take a vacation in Europe and disrupt your plans? No. I'm going after my grandfather, who's sick and confused. For once you'll have to change your plans, take care of yourself for a while."

Zita stalked to the bathroom. Why had she walked in here? She jerked open the door to the linen closet. That's right. Though she probably wouldn't need it, she was going to take an extra hand towel, just in case.

"I could go with Tracy and Linda to see *The Vagina Monologues* this weekend," Peter said.

"Good," Zita said, folding the towel. She pushed it against her face. It smelled like the incense she kept in the closet. She rolled her shoulders, trying to relax. Why were she and Peter fighting like this? She remembered when they'd first started dating, if one or the other of them was going to be gone, the night before, they'd act as if it would be their last night together. What had changed?

"Although, it would be more fun if you were there too. I feel like a fifth wheel with them sometimes. They're so attached at the hip, you know?"

Zita smiled. That was more like it.

"Why don't we plan on going the night you get back?" Peter continued.

Zita closed her eyes and shook her head.

Peter and his plans. Though Zita got stuck in her own rut sometimes, she wasn't as planned as Peter. No one was. And there were times when it was impossible to be planned. Take this trip for example. Though Zita had a ticket, she didn't have a hotel room. The travel agency her company used couldn't book a room at their usual hotel due to some convention. They were trying to get her booked at the Marriott instead, and wanted her to call them back in the morning for the reservation. Zita had agreed, not remembering until it was too late that her plane left at

6:30 in the morning, long before the agency was open. She would have to call them during her layover in Denver.

Peter wouldn't have been so disorganized. Zita opened her eyes and looked at him through the bathroom door. He no longer wore his soft brown hair long enough to fall into his eyes, like he used to—claimed it wasn't the look most agencies wanted. He'd lost weight since college too—his cheekbones were sharper, as was his nose. His lips were still skinny, sensual, though she couldn't remember the last time he'd kissed her. He stood ramrod straight, not quite tense, but precisely arranged. He never talked with his hands or did anything without a reason.

Zita had needed his ability to force order on a chaotic world at one point in her life. She'd relied on him to choose a path for her when everything had come crashing down, when she'd gotten so sick, when her grandfather had grown old, when her stepgrandmother had died. Peter's regimens had supported Zita when she'd failed herself and everyone around her.

They felt like restraints now. She needed to loosen the ties between them. She must stand on her own.

"Peter," she started, walking back into the bedroom and putting the towel down on the bed. Fear manifested in the pit of her stomach. Was she really thinking of leaving him? How could she ever detangle the life they had together? He needed her.

She could use this trip as a start. She looked at what she'd packed, then started taking things out.

"What are you doing?" Peter asked.

Zita didn't respond. She took out the practical blouses, the scratchy pants. The clothing that Peter had helped her buy. She went back into the closet and picked out her favorite clothes: the crimson silk camisole that felt so good on her skin, the long muted brown skirt with the elastic waistband that went with everything, the elegant blue-green tie-dyed blouse that didn't look tie-dyed. She went back into the bathroom and grabbed a small container of bath beads, another of her favorite luxury items.

"Why are you doing this?" Peter asked. He shifted from one foot to the other.

Zita wondered if he could tell the type of clothes she was leaving behind, what kind she was taking. Or if it was just her attitude, the way she held herself, that made him realize something had happened, something was different.

She was changing.

"I'm going, Peter," she said.

Peter bit his lip and shook his head, as if he didn't want to hear any more. "Just for a while."

"At least for a while," Zita replied. She couldn't break all her ties. Not yet.

"I, umm, I respect your decision," Peter said.

Zita turned to him. He almost sounded like the old Peter, the one she'd first met, so tall, strong, gentle, and loving, all at the same time.

He continued. "I'll support you in any decision you make." It sounded like a curse. He walked out the door.

Zita pulled her hair over her face, rubbing the softness against her cheek. Peter had been so close. He'd almost responded the right way. If only he could bend a little. . . .

Zita knew he couldn't. He'd never bend. And she could no longer grow in the path he'd set for her.

Chapter 5

Ephraim

"Morning, Janet," Ephraim said in his most chipper tone, trying to keep the hangover out of his voice. "How are you?"

"You okay?" Janet asked.

"Sure. Everything's great," Ephraim lied. He was glad his ex-wife couldn't see him. She'd be shocked at his appearance: unshaven, black circles going from under his eyes to halfway down his cheeks, his shoulder-length hair full of knots. He'd checked himself in the mirror when he'd first gotten up, certain that he'd be able to see his head splitting apart from the pain.

"Actually," Ephraim continued, "things are better than they've been for a long while." The smile creeping across his face hurt his head, but then again, everything hurt his head.

"You've just never called me during work hours before," Janet said, concern in her voice.

So that was it. He sighed quietly, relieved.

"Today isn't a workday for me. I got laid off," Ephraim said, surprised at how easy it was to say the words out loud. He stood up and hooked his portable phone to his belt, blessing his friend Syl who'd insisted that he get a phone with a headset. He picked up the half-empty glass of rum from his desk and carried it at arm's length toward the kitchen. The smell made him more nauseated than walking did.

"Oh, Eph, I'm so sorry. I heard about the layoffs last night. I didn't think they'd do something so stupid as to lay off half the people from R&D."

"Yeah, sometimes management is just stupid." Ephraim poured the rum down the sink slowly so Janet wouldn't hear. He ran a little water after it, to chase away the smell. "Not only did they lay off the most productive portion of the R&D department, they didn't give us proper notice. They've opened themselves up for lawsuits."

"What do you mean?" Janet asked.

"I think if you lay off a certain number of people, you're supposed to give them ten days' notice or something. And they didn't. They just called us into a meeting while security people stationed themselves at our desks." Ephraim's personal effects hadn't even covered the bottom of a single box. He had no pen holder at work, no photographs, no plants, nothing he'd have to move when he wiped down his work space every morning and every evening. He had an urge to spread pens, clips, and knickknacks all over his desk at home, then keep them there, just to force himself out of his habit. A little dust wouldn't kill him.

"How awful, to be treated like criminals! When they're the ones breaking the law," Janet said.

"Yeah," Ephraim said. He cleared his throat, then continued. "Janet, I, umm, wondered if you could do me a favor." Ephraim picked up the empty bottle of rum sitting next to the sink and put it in the recycling bin. He picked up the container, testing how heavy it was. He could still lift it. Maybe he could go an extra month. Ephraim always took the paper and glass he'd saved to the recycling bins the first Saturday of every month. But he'd be in Budapest then. He shook his head. He didn't have to wait until the first Saturday of the next month to take the recycling in. He could do it anytime. The relief he felt, just loosening his routine a little, made him stand up straighter.

"Sure," Janet said. "You want me to organize a protest or something? Or do you need a lawyer? I can contact Sam. He's good. He donates half his income to the Center for Biodiversity."

Ephraim held up his hands to stop the onslaught

from Janet. His fingers curled, an unconscious warding. He shook his hands, releasing the pattern. "No, I don't need anything like that. Thanks though." It was so like Janet to try to turn him into her newest cause. Ephraim was touched. She still cared. "No, I'm going to be gone for a couple of weeks. Can you come over and water the plants?"

Ephraim nearly laughed into the sudden silence. He could see Janet sitting back, that perplexed look on her face that she got when the world shifted. She'd been steaming away in one direction, and he'd just passed her sailing the other way.

"Where are you going?" she asked.

"On vacation," he said, grinning. It was still so much fun to tease his ex-wife. He walked back to the living room and stared at the remnants of the previous night's party.

"Where?"

He couldn't stop himself from replying, though he wanted to tease her more. "Budapest," he said, trying the Hungarian pronunciation, saying "pesht" instead of "pest."

"Why?" Janet asked, stretching the one word out to a full sentence.

"I'm going to, well, I told you about Grandpa Ferenc, my maternal grandfather, right?" Ephraim asked, finding it difficult to put his crazy plan into words. He stacked the plates quietly and carried them to the kitchen.

"No."

"He came from Hungary, from Budapest. He told me a lot of stories about it when I was a kid."

"Eph, I'm shocked," Janet said. "You've only ever talked about your mom before. I don't think you mentioned any of your other relatives the entire time we were together."

Ephraim thought for a moment. His paternal relatives had disappeared with his father. His maternal ones had passed away before he'd completed college. There had to have been some reason why he'd never mentioned them to Janet, other than the fact that they were no longer around. He vaguely recalled making a deliberate decision to stay silent on the subject.

"I'm not sure why I never told you about Grandpa. We lived with him for a little over a year, right after my father left. My grandpa and my mom made a bargain. He agreed to babysit me after school if he got to teach me Hebrew and prepare me for my Bar Mitzvah."

Ephraim put down the plates he'd been holding and smiled. That had been a wonderful year. His grandpa had died a few months afterward. That's when Ephraim had chosen to keep his Hebrew name, Ephraim, rather than his American name, Earnest. Had he never told Janet about that? Surely he must have. That had also been the year he'd been hurt. He rubbed the long scar down the inside of his left arm. He must have told her how he'd gotten that.

"So you're going to Hungary to visit family?" Janet asked, still puzzling it out.

Ephraim forced himself to continue. "Not exactly. I don't believe anyone on my grandfather's side survived World War II."

An awkward pause emanated from the other end of the phone. Suddenly Ephraim remembered. Janet's relatives were from Germany. Some had been prominent Nazis. It was one of the reasons she was a dedicated activist, to atone for her family's heritage. She was a complete pacifist, arguing that no cause was ever worth someone's life.

Though Ephraim had had a Bar Mitzvah, he and his mother hadn't kept kosher. Soon after his grandfather died, they'd stopped going to synagogue, holding Shabbat, and celebrating with the rest of their community. Within a year, they'd led secular lives again.

Ephraim hadn't thought much about his Jewish heritage and had let what little he'd remembered slip away because he couldn't stand Janet's guilt. Again he shook his head. What else had he given up for her, for the sake of a peaceful life?

"Anyway," Ephraim said, forcing himself to continue, "as I said, Grandpa told me a lot of stories. Some of the stories, um, were about, um, how our people used the caves in Budapest to escape the Nazis."

Ephraim paused. He didn't want to go on. He didn't want to make Janet feel any worse. If they were talking face-to-face, he knew that she'd be biting her lips together, eyes downcast, guilt making it hard for her to swallow. He knew of no ritual that actually worked to remove pain, though he'd tried plenty. Plus, now, in the bright morning sunlight, his idea of going searching for gold in the caves seemed too crazy. Saying it out loud gave it too much strength. Ephraim wandered out of the kitchen and back to his desk.

"The caves? The ones on the Buda side of Budapest?" Janet asked, copying Ephraim and using the Hungarian pronunciation.

"Yes," Ephraim said, surprised and also pleased that Janet hadn't stayed focused on his Jewish heritage.

"Did you know that when the Communists left, the Hungarians discovered that some of the caves had been used as a toxic-waste dump?"

"No, I didn't," Ephraim said. No wonder Janet knew about the caves. She knew about every toxic site in the world. "But they've been cleaned up, right? I could still go visit them?" Ephraim didn't have to be in the same room as Janet to feel her glare. It came through in the silence from the other end of the phone.

"The Hungarians aren't going to do anything about it until someone forces them to. I mean, look at how they treat their own people. Gypsies comprise six percent of the population, yet are fifty percent unemployed, while the national unemployment rate is about ten percent. Life expectancy for gypsies is ten years below the national average. One of the reports by the EU Commission stated that it was generally in favor of Hungary's entrance into the EU, except for its human rights record."

Ephraim sat down on the edge of his desk under the attack of statistics. Of course, Janet would know about the human rights in Hungary. She was a walking encyclopedia of facts about every atrocity currently being committed.

This argument had a familiar feeling to it. Janet always knew more and was always right. He hated her for it. He hated himself too. He usually let her win this sort of argument.

Not this time.

Or maybe they could come to a draw. He pushed himself off his desk. He held his hands down at his sides, refusing to give in to habitual, ineffective gestures against his ex. He straightened his back as if standing up to her and asked, "Is the Hungarian government doing anything about the gypsies?"

Janet sighed. Ephraim heard the exasperation in her voice.

"They're studying it, drawing up a plan."

"So they aren't hiding it; they're doing something," Ephraim said, trying to drive his point home.

"Never enough and always too late," Janet replied.

On the one hand, Ephraim knew that Janet might be right. Governments often didn't move fast enough, and when they did start making progress, they generally made the wrong choices for individuals. That didn't automatically make them evil. Or their countries not worth visiting.

"Wait a second," he said, sitting down and turning on the monitor to his computer. It had driven Janet crazy that he left his computer turned on all the time. She insisted that it was a waste of electricity. However, if he didn't turn it off, he always had an instant connection to the Internet through his DSL line.

"When I was doing research last night, I think I found an article about the gypsies suing the government and winning. Their children had been segregated, put in a class with remedial students. They got that policy reversed." Ephraim paused. "I'll send it to you if I find it." The bookmarks he'd filed under

"Hungary" was a mishmash of URLs, everything from dictionaries to sites about history to lists of Hungarian poets, as well as items just titled "Index."

"So? That was one instance," Janet said.

"It means things can change. Yeah, it'll be slow. But reform is possible," Ephraim replied.

He could change. He could transform himself. He didn't have to be mired in a rut.

A new idea struck him. Maybe Janet couldn't. She was the same as she'd been when he'd first met her in college. Still fighting the good fight.

Pleasure filled Ephraim at his revelation. It also made him anxious, unprotected. His world *was* changing. Without thinking about it, he made a circle with the thumb and first finger of each hand. He raised his hands up above his forehead, touched the two circles together, then slid the finger and thumb of his right hand over his left, so his two hands were joined.

"Are you circling?" Janet asked.

"No," Ephraim said, whipping his hands apart and bringing them down to his sides.

"Eph, you do it every time you argue with me."

"Janet, I didn't call to argue with you," Ephraim said, trying to forestall her next attack. "I called you to ask a favor. And," Ephraim said, pausing for emphasis, "to let you know I was going on an unplanned, unexpected vacation. I thought you'd be happy for me."

"What do you mean?"

"You always said I needed to be more spontaneous. You've accused me of living for my habits, instead of just living. I'm going to Budapest. Isn't that different enough?" Ephraim asked.

"Have you really broken out?" Janet asked. "I mean, it sounds like you've done just as much research as you usually do."

Ephraim chuckled quietly. He couldn't help it. If he hadn't done any research at all, she'd call him an uninformed, stupid American.

"Are you really being spontaneous?" Janet asked, pressing her point.

"I'm leaving tomorrow morning," Ephraim said. "I made the decision last night and bought the ticket then. By bidding on it."

"That is different," Janet conceded.

"So you'll come and water my plants for me while I'm gone?"

Janet laughed—the happy laugh that Ephraim remembered from their college days, that he'd heard less and less often during their time together.

"Yes, I'll water your plants for you. I'll even drive you to the airport," she said.

"Thanks for the offer," Ephraim said, "but my flight leaves at six fifteen in the morning. I'll take a cab." Janet was never on time. When they'd first started dating, Ephraim had thought she'd been late to needle him. After a while, he'd learned not to take it personally. He'd started planning around her, making contingencies if they were five, ten, twenty minutes late. It was just how she was. Her rut.

"Okay. Have a good trip," Janet said. "Call me if you need anything."

"Thanks. Bye."

"Bye."

After Ephraim hung up, he pulled the phone from his belt and held it for a moment. Did Janet have a key? He hadn't changed the locks. It was one of the ways he'd stayed tied to his old relationship. No more. He vowed to hire a locksmith the day he returned from Budapest.

Ephraim put the phone down and shook his head. Those arguments. The one they'd had this morning had been a faint echo of their previous fights. They'd often said insulting things during them. When Ephraim had withdrawn, refused to fight, and just gestured at her, Janet had continued to poke at him, sometimes making him angry enough to continue. She claimed sparring with him kept her sharp, in form, on her toes.

Ephraim didn't want to fight anymore.

He started going through the Hungarian bookmarks

on his computer. Most of the sites looked vaguely familiar. He browsed for a long time through Rozska's Complete Guide to Hungary. It was the most extensive site he'd found.

Ephraim began taking notes. Then he got out his calendar. He'd arrive in Budapest around noon on Sunday. He could spend two days in Budapest, go to the national museum, to the Jewish museum, maybe to the opera. Then he could go to Visegrád, maybe as a day trip, same with Eger, then down to Pécs. . . .

Ephraim made himself stop. He forced himself to put his pen down and close his calendar. He'd started planning. Overplanning.

He shook himself, closed the browser, and turned off his monitor. He would not allow himself to plan anymore. He was just going to Budapest. And while he was traveling, he would get up every morning and decide at that point what the day would hold.

So—what should he do instead? The general mess from the night before called to him. He walked to the kitchen and started putting the plates into the dishwasher. He positioned each plate in its place, large plates next to large ones, and small plates next to small ones. He ordered the glasses in a similar rigid fashion, with spaces when there wasn't a dirty one of the right size. He loaded the silverware with handles down, knives and forks in the back, spoons in the front, each turned precisely.

He poured in the dishwasher liquid, closed the door, then unlocked and locked it three times without thinking about it. Then Ephraim placed his hands on the counter above the dishwasher. He stayed that way for a minute, pushing his breath through his palms, as if willing the dirt and germs to leave the dishes.

As he lifted his hands from the counter, he realized what he'd been doing. He justified his actions to himself: his dishwasher was old, and his dishes always came out cleaner if he ordered them and did his ritual. He had empirical proof that it worked.

It was still crazy.

Ephraim had been so certain he could change when he'd been talking with Janet. He'd even felt a moment of superiority thinking that maybe she couldn't. He wasn't being fair to Janet. She did change, all the time, if not her ideals, at least her causes. Every week was different for her. Was that what he wanted?

The only thing he knew was that he wasn't sure what he wanted. For his rituals to work? Or not to be compelled to do them? To plan only the required amount? Or to be able not to plan at all?

Maybe going to Budapest to search for fool's gold was a stupid idea. He'd already bought his ticket though. He was committed. Whether it was smart or not, the right thing to do or not, he was going.

He felt the urge to make a gesture, but it wasn't as straightforward as usual. Part of him wanted to do a warding, protecting motion, circling, as usual. Part of him wanted to do a new sign, which ended with a pulling motion, as if drawing his fate to himself.

He did neither.

Chapter 6

Laci

The green-tinged light puzzled Laci. It reminded him of . . . something. Laci stopped and gazed at the wall of the terminal, following it up to the curved ceiling. He threaded both his arms through the straps of his backpack. There was something classical about the white strips between the panes of glass, something unsoiled, maybe even sacred. He adored the misty light from these windows. The quality of it mesmerized him. Laci wanted to live in a house that had windows similar to these, watch the snow fall on pure winter mornings.

A child's angry screams echoed through the terminal, catching Laci's attention. He looked down, but didn't see the child. The muted roar of all the conversations in the enclosed space pounded against his ears, a dull sound, like ocean surf. A teenage boy, face covered in acne, head covered by a yellow-and-orange knit cap and headphones, swerved to avoid Laci. The boy needed a bath.

Suddenly, Laci was transported.

He stood on one of the platforms of the Budapest Nyugati train station. He couldn't connect one place to the other until he looked up. The same rounded ceiling arched above him, the same cloudy greenish light shone through. Black iron strips separated each glass pane, yet the windows held the same classy look as . . . as . . . that other place, where Laci had been, that he didn't quite remember now.

The air smelled differently here in the station than in that other place. Here, the scent started with burning coal, exhaust, and a hint of ozone, then mingled with the vinegar from the pickle seller behind Laci, joined to the sourness of the soldier standing next to him, and finished with the darkness of the thick sludge they sold as coffee at the end of the platform.

Laci straightened up, reveling how his young body felt, strong and quick, his nose even more sensitive, his hands always in motion, either fiddling with the small change in his pocket or combing through his then thick black hair. He no longer wore hand-me-downs from his uncle. His mother had married again after the war, making it possible for Laci to go to university. They'd changed their name as well, not so their relatives couldn't find them, but so no one could accuse them of impure blood or being on the wrong side during the war. Laci both understood and resented the necessity.

He made his youthful self touch the small scar between his eyes, the patched-over skin. Something squishy and sleepy lived there. Laci brought down his hand quickly, afraid to awaken it.

Why was he here, at the Nyugati train station? Where was he going? It wasn't to visit Grandmother Zita, his mother's mother. The Germans had killed her during the war, coveting the high land her farm sat on. He still remembered the fiery stomach pain that had come the night she'd died; it had grown and amplified until it destroyed the world. His other relatives were similarly gone, so he wasn't traveling to see them either.

The platform trembled. Laci saw a train approaching. Maybe he wasn't going anywhere. He looked around him. He didn't have any luggage. He didn't recall the backpack still strapped to his body back in Chicago. Was he waiting for someone?

The train stopped with a clunk and a hissing release of the hydraulic brakes. People came streaming out of the doors. Laci stood still in the flow of people, something familiar, almost reassuring about it.

Someone called his name. Farther down the track

he saw her. Judit. His wife. She wore a light pink
dress, one he hadn't seen before, with a matching
sweater. It was pretty, frivolous. It was just the kind
of thing to get them noticed, and possibly harassed,
by the AVO—the secret police.

She raised her hand and beckoned him to draw
near. He heard her voice, impossibly soft through the
roar of the departing passengers.

"Let's go," she said.

He pushed his way through the crowd, against the
surging travelers. He tried to rush, afraid he might
lose her again. She seemed impossibly far down the
platform, just a pink smudge now.

Understanding shook through Laci. He needed to
get away, run away from the darkness he knew lay at
his back. He could escape with Judit. He didn't know
how long she'd been gone, but it seemed like forever.
It would be so good to smell the musk of her skin, to
nibble at her fingers, to follow the curves of her hips
with his hands. He groaned and stumbled forward,
cursing the crush of people between him and his love.

A train arrived at the adjacent platform. The crowd
swelled. A man in a business suit bumped Laci's left
shoulder hard and walked on without an apology.

Laci stopped for a moment, then pushed himself
forward again, straight into the path of a second man,
who grabbed Laci's shoulders and shook him. "Where
are you going?" he asked.

For a moment, Laci thought he saw a spark in the
man's eyes, red and inhuman. Pain burned through
the scar in the middle of Laci's forehead. The world
grew red and hot. The trains on either side of the
platform bulged, their black shapes jostling the edges
of Laci's sight. A roll of thunder issued from the
clouds boiling above the curved ceiling. Darkness
crowded closer. Laci felt his breath bake away. He put
his hand on the arm of the man holding his shoulders.

The touch calmed Laci. Color drained out of the
vision, as if washed away by the rain. The murky
light cleared.

Laci stood back in Chicago. He no longer waited in the hall with the beautiful green glass windows. Instead, he stood in front of an airplane gate with exiting passengers.

"You okay?" the man holding Laci's shoulders asked in a kind voice. "Do you want me to call someone?" He wore a uniform, blue and plastic, with a matching shirt and red power tie.

Numbly, Laci shook his head. His cheeks flared with an embarrassment he hadn't felt since he'd been a teenager. He'd been trying to run away. All his firm resolve out the green-tinted windows.

The man escorted Laci out of the stream of passengers. Laci stood and breathed for a moment, trying to regain his composure. He stiffened when he saw the man holding his arm reach for the walkie-talkie at his belt. Laci needed to stop him from calling anyone. He must be allowed to continue his journey.

"I'm flying to Budapest," Laci said. "Can you help me?"

The man looked at Laci for a moment, then nodded. "You want the international terminal," the man said. He proceeded to give directions on how to get there.

Laci didn't listen to the explanation the man gave. Instead, he scanned the crowd around him. He knew he'd seen a demon. That's what had brought him back. He waited until the man finished his recitation before saying, "Thank you. You've been most kind."

Pulling on the shoulder straps of his backpack, Laci headed into the crowd of people. It didn't matter if the demons were at the airport or not. They were in America, and had threatened his granddaughter. He couldn't run away this time.

He shivered as he walked, remembering Judit. How he missed her. He hadn't just run from the Communists in 1956. They had killed his Judit, shot her while she'd been standing in a line outside a bread shop. He hadn't been able to abide living in a city that held so many memories of her.

He didn't look forward to reopening his old wounds.

Laci followed the signs pointing to the international terminal without paying much attention to where he was going, still wrapped in old grief. He watched his fellow travelers, looking for evidence of demons. When the light dimmed, he realized the escalator he rode was going down to a tunnel.

Orange, pink, pale blue, and yellow colored lights chased each other across the ceiling, looping through fine glass structures. Moving walkways carried people from one end of the tunnel to the other. A cacophony of sounds struck Laci as he followed the herd: chatter from travelers on phones, salesmen plotting their next victory, mechanical voices toning over and over again about the walkway ending, kids screaming—with delight or anger, Laci couldn't tell.

Slowing for a moment, Laci tried to decide which way to go. Should he move through the hall on his own two feet? The crowd behind him pushed him forward, and he took a fearful step onto the walkway. Going on it would be faster, though he wouldn't be able to get away if a demon chose to torment him. He ducked the first time he passed under the weird lights. No one around him paid any attention to them, so he tried to ignore them too.

A brisk but polite feminine voice from behind Laci said, "Excuse me."

Laci turned. A woman stood there, dragging her luggage behind her, obviously wanting to go around him. Laci moved to the right so she could pass, then followed her. Walking on the moving belt was even faster than waiting behind those with mountains of baggage, content to let the walkway transport them. The woman in front of him cleared the way.

Fear made Laci avoid the eyes of the people going the other direction. Eerie colors chased each other across the ceiling and cast strange shadows on their faces, elongating noses and hiding eyes. Arrows of light flickered on either side of the tunnel, as if showing the way to hell. The noise bounced off the walls, getting louder with each echo. A mechanical voice warning of the termination of the walkway kept dropping words until it intoned, "The end is near."

Laci could move only as quickly as the woman in front of him. As they neared the end of the tunnel, she was forced to slow down. More people joined the walking line, racing for the bright open area in front of them. Laci kept his eyes on the bag the woman pulled behind her, afraid to look at her shoulders, scared that the shadows there would congeal into a leering face.

When Laci reached the escalator, he didn't let it take him up passively. He climbed the stairs two at a time, stretching his legs, passing the people who had slowed him down. When he reached the top he paused, bent over, panting a little.

The woman Laci had followed crested the elevator. Her blond hair lit up in the sudden light, like Zita's. The memory warmed Laci's heart. She smiled as she walked, as if remembering a pleasant conversation with a loved one. She ran her hand through her hair, pulling it out of her face.

A trick of the light made it seem as if her hair didn't lay down flat after she passed her hand through it, but stood up straighter. Laci watched it twist and elongate, growing into the light like a plant. The woman's hair continued to coalesce until it metamorphosed into a set of graceful antlers, vibrant and glowing. Laci stared. A child of the *csoda szarvas*? He took a step in her direction.

A business man in a dark suit bumped into Laci. "Sorry," he said as he passed.

Laci stopped mid-step, his attention arrested by what he saw. A monster stood before him. Huge powerful thighs tensed to leap, interlocking spines bristled along its arched neck, and its head nearly touched the ceiling. How had such a creature snuck into a crowded, public place? Bélusz had grown bold. Laci looked around wildly to find the woman with the marvelous antlers, but she'd disappeared into the crowd.

Laci swung back to the demon flexing his fingers, preparing to do a revoking gesture, something to send the minion back to where it had come from.

Why hadn't the thing attacked? Laci stood in plain sight. It stayed frozen, unmoving, still, like a . . .

. . . a statue. It was just a statue. A dinosaur. The ancient peered without malice at the present. Laci sighed and rolled his shoulders. He should know better. Bélusz' minions wouldn't attack him as long as he kept his momentum, going back to Budapest. Why, he wasn't certain. Though he wanted to know, he was sure he wouldn't enjoy the learning.

The weight of his task settled onto his chest, and he started walking again.

Though the terminal Laci had arrived in had been built according to older architecture models, it still felt more modern than the international terminal. There was a late-sixties style to the square counters and white polished floor. As Laci had checked in all the way to Budapest, he didn't have to stand in the ticket line again. He could go straight through security, then past customs.

To Laci, going through customs meant leaving America for good. He'd never come back to this fair land. He felt it in his blood. Longing struck him. He wanted to say good-bye. He hadn't been able to properly say good-bye to his family, though he'd tried, with the bouquet for Zita.

Laci decided to go outside one last time, just for a moment, just to feel he wasn't abandoning this country too.

The wind struck Laci with gale force as he walked out the doors. He toiled through it, forcing himself into a clear bus stop shelter. The walls of the shelter didn't go all the way to the ground. Wind sliced at his ankles. Laci leaned against a wall, his backpack protecting him from the cold. Thunder rattled the enclosure.

Laci closed his eyes. How could he leave this wonderful sheltering land? He loved its natural places, its deserts and forests, even its people, sometimes. He smiled, remembering the night with Edna.

America was a land of opportunity, the fabled land of plenty: plenty of food, land, and family. He ached to hold Margit one more time, to touch Zita's golden hair. He wished he could prove to his granddaughter that he wasn't a crazy old man, yet at the same time, he was glad she'd never developed her sight, that she couldn't see the things he saw. He hoped she'd stay here, in this country, and not follow him. He knew she would, but if she listened to Peter, she wouldn't go for a few days at least. Not until he'd taken care of everything.

He heard Grandmother Zita's words, one of her Hungarian sayings. "*Tartozott az ördögnek egy úttal.*" Literally, it meant that someone owed the devil a journey. It was usually said when someone took a trip in vain. Laci didn't know if the literal or applied meaning was more relevant to his situation.

Rain struck the shelter in hard, small pellets. The wind drove it under the shelter walls, lightly coating Laci's shoes. It washed off the dust from the desert. He had to leave it here, like everything else. America had been his home for a long time. Most of his adult life. Now he must return to his childhood home. His beloved Budapest.

"*Hazamegyek,*" Laci said aloud. Going home.

There was no reply, no laughter or rushing of wings. Just the steady rain.

Laci went back into the terminal, through security and customs. He boarded his plane as quickly as he could. He dreamed of warm, sunny places the entire flight—places he'd lived, places he'd never return to.

Part II

Entrance,
Sink Hole

"Race you," Laci said, then took off running across the open meadow before János replied. He'd show János who was scared. Yes, the Nazi soldiers in the woods behind them frightened him. It was late, and the moon only peeked through the clouds every now and again. But he wasn't going to run away, no matter how much he wanted to run back to the camp with the other scouts.

He heard feet pounding behind him. Before that spring, János would have beaten Laci in any race. Laci had shot up recently, gaining inches in his legs, and had a longer stride now. He wondered sometimes if he'd be even taller if he and his mother weren't so poor, if the war weren't raging, if food were more available. A deep hunger gnawed at his belly all the time.

Just as Laci reached the rise, his friend tackled him from behind. Laci landed hard on his elbows. He pushed himself up and tried to free his legs. János had wrapped his arms around Laci's thighs. Laci felt János remove one arm and reach up toward Laci's shoulder. Laci sunk his knees into the soft grass and shifted his weight back, lifting himself into a kneeling position. János released his hold and flung himself onto Laci's back.

Laci shook himself like a wet dog, trying to dislodge his classmate. János was smaller, lighter than Laci, and not strong enough to force Laci back to the ground.

Suddenly, János let go and stood up. "What was

that?" he asked, looking behind them, toward the woods where they'd seen the patrolling soldiers.

Laci shifted from a kneeling position to a racer's crouch, ready to spring up and run again. He listened hard. He didn't hear anything.

"What did you—" Laci started to say, turning his head to János. He interrupted himself, bringing up his hands to protect himself from János' charge.

"Umph." Laci landed hard on his back, the wind knocked out of him.

"Yield!" János commanded.

Laci grabbed János' right shoulder with his right hand and pressed his elbow up, forcing his forearm against his friend's throat. "Never to trickery," he said through gritted teeth. Laci had seen János deceive other kids, cheat them out of the *fillér* coins their parents had given them. He and János had laughed about it.

He wouldn't stand for János trying to fool him.

Anger lent Laci strength. He pressed up, leveraging his hold on János' shoulder, choking his friend. János' grip loosened. Laci struggled to lift himself from the ground.

János abruptly let go of Laci. He turned his head and looked at Laci's hand, still gripping his shoulder, then at his friend, right eyebrow raised.

Laci let go of János. János stood and brushed off his pants.

Laci stayed reclining in the grass, looking up toward the sky. The moon wasn't quite full; a piece was missing from the side, as if a knife had nicked it. Beyond the moon, in the open patches of the clouds, he saw many stars. The quiet seeped into his skin. Wind spoke in the trees behind him, but he didn't hear any cars, or more important, any planes.

Momentarily content, Laci pushed himself up to a sitting position. The nearly full moon shone on the empty meadow, tipping the new grass with sheaves of white. Just below, the dark band of the Danube separated the city of Buda from the city of Pest. A few lights twinkled in Pest, the flat industrial side of the city. Even fewer lights shone on the Buda side, with its hills, trees, and large rich houses. Laci sighed. He'd been in the hills of Buda before the war, and remembered the carpet of lights the city had been during the evening. The darkness reminded him of the war and the danger. All light and hope had been shuttered against the fear of another Allied air raid.

János sighed loudly, then asked, "Why are you still rolling around on the ground like some rube? Haven't you learned anything living in the city?"

Laci stood, grimacing. János constantly reminded his friend that he hadn't grown up in Budapest, that his family was from Miskolc, that he'd spent every summer and every family vacation on Grandmother Zita's farm. They'd only moved to Budapest because his father had been killed and they'd been forced to live with his mother's brother.

János started walking down the hill. Laci stayed where he was. After a few steps, János stopped and looked over his shoulder at Laci.

"Coming?" he asked.

"We should get back," Laci said. They were on a camping trip with the scouts and had snuck out with some of the other boys. The original plan had been for Laci and János to lead the boys into the woods, get them lost, then sneak back to camp by themselves. The plan had backfired when they'd seen the Nazi soldiers. The other boys had gone back immediately. Laci had wanted to go back too, and had only continued after János had accused him of being chicken.

"You said you would show me the Dead Man's flower," János said.

Laci bit his lip. Though János might tease him about his rural upbringing, his classmate still sought Laci's knowledge. Grandmother Zita had taken her grandson on long rambling walks when he'd visited, teaching him the names and properties of every plant and herb they saw. You used the Dead Man's flower in a spell to bend a ghost's will to the casters. Grandmother Zita had instructed Laci that it should be used only to send a ghost to heaven, or back to the Tree of Life to await rebirth. When Laci had told János about it, his classmate had wanted to try to make a ghost aid them, like finding out the answers for a math test. That is, if the boys could find the flower. And a ghost.

"We'll find one tomorrow," Laci said, turning around. His mother would kill him if he was kicked out of scouts.

He took a slow step, planting his foot carefully. Then another. Sure enough, János tried to jump on him again. This time, Laci was prepared. Instead of falling forward, he fell back, pinning János underneath him. However, János' legs and arms were still free to hit at Laci. Laci rolled, trying to capture at least one of János' legs. János pushed at the same time, and they tumbled a short way down the hill. János ended up sprawled on top of him.

Laci pushed János off roughly. A wink of bright metal caught his eye. "What's that?" Laci said, pointing.

"Oh no, old friend, I won't fall for that trick," János said, bunching himself up for another attack.

"Are those lamps?" Laci said. He watched János out of the corner of his eye, but didn't turn his head toward him.

János heaved himself into a sitting position. "I think so."

Laci stood and walked two steps toward the spot. As he crouched down, János sprang up from where he'd been and shoved Laci so he fell on his side. Immediately, János jumped on top of Laci, forcing his friend's head into the dirt. "Yield!"

"There's a hole here," Laci said. He'd never have seen it standing. Sheaves of long grass made a natural shield for the opening, hiding it from anyone not looking for it, or crawling.

"Yield!" János called again.

"Get off," Laci said, pushing himself up. János fell

back. Together, they approached the hole. Laci lifted away the grass.

A cave entrance stared back at them.

Dank cold and blackness sucked at Laci from the hole. He felt both drawn and repelled by it. Something foul lived down there. Impure.

Important.

Chicken flesh raced across Laci's shoulders and up his neck.

"Let's go," János said.

Laci turned. János had picked up the two kerosene lamps. He shook them at Laci. Liquid sloshed. "Not only did they provide lamps, but they supplied the kerosene as well."

"We have to get back," Laci said. "The scout master is going to find us missing. Or those Nazis are going to see us." He wasn't about to tell his friend of the uneasy feelings the dark hole before him inspired.

János seemed to sense it though. "That cave," he paused. "We need to go in it. You know that."

Laci shook his head. "Maybe you do. I don't."

"Look, you remember that protection thing you showed me?"

"It isn't real."

János shrugged his shoulders. "Perhaps. But I know that you'll feel better if we do it before we go into the cave. I'll do it with you, three times, like you taught me. And I promise we'll leave at the first sign of danger."

Laci didn't walk away. He wanted to, but he didn't.

János put down the lamps, then stamped down the grass in a wide circle around Laci, creating a space for them to "work." He came back and stood next to his friend, then asked, "Ready?"

"No."

"Come on," János said. He sighed, then paused. "I'll set everything straight with the scout master. You won't be kicked out."

Laci looked skeptically at his friend.

"I'll *arrange* it," János said. "For both of us. If I have to. I won't do anything, though, if we can talk our way out of it."

Laci bit his lip. János' family had managed to hold on to their money through the duration of the war, or maybe they'd just had more to start with. Laci didn't hate his own poverty as much as he hated other people's pity. He took care never to lift his feet too high, so no one could see the holes in the bottoms of his shoes. He refused to wear any of the "charity" clothes his mother found anonymously deposited at their door. After his latest fight, he'd worn his bloody shirt with pride, treating the stains as badges of honor.

János had never pitied Laci, never tried to impress him with his money. He teased Laci, but that was part of their friendship. János could pay off the scout master if they got into trouble. They'd both seen him accept bribes from other boys.

Laci didn't want to accept his friend's money, to be beholden to him. "What about the soldiers?" he asked.

"What about them? If they see us, we can always cry and say we were lost."

Laci snorted. He'd never seen János cry, not even when Csaba, the butcher's son, had grabbed his friend's head and bounced it against the brick wall of their school. Besides, would the soldiers believe they were lost if they found them with lamps? And what about the owners of the lanterns? What if they came looking for them?

"Please," János said. "I really want to go into that cave."

With as much grace as he could muster, Laci acquiesced. János so rarely said please.

The boys stood next to each other, legs spread in a wide stance, yet staying within the ring János had inscribed. Laci made a circle from his forefingers and thumbs, raised the loops to his forehead, then joined his hands together. He closed his eyes and concentrated, reciting the words Grandmother Zita had taught him: "Guard me, protect me, safeguard me, lead a bad fate far from me." With the last phrase, Laci pushed his hands out, as if thrusting away all harm. He did this three times, and didn't open his eyes until the last iteration.

To his horror, Laci saw János didn't push out with his hands, but instead, drew his hands in, bringing his fate to him. His friend had changed the ritual. A shot of terror passed through Laci. He swallowed against it, burying the fear, ignoring his misgivings.

János' eyes were closed. He didn't see Laci watching. When he opened his eyes, he smiled and said, "Let's go." He seemed excited.

Laci shook his head, refusing to admit how hollow his stomach now felt. The protection ritual wouldn't really shelter him from harm, no matter what Grandmother Zita had told him. It was a silly superstition, as his practical mother always said. And János purposefully changing the ending of it didn't mean anything either.

János knelt down next to the lamps and lit them with the found lighter, which he then pocketed. Laci nearly told him to leave it where he'd found it, but without the lamps, the lighter wouldn't be much good. He'd remember to tell János to leave it when they finished exploring.

Laci pushed one of the lamps into the hole. A series of ledges led down, like stairs. Or rows of teeth. Laci wanted to turn back, but it was too late. János put the handle of his lamp in his mouth and descended. Laci followed suit. The wood warmed quickly and tasted of sweet grass. The weight pulled at his jaw. He closed his lips tightly around the handle to prevent the lamp from swaying too much.

After climbing down a short way, they came to a flat place where they could both stand. János and Laci held their lamps above their heads. Laci expelled breath sharply from his belly, trying to see if it was cold enough for his breath to steam. It wasn't, but it felt as though it should have been.

Melted rock covered the walls. Long icicles of slate gray, tan, ocher, and beige dripped down on all sides. Faint olive-colored patches, like knobby ears, peeked out between the rock fingers. A dark hole on the far side of the chamber beckoned.

"Isn't this great?" János said, still excited. "I'll go first." He indicated the tunnel leading out.

Laci shook his head. They should leave the cave now. Something still didn't feel right.

"Don't worry. I'll protect you."

With a glare Laci replied, "Don't need your protection."

"Then if you'd like to lead the way?"

Laci pushed himself forward. "Most kind of you, sir," he said, using the most formal words he knew. He refused to show János how scared he felt. He wouldn't run away.

A maze of columns and huge boulders awaited them. Twice they had to wade through bone-chilling knee-high water. There seemed to be only one way to go, so Laci wasn't worried about getting lost. Darkness ate at his courage. Sodden air pushed against him. He wanted to go back, again and again. But János was behind him, egging him on.

They reached a small chamber with two holes leading out of it. The hole leading to the left went up, while the other went down. Bubbly rock bulged between the two holes. A sharp edge toward the center pulled Laci forward. A shell from some ancient sea creature lay trapped in the rock. Dripping water echoed off to his right, reminding Laci of his thirst. He spat, trying to clear his mouth of the dust he'd inhaled.

Laci turned to János. Streaks of dirt lined his friend's face, hollowing out his cheeks. For an instant, János' eyes reflected the light like an animal's, red and wary.

"It's time to go back," Laci said.

János looked at Laci, disgust and contempt mixed equally on his face. "You're such a momma's boy," János said.

"Am not."

"Are too. You're always running back to your momma."

Laci had had enough of János. Bad things awaited him down here, things that not even Grandmother Zita's spirit could protect him from. He turned to go.

János called out after him, "That's it. Run away. Just like your dad did."

Was János accusing his father, a war hero, of cowardice? How dare he! Laci turned back, ready to fight.

He didn't see János anywhere.

Laci walked up to each opening, listening hard, but he couldn't tell which one his friend had taken. Should he call for János? No. That would only bring whatever was waiting in the caves to him. Or possibly the Nazis waiting in the woods above him.

He still couldn't shake the feeling that something lived down here, something not human. Something that waited for him.

After another minute of studying the two trails, Laci chose the path going down. It looked easier, so he figured that would be the path János chose.

Laci moved cautiously, watching the trail, placing his feet carefully along the rock-strewn path. It seemed blacker now that he explored alone. He shook the lantern. Oil still sloshed. How long before it burned out? His wet pants clung to his legs, chaffing his calves.

When Laci reached the next juncture, he held his lamp high and listened. He didn't hear János. He still didn't want to call for his friend, to break the silence of the cave.

Then he heard a sound. A faint cry, like an infant's. There couldn't be a baby down here.

The main path went around to the left. A smaller trail went to the right, down a small hole. Laci crawled a short way, then ran into a dead end.

He sat down to rest. He didn't want to abandon János, but he didn't want to go through the cave anymore either. He decided to go back. He'd proved he wasn't a coward. János was just being stupid. Laci wasn't going to fight with him anymore.

Laci leaned forward to push himself up when he heard a wheeze, the kind an old man makes in his sleep. Laci picked up his lamp and shone it on the wall. A chink sucked at the light. Laci found he had to wrap his body around a boulder to look through the hole.

Beyond the wall stood another chamber, full of long rocks.

Then one of the rocks moved.

A horrible realization pushed Laci away from the wall. Fear dried his throat, making it difficult to swallow. He suddenly knew what he'd seen. It was a group of people, lying together, either sleeping or frozen in terror.

Everything came together in a rush. The soldiers. The hidden lamps. The fear he tasted in the air.

These were Jewish families, hiding.

Laci backed out of the hole fast. In his haste, he turned the wrong way down the main path. Instead of going to the left, back up and out of the cave, he turned to the right, going deeper into it.

After walking around two or three curves, Laci saw a light ahead of him. It beckoned Laci forward. He knelt and peered through the tunnel. What looked like an open chamber stood on the other side. And someone there had a lantern.

It had to be János.

Laci didn't consider that it might be his fate.

Chapter 7

Zita

Cold. The nightmares always started with Zita standing in an underground tunnel, and cold. Zita had never been in a cave, she didn't know if they really were freezing or not, but in her dreams, a soul-numbing iciness swaddled her in an arctic cloak from which she couldn't break free.

The weight of the rock above her assailed her next, pushing down on her, diminishing her. She grew smaller within the confines of her own skin. The rock was so great, and she was so tiny, she felt insignificant, crushed. The pressure made her feel that it was impossible for her to succeed, as if she'd failed before she'd ever begun.

Then came the noises. Clicking, scraping, and gnawing sounds slithered around her. She had to get away. She feared the makers of the noise. She knew that seeing them would change her. She didn't know the exact progress of her metamorphosis, but she knew it would be final. Complete.

So she ran. She always started with a flashlight. Sometimes she lost it and ended up curling in upon herself in blackness so complete that she quickly forgot what the sun looked like. Even with her light, there were still chambers so filled with darkness that she couldn't see in them. She knew better than to try to enter one of them.

Scrambling noises pursued her. Tendrils of glacial air brushed across her face, as if she ran into unseen, frozen spiderwebs. Wider, silk cords of cold would wrap around her and release her as she ran, teasing her, as if to let her know that they could stop her at anytime, but it amused them more to let her run.

Sooner or later she always noticed that she couldn't smell anything, no mold, no rain, no ice, nothing. She ran to regain her sense of smell as much as anything else. She felt outside herself every time she made this discovery. She'd always had a sensitive nose. Grandpa had told her it came from her namesake. That it would lead her to the truth.

She ran faster, swerving around outcroppings of rock, dropping to her knees and crawling as quickly as she could when the tunnel grew too small. She refused to look behind her, to see if the things behind were closer. She could hear them. She knew they were there.

The end always surprised her, coming sooner than she expected. This time, the tunnel she'd run down ended in a T. One side led to one of the dark chambers that would suck her soul out of her body, as the monsters sucked the marrow out of her bones. The other was merely a dead end. She stood with her back pressed against a harsh wall, trapped. She shone her light, hoping to illuminate her attackers, to face fear, but the light faltered. She stood in the dark, alone, afraid, while the edges of her skin tore.

The ripping of her blouse mingled with a static sound, as if it had been made of paper. A grumbling echoed through her, like one of the beasts had just cleared its throat. Icy claws pierced her shoulder, reaching for her soul. She jerked forward; her head slammed down on her chest . . .

. . . and Zita awoke.

She blinked and looked around. She sat in a seat on a plane. The pilot had just come on again, to apologize for their delay. She leaned her head back, afraid to close her eyes and return to her nightmare. A yawn started in her throat, expressed itself as she opened her mouth, then caused her whole body to shudder. She was exhausted. That was it. That was why this nightmare had been so bad. She refused to think any more about it.

This had to be the worst trip she'd ever taken. She'd missed her connection between Denver and New York, strained her right ankle on her race through LaGuardia, and now lightning strikes kept her final plane, from Amsterdam to Budapest, on the tarmac.

According to her original itinerary, she should have arrived at her destination midday. Now, it looked like she'd be lucky to get there by six p.m. To top it off, due to all her travel hitches, she hadn't called her travel agent. She had no place to stay when she finally got to Budapest. She wondered idly if her awful day was the price for breaking her promise to her grandfather about going to Budapest. If—no, *when*—she found him, he'd be disappointed in her, she felt certain.

Zita felt her stomach knotting, as if it chewed on itself. She was starving, but the attendants wouldn't serve food while they were on the ground. The woman sitting next to Zita didn't speak English. She filed her bright red nails and looked out the window. The thin blanket Zita had snatched from one of the seats as she passed didn't warm her at all, or stop the occasional shiver she retained from her nightmare. Frozen claws sank into her shoulder every time she shut her eyes.

Zita dragged out the romance novel she'd bought in the Tucson airport. She couldn't read much more than a paragraph before putting it down and checking the weather outside again. The pilot continued to come on every twenty minutes or so to apologize for their delay.

Three hours later, Zita's plane finally took off. When it landed in Budapest, she felt as though all the fight had been knocked out of her. She'd been sitting all day, but she was as exhausted as if she'd done four, hour-long jazzercise classes back-to-back.

The lines through passport control all looked the

same, extending forever in a harshly lit, echoing hall. Thin steel lines and white squares crisscrossed the black synthetic marble floors. Guards stood against the walls, watching over the herd of passengers. A few more stood at the entrance, guiding those that looked particularly lost.

Zita knew it didn't matter which line she picked. Any line she chose would end up being the slowest. Even if she switched to a quicker moving line, the three people in front of her would turn out to be spies and she'd be stuck there forever.

She still tried to escape her fate by picking the shortest line. Then she watched the lines on either side of her start processing people like water through a mill, while she stood still.

Zita rolled her shoulders, trying to loosen them. It was so late. Would there be any taxis? Would she be able to find a place to stay? She moved forward another inch, then stopped again, rocking from one foot to the other. She found her shoulders hunching up, so she rolled them again and rubbed her neck. It didn't help. Tension crept back into her body. A point between her shoulder blades blazed, as if pinpointed by a laser sight. Zita shrugged again, trying to relieve the discomfort. Eventually it occurred to her what could be causing it: someone watching her.

Zita tried to blame her paranoia on the cola she'd had on the last leg of her journey; she should never have had caffeine on a mostly empty stomach. She casually looked around. No one was watching her, not the guards, not even the other people in line.

After forty minutes, Zita got through passport control. Retrieving her luggage didn't take long: it lay circling the carousal by the time she got there. She still couldn't shake the feeling that someone was watching her. The spot on her back still burned.

In the corner across from the luggage carousel was an official booth for changing money. It was closed.

A long hall with stainless-steel tables on either side

served as customs. Men and women in pale green uniforms stood behind the tables, chatting to each other as the passengers walked by. They didn't stop anyone. With a sigh of relief, Zita walked through the sliding doors into the airport lobby.

To Zita's left, a crowd waited behind a barricade formed by straps running between waist-high metal poles, like people waiting in line for a glimpse of a movie star. To her right ran a dingy reflective wall. It looked like a cheap one-way mirror. It didn't distort her image as much as one in a fun house would, yet it made her head look smaller than it was. An image came to her, that of a golden-haired mouse poking its whiskers out of the nest made by the green silk scarf tied around her neck.

She looked beyond herself to the other people reflected in the wall. She thought she spotted a person watching her. The mirror distorted his features too. He had a long, almost phallic nose, with small ragged wings for ears, large teeth, and black staring holes for eyes. When Zita looked directly at him, she saw only a trio of electricians, dressed in bright orange overalls. They were finishing their work for the day, gathering up the white and yellow cones that separated them from the rest of the people in the lobby. None of them watched her.

Zita hurried past the crowd, not looking at the electricians or in the mirror again. She turned toward the doors leading outside, then stopped. Humid air blew around her ankles as the doors swished open. She smelled rain. It seemed so *dark* out there. Where was she going to go? Conversations erupted around her, none of them in English.

A small booth to her right caught her eye. Its white-and-blue sign offered hostel reservations and a minibus service into the city. No one sat behind the desk though. Zita turned up the collar on her jacket and wrapped the scarf around her neck tighter. The lobby seemed chilly, all white marble and black counters, with spotlights set in the ceiling. Zita suddenly longed to touch bare ground, to call an earth goddess to her defense. She shook herself, told herself not to be silly.

She walked toward the booth for the hostels. The white-and-blue sign was still lit. Maybe someone would come. She looked around the lobby again. The electricians still stood there, putting away their supplies, though most of the rest of the lobby had cleared out. The gray Formica counter chilled her hands as she pushed against it, going up on her toes, trying to look over the counter. Everything lay in neat piles—nothing was out, no pads of paper, no pens. Maybe they were gone for the evening.

"May I be of assistance?" came a voice from behind Zita. It had a strong British accent.

Zita turned. An older gentleman stood there. He wore a tailored smoke-gray suit. A cream-colored shirt open at the collar set off his olive skin. His face was smooth, the skin tight, as if baked on, though Zita had the impression the man was older than he looked. His thinning black hair was slicked back on top and retreating from his temples.

"I can drive you wherever you want to go," the man offered. He gestured toward the door.

The grace of his movements mesmerized Zita. She wondered if he were some kind of royalty. He smelled of red wine and dark European cigarettes, a romantic scent. She didn't know what to make of him.

"Do you always hang out at airports, helping stranded tourists?" Zita asked.

The man shook his head sadly. "I missed an old friend earlier. I couldn't get here in time to greet him personally. But something told me to wait, that a new friend would be along shortly."

As pickup lines went, it wasn't the worst Zita had ever heard. She wasn't interested in any kind of romantic interlude. But to have a friend here to help her with her search . . .

Zita peered at the man. There was something wrong with his eyes. Faint red lines ran across the whites, as if he'd taken ineffective drops to mask how bloodshot they were. His smile didn't fill his whole face either. While her grandfather had dark eyes that seemed full of light, the man before her had a countenance full of secrets. His happy expression hid, rather than revealed, his true nature.

Zita took a deep breath. The man's scent rolled over her again. An earthy smell came with it this time, not of freshly turned soil, ready for planting, but of molding corpses in graveyards. An outline of corrupt stone superimposed itself on the man's face. His shadow stretched behind him, like the train of a great cloak. It reminded her of her recent nightmares, the darkness flowing like water through endless tunnels.

Zita shook her head. She was just tired, hungry, seeing things. Yet a phrase came to her, something about looking fair while feeling foul. Though this was a man with power, and could possibly help her find her grandfather, it wouldn't be worth the price he'd ask of her.

"I'll find my own ride. Thank you," Zita said, pushing off the counter and heading for the door.

A row of cars with taxi signs on them waited at the curb. Several men leaned against the pillars, smoking and talking with each other. They ignored her.

"My car is this way. My driver is waiting for us," the man said, indicating a limo to her left.

Zita resolutely turned to the right. She wasn't about to get into the backseat of a limousine with this strange man, no matter how charming he might seem on the surface.

A warm hand touched her elbow and a deep voice asked, "Do you need a taxi?"

Zita pulled back. A small, weasel-like man with a sharp chin and sharper nose stood next to her. Laughter from the men next to the other cars sliced through the air. The man before her smiled as if he were in on the joke.

"Can you take me to the Marriott?" she asked. That was where her travel agency was supposed to book her a room.

The man standing next to the limo called out, "You don't want to go with him."

Zita ignored him.

"They're full," the taxi driver said, reaching for her bag.

Zita hesitated.

The man continued, his accent coming on more thickly with phrases that he didn't use all the time. "Big conference. School teachers. Or engineers. A group."

Zita remembered her travel agent not being able to book her into their usual hotel because of a conference. She handed her bag to the taxi driver.

"You really don't want to do that," called the other man.

The man in front of Zita waved his hand, dismissing the man next to the limo. "I know a place. Cheap. Peaceful. Run by family. Not a tourist place. Good home cooking. Friendly. Are you friendly?" he asked, his smile full of dingy, crooked teeth.

Zita smiled back, not sure if he was using some literal Hungarian phrase or if he was making a pass. The look he gave her didn't contain a leer, just curiosity. Wasn't it better to support the local economy than some faceless corporation? Zita followed the man to his taxi.

"I warned you."

Zita glanced over. The man stood with his arms folded across his chest, leaning against his car. It was too dim for Zita to see his expression. She was sure it was smug. Shadows gathered around him, as if he was only temporarily carved from the night and would dissolve back into it soon.

The smell from inside the taxi swirled around Zita when the little man opened the door. Zita gulped as much fresh air as she could before ducking her head and climbing in. She wasn't about to acknowledge that the other man might be right, that she shouldn't go with this man. She wasn't going to admit possible failure.

The sweat smells weren't too bad. She could deal with that. It was the other smells that bothered her: the rancid leather, the harsh tobacco, and the musky, wet-fur animal smell. She tried to roll down a window, only to discover the window handle was missing. She gave in to her paranoia and checked the door. It opened. She took another deep breath of clean air before closing the door again.

The taxi took off without signaling, rocketing down the ramp. The driver merged with traffic without slowing down, causing the car behind him to honk angrily. Zita was surprised at the amount of traffic on the road at ten p.m., even though it was Sunday night. Her driver was an egomaniac, not caring about the others on the road, forcing his way through. More than once Zita closed her eyes as he passed vehicles, either on the left—barely missing the oncoming traffic—or on the right, driving on the shoulder. The tape he played at rock-concert level sounded like it had been left in the sun and had melted, the music droning, then speeding up.

At first they drove down a straight road. Zita received half-formed impressions of the buildings they flew by, the ground floors filled with shops and restaurants with their lights still on, supporting black hulking shapes above them. There was more neon than she'd thought there would be.

While waiting at a light—the driver gunning his engine—Zita noticed no meter presided on the front dashboard. She had no idea how much the driver would charge her. She had no local currency, either. Maybe she could change money at the hotel. Or maybe they'd take American dollars. Zita's stomach churned. How could she have been so unprepared? She missed Peter, missed his cool efficiency. Maybe living spontaneously, having no plans at all, wasn't the best idea.

The taxi took an abrupt left, shooting across traffic, going up a small, twisting road. The lights from the buildings halted. Trees lined the road. The taxi continued at its breakneck pace, tires squealing through the switchbacks.

Zita didn't know what prompted her to turn around. They'd just crested the top of a hill, miraculously without the wheels leaving the road. Through the smeared rear window she saw the city spread beneath her, covered with orange-yellow lights, like a fairy carpet. She could see only two of the eight bridges that stretched across the Danube, winging their way through the darkness. The warmth and vibrancy called to her, inviting her to the dance. She caught her breath, surprised. No wonder Grandpa always called it his beloved Budapest.

She remembered that he'd also referred to taxi drivers as the "enemy."

The taxi stopped in front of a dimly lit house. The driveway and garage roosted at street level. An almost vertical set of stairs led to the house.

"How much do I owe you?" Zita asked, opening the door and filling her lungs with clean air.

The taxi driver waved his hand at her. "Pay me in hotel," he said, pointing with his chin.

Zita didn't know if this was normal or not. She got out of the car and walked around to the open trunk. The driver didn't offer to help her with her bag. Zita felt like stiffing him when they got up to the lobby since the ride had been so nerve-wracking, but instead, she grabbed her luggage out of his trunk and started up the stairs. The taxi driver followed.

Zita felt the cracked concrete stairs through her shoes. To her right, the wall of the garage cut into the hill. It, too, felt splintered and broken when she touched it. On her left a handrail survived, made out of a single metal pipe. Bushes reached under it and grabbed at her legs.

After the first set of stairs lay a flat yard. Zita caught another glimpse of the city. Being up on the hill was nice, but she longed to be in the center of all those lights.

Then came a second, shorter set of stairs leading up

to the house. A single weak bulb barely illuminated
the last few steps. The door had a large oval window
in the center of it and at one time had probably been
elegant. Now the gray paint looked swollen, full of
bubbles, and had peeled off along both sides of the
door. Zita had to push hard to open it.

The smell of damp, rotting wood, spilled wine, and
urine beset her. She would have backed out but her
"friendly" taxi driver blocked her way. To her left
stood two chairs with a sputtering light between them.
A large booth squatted opposite the door, wood on
the bottom and glass on the top. The glass had been
reinforced with chicken wire and bars.

Zita couldn't see anyone behind the desk so she
walked up for a closer look. A man sat with his back
to her, watching a soccer game on TV.

Zita said, "Excuse me."

The man didn't turn around.

"Excuse me," Zita tried again in a louder voice.
She looked at the taxi driver. He shrugged his shoulders. Zita rapped on the glass of the booth with her
knuckles. "Excuse me."

The man finally turned around. He looked like a
close cousin to her taxi driver: dark eyes, pointed chin,
and bad acne that spread like a pox across his cheeks
and nose. He glanced at Zita, then at the driver standing behind her. With a nod to the taxi driver, as if
they'd exchanged words, he picked up a clipboard, slid
open a small section in the glass, and plopped the
board down in front of Zita with a thud.

The registration form was written in Hungarian and
English. Zita ran a finger over it. A grease stain blot-
ted out the bottom right-hand side, where she was
supposed to put her signature.

"Passport."

Zita looked up from the form.

The man behind the glass booth held his hand out
to her.

Zita's anger flared. She had no one to blame but
herself. She should have admitted her failure at the

airport and not gone with this man. She shouldn't have gone with the other man, in the limo, either, but taken a third choice, found a different ride into the city.

The greed on the hotel man's face made her even angrier and settled her resolve. "I want to see the room first," Zita said. She refused to hand over her passport to this man.

The man turned to a collection of keys hanging on the wall and picked one, seemingly at random. He walked out a door beyond the TV and appeared in the lobby a moment later.

Zita brought her suitcase with her. She didn't trust the driver not to hold it, and her, hostage. How was she going to get out of this place?

The stairs, once upon a time, had been carpeted. Now, just bare wood showed, scuffed, with dirt in the corners. The same gray paint on the front door covered the walls, and water stains ran down them. The decaying wood smell grew stronger. Zita wondered how long it would be before the stairs rotted away.

The taxi man followed Zita closely, almost stepping on her heels. If she stopped, he'd run over her. There was no way to get distance between herself and him, unless she struck out a sharp elbow. Which she might have to do, soon. She tried to harden herself to the possibility.

Though there were sconces for lights between every door, only every second or third held a bulb. It wasn't dark enough for someone to be hiding in the shadows, but Zita kept turning her head and watching carefully, seeking an escape. Each door was solid wood, with brass handles that needed cleaning. Zita knew that she'd feel a need to wash her hands after she touched one. They passed by a door with beige rope strung across it and a puddle of water seeping under it. The hotel man opened the door to the next room and ushered his charges in.

The room had a bare 40-watt bulb in a holder next to the door. A plain mattress, with no sheets, blankets, or pillows, dominated the room. Zita could taste the mustiness.

A rhythmic bumping noise came from the room beyond.

Zita gulped and turned back toward the two men, the worst of her fears blossoming, choking her breath. However, the two men spoke in Hungarian to each other, paying little attention to her. They gestured toward the wall where the noises came from. Zita didn't need to speak Hungarian to guess what they talked about. The grunting sounds came through quite clearly.

It gave her an idea.

She walked farther into the room and spun, like a princess flaring out her long gown. She beamed at the men. She must lull them into thinking she accepted the situation, so she could get back downstairs and out the door without losing her luggage, her passport, or anything else.

She forced her tone to be light and carefree. "It's lovely. I'll take it." She blatantly looked both men up and down. "Where's the bathroom?" she asked, forcing a sultry tone into her voice.

The hotel man gulped loud enough to be heard over the activity in the next room.

"Down the hall," he said, gesturing with one hand, wonder creeping into his face.

Zita put as much charm as she could muster into her smile. "Thank you," she said, picking up her luggage. "I just need to freshen up. Slip into something more comfortable. You know what I mean. I'll be right back," she added. She flashed her eyes at the taxi man, who leered at her.

Zita walked directly down the stairs back to the lobby, her heart pounding. She didn't hear footsteps behind her, yet. She went out the door into the cool night, not closing it behind her, not wanting to alert the men that she wasn't coming right back. The air caressed her cheeks, as if forgiving her for her wrong decision. She raced down the fractured stairs, going as fast as she dared. The plants growing through the railing reached for her again, but they couldn't stop her.

She took a shaky breath when she reached the street. No sounds came from the "Water Hell Hotel," as she dubbed the place. She walked to her right, hurrying toward the lights. She didn't know where she was, but she had to get away. Maybe she could beg for mercy at one of the other houses. A sudden gust of wind made her shiver.

A car came up the street toward her. It was a taxi, stopping to let some people off, just two houses down from the Water Hell Hotel. Her heart jumped in her throat. Maybe her luck was changing. Zita stepped into the street to flag it down as it left the curb.

Someone behind her yelled. Zita started but refused to turn around.

The taxi stopped.

"The Marriott, quickly," she said, diving into the backseat.

The taxi driver looked at her, then forward, at the place where she'd come from. Two shapes detached themselves from the shadows, hurtling toward the car.

"Of course," he said, flooring the motor as she closed the door. "Marriott good place. Not like that," he said, gesturing behind him as they passed the two men.

Tears welled in Zita's eyes. No, not like that. She found she couldn't stop her hands from trembling. Her exhaustion rolled over her. How many hours had she been awake? With no food, nothing but anxiety in her stomach?

This taxi driver also drove like a maniac, but at least he didn't honk his horn as often as the first one had. No wonder her grandfather didn't like them. Zita wiped the tears from her cheeks, worry and strain threatening what little self-restraint she had left. They flew across the dark expanse of the Danube into the lighted heart of the city. Yellow-and-white street cars trundled down the center of the street.

Zita's spirits rose. Though she didn't consider herself an urbanite, all the buildings and concrete reassured her. She'd escaped. It was going to be okay. Fantastic statues of bearded, muscular men holding up balconies flashed by. Most of the shops filling the lower floors were closed, but as they paused at a light, Zita saw that a flower shop was still open. If only she knew where her grandfather was, she'd buy flowers for him.

Too soon, they pulled into the long U-shaped driveway of the Marriott. Zita pulled out two twenty-dollar bills to pay the driver, not caring if she overpaid. He tried to give her change, but Zita wouldn't take it. It was only money. He'd saved her from an awful fate.

The lobby of the Marriott wasn't as plastic as she'd feared. It looked like something from the forties. Dark wood with recessed panels lined the walls. A slab of gray marble formed the front desk. The clerk was all smiles and proper English. Of course they had rooms available. Of course they would take a credit card. Of course they could exchange her American dollars for Hungarian forint.

Zita dragged her luggage to the elevator, then to her room on the eleventh floor. The bed looked so inviting, she couldn't do more than take off her shoes before she collapsed.

She hadn't completely failed. She had escaped from the Water Hell Hotel, her virtue and belongings intact. As the dark cavern of sleep called for her, she wondered about her adventure. Maybe there was something beyond failure, something about succeeding after first failing. She pulled the covers over her head, too tired to think anymore.

Chapter 8

Ephraim

Ephraim stood up as soon as the fasten seat belt sign was turned off. He shrugged his backpack on, his anxiousness matched by his excitement. He worked his jaw, unclenching it, but he couldn't stop his racing heart.

Here he was. In Budapest. It was only two in the afternoon. What would he do with the rest of his day? He hadn't had free time like this since he was a boy. All his vacations had been a series of planned events: people to visit, museums to see, rallies to go to.

But now—the empty Sunday afternoon yawned before him, full of potential.

Ephraim followed the herd of passengers off the airplane and onto the ramp. He made himself walk slowly, taking in the unfamiliar scents and sights. The air seemed soft, even though it was reprocessed. The new corridor he walked down smelled harshly of fresh paint and carpet glue. He paused and looked out the window, back toward the tarmac. Clouds gathered just above the horizon: it would storm later. Planes sat at terminals on either side of where he stood, being serviced. Humps covered with camouflage tarps lay just past the runway. He watched another airboat land.

As Ephraim turned from the window, a man bumped into him.

"Excuse me," the man said, his voice high and thin.

Ephraim, sleepy from the long flight, tripped when his momentum was interrupted. He put his hands out to stop his fall and grabbed the closest thing—the other man's forearms.

The man looked up at Ephraim with wide, scared eyes. They darted quickly to the right, then back to Ephraim's face. Ephraim followed their path.

The assailant held Ephraim's passport.

"Hey!" Ephraim said, clutching the pickpocket's arms tighter. Ephraim shook the man, trying to make him let go of the passport.

The would-be robber's eyes flashed as red as a rabbit's. Ephraim had a wild impression of flea-bitten ears tucked up under the man's beret. The thief glanced down at the floor.

"No," Ephraim said, taking a wide stance, trying to get his feet out of stomping range.

The man pulled back, trying to free himself. Ephraim tightened his hold, his knuckles aching from the strain. The assailant jerked his arms down sharply, dropped the passport, and kicked it to the right. Then he wrenched his arms in and down, breaking Ephraim's hold at its weakest point, where his thumb met the rest of his fingers. The pickpocket bolted down the ramp.

Ephraim raced to where his passport lay and scooped it up. He put it back in the breast pocket of his jacket, verified his plane ticket still rested there and his wallet was still tucked into his pants pocket, then ran after the man. He quickly caught up to the rest of the crowd from the plane. Ephraim pushed his way through the first group, then stopped. He didn't see anyone in front of him trying to move quickly. If his assailant had slowed and now moved in time with everyone else, Ephraim would never find him.

Scanning the crowd, Ephraim pushed forward. He stepped into the wide passport control hall. No one in the broad room wore a beret. He hesitated. Should he go and tell one of the guards what had happened? He remembered his recent encounter with rent-a-cops. Did he really want another? Besides, what could he tell them?

Ephraim forced himself to consider. Would he recognize the man again? What had the man been wearing? A hat, like a beret, brown wool. What else? A matching suit, it had felt scratchy under Ephraim's hands. Beyond that, all he remembered was an impression of brown. Was the man young or old? What color were his eyes? Was his nose thick or thin?

Disgusted with himself for not paying more attention, Ephraim pushed his lips together and forced himself to join the appropriate line of passengers. He peered at the travelers around him, but he didn't see his attacker. He was so focused on watching everyone else that the man behind him had to tap his shoulder to get his attention when it was his turn to step up to the passport control booth.

"Hello," Ephraim said as he slid his passport through the small opening to the guard sitting at the desk.

The guard grunted in reply. He opened Ephraim's passport to the picture, held it up, and looked at Ephraim.

Ephraim stopped himself from jerking back at the hostility in the guard's expression. Why was he so upset? Ephraim allowed a small smile to creep across his face, trying to keep the game friendly.

The guard glared at Ephraim, his eyes narrowing. "Why are you visiting Budapest?" he asked.

"I'm on vacation," Ephraim said.

"For how long?"

"Two weeks."

"Can you prove that?"

"Here's my return ticket," Ephraim said, fishing it out of his pocket, extra grateful that it hadn't been taken. He started to sweat in the cool air.

The guard scrutinized the ticket, then pulled out a sheaf of papers with columns printed on it. He ran one thin finger down each column, picking up Ephraim's ticket, then his passport, obviously comparing them.

Ephraim told himself that he had nothing to be concerned about, though he had a vision of himself spending all afternoon answering questions in a chilly,

windowless office. Why was the guard giving him such
a hard time? His passport was legitimate, as was his
ticket. The airline had issued it when he'd checked in.
It couldn't be because his last name was Cohen, could
it? He recalled reading something about strong anti-
Semitic sentiment running through all of Eastern Europe. He hadn't expected to run into it first thing.

Ephraim forced himself to take a deep, shaky
breath. It didn't help his knotting stomach. Sweat
trickled down his sides, under his shirt, and he instantly grew clammy. Fear pricked at his shoulders,
sending chills down his spine. He wasn't going to make
it. They weren't going to allow him into Hungary.

His hands, of their own accord, started making small
smoothing gestures below the sight of the guard.
Ephraim couldn't help himself. It was as much to calm
himself as to influence the situation—as if any of his
rituals could.

The guard grunted once, then took a large metal
stamp, opened the passport to a random page, and
validated it with a loud thump. Then he slapped
Ephraim's passport and ticket on the counter and
shoved them through the small window.

"Next," was all he said, not even looking at
Ephraim.

Ephraim grabbed his documents and put them in
his breast pocket, moving quickly beyond the booth.
He didn't know why the guard had stopped harassing
him, whether Ephraim's gestures had anything to do
with it or if he'd just decided Ephraim's papers were
in order. It didn't matter. Ephraim still had more hur-
dles to cross—getting his suitcase and going through
customs.

Relief trickled into Ephraim when he spotted his
luggage on the carousel—still whole, not ripped, broken apart, or stolen. He exchanged money at the
counter opposite baggage claim without any problems,
counting through it twice before putting it into his
front pants pocket, along with his wallet. He didn't
have a money belt for his ticket and passport, but he

vowed to get one as soon as he could, maybe even go look for one at a shop in the airport.

A customs agent stopped Ephraim on his way toward the exit. Ephraim wasn't surprised. He placed his bag as directed on one of the stainless-steel tables. Behind Ephraim, the automatic door to the lobby opened and shut as other passengers streamed by. He felt sure God was teasing him, putting escape so close. The guards lifted his clothes, felt all around the sides of his bag, and opened his toiletry kit. Fear and anxiousness made Ephraim breathe harder. He was certain he carried no contraband, but it had been one of those days. He clenched his fists by his sides, determined not to give in to his habits, not to do anything that marked him as different from anyone else.

He couldn't believe it when the customs agents told him he could leave. Relief made him open his hands. Goose bumps ran across his shoulders, down his arms. His excitement picked up again. Finally, he was going to get into the country and start his vacation. He zipped up his bag quickly . . .

. . . but not quick enough.

A guard came up before Ephraim finished, tapped him on his shoulder, and said, "Will you accompany me, please?" The guard spoke English with a slight British accent.

Disappointment flooded Ephraim. He picked up his bag, cast one last forlorn look out the exit, then followed the guard back into the luggage area.

"Can you tell me what you want?" Ephraim asked as they walked.

"If you'll just follow me, sir." The guard led Ephraim around a corner, then to a forbidding door, painted black. The guard opened it without knocking.

The cold from the room wrapped around Ephraim firmly, as if it would never let go. A metal, industrial-type desk sat on the far side. Two matching chairs with faded beige cushions faced it. Though the bookshelves lining the walls were made from dark wood, and the filing cabinets in the corner were white, Ephraim couldn't shake the notion that everything in the room was washed out, gray. It wasn't exactly the same as the room he'd envisioned while standing in front of the passport guard: the reality was much worse.

The guard took the seat behind the desk, indicating that Ephraim should sit in one of the chairs opposite him. Then the man started questioning Ephraim—friendly questions—as if the guard were just a nosy stranger trying to make small talk. He asked Ephraim about which airport he'd flown from, how his flights had been, where he had made stopovers.

Ephraim didn't know why this man interrogated him, but he didn't want to seem uncooperative, so he tried to respond in full.

The investigator seemed only half-interested in Ephraim's answers. He kept his attention on the papers covering the desk, picking two or three up at random, straightening them, then placing them on a different pile.

The questions continued. How long would Ephraim be in Hungary? Did he plan to visit any other countries? Where was he staying?

Ephraim struggled to maintain a light tone. He felt compelled to hide his fear from this man. This was worse than any bridge tournament. He kept the parts of his body that were visible to the guard loose and relaxed. He had to bluff his way out of this, keep the tricks rolling to his side, though he wasn't sure what game they played. He curled his toes inside his shoes hard enough that they hurt, letting that be the only part of his body that expressed the anxiousness he felt. No matter how urbane his questioner appeared, he was in a position to do Ephraim harm. Beneath the guard's polish lurked something hard and hateful.

"Why did you choose to visit Hungary? Do you have family here?"

Ephraim hesitated for the first time. "No. At least, none that I know of."

"Then why did you come?" The guard looked up, finally giving Ephraim his full attention.

"I, ah, I wanted to visit someplace different. Someplace other than Europe."

"You could have gone to the Orient if you wanted something foreign. Why Budapest?"

Ephraim tried unsuccessfully to release some of the tension in his chest with a deep inhalation. He couldn't tell his intent questioner about his search for gold, so instead Ephraim replied, "I'm interested in exploring the caves in Budapest."

The guard sat up straight and stared at Ephraim. The man's smile melted away. The temperature in the room dropped ten degrees.

"If you'll excuse me a moment," the inquisitor said. He stood and walked briskly out of the room. The door closed behind him with a sharp crack.

Ephraim didn't hear the guard bolt the door, but it didn't matter. He couldn't just get up and leave, as much as he wanted to. He imagined the police telling Janet that he'd been fatally shot while trying to escape custody. Fear burned in his chest with white-hot intensity. He wondered if he'd ever talk with her again.

He glanced at his watch: three thirty. There wouldn't be much, if any, of the day left by the time they finished with him. *If* they ever finished with him. His heart thudded in his throat, making it difficult to swallow.

Certain that hidden cameras recorded his every move, Ephraim closed his eyes, wrapped his arms over his chest, and settled down to wait. He would not put on some kind of "show" for his observers. His anxiety made him squirm, cross his right leg over his left, then vice versa, but he wouldn't allow himself to stand, pace, or panic.

Within ten minutes, Ephraim heard the door open behind him. He refused to turn around to see who it was.

"Sorry for keeping you, old chap," said an older man in a tailored smoke-gray suit as he walked around the desk and sat down.

Puzzlement and surprise filled Ephraim as he straightened up in his chair. A civilian?

The man extended his hand across the desk. "My name is János Szalay."

"Ephraim Cohen." János' hand was smooth and dry. Though he didn't grip Ephraim's hand forcefully, or shake it vigorously, the man's innate power still impressed Ephraim. It radiated from János in waves. This was a mover and a shaker, in charge of something big, not a petty controller like Stu.

"Now, Mr. Cohen, what exactly is your interest in the caves?" János, like the guard, appeared to be more concerned with the papers on the desk in front of him than with Ephraim.

"I read about them. Is there some reason why I shouldn't be interested in them? Why I'm being interrogated?"

"All in good time," János said, waving his hand as if dismissing Ephraim's question. "Where did you read about them?"

"On the Internet."

"Ah, the Internet. Great waste of time that, eh?" The man peered up at Ephraim slyly.

Was János making a joke? The bizarre nature of the afternoon struck Ephraim. His hands wanted to twist, make everything that they said light and unimportant. Instead, he forced them down flat on his thighs and waited.

"So, what did you read that was so interesting?"

"The cave structures are unique."

" 'Unique.' "

"Yes." Ephraim hurried to explain. "Normal caves are formed by water from the surface trickling down. The caves of Buda were formed by steam rising from hot springs."

"Surely there must be some other reason?" János pursed his thin lips like a disapproving uncle.

"Why are you asking me these questions?" Ephraim put his arms across his chest. Fear warred with anger.

"We need your cooperation. Why are you going to the caves?" János' voice hardened.

"What am I being accused of? What do you think I might do in the caves?"

János considered for a moment. He moved his lips silently, and he opened and closed his hands a few times, as if rolling through possible problems and solutions.

János' eyes took on a silver glow.

Ephraim, startled, sat back and rubbed his right hand across his own eyes. It must be some kind of weird reflection. This guy's eyes couldn't really be glowing.

Ephraim's right hand made a warding circle as it came down and joined with his left when it reached his lap.

With a jerk, Ephraim pulled his fingers apart, breaking the circles as soon as he realized what he'd done.

János did not seem amused. His eyes began to blaze red now.

Ephraim told himself it was just a trick of the light.

"There are terrorists in the world, old chap, people who destroy national monuments for religious or other twisted purposes. We have to be careful. The caves are an important part of our heritage."

"I'm not here to blow them up," Ephraim said, exasperated. "I want to visit them, to enjoy them." He steeled his jaw and stared at János, determined to end this.

The light in János' eyes faded. He sat back in his chair and said, "Hmmm." He leaned his head to one side and moved his gaze up and down Ephraim, as if seeing him for the first time. "I suppose we have nothing to worry about from the likes of you."

Ephraim felt the assessment was meant as an insult.

"Just remember, my *very* young friend: the caves can be dangerous. Stay to the marked paths, stick with the tours. You'll be fine. You're free to go." János waved Ephraim toward the door, then picked up one of the papers from the desk and began to read it.

Ephraim stood up, nonplussed. That was it? What had that been about? He opened his mouth to ask more questions, then closed it, turned on his heel, and walked out the door. He didn't give in to his impulse to slam it shut behind him.

This time, no customs agents stopped Ephraim. His unease didn't lessen. A saying came to him. "You're not being paranoid if they're really out to get you." He didn't know if János' minions watched or followed him; he had to assume they would.

Ephraim blinked several times as he stepped into the airport lobby. It was so bright after the badly lit room he'd been in. The afternoon sun streamed through the windows and bounced off the white marble floor.

To Ephraim's left, a crowd waited behind a barricade formed by straps running between waist-high metal poles, like people waiting to catch a glimpse of a rock star. To his right ran a dingy reflective wall. It didn't distort his features as much as one in a fun house would; however, it did exaggerate them, making him look like a caricature of himself. His already sharp nose and chin elongated, while his soft round cheeks grew pudgy. His square European glasses shrank to granny size, while his thin lips and wide smile seemed to take up the bottom half of his face, like a clown's. Only his shoulder-length brown hair stayed the same, still mousy and slightly curling at the ends. He looked ridiculous and immature, like someone you didn't have to take seriously.

Next to his reflection, Ephraim saw a weird tree man, tall, with twigs sticking out of his ears and pasty sap dripping out of the black hole of his mouth. Startled, he looked around.

A trio of electricians wearing bright orange overalls stood to the left. A circle of ashen and ocher cones separated them from the rest of the waiting people. They were in the middle of a job. One stood on a ladder with his head above the drop ceiling, another fed him lemon cable from a spool, while a third steadied the ladder and watched the crowd coming through the door.

Ephraim shook his head. His reason had succumbed to his tiredness and stress. There was nothing out of the ordinary about these men. They weren't watching him, waiting for him, reporting on where he went.

The man holding the ladder continued to stare at Ephraim. He reached into his breast pocket and pulled out a cell phone.

Maybe the workers lived double lives and also acted as János' stoolies.

A Latin phrase from Ephraim's teenage role-playing years rose unbidden in his mind. He mumbled it while making a slight warding gesture with his hands: *"cingi aversabilis malus-contego-obscuro ipse."*

Ephraim continued to walk. By the time he reached the end of the roped-off area, the electrician's eyes had slid off him. He had put his cell phone away without actually making a call and had returned to watching the steady line of people coming through the door.

Just past the end of the pole barricade stood a booth with a white-and-blue sign above it, proclaiming hostel reservations and a minibus service into the city.

Though Ephraim would have liked to save some money by not taking a cab, he felt too vulnerable waiting in the lobby. He wanted to get as far away from the airport—as well as János and his minions—as quickly as possible. Ephraim walked straight out the door.

A row of taxis waited at the curve immediately in front of him. A large silent blue bus hulked to his far left. To his right waited a white-and-blue minibus. As Ephraim watched, the driver entered the minibus and started the engine.

Ephraim hurried that way. A man stood to the side of the van, writing on a clipboard.

"Excuse me," Ephraim said.

The man looked up. "What hostel?" he asked.

Relief crept up Ephraim's back, bringing a smile

with it. Was he really going to escape? Without any more hassle? "More than Ways," he said confidently.

"Which?"

"Excuse me?"

"Which More than Ways?"

Ephraim's head spun. He envisioned the concrete softening beneath him, then hardening again after his feet had sunk into it, effectively trapping him forever.

"Just a moment," Ephraim said, holding up one hand. With the other, he pulled his notes out of his pocket. He remembered writing down the address.

The driver called out a question. The man with the clipboard replied without looking away from Ephraim.

Ephraim felt his chance to escape slipping away. He had to hurry. Frantically he flipped through his papers, his fingers shaking, until he found his list. He handed it to the man. Ephraim was glad he hadn't risked pronouncing Dózsa György.

The man grunted, nodded, then asked, "One way or return?"

"One way, please," Ephraim said, handing the man a bill of medium denomination.

The man tore off a ticket and handed Ephraim his change. Then he picked up Ephraim's bag and tossed it in the back.

Ephraim got in the van. He had to climb over the already-seated passengers to the only available spot, which was the last seat in the back.

Moments later, the minibus took off. It rocketed down the exit ramp, merging with traffic without slowing down. Ephraim tried to catch his breath. He spent a moment reaching behind himself, searching in vain for a seat belt. Not finding one didn't lessen his relief.

He'd made it. He'd escaped, gotten away from the airport, possibly without János following him. He'd wanted adventure. Something different. This was more different than anything he'd imagined. Relief continued to wash over him. He was really here, in Budapest, Hungary. He could start to enjoy his trip. He still needed to buy a money belt—he checked his ticket and passport again—but he assured himself that it was all going to be okay.

The countryside flashed by. At first, wild, not cultivated, fields filled the view. Billboards, some in English, some in Hungarian, lined the road. Then small houses dominated the landscape. Next, they passed some kind of factory. There must have been a fire there earlier that day, because fire trucks filled both sides of the street. Silver tubes carried materials high above the street, from one side to the other. Behind the factory, Ephraim saw miles of these pipes, looping like a crazed gerbil run. What filled them? Ephraim couldn't imagine.

Finally, they reached the city. The abrupt change occurred in about a block, from yards to tall buildings. Shops lined the sidewalk. Ephraim saw some signs in English, but most weren't. Panic and elation burst in him.

He quickly lost all sense of direction. He knew the airport lay east and south of the city and that his hostel was in the north, but the driver made too many turns and stops for Ephraim to keep himself oriented. Eventually, only Ephraim and the couple next to him remained. The driver turned left from the wide tree-lined road they'd been traversing, onto a street not much bigger than an alley. It took Ephraim a moment to realize the driver had said, "More than Ways," the name of his hostel.

The couple got out. Ephraim followed.

A gray stone building towered to Ephraim's left. Chicken wire and graffiti covered the windows next to the street. About halfway down the block, broad stairs went up to a pair of oversized wooden doors. Ephraim trailed the couple, wondering whether his Internet source, Rozska's Guide to Hungary, had lied, or if the place had changed hands and could no longer be considered the best hostel in Budapest.

He paused for a moment, considering. At least this

didn't look like the kind of place the extremely polished János would frequent.

As Ephraim stepped through the doors, he caught a whiff of sour cleaning polish, the kind used in institutions, like his high school. It made him smile. A scuffed coat of tawny paint covered the walls. Maps and notices lined the staircase going into the lobby.

The couple stepped up to a wood-and-glass-enclosed booth located next to a grand staircase leading up to what Ephraim assumed were the rooms. Ephraim waited in line behind them. A large sign in several languages that hung at the start of the staircase read GUESTS ONLY BEYOND THIS POINT. A smaller, darker staircase led downstairs, with a sign welcoming visitors to THE HOLE. A door labeled KITCHEN stood squeezed between the staircases. A pair of faded blue vinyl couches slouched opposite the booth. Two young men lingered there, their well-traveled backpacks resting on the couches while the men stood.

When the two finished checking in, they stayed for another minute or so, asking about some place called Heroes' Square. The person behind the desk gave them full details as well as a map.

Finally, it was Ephraim's turn. Registration went quickly. Ephraim turned away from the desk, then turned back. "Can you tell me about the caves?" he asked.

The woman nodded, bored, and got out another map. "They're all on the Buda side." She drew large circles around the landmarks, wrote down the bus numbers he would have to take, then handed the map to Ephraim.

Ephraim ascended the staircase with a growing sense of anticipation and accomplishment. He'd done it! He'd come to a foreign country, made his way through the Byzantine bureaucracy at the airport, found his way to a nice establishment, negotiated a room. Of course, it hadn't been that difficult. He hadn't had to try his nonexistent Hungarian language skills.

The room was about the same length as the bed, and only one and a half times as wide. Ephraim was glad he didn't suffer from claustrophobia. The only similarity it had to an American hotel room was the white paint on the walls. The window faced east, overlooking the street. The sound of traffic leaked through the glass. Hot pipes ran across the wall at the head of the bed, under the window. The largest pipe had the impression of a sock burned into it.

Ephraim sat on the bed. He bent over and closed his eyes, resting for a moment, exhaustion overriding his stress and elation. He didn't want to sleep yet, not until later that night. He wanted to encourage his body to adjust to the new time zone quickly.

He examined the map the woman had given him. Getting to the caves seemed easy enough. Sticking to the trails, taking the tours—he'd start with that. János, whoever he was, couldn't deter Ephraim from his stated purpose.

He still didn't know why he'd been questioned, what János really wanted. It didn't matter. He'd started making changes in his life, breaking his routine. János' opinion of his worth didn't count.

Chapter 9

Laci

Laci listened hard, but he couldn't understand either the Hungarian or English version of the announcement the flight attendant gave when they landed. The loudspeaker distorted the words, softening the consonants so it sounded like babbling.

Anxious, Laci asked the bored young man sitting next to him, "What did they say?"

The man glanced at Laci, shrugged and said, "Something like 'Welcome to Budapest.'"

"'Welcome to Budapest.'" Laci couldn't help but smile. Here he was. He eagerly stood up with everyone else on the plane, impatiently waiting for the attendants to open the doors, wanting to breathe the silky air of his real home.

Laci shuffled off the plane along with the rest of the crowd, up the ramp, along a glass-enclosed hallway. Everything looked disappointingly new and generic, like every other airport Laci had ever been in. Only the signs hinted that it might be somewhere different: they all had Hungarian versions of their messages.

When Laci reached the large echoing passport-control hall, he almost chose the Hungarian line. He was Hungarian, after all. However, his passport proclaimed him as an American. He'd had to give up his Hungarian citizenship when he'd left the country. He'd sworn to protect his new land, never to forsake it, even though, in his heart, Hungary would always be his home. After a minute's deliberation, he went to the foreigner line. He'd run away, left her in one of her times of need. Never mind that he wouldn't have lived long if he hadn't. The guilt snowed on him as he stood in line. *Gyáva népnek nincs hazája,* a coward never has a home.

The guard sat very low in the passport booth, so far down that he couldn't see the top of the man's head until he was up at the booth. The security agent held Laci's passport under a scanner, reading in his name and number. Laci wondered if it set off any unheard alarms: another prodigal son returns. But the official didn't comment. He just asked whether Laci was there on business or pleasure, then stamped his passport.

Laci exchanged money at the cambio desk while everyone else waited for their luggage. As he gathered up his coins Laci asked, "Where can I buy a bus ticket into Budapest?"

"There's a shop, on your, to your," she hesitated, waving her left arm, momentarily blanking on the word. "*Balra,*" she finally said.

"*Igen,*" Laci said, encouraging her to continue.

With obvious relief, she gave the rest of the directions in Hungarian.

Laci thanked her with the most polite words he knew, as well as his best smile. Shouldering his backpack, he walked past the customs people and out the door.

To Laci's left a crowd waited behind a barricade formed by straps running between waist-high metal poles, like reporters waiting to question a famous politician. To his right ran a dingy reflective wall. It looked like a cheap one-way mirror. It didn't distort his image as much as a fun house one would, but it made his nose flatten against his face, his hair stand up straight and wild like a mane, his pupils elongate like a cat's, and the scar in the center of his forehead took the appearance of a bloodshot eye.

Laci looked beyond himself to the other people in the mirror. Demons stood there, at least three of them. The one watching Laci had a long, almost phallic nose, with small ragged wings for ears. A giant tree man stood next to him. When Laci looked directly at them, he saw a trio of electricians in bright orange overalls, just starting a job. One unloaded equipment from a small cart, another set up a circle of dusty cones to separate them from the crowds, while the third reached into his breast pocket and pulled out a cell phone.

Laci knew there was a way to dislodge the demon's gaze and make it forget what it saw. Grandmother Zita had taught it to him. He merely had to chant a simple phrase in Latin, but he couldn't remember the words. Laci slowed down until he was in the middle of a group of travelers, trying to lose himself. He knew it would be useless. Surrounded by strangers, he moved to his left to go to the shop selling the bus tickets. He checked over his shoulder, but he didn't see the workmen following him.

By asking for the ticket in Hungarian, Laci received prompt service from the bored clerk. He left the store quickly, afraid to be caught alone there, more afraid of endangering another innocent, like Jack.

Laci slipped through the lobby doors and stepped outside. He stopped for a moment and took a deep breath. Though an anxious voice in his head told him to keep moving, he stayed still for another moment, breathing deeply. Something indefinably sweet filled the Hungarian air. Then he turned to his left and hurried to the blue-and-white bus.

People and packages occupied almost all the seats. Laci walked past them: the traveling youths hugging their oversized backpacks in their laps like parents holding their children; the older women in uniforms, just off work, enduring the world with their eyes closed; the laborers finished with their shift, already sneaking drinks out of brown paper bags. Laci hoped he wasn't putting these people at risk, but he had to get into the city.

After validating his ticket in one of the small black boxes bolted to every pole, Laci stood at the back so he could watch everyone getting on and off. In addition, the rear door was right next to him, so if he needed to, he could leave in a hurry. The driver boarded immediately after Laci got on. The bus rumbled to life. Laci felt the vibrations pass up his legs, all the way to his chest. It made him smile. He hadn't taken any public transportation since his first few years in America.

The vehicle bolted down the exit ramp and merged with the existing traffic without stopping. They moved so quickly that Laci wondered if the bus driver was training to be a taxi driver. He told himself he could relax a little, they were safe until they started picking up passengers. He loosened his knees and swayed in accord with his ride, pleased that he hadn't lost his "sea legs."

Billboards, wild fields, and regimented blocks of houses raced by. Nothing Laci saw told him he'd returned to Hungary. He gripped the handrail until his knuckles ached. His head floated up above his body, disconnected, like it had in his dream. He'd known, intellectually, that things had to change. He wanted Hungary to be prosperous, which meant joining today's world, not staying in the past. Regret for his lost childhood home rang through his bones.

More buildings populated both sides of the road now: houses, a school, a car repair shop. The bus stopped to pick up a lanky youth waiting at a green metal shelter. He walked insolently to the rear of the bus, then just leaned against the side of the bus, deigning to hold on to anything.

Laci tried to observe the youth without staring at him. The vehicle slowed to its next stop with a slight roll. Laci allowed his head to swing forward with the motion, then let his gaze wander over to the young man. He wore the ubiquitous teenage uniform: a black T-shirt emblazoned with some odd-named band across the front, jeans, and tennis shoes. His shaggy blond hair drooped over his left eye. Knotted leather bracelets snaked around both wrists, like some kind of dirty brand. Was there something odd about him? Maybe an extra shadow?

The young man met Laci's gaze with what looked

like a genuine smile of friendship. Then he ducked his head as if shy.

Laci beamed at him and crossed his arms over his chest, like a proud father. Maybe the young man did have manners.

As the bus slowed again, the young man leaned over toward Laci and said in good English, "Excuse me, sir. But you look like someone who knows my father."

Laci shook his head, as if still clearing out the pressure that had built up from the airplane ride. Had the youth really just said something so polite? Wanting to be sure, he asked, "*Elnézést?*"

The youth continued speaking in English. "I'm sure you're someone my father knows. Do you have a place to stay? Even if you don't know my father, you'd love to meet him."

Laci's heart ached. He wanted to agree. He wanted to believe this semblance of hospitality. But he knew too well who this youth's "father" was. A shadow lurked on the boy's shoulder, controlling his actions. A creature placed there by Bélusz.

Laci leaned back and stared at the young man, challenging him with his gaze. He wouldn't go with this minion. This was just another demon trick.

The youth's own gaze changed from friendliness to smugness. "You will come see us soon, won't you? Before we have to send someone else for you?" Venom dripped from his words, shaking Laci to the core.

Bélusz already knew he had arrived. Of course. Maybe silent bells *had* gone off in the airport when the guard had scanned his passport.

The youth slouched away toward the back door. He pressed the buzzer, signaling the bus to stop. Laci watched him as one watches a rattlesnake, afraid to look away. They passed under a mass of silver pipes, running from one side of the street to the other.

As the bus slowed, the youth looked back toward Laci and said, "*Vigyáz! Csukd be a szemed.*"

Careful? Watch his eye? Did he mean Laci's third eye, the one that allowed him to see the true nature of people? Or something else? Laci reached up and touched his forehead. As the new scab healed, replacing the old scar Bélusz had given him, he "saw" more and more. He passed his hand over his eyes, pressed upon them for a moment. What was he doing so far from home, in this now-foreign place? He felt so old and tired, incapable of being a hero.

An explosion rocked the bus. The windows along the left side of the bus cracked and shattered.

Dozens of sharp pains stung the back of the hand Laci had over his eyes. The screams from the other passengers on the bus mingled in his memory with air-raid sirens. Behind his closed eyes, he had a vision of glass blowing through the bus in slow motion, like a million crystal snowflakes.

The vehicle abruptly stopped. Laci gripped the handrail, struggling to stay on his feet. Then he launched himself off it, flying for the door. He reached the back exit before anyone else and wrenched it open. Pleas for help followed him out the door. He couldn't stop. He had to see if his deepest fears were real, if he could see Bélusz' hand in this.

Laci walked behind the bus. Still wary from the boy's warning, he kept one hand shielding his eyes and his gaze on the ground, the other hand on the rear of the vehicle, letting touch guide him. Passengers pressed around him. When he felt the heat from the fire, he pulled his hand away from his eyes and made himself look at what had occurred.

Flames poured from the factory on the south side of the street. Men in shirts and ties, as well as in factory overalls, ran every direction, from the building, to the building, to the street, to the water hydrant nearby, and back again. Blood poured down the face of a young woman in a peach-colored suit. A man with one sleeve torn from his blue shirt helped her walk to the curb. Everyone shouted to make themselves heard over the roar of the fire. The factory was only three stories high, but the flames added a fourth, even a fifth, level. Sirens approached from the distance, honking to clear the way.

Suddenly Laci was transported.

Instead of the modern factory in front of him, he loitered outside the apartment he and Judit shared. Three tanks sat shelling a building half a block away. It had been a beautiful structure, with decorations of grapevines strung between the windows. The continual barrage from the big guns echoed inside Laci's head. He couldn't get away, couldn't escape the noise, the irregular beat. He remembered watching it for hours. When the tanks had finished their work, nothing had been left of the building but rubble.

Then he saw the fire in Új-lipót Város, the neighborhood in Budapest where his uncle lived. The gas lines had blown, causing muffled explosions under the street and terrifying blue fires in the houses. The fire had roared like an ancient, mythical beast.

The past and the present mixed together, the same horrible screams, the same roar of the fire, the same awful burning smell. Air-raid sirens sounded again, warning Laci of the coming danger. The snow created by books blown to bits swirled around him. The cold of his stolen childhood froze his hands, worse than anytime he'd gone sledding.

Laci no longer felt the fire against his hand. He pressed forward. Blinded by whiteness, he stumbled over an unseen curb, surrounded by the death of his homeland's ideas, the loss of hope, the limited freedom. His own demise beckoned, an easy way out, with closed eyes and a petrified heart.

Laci's left shoulder stopped moving. He looked at it, expecting to see red blooming on his sleeve, wondering where the pain from the bullet was. A callused and chapped hand rested there, the fingernails bitten to the quick. Laci looked up, jerked back to the present day. A factory worker stood in front of him, silent, preventing Laci from getting any closer. Not a demon or an angel, just a Good Samaritan. Laci took two steps back and peered beyond the man blocking his way.

The factory still burned. Men still screamed and died.

Laci knew this was a message from Bélusz. This terrible tragedy, with all the sights and sounds of a bombed building. A country at war.

What was, will be again. Unless Laci cooperated.

Or, unless he stopped it.

Laci came back to the present slowly, as if he'd started from a great distance. Darkness and smoke filled the room. He sat on a stool, leaning against something. His elbows ached: he must have been there for a while. Rows of bottles stacked like dominoes lined a shelf just beyond the rounded piece of polished wood Laci rested on. A mirror hung on the wall behind them. Laci could barely see his own reflection in the shadowy light, let alone the rest of the room.

Slow fingers of cognizance crept into his skull. He was in a bar. He picked up and sniffed the glass of red wine before him—Kék Fránkos. What was he doing here? How long had he been loitering? He straightened as worry and panic took hold.

"The important thing is, you got away, right?" said the man beside him.

Laci didn't know if the man was talking to him or not.

"I mean, you're still free. You still have a chance to defeat this demon."

"Excuse me?" Laci asked.

"Bélusz. You know, the demon."

How did this man know? Had Laci been talking with him? Laci peered at his companion. Merely human.

Laci relaxed a little. The man spoke truly. Laci still had his freedom. The demon hadn't captured him. It didn't hold him prisoner in its cave. Laci couldn't remember what danger he'd been in, or his escape. He tried to squelch his swelling panic. He didn't know the bar he sat in, how much time had passed, or how he'd gotten there.

"So, how are you going to do it? Kill the demon?"

Laci tried to respond normally, as if he'd been following the conversation all along. "Kill Bélusz? Without killing myself? That's the tricky part." Laci took a sip of his wine. It warmed his mouth, soothed his throat, and diminished his panic.

"You said he was made of stone, right? So what if you took a jackhammer to him?"

"Hard to sneak up on someone if you're carrying a jackhammer."

"True. How about acid? Something that would dissolve rock? I have a neighbor who's a chemist. Maybe he could create a dissolving agent."

Laci sighed and shook his head. "It isn't just the demon's physical form I'm concerned about. The magician who bound Bélusz could have broken the demon's body to pieces once it was frozen, right? I think I need something more."

"Like another magician," the man said. "A stronger one."

"Exactly." Laci's newfound friend had pierced the issue. Laci needed a powerful magician, not one who would merely rebind the demon, but destroy it.

"You might try the *Daily News*," the man said. "You can buy anything in Hungary these days."

Laci chuckled, then found himself laughing aloud. He'd missed the dry humor of his countrymen. Americans usually joked about obvious things. Laci raised his glass in a toast to his friend.

The man raised his glass in return. They shared a companionable silence for a moment, savoring their drinks.

Laci couldn't sit in peace for long. The threat of Bélusz tugged at him. He'd come to Budapest to protect his granddaughter. Now his task seemed bigger. He wasn't just saving Zita. He must also save the city of his heart. "What am I going to do?" he asked, knowing he was repeating himself and not caring.

"Why is the demon attacking now? If you knew that, it might help you figure out how to kill it."

"The plaque," Laci said.

"What?"

"The plaque. They've found the last plaque. That binds the demon." He recalled seeing an advertisement for a new display someplace on Castle Hill, a newly discovered Roman curse tablet, like the hundreds found in the Óbuda graveyard. Grandmother Zita's spirit had whispered to him that it was the last plaque. And also, that he had a day or two. The demons wouldn't break the plaque until the new moon.

"You have to do something," the man said.

Laci let his head fall down to his chest. He knew. It was his responsibility, his fate. He'd run halfway around the world trying to escape it. It had followed him and dragged him back.

"Ah, friend, no reason to be so sad. Much water will flow in the Danube between now and tomorrow."

"I still have to . . ." Laci let his words trail off, confused. "I need a plan."

"Do you?" his friend asked, suddenly looking up. "Do you need a plan? Or just attitude?"

"Like some obscenely muscled American kickboxer?" Laci asked, grimacing.

"No, like Jesus in the garden. Remember? God wouldn't take him until he was willing to die. Maybe you don't need a magician. Maybe you just need the proper attitude."

"Like a lamb, not a lion, to the slaughter, eh?"

"Exactly!"

Laci nodded, considering. Perhaps that really was all he needed to do. No mater what bravado he showed to his companion, Laci knew the new moon heralded his death as well.

"There's no medicine against death. Not even this," his friend said, indicating his wine, using old terms like in the folk saying.

"Ah, but in wine, there is truth," Laci responded with another old saying.

His companion recognized it and grinned.

Laci took another sip of his drink, comforted. It was good to spend time with another Hungarian before he died. His friend had the grizzled look of someone who spent too many nights in bars. Laci wondered who paid for their drinks, then decided it didn't matter. He wanted to share company with someone tonight.

The beautiful bridges spanning the Danube, the magnificent architecture of the city—they didn't constitute the true Budapest. The heart of the city was its people.

Laci took deep breaths as he made himself walk up the hill—Szarvas-hegy—toward the cave. The early-morning sunshine lent the air that special shimmer that came to Budapest in May. Not as many birds sang in the trees, or at least, not as many as Laci remembered from childhood. The thickness of the woods had diminished as well, but that could be because he was no longer a child and so much smaller. The smell of dew on the grass, the mulching earth under the trees, and a few late-blooming lilacs, those scents remained the same. They made Laci feel like he had come home, more than walking through the city itself had.

Bramble, bushes, the occasional wildflower, the insects, all the living things caught and held Laci's attention. Though this might be his death march, he hadn't died yet. The sky peeked through the trees, an unbelievable blue, full of hope.

Laci didn't have a plan. Or, if he had come up with one the night before in the bar, he didn't remember it now. He knew attitude—a sacrificial spirit—took precedence over all else, without recalling exactly why. He trusted Grandmother Zita's spirit to guide him.

The edge of the forest came sooner than he expected. He didn't think he was mistaken: the woods used to go farther into the meadow. They'd retreated. He paused for a moment, studying the trees nearest the edge. Spring had already passed through Budapest; however, most of the branches at the edge were bare. Sickly yellow leaves sprouted from the few that had bloomed. The tree trunks pushed upward more or less straight, but their limbs curved and bent, like misshapen old men. Just a few feet away from the open space, healthy trees grew.

Something poisoned these woods.

One of Grandmother Zita's sayings came back to Laci: *Csúnya madár, amelyik a saját fészkébe piszkít.* An ugly bird fouls its own nest.

Laci thought he knew which fowl would do this.

He expelled himself from the woods into the meadow. He felt exposed. The wide field dipped down, as it had the first time he'd been here. Just below the crest would be the entrance to the cave. Laci struggled forward, walking slowly. Anxiety twisted his gut. He wouldn't allow himself to think about what he was about to do. Attitude. Sacrifice. Grandmother Zita holding his hand, making everything better, as she always did.

Laci marched across the meadow, not noticing where he placed his feet. The cave entrance filled his vision, ribbed with ledges, like the gullet of a great snake. The blackness sucked him down, muddied the light, until all he saw was the horror of the corrupt rock creature waiting for him. It hadn't all been a dream. The kerosene lamp he held in his fourteen-year-old hand flickered. The ancient alchemist behind him twisted his arm and pushed him forward. The magnificent stag awaited him, witness to his sacrifice. Just a little while longer and he'd be engulfed by that foul breath. Just a few steps more . . .

"Hey, *nagybácsi. Hova mész?*"

A voice interrupted Laci's reverie. Startled, he rebounded into the present.

Several workers surrounded Laci. Less than two feet

in front of him rested an iron fence. Laci shook his head and punched out a laugh.

"Don't know where I'm going," he replied in Hungarian. "It's just too beautiful a day to sit." He paused, then added slyly, "Or work inside."

The workmen around him chuckled and nodded in agreement. They went back to their lunches. The foreman, a friendly looking man with a flat red nose and broad cheeks, came over. Laci took out a pack of American cigarettes he'd bought for this type of occasion and offered the man one. He took it and lit up.

Laci pointed with his chin toward the fence. "What's beyond this? I"—he paused, not sure how to continue—"I remember a cave around here."

The foreman nodded. "Yeah." He didn't seem inclined to comment more, drawing on his cigarette instead.

"When I was a boy," Laci started. The foreman didn't roll his eyes, but Laci could tell he was already bored. He hurried on. "My uncle made me join these sissy scouts. We went camping up on this hill. A classmate and I discovered this cave, but the *néni* scoutmaster wouldn't let us explore it. Then, between the Allies and the war, well, I never got back."

The other man grunted. He finished his cigarette, crushed it under the heel of his boot, and peered at Laci.

Laci handed the man the rest of the pack of cigarettes.

The foreman put the pack into his breast pocket. "We're working on improving a cave. Don't know if it's the same one or not," he said. He turned and walked through the gate.

Laci followed him.

A deep black hole lay hidden by mounds of dirt on all sides. Before, where there had been many shelves, was now a smooth throat, a straight shot into the acid pit of the stomach of a demon. Laci grunted when he saw it. Without the teeth ledges, it appeared more evil.

"Might be it," Laci said, though he was sure it was. A cold miasma issuing from the pit clutched at him. "How do you get down?" he asked.

The workman pointed to a solid ring bolted to the ground. Coiled ropes ran through it.

Laci shook his head and spoke before he thought. "Why aren't there stairs?" He hoped the foreman didn't take his statement as a slur on his industriousness.

The foreman laughed. "There are some stairs. At the bottom. This is just typical Hungarian construction, in this capitalistic age. This is the second?" He paused for a moment, then answered his own question. "No, third time construction's been started here. You see, they raise enough money to do conservation work for the cave; then, before the work's finished, the money disappears. Maybe the director has a new car. Or his mistress does. So the project closes. Then more money is raised." The workman elegantly shrugged his shoulders. "You know how it goes."

Laci nodded in grim agreement. He worked on projects in America that had been run the same way.

"Who's the director this time?" Laci asked.

The foreman pointed to a large sign on the far side of the iron wall. Laci went to read it.

Under the names of all the sponsors lay the name that he'd half-suspected, half-dreaded he would find.

Szalay János. His old classmate. The one who'd found the cave with him. The one who had turned traitor. The one Bélusz had corrupted.

It wouldn't be enough to stop Bélusz. Confronting János was part of his fate as well.

And merely an attitude of sacrifice wouldn't be enough.

Part III

Stalactites, Stalagmites

Laci pressed his forehead hard against the table, hurting himself deliberately. When white lights arched across the backs of his closed eyelids, he pushed himself up. He sat straight for a moment, then let his head fall back toward his chest. He couldn't stay upright. His spine had lost its ability to stiffen.

They'd killed Judit.

His sorrow threatened to overwhelm him again. He wanted to sink through the table, prostrate himself on the ground, and empty himself of his pain. He felt like a thin sheaf of skin wrapped around a core of hurt. He couldn't envision the days without her bright smile, her laughter, her witty words tugging the best out of him, giving him hope.

Despair sluiced through him, no floodgate adequate for his grief. The Russians had returned, after Hungary's brief fling with freedom. The West had encouraged them with words alone. No one had come to their aid.

The fighting had continued for a while in the cold November nights. Laci had helped disassemble fallen tanks, stripping them of guns, wires, and treads. Now it was over. Laci assumed it would be just a matter of time before the secret police came for him, whether for crimes he'd committed or not, it didn't matter. Nothing mattered.

They'd killed Judit. They'd demolished his and Judit's apartment. A passing tank shell had destroyed what was left of his heritage, blown all the antique books to whirling pieces.

He slumped forward again.

"No you don't," someone ordered.

Laci looked up. He'd forgotten his mother was with him in the kitchen. He watched her walk around the cramped space, pulling unrecognizable items off the shelves, considering them, then either stuffing them into the knapsack she held or discarding them.

"You are not going to waste any more time. You can grieve later. I've lost my daughter-in-law. I'm *not* going to lose my only grandchild." She stopped and faced Laci, arms akimbo. "You're leaving as soon as I finish packing."

Laci blinked, confused. Leaving? Where?

"West. Go to the West. All the way to America. She's going to grow up free. You've got to keep my granddaughter safe."

Laci swallowed hard. How could he take Margit so far away from her family? She'd miss her home, her friends.

Her mother.

A lump formed in Laci's throat. He forced his objections out around it, his voice sounding harsh even to his ears. "She's just a child. How will she make it, walk the miles we'll need to? The crossing isn't safe. It's November. The nights are too cold. And there's no guarantee we'll find a good life in the West. What happens if we're shot? It will all be for nothing."

Laci's mother pursed her lips. "You'll make it." She said it with such finality Laci wondered if she'd seen the future, like Grandmother Zita claimed she could.

"People will call me a coward," Laci said. He could see Sandor, the engineer he shared his office with, curling his lip with disdain when he heard the news. And what would Izolda, the secretary of their company, say? She spread gossip faster and farther than Russians could spray bullets.

"Let them talk." His mother stood very still, as if the slightest movement would rain disaster on her head.

"Excuse me?" Laci asked, surprised. Even during

the war, no matter how many fights Laci had, how he'd torn or bloodied his clothes, she'd always cleaned and repaired them, battling all the outward signs of their poverty.

"You must live with more than an appearance of freedom. Otherwise, you're not living."

Laci recognized the tight way his mother carried herself. He'd seen it during the war, after the big fire that had burned his uncle's place. After they'd lost everything except for two dozen books and the clothes on their backs.

"*Anya . . .*" Laci didn't know how to comfort her. "I'm not a coward." He couldn't fight her. He could only war against how he longed to run away.

An impatient knock echoed through the apartment, interrupting their argument.

Laci's mother pointed at him, commanding him to silence and to stay seated. Laci bit his lip and nodded.

"*Csókolom.*" The old-fashioned greeting—an offer to kiss the other's hand—given in that smooth voice, that cultured accent, sent chills down Laci's spine. He found himself sitting up, ramrod straight.

János. Bélusz. The fourth plaque. His old classmate had warned Laci that they'd found it. The return of the Russians signified that János had broken it.

Laci didn't hear his mother's reply, if she had even said anything. Silence ensued.

"May I come in?" János finally asked.

"It's late. My son isn't here." The tiredness in his mother's voice wrenched Laci's heart. She would repeat that phrase again and again after he left. It sounded as though she'd already started practicing it. Unless she could come with them . . .

"I wanted to express my condolences for your loss."

More silence. The loneliness of the empty kitchen engulfed Laci, his grief doubled by the recognition of his mother's losses.

"When will Laci be returning?"

"I don't know."

"I see. West, eh?"

"Couldn't say for sure."

"He'd risk that crossing with his daughter?"

His mother issued a sharp bark of laughter. It careened through the apartment, an unnatural sound, harsh and mocking, not like his mother at all.

"She's dead. She was standing in the bread line with Judit when the soldiers drove by and shot them."

"Ah, that's too bad. She would have grown up into such a beautiful woman." János paused. "I saw the signs of it, even though she was only five. She would have had powerful children."

Laci's heart drummed in his chest. János' unhealthy interest in Margit frightened Laci. His skin crawled with goose bumps, as if a cold wind had sprung up around him. He willed himself to see nothing but the darkness of woods, to hear only the quiet of the night, as if he'd already started his journey.

"Do let me know where Laci lands, eh? I'd like to keep in touch with him."

Laci's mother shut the door gently; then she threw the lock with much force, a loud banging *thunk*.

Laci stood up. His mother came into the kitchen, her face white with anger or fear, Laci didn't know.

"Get Margit," he said.

The fierceness of his mother's expression softened slightly. Expectations shone there briefly, then aching overlay them.

Laci opened the pack to examine what his mother had enclosed in it. Dried food, mainly. Some tea. A small bag of sugar, to put on bread for Margit. A gold wristwatch, one of the few pieces of jewelry that had survived not only World War II, but the aftermath of the Russian soldiers. No money—not like it would be worth anything across the border. Laci closed the pack and slipped it on.

His mother came back into the kitchen holding her granddaughter. Margit still slept, her head resting on her grandmother's shoulder. She wore street clothes. Her grandmother had covered her with a thick blanket.

Laci reached for his child. She expressed his heart, his hope, his only reason for living now.

"Don't wake her," his mother said.

"But—"

"Let her sleep as long as she can. She's going to have to wake soon enough." His mother smiled sadly at him. "Even if we woke her, chances are, she's too young to remember saying farewell. It would just be for me. And I've said my good-byes."

"Come with us."

His mother shook her head. "No."

"Why—"

"Someone has to stay here. Someone has to keep the beasts off your track. Off of *her*."

Laci nodded. There had been too much chaos in the city for an official report of Judit's death. Soon though, order would return, forms would have to be filled out. His mother needed to propagate the lie that the Russians had also killed Margit. His mother would protect them.

"It's never been my place to go," she added softly. "Grandmother Zita told me before she died that I would always have to stay."

With closed eyes, Laci reached out with one arm and hugged his mother to his chest. He wanted to argue with her, but he knew that tone in her voice. Nothing he could say would change her mind about going now. Maybe he could send for her later, once they got settled.

Laci rested his chin against her hair. She'd just washed it, one of her weekly rituals. The softness and the hint of sweet shampoo cut his heart. She should have been able to bathe in perfume every day if she wanted. She had suffered as much, if not more than he had, under the Communist reign.

And now she had to suffer alone.

"It will be worth it," she said, as if responding to his unspoken pain. "Knowing my grandchild is safe. Knowing that you're free, living where you can read anything you want to, see every play that's produced, and listen to dissenting opinions. I will live happily knowing you're both safe."

Laci accepted the burden of his daughter from his mother. Margit shifted in her sleep, but stayed wrapped in dreams. It was better this way. She'd wake up and they'd already be on an adventure, in the countryside some place. She wouldn't start her regrets until after the excitement had died away, after they were in the West.

The chill János had brought had settled into Laci's bones, freezing his resolve more solidly than midwinter ice. He had no thought of backing out now.

Laci waited just inside the door while his mother checked the hallway; then he followed his mother to the street. The people scurrying there went their own way; no one paid any attention to the breaking family.

Laci reached out and gave his mother a quick hug, as if this were a casual parting. Then he walked away without turning back.

Laci's warm breath steamed in the quiet night air. He tugged the blanket around his sleeping child tighter. He was leaving. Leaving Budapest. Leaving János. Leaving Bélusz and the nightmare of his death behind.

Maybe in a faraway land the strength of the demon's curse would lift. Laci would be free to die there, and take the demon with him. Then no more disasters would overcome his land. No more people would be killed as portents of the times, sacrificed to the demon's freedom.

He should have paid more attention to János, to his warnings of the bad times coming with the breaking of the fourth plaque. Laci couldn't have known what his old classmate had meant with his dark words. Laci should have been more careful. He should have kept Judit safe, at home.

The time for wishes had passed.

Laci hurried through the dark streets to the train station. He would get a ticket on the last train West if he could, or spend the night in the station and take the first train in the morning. He'd go as far as he could using public transportation, then walk from there.

Ten thousand doubts assailed him while he stood in line for their tickets. He nearly turned back. How could he leave like this? His country needed him. He hated running away.

He told himself he had to go. For Judit. For his mother. For Margit.

For himself.

Chapter 10

Zita

The old man in the crumpled beige-and-green-wool jacket jerked his head up when his name was called, then rose out of his chair slowly. Zita put the tips of her fingers under her legs, certain that if she didn't sit on her hands, she'd give the ancient relic a shove to get him to move faster. He reached down and picked up the cracking brown leather satchel on the floor next to him. A small dog's head, tan and white, popped out of an opening between the handles, yipped once, then disappeared again. The man stopped his forward progress to lift the bag and whisper into it.

Zita opened her mouth, then snapped it shut. She would *not* scream or tell him to get going. She forced herself to look away instead. At least now only two people comprised the line in front of her to see someone on the embassy staff. There had been more than ten when Zita had arrived at the American Embassy that morning.

The minutes dragged on. Zita brought her hands up and gripped the sides of her chair until her knuckles hurt. She tried to calm her knotting stomach with deep breaths. The sickly sweet lemon scent left over from the cleaning solution the night crew had used nauseated her.

Zita feared that every minute she wasted not physically looking for Grandpa was another minute he'd spend in trouble. She couldn't stop thinking that her grandfather was in horrible condition, fighting demons in a dingy alley while thugs had already removed his passport and his money from him. For some reason, she didn't know why, maybe a scent in the wind that morning, she believed he still had his wits and his belongings. She didn't trust that feeling though. She *had* to find him.

Bright morning sunshine streamed through the windows, lighting up columns of dust motes. The polished black-and-white-marble floor reflected the heavy metal desks spread across it. The walls went up forever, creating shadows near the ceiling.

Zita craned her neck, searching for the cameras that her prickling unease told her about. Unseen eyes had peered at her all morning. She couldn't prove she'd been followed to the embassy. Yet she was certain she had been. Not by the men from the Water Hell Hotel but by that strange suave man from the airport. In her mind's eye she saw him again, a small figure with an aura of caves and deep-buried death flaring out around him like a huge cape. He'd been in her nightmares the previous night, joining skeletons and unseen things that slobbered and panted, who had chased her through cave tunnels into a dead end, then had piled rocks over the opening so she'd never escape.

Finally, a smartly dressed assistant called Zita's name. Zita rose quickly, then practically walked on the heels of the woman leading her. The office she came to had the shades drawn against the dazzling light coming in the windows. Zita hesitated in the doorway. Cool damp air emanated from the office, reminding Zita of the cavernous prison from her dream. A spike of fear drove through her chest.

The young man from behind the desk looked up. "Come in. Come in," he said in a cheery tone, beckoning Zita.

Zita told herself that there was nothing to be afraid of. She forced herself to walk into the room.

"I'm Mr. Farkas," the man said, half-rising and extending his hand.

Zita returned the quick handshake. "Zita Gárdos."

Papers blanketed the man's desk. Shelves filled with

books and more papers covered the walls to his right and his left. Two padded metal chairs stood before the desk. Zita sank into the one on the right as the embassy man sat back down.

"What can I do for you?" Mr. Farkas asked, focusing on Zita.

Zita had the impression that the man had just blocked out everything—the papers on his desk, the noise from the corridor, any appointments he might have had—just to concentrate on her. She relaxed a smidgen.

"I'm looking for my grandfather," Zita started.

"Do you know his last name?" Mr. Farkas asked. He kept his eyes on Zita while he opened one of his desk drawers. He pulled out a phone book and thumped it onto his desk.

"He doesn't live in Hungary anymore," she said quickly. "He lives in America. He immigrated in 1956. But he recently came back here."

"Why? Was he in trouble? Is he running from something?"

"No, nothing like that. He's old. And"—Zita hesitated—"he doesn't always know where he is."

"Did you travel here together?"

"No. He came by himself."

"If he can fly by himself, I'm sure he's fine." For the first time, Mr. Farkas' eyes left Zita's and returned to the papers on his desk. He leaned back in his chair. "He'll show up in a day or so."

"Could you check for me?" Zita said. She would not take this abrupt dismissal.

"Where?" Mr. Farkas asked in a tone that implied the ridiculousness of Zita's request.

"Could you call some hospitals for me? As I said, he doesn't always know where he is."

"Will he hurt himself?"

"He did, once, a few weeks ago. But he's been okay ever since."

"Then I suggest you go back to your hotel room and wait. I'm sure he'll be fine."

"But I don't know where he is!"

Mr. Farkas looked at her coldly. "If you don't know where he is, then why are you so certain he came to Budapest? Was he born here?"

"No, he was born in a town north of here."

The embassy man looked around his office. Zita watched the pressures of his job manifest and his calm evaporate. Zita was no longer his first and only priority.

"Why wouldn't he go back there?" Mr. Farkas asked.

Zita refused to tell this distracted young man about her grandfather's demons. "He'll come here. The caves are here."

"Then I suggest you check the caves."

The woman who had led Zita to the office stuck her head through the door. "Mr. Farkas, I'm sorry to disturb you, but—"

"That's okay. We're just finished here." He stood up and held out his hand to Zita.

Zita stayed stubbornly sitting in her chair. "I want you to call all the hospitals to see if my grandfather is there."

The man blinked. He obviously hadn't expected any resistance to his dismissal.

Zita crossed her arms and stared at him.

"Yes, well, I see." He rattled something off to the woman in Hungarian. She replied, then walked off.

"Hospitals, eh?"

"Yes."

He shook his head, but replied, "Okay."

Twenty minutes later, Mr. Farkas hung up the phone with a tight smile. "He isn't there either."

Zita knew she'd grasped her last straw. She couldn't expect any more help from Mr. Farkas.

"I suggest you either go back to your hotel and wait for your grandfather to call you, or go back to his hometown and look for him there."

"Or I could go to the caves," Zita said, admitting defeat.

Mr. Farkas stood again. This time Zita accepted his verdict. The harsh responsibility of finding her grandfather rested solely on her.

Zita made her way out into the day. She blinked to clear her eyes after being in the darkened building.

She didn't want to go the caves.

Her rational side derided her. Nothing horrible would happen if she did go. She couldn't let fear dictate her actions. No monsters would chase her down endless tunnels; the lights wouldn't fail and leave her stranded in the dark forever. But the thought of them chilled the bright morning air.

Continually looking over her shoulder, Zita tried to distract herself from her apprehension by searching for the people following her. She didn't spot anyone, but that didn't mean they weren't there.

Zita took a cab back to the hotel, shocked at how much the ride cost. The cab from the hotel to the embassy had cost only half that amount. She'd tried arguing with the driver, but he only pointed at the meter. Disgusted, Zita paid, but she didn't tip him.

She went back up to her room and packed a small day pack, remembering to take a picture of her grandfather as well as the small English-Hungarian dictionary she'd bought in the hotel gift shop.

When Zita came back to the lobby, she asked the hotel concierge about the caves. He tried to talk her into a bus tour of Budapest instead. His offer tempted her. On one hand, it would give her an overview of the whole city and maybe some additional ideas of where her grandfather could be. On the other hand, it wasn't actually looking for her grandfather. Plus, it sounded like the sort of thing lazy tourists would do, the kind of tourists who complained about no one speaking English in a foreign country, the kind of tourist Peter had accused her of being when he'd found out she was staying at the Marriott. So she asked the concierge again about the caves.

The two most popular were Pál-Völgy and Szemlö-hegy. A cave also existed on Castle Hill, though the

concierge didn't know if it was open, as well as something called the Labyrinth. The concierge offered to
hire a taxi for Zita for the day, but she balked at the
price. It cost more than what she'd paid for her hotel
room. One taxi had already ripped her off that day.
She refused to take another.

After Zita pressed the concierge further, he told her
about a seven-day tourist pass that would be good on all
the buses in the city, as well as the metro. He drew the
route to the caves on a map, spelling out the bus stops.

The first hurdle Zita had to overcome was buying
a pass. Certain she'd never find the station without
getting lost several times, Zita stepped out of her
haven of Americanism and into the streets of a foreign
country, prepared, this time, to go explore. Her heart
pounded, and for a moment she felt glad she'd come.
She couldn't describe this as a vacation, but it was still
so different than her everyday life.

Was someone still following her? Did it matter?
They were about to get as lost as she was.

Booths sat between the river and the hotel, as well
as in the square north of the hotel, selling everything
from uncut sheep pelts to colorfully embroidered
blouses. Zita had seen them through the restaurant
windows at breakfast and decided to walk that way
on her way to the metro.

She followed the stalls around the edge of the
square. Next to the street, an ancient man wearing a
gray wooly hat and a dirty suit bent over a small table,
playing an odd-shaped flat piece of wood with an
inlaid-pearl design on it and wires strung across it, like
a zither. The tune had an peculiar rhythm—a lot of
Hungarian folk music is in 5/4 time. It reminded her
of the dancing waves on the Danube.

She dropped a few coins in the cup sitting next to
the instrument and blinked back tears. She hoped the
old man had a granddaughter waiting for him at home.

By the time Zita found her way to the second bus
she felt like an experienced world traveler. The metro

had been easy. Colors differentiated the subway lines, and once she figured out the name of the last station, she knew which train to get on. She'd been delighted with the wooden slats on the escalators, the foreign advertisements lining the walls, the compressed rush of wind as the train approached, the strange foreign warning that came on the loudspeaker just before the doors closed. It had felt good, finally doing something, actually searching for her grandfather.

The first bus had been easy to find. Determining when to exit the moving vehicle had been a different issue. Large plastic signs hanging next to both doors listed the stops. However, once the bus started, Zita couldn't find any street signs and couldn't figure out which stop was which. She hung on to one of the poles next to the rear exit and looked around. An older man standing there smiled at her. Zita got an idea.

She pointed to the sign, to where she wanted to get off, then back to the door.

The old man shook his head and said, "*Harmadik állomás.*"

Zita shrugged her shoulders, not understanding.

The man held up his hand, showing her three fingers.

She was three stops away. She smiled and nodded, struggling for the Hungarian. Finally, she remembered. "Thank you—*Köszónóm.*"

The old man grinned at her, showing her uneven gapped teeth. When the time came, he rang the buzzer for her and waved good-bye.

Back on the street, Zita carefully waited to see if the mysterious stalker still followed her. She was the only person to get off the bus, and it hadn't stopped again until she lost sight of it. Maybe just paranoia pursued her. She put it out of her mind and concentrated on finding the next stop.

Not as many people filled the second bus. Empty seats lined both sides. Still, Zita chose to stand near the rear door again.

The bus sped up the hill. Zita feared that the driver

passed stops without slowing because no one wanted
to get on or off. However, the driver's deep bass voice
rang out just a moment later, announcing the stop as
they approached it. Zita felt certain she'd recognize
Szikla when she heard it. Feeling less worried, she
examined her fellow passengers.

An extremely cute guy stood close to the front door,
listening to the bus driver's announcements. He had
shoulder-length brown hair, square European glasses,
a large nose, and skinny lips. He appeared too old to
be a student, though he had a scholarly air about him.
Maybe he was a rabbi on holiday. He wore a polo
shirt and jeans. Zita decided he must be German or
Austrian. He looked too neat to be American.

That had been one of the things that had first attracted Zita to Peter. He didn't wear jeans and T-shirts.
He always dressed nicely.

How to untangle their lives? No question remained
about her leaving him. The infamous last straw had
been placed, like a gauntlet, between them. There was
no going back, no fixing things up. Particularly now
that Zita had had a taste of freedom. Giddiness tugged
at her. And why not? She was navigating her way
through a foreign city and had rescued herself the previous night. She was succeeding on her own, without
Peter. Worry about her grandfather tainted her mood,
yet she still felt more confident than she had in years.

How could she be so calm? Maybe it was the jet
lag. After she'd had enough rest, all the horror and
stress of her situation would probably come crashing
down on her. She'd failed her grandfather, letting him
get lost here alone. Her relationship, all her stability,
had vanished. Her job still depended so much on others as to make it impossible to do it well.

The morning abruptly didn't seem as bright as it
had. Zita pulled on her hair, smoothed it down over
her cheek. She rubbed it over her eyes, enjoying how
silky it felt. She reveled in it for a moment. But her
hair couldn't protect her from her life. She pushed it
behind her ears and pulled it off her neck. For the

first time in ages, she thought about cutting it. Wouldn't that give Peter a turn.

Zita sighed. She had to stop doing things because Peter would or wouldn't approve. She needed to do a thing for the rightness of the thing itself.

It turned out the cute guy got off the same time Zita did. He resolutely walked downhill from the bus stop, as did a group of three young people, all wearing dreadlocks. Zita decided to follow them. About half a block away, she saw the Hungarian symbol for cave—similar to an omega—as well as a sign that said BARLANG.

To the left of the entrance stood a large cliff face, ashen limestone rocks peeking out of the flowing greenery. At the bottom, a small door led into the Pál-Völgy cave system. To the right, up some stairs, was the ticket booth. To her surprise, the cute guy spoke with an American accent. So much for looks. She scolded herself for even speculating about him. She hadn't officially broken up with Peter, except in her head, right?

Zita hung back until all the people from the bus had bought their tickets. Then she walked up to the booth, showed the photo of her grandfather to the man selling the tickets and asked, "Do you speak English?"

The man shook his head no.

Zita took a deep breath and tried Hungarian. *"Tudsz Nagyapa?"* She knew she used the wrong phrase, that she wasn't asking if he recognized her grandfather, but if he knew him, or something like that. It was the only thing she knew how to say.

The man in the booth gave her a blank look.

Zita pressed her hand against her chest and repeated, *"Nagyapa,"* knowing that she could at least pronounce the word for grandfather correctly. Then she pointed at the picture and said again, *"Tudsz Nagyapa?"*

The man seemed to understand. He looked closely

at the picture and shook his head. *"Nem."* He said something long and involved in Hungarian.

Zita had no idea what he said, but she knew he hadn't seen her grandfather. As she put the picture back in her backpack the man in the booth said, in English, "Ticket?"

"Yes, one please," Zita made herself reply. She didn't know if her grandfather would be in this cave or not. She didn't think he would be. She remembered the cave he had talked about had been on a different hill, one that had started with an "S" sound. But he might be here. She had to check.

Even if going into a cave terrified her.

Zita gulped back her panic as she took the ticket from the seller. She told herself that she had nothing to fear about going into a cave. The anxiety inspired by her nightmares had grown out of proportion.

She thanked the young man and walked to the cave entrance. Only then did she find out that guides took groups through the caves every hour, on the hour.

Zita hesitated. Her grandfather wouldn't go on a tour of a cave. He'd only go to an undeveloped cave system that he could haunt alone.

Her relief at the thought of not going into the cave made her stay. She spurned the idea of being scared of caves just because she'd had a few nightmares.

As she stood there, the trio of dreadlocks came up, followed by the cute American. What looked like two Hungarian families joined them next, though she wasn't sure. The kids seemed interchangeable, going from one set of parents to the other, and there seemed to be at least one unattached adult.

Their guide showed up two minutes after the hour. He wore jeans, leather hiking boots, and a gray T-shirt over an olive-green long-sleeved shirt. He introduced himself in Hungarian, then continued to speak in that language. The girl with the long blond dreadlocks interrupted him, asking him if he spoke English or German.

The guide said, "No. No English. Come. Please. Come." His eyes pleaded with them.

The blonde said, "I'm getting a refund. Let's go." She marshaled her group and walked away.

The guide pressed his lips together, watching the trio leave. One of the Hungarians leaned over and said something in a scornful voice. The guide didn't acknowledge him; instead, he glanced up at Zita, his eyes entreating her to stay. Maybe his salary was based on the number of people in his groups.

Zita looked at the trio, then back. The American guy caught her eye and shrugged, as if to say, "What can you do about such bad manners?"

Resigned, Zita trudged into the cave.

Stairs went down from the entrance to a small platform. The guide made everyone stand there while he talked for a moment. Zita assumed they waited for people's eyes to acclimate to the darkness. The temperature felt noticeably cooler, even just a few feet inside the cave. The damp air draped itself over her shoulders like a wet cloak. Zita shivered and wished she'd brought a sweater. Her nightmares had warned her how cold it would be under the earth.

At the first stop, the guide used a flashlight to show them some structures. The subtle colors—gray shades bleeding into tans and rust—reminded Zita of the desert. Nodules bulged out of the walls like rock muscles. Stalactites reached down from the ceiling, tapered like fingers. Water dripped from the tips onto stubby stalagmites growing out of the floor. The rock oozed in places, as if it had once been liquid. In other areas, small bumps and blemishes covered the walls, like diseased skin. Zita stayed behind for a minute after the rest of the group left.

Suddenly, she saw a face in the wall: the bulges grew eyes that watched her, the stalagmites formed the sallow teeth of a hideous mouth, and the cold enclosed her like demon's breath. She backed up without thinking and bumped into the handrail behind her. Startled, she looked up and saw an assembly of demonic faces staring down at her. Stalactites, curved like claws, reached out to snag her.

Zita forced herself to take a deep breath. She closed her eyes, willing the world to return to normalcy. It was just a cave, she told herself sternly. Demons didn't exist anywhere except in her grandfather's imagination. Her tiredness and stress just played tricks with light and rock.

Now she understood how a scared young boy, without a steady light, could believe he'd seen terrible things in a place like this.

Zita opened her eyes and without looking around, hurried to catch up with the group.

For the rest of the tour, Zita again felt something watching her, eyes that didn't belong to the other people on her tour, eyes that lived in the cave. She tried to convince herself it was just her imagination working overtime, that leftovers from her nightmares had dripped into her consciousness. She'd been paranoid the entire trip, first thinking that the strange man from the airport had followed her, now this.

She couldn't shake the feeling.

Zita held back her impatience every time the group stopped, willing the tour to be finished, wanting to get out before something got her.

One of the last stops on the tour took place at the bottom of a ravine. Above them protruded several large ledges. The stone was light colored, almost white. Zita thought it looked like the inside of someone's stomach. Just as the guide finished, the American guy asked a question Zita didn't quite hear. The guide thought for a moment, then said to both Americans, "Big war. Planes." He paused for a moment, then waved his hand at the ledges. "This, hospital."

Zita understood. When the Allies, at the end of World War II, had bombed Budapest, the Hungarians had used this area in the cave as a hospital, putting patients on the ledges.

Stepping into the bright sunlit meadow felt like being freed from prison. Zita stood gulping air for a moment. She hadn't been in any danger in the cave, yet she'd still felt threatened. Memories of skeletons, that strange man from the airport, and being trapped, returned. The world of caves was beautiful, colorful, flowing. A whole new universe to explore.

A region that she would just as soon leave to the demons.

Zita reluctantly signaled the waiter to bring her bill. She didn't want to go into another cave, but it still seemed like the best option for finding her grandfather. The second cave she'd gone through that morning had been scarier than the first. She'd made it through only by clenching her hands into fists, prepared to pummel anything that grabbed her. She hadn't felt claustrophobic: she knew that the rocks and the things she imagined didn't breathe, that nothing was stealing the oxygen, that there was plenty of air down there. She'd just been horribly afraid of something trapping her belowground. Her nightmares continued to chase her.

The Labyrinth on Castle Hill was the next tourist cave she had to check and the last on her list for the day. Tomorrow she would try to find someone to guide her through the less-developed caves, the ones that were accessible to the public only with proper spelunking equipment.

Zita shivered at the thought of having to crawl through small spaces, the weight of the walls pushing down on her, the rock enclosing her, grabbing at her. . . . She shivered again, and told herself that she was just cold. The core of her being felt as though it still bathed in glacial air. Even the spicy *gulyás* she'd had for lunch hadn't warmed her up.

Zita sighed and sipped her coffee, looking out on the street. She'd enjoyed the romantic setting, sitting in a street café, across from the castle's crenellated walls, watching people from every nation walk by.

If only her grandfather had been there to join her. The enormity of her task crushed her will and darkened the sunny street. How was she going to find Grandpa? She was failing him, as she'd always known she would. Foreboding crowded out rational thought. Those walls *had* watched her this morning. She wished her mother, or even Peter, sat next to her, holding her hand, making the monsters go away. She longed for a friend on her search.

Bravery didn't prompt her to rise, pay her bill, and start walking. Stubbornness did. She'd never considered herself courageous. However, she had said she would explore the caves of Buda to find her grandfather. And nothing, not even real demons, could keep her from that task. She refused to be the failure her grandfather had accused her of being.

Zita followed her map to Úri Utca, the street the Labyrinth resided on. She turned away from the crenellated castle walls and down a narrow street. After walking half a block, she came upon a small sign flush against the wall of a mustard-colored building that told her she'd reached her destination.

The steep stairs descending into darkness were made of a brown-red tile that looked as if it had been stained with blood and not washed clean. Zita trembled as the cold rising from the depths reached for her. She didn't want to go under the earth again. She looked to her left, back along the way she'd come, toward the sunshine and charming cafés. Damn it. Nothing but her own fear had attacked her.

Zita walked down the stairs, gritting her teeth as the numbing air engulfed her.

The way to the ticket desk passed through a small eatery. A pair of couples dined in a small alcove with rock walls and fancy iron gates, like a cage. Zita couldn't imagine having a meal, even a snack, down there. Hadn't there been some Greek goddess who'd eaten six pomegranate seeds while she'd been captured underground and therefore had to return for six months every year?

The cute American guy who'd been at both the caves Zita had toured that morning stood in front of the desk. She came up just as he asked the women at the ticket booth about World War II.

Using very good English, the ticket sellers told him that the people living in the area had used the Labyrinth as an air-raid shelter and assured him he'd hear more about it on the tour. They also talked about a brand-new exhibit, one that had opened just that day—a room with a Roman curse plaque embedded in the wall.

The cute guy thanked them and wandered to one side. Zita pulled her grandfather's picture from her backpack as she approached and asked, "Have you seen this man? He's my grandfather. He might have gone on one of the tours."

Both women examined the picture, but neither had seen him.

"Is he lost?" the one with the long black hair asked.

Zita sighed. How could she explain her grandfather's delusions without making him sound dangerous?

"He's a little senile," Zita said. "He sometimes thinks he's a teenager, still living here, during World War II."

"Ah," said the other woman, the one with shorter hair. "My grandfather's like that too." She looked at the picture again. "I don't recognize him, but he might have gone through the Labyrinth on his own, looking for one of the old shelters. Why don't you come on the tour? Maybe you'll see him."

Zita bought a ticket and waited in the frigid cavernous space next to the ticket desk. The American guy returned carrying a soda. Zita irrationally felt like warning him not to eat or drink anything while underground. His cuteness shouldn't be stuck here.

The tour guide gave her talk in Hungarian first, then in English. Zita enjoyed her spiel. Many people had lived in these caves at different times: Neanderthals, Romans, gypsies, as well as Hungarians escaping both Nazis and air raids. People had also used the caves as wine and root cellars. During the Cold War, the Labyrinth had been part of a military underground facility.

Zita nearly turned around and walked away as they entered the Labyrinth. A loud beating heart echoed through the wintry halls. The overtones had a mechanical edge to them, staccato, not the comforting reverberations of a living heart. She didn't like it at all. She especially didn't care for the tour guide's explanation that this sound represented the heart at the center of the world. It was too monotonous and aloof for that.

Around a sharp corner came representations of famous cave paintings from Europe. The thick walls muffled most of the heartbeat. Zita wished briefly that she could share this with Peter. He would appreciate not just the pictures, but the atmosphere and the way they were presented.

Then the guide led them to a closed-off part called, the "Personal Labyrinth." Echoes of the world heart sounded louder in the dark room. The obscured light made Zita anxious. Her own heart started to race. She took a deep breath, told herself not to be silly, and forced herself to look around.

Smooth man-made walls surrounded her. No eyes watched her here. Men had also made the figure behind the altar. It didn't seem demonic at all. It struck Zita as people deliberately trying to scare themselves, like children in a haunted house. The tension that had frozen in her chest started to thaw. Maybe she didn't have to be afraid of all caves. She relaxed further when they left the Personal Labyrinth and went back into the regular cave tunnels.

Zita peered at all the people the tour passed, hoping that her grandfather wandered here. She didn't see him, or many old people for that matter. Most of the other patrons seemed to be teenagers, escaping school for the afternoon, or tourists.

Zita started when she heard the guide start talking of the *csoda szarvas*. They'd arrived at the Path of the Magic Deer. Her grandfather had talked about this creature. She remembered the tiny altar he'd set up on his dresser, the compelling picture of the horned deer he'd put up.

The Labyrinth's representation was part man, part stag, done in bas relief. It looked ludicrous to Zita, particularly with its azure body. It couldn't be the same stag her grandfather had seen as a boy—he'd described it as a free-standing statue. Besides, this one had been built after her grandfather had left Hungary.

The guide continued, telling how the mysterious creature had brought the seven tribes to Hungary and had been a kind of guardian, supposed to oversee their nation through all their hardships. The guide made a joke about it not doing a good job in the recent century.

Zita stopped listening to the guide again, instead, staring at their representation of this shaman from an earlier time. Would her grandfather come here? To visit this version? Zita didn't know. She resolved to return every afternoon, just in case he might. She reluctantly left the figure and hurried to catch up to the tour. She nearly walked right by them, as they'd taken a sharp turn into another darkened room.

A semicircular wall jutted out next to the entrance, like half a well. Above it, lit with covered reddened lights, hung a blackened lead plaque, approximately a foot square. Too many people gathered close to it, so Zita stood at the rear, waiting for their guide to repeat her talk in English.

"Recent archaeological work in this area of the Labyrinth uncovered this plaque. It's a curse tablet, similar to the ones found in the graveyards in the old Roman town Aquincum, in Óbuda, just north of Budapest. It curses Beilum, binding him to stone."

Beilum? Was that the Latin name for Bélusz?

Zita pushed her way to the front of the group and leaned forward, leaning against the half wall, trying to get a closer look. The lights were low so as not to ruin the plaque, exposed now to the air for the first time in centuries.

The American guy stood next to Zita, also leaning forward. He muttered to himself. Zita wondered if he could read the inscription.

"Can you make out the name? The name of the, ah, person being cursed? Is it, um, Bélusz?" she asked.

The guy jumped at the sound of her voice. He turned and blinked at her several times, as if he'd been in deep concentration. His blue-green eyes shone with light from a distant place. Then he turned back to the plaque. "Well, Beilum is what's written here, because the name is the direct object. If the name was used as the subject, the 'um' could change to an 'us,' so I guess it could be Beilus," he said.

Bélusz. Zita pulled back from the wall. The tour group shuffled out, going to their next stop. Zita turned to join them, but then the American started reading the Latin aloud.

Vincio neque Beilum liberabo. Beilum quinquies lapideis catenas vincio. Qualis statua haec et sedes regia unus sunt, sic ad sella regia Beilum restringo. Capellum suum, frontem, supercilia, oculos, nasium, genas, labia, linguas, orem, orationem vincio, ut non caput agitare posset . . .

The words rolled off his tongue, echoing in the small room. The man had a beautiful voice, not deep, but full and clear. He sounded like a priest at high mass, casting a spell of God, bringing light to the darkness. Zita could almost smell the incense. She smiled and hugged herself, stepping back next to the guy, delighting in his recitation.

Something moved.

Zita saw it only out of the corner of her eye. She turned her head. Nothing was there. Silly. She took a deep breath to calm her heart, which had started beating fast again. The American guy continued reading, almost as if the text had caught him, compelling him to finish it. Dusky light reflected off his glasses and hid his eyes.

The edges of the room blurred. Thin smoke flowed up and out the half-circle wall, covering the light.

Zita blinked. Shadows moved in the depths of the dark space before them. It reminded her of her nightmares, things materializing out of the mist.

The man next to Zita continued to read aloud. His voice sounded strained. He looked conflicted. His hands clutched the wall, holding him in place, yet, at the same time, he arched his back and leaned away, as if trying to escape. Zita tried to call out. The gloom strangled her voice. The man's chanting attempted to hold back the blackness, but it was as futile as a sword cutting through fog. The darkness always welled back up in the holes the words made, filling the space.

Zita turned away. She should leave the room, find the tour guide. When she turned back, out of the corner of her eye . . .

. . . she saw them.

The demons.

The smell of decaying garbage flowed with them, spiked with the scent of acid smoke and rotten flesh. The proof of her nose convinced her more than her actual viewing of them, though their actuality still astounded her. The one in front had an empty hole for a nose and long sharp teeth, dripping and pale, like stalactites. It reached out with one bony arm—covered with floppy, pockmarked skin—for the chanter. The talons on the ends of its fingers glistened. It advanced in slow motion, a fraction at a time, as if it moved through a semisolid morass.

When Zita looked directly at the demon, she couldn't see anything. She deliberately turned her head and looked out of the corner of her eye again. The monster would rip out the cute American guy's throat once it reached it.

Other demons swarmed around the plaque, all moving sluggishly, as if they traveled through water. Half-man, half-animal monsters, all bones, fangs, claws, and impossible eyes. They shook their fists and jeered at the plaque. A grotesque stork creature with a beak for a mouth even mooned it. It reminded Zita of the boys who had defecated in her fountain back in Tucson.

A feral wolflike demon appeared. It snarled at Zita, its low growl raising the hairs on the back of her neck, the clear threat swimming under the American guy's chanting. Hunger filled its storm-colored eyes. A slime-covered tongue licked its elongated fangs, as if cleaning them of blood. Zita caught her breath and shrank in on herself, instinctively trying to make herself a smaller target.

The wolflike demon held up a jar of blackness that sucked in the remaining light in the cave. It seemed to be a piece of true void. Arctic air pushed across the room, brushing against Zita's cheeks. She took a step backward. The demon gave her a broad, long wink, then with a languid overhand, threw the jar against the wall, above the plaque. Horrible sizzling lines of darkness dribbled down the wall, making sucking noises, like a heart wound.

The chanting stopped. Suddenly, all the demons could move at normal speed. The one reaching for the American grabbed him by the throat and pulled him forward, toward the bubbling blackness now covering the plaque.

"NO!" Zita screamed. She pushed herself forward, into the thin ink cloud rising out of the well, the cold chilling the back of her teeth, freezing her joints. She came at an oblique angle, bodychecking the American, yanking him free of the demon's grasp, away from the wall. He turned slightly, twisting free.

Zita tripped from her own momentum. Instead of falling into the room, she slammed her back against the wall. The smell of burning hair filled the room. Zita screamed as the acid bit into her neck.

The light brightened. The chill disappeared. Sound returned. The edges of the room sharpened.

Zita looked at the American guy. He stood bent over, breathing hard, like a fighter trying to shake off the blows that had landed. Maybe he'd had a fit or something. Maybe there hadn't been any demons after all. Maybe they'd all been in her imagination, leftover images from her nightmares.

Then she looked at the ruined plaque, smelled her burnt hair, and knew that her world would never be normal again.

Chapter 11

Ephraim

"It wasn't us," Ephraim repeated again.

"It was those three boys," the American woman who'd risked herself to save him blurted out. Zita. The woman with the golden hair, now burned and splotchy from the acid.

"Didn't you see them?" Ephraim asked. He didn't know where Zita was going with this, but he could play along.

"They were dressed in bulky camo. Like they hid stuff. When we saw them, we waited in the room to make sure they didn't do anything. Then one got out that jar of acid, and this man tried to stop him. That's when they attacked us."

Ephraim stretched his neck, though it hurt to do so. Zita had told him that black bruises already covered it. He'd pointed out, more than once, that if he and Zita had been the vandals, how could he have gotten such an injury?

Zita continued, giving a thorough description of the youths. Ephraim suspected she hadn't invented the trio. The disgust in her voice told him that she'd seen these three do something destructive.

What *had* happened? Ephraim swallowed painfully. He wanted to believe he'd dreamed it all. He yearned to forget how the stanzas had gripped him and pulled him into a world other than this one, a place of flickering lights, incense, and magic. His high-school Latin had come pouring into his head. He would never forget the mad look in the demon's eyes when it finally broke through, its foul breath overwhelming him, its dripping talons crushing his throat, choking off his breath.

Ephraim couldn't convince himself that nothing had happened. When he did a ritual, sometimes the effect he wanted did occur, but he'd always explained it away, saying it was just coincidence. Not this. Too much physical evidence existed to the contrary. To start with, there was the plaque. They'd been lucky: the acid hadn't completely destroyed it. The first two lines of the curse had been made unreadable, but the rest survived intact. Then there was Zita's hair. The acid had ruined her mass of spun gold, though at least the stink from it had died down. And his bruises continued to blossom.

After the police had written down Ephraim's and Zita's hotel addresses, as well as photocopied their passports, they let the two go. The woman who had run the tour gave them dirty looks on their way out.

Ephraim followed Zita up the steep stairs to the street. She stopped for a moment, then reached up to touch her hair. Her hand stiffened as it reached the burnt part. Her hair looked spiky where it had been burnt off. The material that remained covered her hair like tar.

"Excuse me, miss?" Ephraim asked as gently as he could, coming up from behind her. "Please, let me buy you a drink."

Zita gave him a small smile. The hair in front of her face came down over her eyes. She seemed like she might be beautiful if she pulled it back. For now, anxiety masked her features.

"Zita, right?" Ephraim asked as they walked up the street. "I'm Ephraim," he continued, forestalling any embarrassment she might feel asking his name. He got a relieved smile for his effort. "How long have you been in Budapest?"

"I arrived yesterday. It was the trip from hell," she said.

"Really?" Ephraim asked. Maybe a previous disaster would distract her from her current one.

"Yeah." Zita told him about missing her plane in Denver due to her time-zone confusion, her mad sprint through LaGuardia, then being grounded in Amsterdam due to lightning. Ephraim paid close attention, sympathizing with her exasperation, encouraging her to embellish the story. He did it consciously, trying to distract her, so she wouldn't notice how the people sitting at the tables in the street café stared at her.

He didn't succeed. She'd just started taking about a strange man trying to pick her up in the lobby of the Budapest airport when she broke off her narrative. Ghosts of the terror returned to her eyes. She tugged on her hair, pulling it farther over her face, rubbing it on her cheek.

"It's that awful, isn't it?" she said.

Ephraim had to agree. Her hair resembled a bad punk hairdo.

A crowd of Japanese tourists got off a bus just in front of them. Two of the men pointed. Zita shrank back. They wouldn't try to take pictures of her, would they? Ephraim wanted to make a joke about it, but knew Zita wouldn't take it well. He wished he knew of a ritual to reduce her pain.

An image of his hands pressing together, palm to palm, against her heart, came to him. He shook it off. He'd started to believe in the magic he'd seen, but he couldn't afford to. It meant changing his world too much. None of this could be real. Maybe youths in costumes, dressed up as demons, had attacked them. It had been very dark in that exhibit.

"I know," Ephraim said, taking Zita's elbow and turning her around. "Let's get your hair fixed. I'll pay. I figure I owe you that, after you saved my life." He couldn't read the look Zita shot him. Was she pissed off because he'd offered to take the lead? Ephraim dropped her arm.

Zita didn't say anything, but she did walk after Ephraim as he led them toward the crenellated castle wall. An almost vertical staircase provided passage to the street below. He started down the steps. They smelled like urine and rotten wine. Zita followed.

"I know there's a hair salon at my hotel, but I don't want to go all the way back there, not looking like this," Zita said.

Ephraim stopped on a landing. "I could buy you a scarf . . ." he offered, turning around.

"No, thank you," Zita said. She shook herself, then walked past him, continuing her descent.

When they reached the bottom, they looked at each other, then up and down the street. Both directions appeared to be the same, castle wall on one side, business buildings on the other, trees and cars scattered between them.

Zita pulled the hair out of her face for a moment and sniffed the air.

Ephraim's palms itched. The memory of the finding ritual he'd done at the start of his trip rushed by him. Before he could think about trying to hide his action, Zita nodded and said, "This way."

After a few steps, Ephraim also smelled the chemicals that marked a beauty shop, that unique combination of hair spray, powdery makeup, and sweet shampoo. Ephraim smiled. Zita had just done exactly what Janet would have—that is, take charge once she recovered from her emotional outrage.

Two young women sat in chairs before mirrors in the small shop. They wore the same uniform: white shirt, black vest, black pants. Ephraim had seen larger walk-in closets. They jumped up when Zita and Ephraim came in. One ran forward, toward Zita, while the other went to the back of the shop. She *tsk*ed over Zita's hair, touching it gently, stroking her shoulders, and looking sympathetic. She didn't speak English. An amiable man with tightly cropped curly hair and a large mustache came out of the back. He appraised Zita's hair in a professional manner, then ordered the women around.

One of them led Ephraim to two chairs set against the wall, then directed him toward an overflowing stack of magazines. They were mostly beauty magazines, in French or German, but after he dug awhile, he came up with an ancient *National Geographic* in English.

"*Kavé? Teá?*" the woman asked, hovering.

"Water? *Agua?*" Ephraim asked, wondering if she'd understand.

"*Víz.* Moment," she said, and scurried off.

The woman came back with a small glass bottle of chilled mineral water and a paper cup. Ephraim thanked her. She smiled at him, then hurried back to her companions.

The hairdresser sat Zita down in front of the mirrors for a consultation in pantomime, showing how short he must cut her hair, asking how she styled it, which side she parted it on. He studied her face, took measurements with his fingers against her cheek, nose, and forehead. Then he'd whisked her into the back. Ephraim heard feminine giggles and the sound of water. He hoped everything would be okay. There wouldn't be demons here, would there be?

Ephraim crushed the thought. Demons did not exist. He wasn't a magician, not in cards or in real life. His rituals didn't do anything but make him feel better.

The golden light Ephraim remembered from reading the stanzas lessened. He nodded. He must reside in *this* world, not some imaginary place. He exhaled and pulled himself in. He felt his soul shrink, as though it had to grow smaller to settle back into the mere boundaries of his body. An image came to him—that strange man from the airport, János. Ephraim bristled at the memory. He hadn't liked János dismissing him as so insignificant. Yet here he was, diminishing himself.

He sighed again. It didn't matter.

He returned to his magazine, trying to interest himself in an article about Chilean mummies. He found himself glancing up frequently, wondering how Zita faired.

Finally, Zita came out. Ephraim forgot whatever he'd been reading. She wasn't just pretty with all her

hair pulled away from her face: she was stunning.
They'd spiked her hair a little, making an interesting
frame for the soft curves of her cheeks, her petite
nose, and full lips.

"Wow," Ephraim said, hoping that she'd understand his statement for the compliment he meant to
say. The hairstylist had performed magic as powerful
as any Ephraim had felt. Because of the volume he'd
given Zita's hair, even though she had the full curves
of a woman, all her parts aligned in brilliant proportion with each other. She looked beautiful.

"Wow," Ephraim repeated. He couldn't stop staring
at her. She blushed and hung her head. She reached
up—maybe out of habit—to draw her hair in front of
her face, but stopped short of touching it.

Ephraim paid the bill without even trying to convert
it to dollars. It didn't matter how much it cost in
"real" money. Any amount was worth this trans-
formation.

As they left the store, Zita said, "Thank you. I've
wanted to get my hair cut short for a long time, but
Peter . . ." She paused.

The sunshine grew a little colder.

"But Peter?"

"Peter," Zita said, her eyes unfocused. "He's my,
my ex-boyfriend."

The day brightened again. Ephraim swallowed
around the unexpected lump in his throat and told
himself that this was the perfect time to ask her out
to dinner. He took a deep breath, preparing himself
for the rejection.

"Thank you again," Zita said. "I, ah, need to go."

Ephraim stood, blinking, not sure what to say.

"I need to keep looking for my grandfather."

"That's right. I remember you asking about him.
What happened?"

Zita gave him a grateful smile, then turned and
started down the street, back the way they'd come.
Ephraim came up beside her. Zita told him about how
her grandfather had started losing his mind, the awful

condition of his house. How he lived in the past, fighting Communists. She told him that her grandfather had been born in Hungary and had come back to his childhood home.

They reached a cross street. Zita pulled out a map and examined it.

"What are you looking for?" Ephraim asked.

"The nearest metro station. I should go back to the American Embassy, see if my grandfather has gone there, or if they have any news about him."

Zita sagged as she talked about the embassy and her grandfather, the joy of her new look banished by her worries.

"Would you like some company?" Ephraim asked.

The smile she gave him eclipsed the sun.

The embassy was closed by the time they got there. Ephraim didn't like the panicked expression Zita wore and suggested dinner. They strolled back to the main avenue, to a tourist place, with an English menu and French food. The wine and the atmosphere made them both relax. Ephraim hadn't realized how tightly he'd been holding himself—muscles coiled so he could run at the first sign of attack—until after he'd finished his first glass of wine. The memory of the demons faded fast among the sparkling chandeliers, starched linens, and heavy silverware. Every once in a while, he'd turn his head and the pain he felt in his neck would remind him that not everything was normal. Both he and Zita avoided the subject though, talking instead of their lives, their jobs. Budapest had helped both of them break out of ruts.

They had a wonderful time. Zita hadn't wanted to talk about her grandfather while eating, explaining that she'd feel more guilty about having a good time while he was out someplace, lost. Ephraim accepted her story, but he knew she held something back, something about the real reason why her grandfather had come back to Budapest.

Toward the end of dinner though, Zita began obsessing about her grandfather. He hadn't been at any of the caves she'd checked. She knew of other caves, that she'd need proper spelunking equipment for, but she didn't think he'd be there either. She didn't know where else she should search.

Ephraim pulled out his map of Budapest. "Let's take a look."

They pushed their coffee cups to one side and spread the large paper between them.

"Maybe he's visiting a graveyard, saying good-bye to his mother. Or his sister," Zita said.

"You don't want to go to a graveyard at night," Ephraim said. "They aren't safe."

Zita shot him a questioning look.

Ephraim hurriedly explained. "Graveyards generally don't have any streetlights. They're really dark. In the U.S., a lot of drug deals go on in graveyards."

Zita nodded. "Okay. We'll check them tomorrow then."

Ephraim warmed at her use of the word "we."

"But where would he be now?" Zita said.

Ephraim pointed to a spot north of them. "Could he have gone to Heroes' Square? To find a hero?"

"Why would he be searching for a hero?" Zita asked slowly.

"You said he was living in the past, still fighting the Communists." Ephraim smiled, hoping she would see the joke he tried to make.

"That's a great idea. Let's go," Zita said, standing.

"Okay," Ephraim said. They'd already paid their bill. He should have known that Zita was a woman of action.

They found the closest metro station, then switched to the yellow line. Both Ephraim and Zita laughed at the cars that chugged up the tunnel. They both thought it looked like some kind of animal. They could imagine its headlights as eyes, the metro symbol in the center made a great nose, and the bumper looked like a mouth. The oldest underground system on the European continent had been recently refurbished. Sunshine-yellow coated the outside, thin wooden slats covered the floor, brick-red leather loops dangled from the ceiling, while beige leather encased the seats.

Ephraim swayed as the cars raced along, bumping into Zita, at first accidentally, then on purpose. The train turned a corner, forcing Ephraim to adjust his feet so he wouldn't lose his balance. He caught Zita's hand in the process. This time, she didn't scowl at him. Instead, she smiled and squeezed his hand in return. He shivered. Things were going fast, not planned at all. His head spun with adrenaline. He brushed up against her arm again. God she smelled good, of wine, coffee, and sweet shampoo. The acid smell from that afternoon had disappeared. The memory would fade faster than his bruises if he let it.

Only two working neon bulbs lit the subway station where they got out. A group of youths stood at the far end of the platform, listening to loud music and smoking. Ephraim wondered if he and Zita had made a mistake, if maybe Heroes' Square was in a bad part of town. They climbed the stairs and out into the night. Traffic swirled around them. Across the street stood a large, brightly lit monument.

"Come on!" Zita said, tugging at Ephraim.

Ephraim opened his mouth to suggest using a crosswalk, then shut it. Time to be more spontaneous. "Let's go!"

They ran to the other side without incident.

"This version of Heroes' Square was finished in 1956. But it's been around since the 1880s. This way please," Ephraim said, playing tour guide.

Zita giggled.

Ephraim smiled broadly, enjoying her company. He pointed out the statues on the tops of columns, representing peace, war, labor, and knowledge.

"How do you know all this?" Zita asked.

"I read it in my guidebook last night. I remember most everything I read," Ephraim said.

Three men came up to them as they approached the large center memorial.

"Postcards? Souvenirs?"

"No thank you," Ephraim said, turning away. He caught Zita's hand again.

The man persisted. "Pictures? Pens?"

Ephraim turned back, "No, leave us alone, ple—"

He recognized the men. He'd seen them before. Their overalls. Orange. Like the ones the trio of electricians in the airport had been wearing.

But something was wrong with these men. Their jackets bulged, as if hiding weapons. Nausea struck him when the next thought arrived—or extraneous body parts. Sickly amber tinted the men's eyes.

"You're not real," Ephraim hissed.

"Oh no, we are very real," replied the one with the crew cut. He pulled a glass tube out of his jacket pocket. The thin bottle radiated waves of cold, like it contained the vacuum of space. He heard Zita gasp.

Ephraim hadn't seen the jar the things from the Labyrinth had wielded—he'd been too caught up reading the curse. He assumed this tube held the same substance. He wondered how badly it would scar, if he'd be recognizable after it worked its way across his face.

While demons might not be real, that acid had been.

The one with the tube opened the top of the bottle and shook it at them, like a frat boy might shake a can of beer to spray on his brothers. Black liquid flew out. Ephraim and Zita both jumped back. Ephraim put his left arm out to block the youths, in case they came any closer.

A sizzling sound issued from his jacket sleeve where a few drops of blackness had touched it.

Ephraim shook his arm, hard, hoping to keep the acid from burning through. The scar on his forearm ached. He didn't want to take off his jacket to check it. What if they threw more blackness? His light cotton shirt wouldn't protect him at all.

He glanced over his shoulder. The center memorial, with life-size bronze statues representing the seven tribes of Hungary, stood directly behind them, blocking their freedom. Ephraim angled his steps, hoping to get around it. He took Zita's hand and pulled her in the same direction.

"Excuse me, sir. Is there a problem?" Ephraim jumped at the voice appearing at his right. It took him a moment to process that the words had been said in heavily accented English.

A policeman stood at the corner of the monument.

"Yes, Officer. These men were bothering us," Ephraim said. He glanced at the trio, expecting to see them backing away. Instead, they grinned and pulled out a large laminated card.

"Our license," one of them said, handing it to the policeman with a flourish.

Zita tugged on Ephraim's hand, pulling him back. He couldn't understand why. These scum might have a permit, but they'd still burned his jacket.

"What?" he asked, glancing over his shoulder at her.

She pointed at the cop.

The policeman didn't have the same bulky form as the men. His body appeared perfectly normal. Ephraim couldn't see anything wrong with him.

Then he noticed a halo around the cop's hat. No, not the cap. The gold badge in the center. It glowed for another moment, an infected white.

The light parted. A bloodshot eye opened and stared at Ephraim.

Ephraim couldn't break away. The eye hypnotized him, like a snake held a rabbit. He stood frozen, merely prey, waiting to be plucked.

Something insignificant yanked on his arm. He didn't know what it was anymore. He no longer saw the square. He couldn't look away from that eye. It told him all about his life—his useless rituals and his pathetic attempts to break free from his old habits. Ephraim was as worthless as he'd always feared. Maybe more so. No woman could ever be his true companion. He didn't deserve a mate, or children. He didn't deserve anything. Not even to live.

The eye swallowed him. And soon, he knew in his gut, it would consume everything. Grey dust rained across his vision, smothering hills and fields alike.

Someone—Ephraim later realized it was Zita—bodychecked him like she'd done that afternoon, breaking the gaze.

The cool of the evening returned. Ephraim found he could breathe again. The world retook its normal colors and shapes.

"Run!" Zita said.

A group of Japanese tourists following a young man holding an umbrella above his head approached the tomb just south of them. Ephraim and Zita ran and joined the crowd, pushing their way into the middle of it.

The group pooled around the leader as he spoke to them in Japanese. Cameras clicked and whirred all around them. Ephraim clenched his fists, then flexed his fingers, trying to make his hands stop shaking. He didn't know any rituals to defend not only himself, but Zita, from four assailants at the same time. He glanced behind him. The policeman and the youths stood at the edge of the crowd, waiting for them. Ephraim turned away quickly before the terrible eye could capture him again.

"What are we going to do?" Ephraim whispered to Zita.

Zita had a faraway expression on her face.

"Do you remember how the demons couldn't move quickly while you were reading the curse? From the plaque?"

"Yes," Ephraim said, closing his eyes for a moment. He could still see that long, clawed hand reaching for his neck, inching forward, torturously slow. Pain from his bruises danced around his throat.

"I don't know if it will stop these guys, but it might. Do you think you could chant it again?"

The words rolled by in a flash of solid gold. He nodded.

"Keep it ready."

The leader of the Japanese tour finished speaking.

He raised his umbrella like a baton and walked toward the large bus waiting next to the square. Zita and Ephraim stood still and let the group dissolve around them, like water running past a stone.

When the crowd had gone, they confronted their attackers again. The four approached, danger in their eyes, aggression in their menacing walk. The one with the bottle held it up over his head.

"Now," Zita said.

Ephraim let the binding flow from him. He raised his voice, pitching the words higher than his normal tone, almost singing them.

The four stopped. They seemed to be struggling to move, but they couldn't.

Zita tugged on Ephraim's sleeve and pulled him to the right, around the men. Ephraim kept chanting as he walked, binding Beilum, binding its hair, its forehead, each eye—all five of them—both ears, its nose, lips, teeth, chin.

Once they reached the far side of their attackers, Zita pushed him and said, "Go."

They ran. Ephraim heard the possessed men following them after just a moment. He pulled on Zita's hand, running faster. He didn't dare look back, afraid of that eye trapping him again, as well as of seeing how close their pursuers were.

At the far end of the square, the constant stream of cars forced them to pause. With a daring burst, Ephraim and Zita ran across the street. The men stood on the other side, traffic blocking their way.

Something rumbled beneath his feet.

"This way!" Ephraim said, pulling Zita down the stairs to the metro station. The possessed men wouldn't attack them in a crowd, and there were sure to be other people on the car. Zita and Ephraim rushed onto the train.

The doors closed and the car pulled away just as their pursuers came down the stairs.

Ephraim and Zita clutched at the leather loops above their heads, barely holding themselves upright.

Ephraim took a deep breath. "That wasn't real. It couldn't have been real. Latin binding spells don't really work." He didn't know who he tried to convince.

Zita pressed her lips together into a thin line and tugged on Ephraim's left arm.

He transferred hands on the strap above his head and brought his arm down.

Zita made him look at his sleeve.

Holes burned by the acid stared at him. His neck suddenly ached again.

"We need a plan," she said.

Ephraim pulled Zita's hand back just before she inserted her key card into her hotel room door.

"The threshold," he said.

"Excuse me?"

"The threshold. Old Roman superstition. Demons live in thresholds. That's why we carry brides over them, so the demons can't attack."

Zita gave Ephraim a wry smile. Ephraim hung his head. He knew how ridiculous he sounded. After what had happened at Heroes' Square though . . .

"What are you proposing? That you carry me over the threshold? Do you really think that's necessary?"

Ephraim made himself look up. He wished he hadn't said anything. He didn't want Zita to think he was propositioning her. Her beauty crowded against him. He felt drawn to her, with ties stronger than gravity. However, their situation complicated everything. His affection didn't fit right now.

"Just walk over quickly," he said.

Zita opened the door, then to his surprise, jumped over the threshold, like a child in a sack race at the finish line.

"Are you coming?" she asked, holding the door open.

Feeling silly, Ephraim did the same. Zita closed the door behind him, then slammed the deadbolt home and put on the chain. Ephraim took off his jacket, rolled it, then pushed it against the foot of the door, blocking the crack there, covering the door jam and threshold.

Zita nodded in approval, then said, "I'd offer you a drink—I think we both could use one—but I'm fresh out. Could I get you some water?"

"Yes, thank you," Ephraim said. He waited awkwardly in the vestibule, unwilling to go farther into Zita's room without an explicit invitation. His heart beat a little faster than it should, and his palms started sweating. Ephraim had a memory of when he'd been sixteen, waiting at the foot of the stairs for his date while her father sat at his desk, staring at him.

Zita emerged from the bathroom with two full glasses of water.

"Please, come in. Sit down," she said, indicating a chair on the far side of the room.

Ephraim slid into the seat, grateful not to be standing. Zita obviously had no idea of his attraction to her, not that she would return it even if she did know. That sickly eye from the cop's cap had reminded him of his worthlessness.

Zita absentmindedly handed him a glass of water, then took a sip from hers and put it down on the table. She didn't sit, but instead started pacing.

Without preamble, she told him about her grandfather and his insistence that demons persecuted him. She told the story of how he had found the cave, the Jewish families, and the demon Bélusz, how it had scarred him, and how he'd injured himself in order for his "sight" to return. She told Ephraim that her grandfather had left America to destroy the demon, and himself.

"Demons don't die," she said. "They have to be killed."

"But they can be bound," Ephraim said. "The plaques your grandfather talked about, and the one in the Labyrinth, bind the demon to its throne. Maybe we don't have to destroy Bélusz. Maybe we could bind it again."

"Do you think so?" Zita asked, pausing for a moment. "If we bind the demon, and don't destroy it, then maybe Grandpa . . ."

She couldn't continue. Ephraim didn't need for her to. When the demon died, so did her grandfather.

"I think that would work," Zita said. "Why didn't Grandpa think of that? Why didn't he try to find a plaque and rebind the demon himself? Or maybe only extraordinary individuals can make the magic work."

Ephraim bit his lip and hung his head, unsure of what to say. Maybe he was special. A lifetime of self-effacement stood between him and that possibility.

"Grandpa said he used to play at being a magician. With his best friend. He probably could have made the magic work. But no. He had to come and kill the demon instead. Of all the stupid, macho things . . ."

Ephraim tried not to laugh. Zita reminded him so much of Janet—her power, her focus, and her passion. In fact, that was what he'd loved in Janet. Her passion.

Zita's words faded to silence. Ephraim felt like a drop of water at the end of a stalactite, gathering moisture and mass for years before finally splashing down onto the waiting surface below. Cupboards opened in Ephraim's mind and memories flooded in. The good times with Janet, the happy times, the times he'd forgotten about. Her search for the next injustice, the next battle. How he'd loved her anger and her determination to do something about the problems she saw. How he hated that anger when she'd directed it at him. It swept through like wildfire, blooming quick and fast across the dry forest, always seeking new fuel.

Janet had been as much of a victim of her passions as he'd been. When they'd shared that passion, it had been marvelous. She'd soon burned out on their joint cause though, gone looking elsewhere, and had left him behind. They shouldn't have gotten married after that first glorious summer. They should have let the relationship fade away and die. She didn't control her passions. That, too, had attracted him at first, and it had burned him in the end.

In that instant of understanding, he forgave his ex-wife, forgave her for her passions, for her anger, and her lack of control.

And himself, for loving her.

His well of self-loathing suddenly drained. The stagnant water receded and dried up. He felt cleansed.

A new thought occurred to him. Maybe he was worthy of love. Maybe he always had been. The amazing golden magic light hovered close enough for him to grasp it.

Ephraim tuned in again to hear Zita propose going shopping the next day for a hammer and chisel. They needed to steal the binding plaque and take it away, someplace where the demon's minions couldn't destroy it. That way Bélusz would stay bound.

Was she really suggesting theft? Ephraim might be enamored with her, but he couldn't seriously go along with this plan.

"Why don't we both think about it tonight," Ephraim said, standing. "I'll meet you here for breakfast, okay?"

"Do you think it's safe?" Zita asked, pausing midstride. "You could spend the night here," she said.

Ephraim smiled at her offer. "If I stay, will you stop pacing and planning long enough to let us sleep?"

Despite the inadequate light in the room, Ephraim could tell Zita blushed.

"I don't know," she said. "I do get focused sometimes."

"I noticed," Ephraim replied. "And so do I, sometimes. But even with all we've been through tonight, I can barely keep my eyes open." He knew the stress and revelations of the day contributed to his exhaustion. His body craved an escape from his overworked mind and emotions.

Zita nodded. "Okay. I promise to let you get at least a couple hours of sleep."

Ephraim looked sharply at Zita. He couldn't help but be disappointed when he realized she wasn't flirting with him. The throes of her current passion still held her, not passion in general. As it should.

With a sigh, Ephraim trained his thoughts away from love, lust, and worth. He concentrated instead on the mechanics of preparing for bed, all the while hoping to dream of his new possibilities, not the nightmarish task ahead of them.

Chapter 12

Laci

Laci recognized his old school: the plain brick building held the same stodgy, disapproving appearance he remembered from his years there. Though Laci was no longer a child, he still felt slightly intimidated. Shops crouched closely on either side of the building, covering what had been the school yard. Graffiti colored the nearby walls, even the sidewalk leading up to the school, but not the building itself—it was as if the school held itself above such common tags.

The doors held the same weight and resistance in the heavy oak that his younger self had always noticed. He stood for a moment just beyond the entrance and watched a group of children walk by. The young ruled here, not sad old men. However, his connection to János had started in this school. Hopefully a trail still led from there to his old friend.

Laci stepped farther into the building. The hallways appeared smaller, the walls held pictures he didn't recognize, and the dull roar of students moving from one class to another hurt his ears. The chemical smell of floor polish, the sweat of innocents learning, and the spring breeze carried in by the open windows, reassured him though.

The headmaster still held court in the squared-off rooms at the end of the first floor hall. The same broad desk separated the heathen from the ordained, the same dark carved doors hid his exalted highness, and the same scuffed chairs for the condemned waited outside those doors.

But signs that the office had changed flourished.

Books and papers lay on every available surface, something that never would have been allowed in Laci's youth. A computer terminal with a blinking orange cursor sat next to the sign-in sheet on the desk. Yellow stickies hung from every shelf. The phrase "ordered chaos" came to mind.

The secretary had the look of all harried assistants: stern hair escaping its ties, glasses smudged with fingerprints, lipstick half-erased. She didn't seem disturbed by Laci's presence. "May I help you?" she asked in a mechanical tone.

"I went to school here, many years ago," he started, then hesitated.

"What years?" she asked, already turning away.

"From 1944 through 1947," Laci said. "When the school was open, that is, when there weren't bombings."

The secretary peered at a shelf lined with three-inch-thick volumes, then pulled one from the shelf. Placing the ledger on the desk in front of Laci she said, "A lot of student information is missing because of the war." Without another word, she sat back down at her desk.

Laci turned the book around and opened it. Records of the students from his class filled its pages, all written with a neat hand. Names, occupations, current addresses, all listed there for Laci to peruse.

"Thank you, from my heart, thank you," Laci said, his voice hoarse from emotion.

The secretary looked up, and for the first time, seemed to really see Laci. She smiled. "You're welcome. I know how much this means to you. That's why I try to keep them up. If you give me your name and address, I'll make sure it gets included." She shrugged helplessly, indicating the mess around her. "When I have time."

After Laci shared a laugh with her, he went back to finding János. It didn't surprise him that his former classmate's entry was up-to-date. János understood the value of connections. He lived three blocks away, in a building that had been occupied by Jewish families before the war.

Laci wrote down his own contact information on a yellow sticky, mainly out of kindness, not because he expected anyone to be able to get in touch with him. The secretary placed it in the book. Laci thanked her again, then went to locate János, before his courage left or his mind went wandering.

What could he say to his old friend? Threats were useless—what did Laci have to threaten János with? Maybe Laci could bribe János by bluffing him with savings in America that didn't exist. Laci had no illusions about János staying bought, but, it might give him enough time to do something about Bélusz, whatever that might be.

A broad arched doorway marked the entrance to János' building. People living in the building could drive through it and park their cars in the courtyard, just past the small green garden standing in the center. To the right of the entrance stood a well-lit alcove. The apartment numbers and names were clearly written on the mailboxes. No security gate blocked Laci's access to the stairs. He had no excuse to turn around and leave. He wasn't sure what he feared most: seeing his former friend so corrupted, or the real power that János might now wield.

The building János lived in had either been restored, or, more likely, had never been stripped of its marble and fixtures, either by Hungarians during the war or by the Communists afterward. Laci felt like he'd stepped back in time. He walked up the staircase slowly, admiring its beauty. He loved the iron art deco stair rail, with its elegance and sudden curves. Laci didn't know for certain, but he guessed that the grape-and-ivy-patterned molding around the ceiling was hand carved. Ice-green wallpaper with golden swirls dancing through it covered the walls. No graffiti had ever made its way into this sanctuary.

János lived on the top floor, just past an apartment oozing with medicinal smells. Pink and white petunias bloomed in the window box next to János' brightly painted red door. It looked so homey, so normal.

Was that the sound of children playing ball in the courtyard?

Suddenly, Laci was transported.

He watched himself as a teenage boy in stained clothes kicking a rag ball around the courtyard. Old newspapers, construction rubble, and rusted metal pipes lay scattered around the edges and in the corners. Broken glass glittered in front of the "goal." Other children just as ragged, but none as determined, chased after the boy. Their shouts echoed off the walls and up to the gray winter sky, like a chanted prayer.

The sound of a car starting broke Laci's reverie.

He came back to the green of the afternoon, the warmth in the air, and the job he had to do. He shook his head, trying to shake off his surge of anger. He and János had never played soccer together. János had belonged to a club and played with proper equipment. Laci had never even kicked a real ball.

Laci turned away from the courtyard and his past. He jammed his thumb into the doorbell.

A faint voice responded, *"Szabad!"*

Laci hesitated. János couldn't be expecting him.

The voice repeated itself. *"Szabad!* Come in!"

The brass knob chilled Laci's hand as he turned it. The door swung open freely.

"Back here," the voice called.

Laci closed the door behind him, shutting out the sunshine. Through an arch to his immediate left stood an airy kitchen. Smells of garlic, oregano, and peppers floated from it. A closed door stood to his right.

Straight ahead of Laci stretched a long unlit hallway. Darkness hid the tall ceiling above him. Black-and-white photographs of nude women hung at eye level on both walls, like in a fancy gallery. Laci tried not to look at them when he realized the women wore handcuffs, ropes, and no smiles.

The hallway spilled out into a large, octagonal room. Diffuse sunlight shone through the lace curtains. Rose-patterned Oriental rugs covered much of the pale wooden floor. A pea-green velvet couch with wood accents sat behind a low table in the center of the room. Formal chairs, with and without arms, were placed with careless precision around the edges of the room, as well as the occasional table and reading lamp.

A door to Laci's left opened. János walked through and crossed over to Laci, hand out. Laci responded automatically, and found himself on the receiving end of an enthusiastic handshake.

"It's so good to see you," János said, holding Laci's hand firmly with one hand while he grasped Laci's arm with his other. "Just so good."

Laci examined János. The years had been kind to him. Though his black hair had thinned and receded from his temples, his skin still looked sleek, as though time had baked and shrank it instead of loosening it in wrinkles. Age hadn't blunted his features either: his eyebrows still rose sharply against the curve of his forehead, his nose still peaked from the plane of his face, and his lips still held a pointed smile.

No demon rode János' shoulder. Yet Laci knew there was something wrong with János, something twisted, something . . . not human. He released his old friend's arm, took a step back, and looked into János' eyes. A soft brown worried gaze met his. Normal eyes. Human eyes.

Eyes that started to glow.

Laci was instantly mesmerized. What could be wrong with eyes that shone like that? The beautiful light reminded Laci of sun on a hill blanketed with dried grass—a soft autumn color, restful and soothing. It pulled at Laci, making him want to relax, give in and prepare for a long winter's sleep. He longed to slide into that light, surround himself in it, and never leave.

The color shifted and darkened. It gained weight as Laci fell into it. The light lived on all sides of him now, becoming mud brown as it drew closer.

Laci regretted the loss of the original color, the warm gold. He wanted to make his way back to that, but the light around him was too heavy now. Longing shook him. If only he could go back, bathe in the amber radiance. A trickling sense of softness ran across his fingers as he struggled to return. He had a sudden image of Zita, seeing her in his backyard, her hair shining in the bright sunlight.

Thinking of his granddaughter made Laci realize that something was wrong.

The light. It blinded him, calmed him, and made him want to nap. It was deceiving him. He wasn't in bed, he wasn't in America—he was somewhere else. He needed to wake up.

Slowly, feeling as though he moved through layers of sand, the old man circled his fingers together and willed himself to see beyond the illusion, force his way past the light, and look into the heart of the thing.

His vision cleared. Laci saw the face of his old friend. János' pupils had elongated, like those of a cat, or a demon. Light poured from them, golden in color, with a black heart in the center.

Laci pushed himself back, away from his old classmate. He closed his own eyes and looked away, drawing a deep shuddering breath.

When he turned back, János had returned to normal. Faint bloodshot lines ran through the whites of his eyes.

János shrugged and turned abruptly. "Please, won't you sit down, old friend?" He gestured toward the couch with a shaking hand. "Let me pour you some tea. I've been expecting you." He collapsed on the seat, as if suddenly exhausted.

Laci hesitated, then walked around to the other side of the table. He sat as far away from János as he could, his hands at the ready, the protection rituals his grandmother had taught him suddenly coming back to him.

"Expecting me?" Laci asked.

"Yes. I knew you'd come home. Sorry to have

missed you at the airport," János said. He removed a white porcelain pot from a purple-and-jade-knit tea cozy and poured a light brown liquid into two glass-and-steel cups. "I'd assumed you'd fly direct." János picked up his cup and held it in a toast to Laci. "To you, old friend. For coming back so quickly in our time of need." János paused and sipped his tea. "Chrysanthemum. I hope you like it. It's one of my favorites."

Laci picked up his cup and sniffed it warily. The tea had slight overtones of sweet flowers, mingled with a roasted scent that came from drying them. Laci doubted it contained poison. Bélusz would want to watch him die. There might be some kind of soporific in it though, something that János had built an immunity to. Or that wouldn't affect him. Laci couldn't tell how much humanity János retained. Was his face just a mask? Could Laci not see a demon on his shoulder because János carried it inside himself?

János sighed after sipping his tea. "This is just lovely. It's so good to see you. I'm so glad you came."

"Why?" Laci asked, putting his cup down again, its contents untasted.

"Ah, you have been in America for a long time, haven't you? So direct. I respect that. So let me tell you directly.

"Bélusz has figured out a way to kill you without killing itself."

Laci sighed, letting János' words settle onto his shoulders. Of course. No wonder the demon wanted him back in Budapest so soon after finding the last plaque. Just finding the plaque wouldn't have been enough. No, the demon had to be able to use the plaque against Laci.

"How?"

"Well, it's complicated, old friend." János rolled his shoulders, first one, then the other. Laci recognized the gesture from their childhood together.

János was preparing himself to lie.

"You see," János started, then paused to lick his

top lip, like a cat when it smelled something good to eat. "Bélusz is a demon who turns things to stone. It has an affinity with the earth."

Laci couldn't stop the shudder that came over him. He disagreed with János, but he didn't say anything. Bélusz didn't have a natural association with rock. The demon corrupted the stone that encased it. Laci remembered the contrast between the demon on its throne and the magnificent stag standing before it.

"So what would happen if Bélusz' powers were reduced? Say, if it could no longer turn things to stone? If Bélusz is no longer the demon you cursed, will the curse still work?"

"Years won't diminish the strength of a curse," Laci said. Time might be slippery for him, but Grandmother Zita still held his hand.

"I'm not saying that," János said impatiently. "But what if the essential nature of Bélusz changed? What if it transferred its affinity with stone to someone else? Might not the curse follow the essence of the demon?"

Laci shook his head, still not understanding.

"Suppose Bélusz gave someone else its ability to change things to stone. Then that person lets himself be sacrificed. The brave soul dies of your curse when you die, and Bélusz continues to live."

Laci sat back, his breath growing shallow as the horror of what János told him seeped in. "Bélusz is going to consign its powers to you," he said. "It's 'essence.' Then you will die from the curse, instead of it."

János grinned large enough to show all his teeth. "Brilliant!" he said. He wagged a finger at Laci. "Still as sharp as ever."

"It won't work." The words floated through the room.

"What do you mean old friend? Of course it will work." The smile that had never touched Janos' eyes slid a few degrees colder.

"You'll ruin the transfer," Laci said, realizing the lie that János told. "You'll rush it, or something. When I

die, the curse will kill Bélusz. And you'll be left holding all the demon's power."

János sat back, his smile smaller but more genuine.
"Of course you'd see through to the heart of it, old
friend. Gosh, I've missed you.

"You'll help me do it, won't you? Once Bélusz has
given me its powers, it will be much more frail. We
can kill it. I can't do it properly without you."

Laci stared off into the distance, the sunny room
growing cloudy. János offered him a dream, a wonderful fantasy. His old classmate—a magician, one with
power—helping Laci kill Bélusz.

Only to inherit all of the demon's abilities.

Dread churned Laci's stomach.

János, with Bélusz' capabilities, would be ten thousand times worse. The demon wanted only its freedom, to be warm again, to walk in the sun. János
desired power. Bélusz was less directed than János.
Though the demon would cause great ruin, it would
be a casual thing. János would actively destroy anyone
and anything that stood in his way. Laci knew János
from when they'd been boys together. Looking at the
man now, Laci could see that his friend had never
outgrown being the spoiled prince.

"No."

"What do you mean 'no'? Think of all the good I'd
be able to do. To protect our sweet motherland. To
get revenge on our enemies. The Germans. The Communists. Hungary shall have her proper borders
again."

The scene blossomed across Laci's mind's eye. It
would be like the Great War. But there would be no
end. Mushroom clouds would fill the sky from horizon
to horizon.

Laci examined János, willing himself to truly see
his classmate.

The demon's shadow overpowered the man, like an
overlarge cloak. Little of his old friend remained. The
weakness he'd shown after using his power, his shak-

ing hands, how he'd collapsed onto the couch—no, only a trace of humanity stuck to the shell of what used to be a man. Once Bélusz was gone, János would be diminished, no longer a threat. If only Laci could kill Bélusz without János' aid, or hindrance.

"I can't help you," Laci said. He must find a way to kill Bélusz on his own.

"You must," János said. He put his cup down on the table and filled it again with tea.

Laci merely shook his head. Chills ran down his back. Flames enveloped János. Laci knew they weren't real, they existed only as the shadow of what might come. If he let it.

János sighed with impatience and took a sip of tea. "I don't want to do this," he said.

Laci knew János still lied.

"Tell me about America, your family, your beautiful wife," János said in a congenial tone, abruptly switching tracks.

"She's dead," Laci replied, hoping the monotone he used would dissuade any further questions.

"Yes, Judit. I knew that. That was why you left, wasn't it? But didn't you remarry? An American?" János asked.

"She's dead too."

"Ah, I see. What a shame. And your children?"

"I don't have any children," Laci said, willing himself not to think of Margit.

"Didn't you have a daughter . . . ?" János asked, with a quizzical expression.

"Who died during the war," Laci said. "The Communists killed her, along with her mother, while standing in that bread line." Laci made his tone as deadpan as possible, forcing himself to believe the lie.

"Terribly sorry. So you have no family left?" János asked, leaning forward.

"None." Laci said. János couldn't know about Zita. He must protect her. A sinking feeling churned Laci's gut. Fear as great as when he'd faced Bélusz the first time overcame him. He stood up to go.

"Are you sure you have no family left?" János asked.

"Of cour—"

"Because I could swear I saw your granddaughter at the airport," János said, interrupting Laci.

Laci stared straight ahead. The door out of the room, his only escape, seemed as far as an ocean away.

"She's a blonde, right? Pretty. If only she'd pull some of that hair away from her face. Full-figured, like your mother's side of the family, eh?"

Laci took a deep breath. He sat down again.

"She'll be safe, you know. If she's with me."

"Don't do this."

"I must, old man. I must. Your only way to save her is to agree to help me."

Zita. Laci had a vision of her with the gold leached out of her hair by days spent underground in János' thrall.

"I want to see her." Laci could face his death if she were safe.

"You will. If you'll help me."

"Where is she?"

"You'll meet her. By the Danube. Later this morning. Near the place where the water turned red the night we killed the Jews."

Hope flared through Laci for a moment. His granddaughter still breathed free air. Maybe she could get away.

He quickly squelched the thought. Just saving his granddaughter wasn't enough anymore. He had to stop the coming apocalypse. János would destroy not only his beloved Budapest, but the world.

"Come to the cave tonight. Alone. Follow my lead. And Bélusz will die. It's what you came back to do, right? Kill the demon?"

Laci hesitated. He didn't want to agree, but he had to see Zita. He had to keep her safe. Finally, he nodded his head. He couldn't commit such travesty to words.

"It was so good to see you, old friend," János said,

clapping Laci on the back and squeezing his shoulder. "So good."

Laci walked out János' door. He closed it quietly behind him, his shoulders shaking as chills chased across his torso.

For a moment, Laci had almost believed János when he'd said it had been good to see him. Almost.

Keep my granddaughter safe.

He heard his mother's words again as he walked. She'd said them as she packed the bag of food to carry them to the West, condemning herself to a lonely future, dying during one of the winters when there wasn't enough fuel or food—artificial shortages caused by the Communists.

How could Laci save the world? His age and confusion came crashing down on him. Zita. He must see Zita again. He must keep her safe, get her through the frozen marsh and across the bridge to the West, to safety. But hadn't he already done that?

He'd run away when his country had needed him, run in fear of János and his plans. Laci couldn't leave this time. He refused to run away, but why did he feel as though he was?

He strolled along the Danube, watching the sunlight play with the waves. His vision darkened, as if a cloud boiled across the sky. Red streamers swirled through the water. Laci shivered. He'd never seen this with his own eyes, the night the Arrow Cross had taken as many Jewish families they could find, as well as people they didn't like and could kill without repercussions, and brought them down to the Danube. The water had cleared quickly, but the scent of the dead had lingered.

Suddenly Laci was transported.

The decay turned to a burning smell, like a bonfire. The blackness of the cave engulfed him, but he had to keep climbing, feeling his way for one ledge after another. He had to get out.

He'd met soldiers on his mad dash away from Bé-

lusz. They'd let him carry his lamp to the gullet entrance, but then they'd made him climb up without it.

Able to breathe clear air again, Laci fell on his
knees and put his hands to the earth, to receive her
blessing. But he couldn't touch her, like before, when
he'd had his sight. The reverberations of his loss had
just begun.

Unkind laughter cut through the night. János had
beat Laci out of the cave. He stood, laughing and
smoking, with more soldiers. Even without his special
vision, Laci knew his classmate had changed. Shadows
caressed him. His destiny ruled him.

"So good of you to scream like that, old friend.
Made our job so much easier."

Laci couldn't stand to see the stone filtering into his
friend's blood. He glanced away from János to the
soldiers' faces. The firelight distorted them. With their
mouths open in parodies of joy, it seemed like the
demon had already taken them as well.

János' words sank in. The Jewish families. He'd condemned them by screaming, alerting the soldiers. Now
their blood would overflow the Danube.

Laci backed away from János and ran to the woods,
the laughter riding him as hard as any demon. He ran
and ran, back to the camp, back to a world without
his special sight, into a world where the heaviness of
the demon's curse lay on his soul, all the way back to
the present day.

Laci looked again at the Danube, the day clear, sea-
gulls dipping into the water. The day appeared too
bright to be his last.

Suddenly, he didn't want to see Zita. She'd be disgusted at his acquiescence. He'd been responsible for
the deaths of those families. He didn't want her to see
him like this, colluding in the death of more innocents,
just to save her. He turned away from the river, back
to the busy streets. He'd buy some paper, send a note
to Zita, and hope she'd understand that he'd chosen
not to run away this time. All he wanted was to keep
his granddaughter safe.

A light outside the stationery store caught his eye. A golden spot—sunlight on a young woman's hair, cut short, above her neck. She turned, laughing, to the dark young man standing next to her. She moved in slow motion, her face gradually coming into focus, her smile cutting through Laci's fog. Recognition broke through the layers of darkness swaddling Laci.

Zita. No longer hiding behind her hair, but blooming in independence. She placed her hand on the young man's arm, just for a moment, a shared caring.

She still lived free.

As he could. He didn't have to run away. And going back to the caves, alone, agreeing to János' plans, constituted running away. Acknowledging responsibility wasn't enough. You also had to do something with it.

"Ne csak tudd a jót, hanem tedd is."

Laci's bones, brittle with age, suddenly hardened. He stood up straight once again. Like a stalactite growing centimeter by centimeter, he found the power buried deep within himself. He didn't know how to kill Bélusz, defeat János, or make the mushroom clouds of his visions disappear. But he would.

The resolve in him baked solid as Zita caught sight of him, her face shining in relief and love.

He would fight and probably die.

But maybe he could win.

Chapter 13

Zita

"Grandpa!" Zita called out. She ran toward him, but stopped a foot away.

He looked awful. Ashen sagging skin covered his face. Was that wine staining the front of his shirt? Or blood? His full hair stood all on end, wild and untamed. Where had he been?

"Zita," her grandfather said. He breached the distance between them by reaching out a rough hand and stroking her cheek. "*Édesem.*"

Zita pulled him close to her. He smelled of cigarette smoke and sweat.

And fear.

"Oh, Grandpa," Zita said. He held his arms loosely around her, as if his bones didn't contain strength. She started to pull away when he gripped her tightly. He kissed her hair. When she did pull back, his eyes brimmed with tears.

"I wanted to see you again," he said.

Zita shuddered at his ominous words, the unspoken part of his sentence, "before I die," echoing around them.

"I'm glad you're here," he continued.

Tears threatened to overcome Zita. She felt like a little girl again.

"You're, you're not disappointed in me? I didn't fail you?" she asked, her voice meek. She'd meant to ask about her being there. The question she asked was the real one though, the one she'd always wanted to ask. The one she had to ask, before he died.

"I've never been disappointed in you," her grandfather said. "Never." He pulled her close again and kissed her forehead.

The warmth from his lips passed through her skull, down her body, and settled into the core of her being.

"I've always been proud of you," he added.

Zita felt lighter, as if weights that had been strapped across her chest had dissolved. Years of doubt and failure sloughed off her, leaving her pure and clean, capable of real choice.

Laci said something more in Hungarian that Zita didn't understand. A blessing? He kissed her right eye, then her left.

When Zita opened her eyes, a golden flash momentarily outlined her grandfather. Strength filled that light, enough to bulldoze mountains. Then it collapsed. A flickering blue glow remained, a determination that nothing, not even death, could conquer.

Was this what her grandfather saw? With his special sight? For a moment, the wondrous colors enchanted her. Then her shoulder started aching again with the treacherous memory of her latest nightmares.

Demons that chased her, threatened her grandfather, they weren't good, but at least they were outside, external. How could she get rid of a demon that lived under her skin? Visions that she had no control over?

She opened her mouth to ask her grandfather about what she saw when she noticed him peering over her shoulder.

Ephraim.

"Grandpa, this is Ephraim," she said, turning, momentarily embarrassed. What was his last name? Her shame disappeared when she saw him. The flickering blue that surrounded her grandfather also wrapped around her new friend, though it was both more mellow and stronger at the same time, a casual resolve woven into the core of his being.

Zita blinked. The sight faded. She didn't know if she had the ability to will it to return. Or to fight it off if it came on its own.

"Ephraim Cohen, sir," Ephraim said, sticking his hand out. "I'm very pleased to meet you." The two men shook hands.

Ephraim's formality surprised Zita. How had he known that would be the best way to greet her grandfather? But then again, didn't Ephraim often seem to know what to do or say? She'd never met anyone who had as many moments of natural grace as Ephraim.

"Cohen, eh?" Laci said. "Long history of magicians in your family."

Magicians? What was her grandfather talking about?

Zita shook herself mentally. She had more important things to worry about. They had to get Grandpa cleaned up. When was the last time he'd eaten? Would he know?

"Why don't you come back with us to my hotel? It's just a couple of blocks away," she said, taking his arm. "Where are you staying?"

"I . . . It . . . doesn't matter," Laci said.

Zita wondered if he didn't remember where or if he'd been sleeping in a park. His clothes certainly looked that way.

Laci stopped. "You should leave?" he said, as if unsure. He examined Ephraim, then Zita.

"Yes, we'll all leave," she said, tugging on him. He started walking again. She looked back and gestured for Ephraim to join them.

Ephraim bent down to pick up the bag at his feet. Zita took a deep breath. The package contained the hammer and chisel they'd bought. She'd sweet-talked the clerk into giving them a large bag so they could hide the plaque in the bag after they'd stolen it from the Labyrinth.

Zita's stomach knotted. She'd momentarily forgotten everything. A great weight returned to her shoulders, pressing her down. As happy as she was to see her grandfather, they couldn't abandon their quest. The demons existed.

Which meant the curse, the one tying her grandfather to Bélusz, existed as well.

Zita's chin rose. She wasn't just going to stop the demons. She would save her grandfather. If they could get the plaque, her grandfather wouldn't have to die. Not yet. Not for a while.

Not ever.

"Grandpa . . ." she said, then hesitated. How could they talk about demons in the bright sunshine?

"You've seen them," he said.

The dread in his voice chilled her heart.

"You must leave. So you'll be safe. János, my old classmate, he knows you're here, he—"

"János?" Ephraim asked, interrupting.

"Have you met him?" Laci asked, rotating toward Ephraim.

"A man named János questioned me at the airport. He wore an impeccable suit, had dark skin and weird eyes."

"He recognized the power in you. He hates magicians."

Zita's breath caught in her throat. "It sounds like the man who offered me a ride from the airport in his limo."

"Yes, he saw you there."

"It doesn't matter. We have a plan," she said, striking out again. "They don't have the last plaque yet."

Her grandfather nodded as he came after her. "They've found it," he said.

"But it's still hanging in the Labyrinth," Zita replied. "They tried to ruin it, but we stopped them."

"It doesn't matter," he said.

"Yes, it does. What if we got the plaque before they did? And stashed it someplace safe, where they couldn't get at it?"

"There's no safe place, *édes*."

Zita turned to Ephraim. He shrugged. He hadn't been thrilled with her plan to steal the plaque—he'd argued against her plan all morning—but he'd finally agreed to go along with her.

"We can get it away from them. At least for a while. So we'll have some time."

Her grandfather sighed and shook his head. "It won't work."

"But we can try. We have to do something. We can't just let them win."

The joy that filled the smile her grandfather gave her stunned Zita.

"I love you," he said.

Zita still heard the doubt in his voice. "Grandpa, it'll work."

They crossed the street in silence, then turned toward the hotel entrance.

Laci looked past Zita to Ephraim. "What's his name?" he asked.

"Ephraim," Zita said, biting her lip. Though her grandfather's hair still stood up on edge, the rest of him was deflating. The excitement of their meeting could carry him only so far before he cycled down again.

"Where did you meet him?" he asked.

"At the Labyrinth, where the plaque is being displayed."

"He's Jewish, you know. And a magician," Laci said blithely, as if Ephraim couldn't hear. "I couldn't save the Jewish families, down in the cave. But he can."

Zita gazed at Ephraim. He shrugged his shoulders. She tried to smile at him, but couldn't. A chill gripped her. Why hadn't she seen it before? His strength. His grace.

He resembled her grandfather.

Who saw demons.

As much as she might be attracted to Ephraim, he could call up magic and cast spells. She'd seen it. Whatever warm feelings she might have for him had to be checked, stopped now, if she ever wanted to return to a normal world, a world without magic and ancient evil. Her own short burst of special sight made her anxious enough. She didn't want to be marked, scarred like her grandfather, for seeing more than others could.

"We need a magician. One who's strong enough to fight János. Otherwise, it won't work."

"What won't work?" Zita asked.

"It's so good to see you *édes*."

Zita looked at Ephraim, signaling with her eyes that he should ask the next question. Maybe if a query came from him, her grandfather would answer.

"What might work, sir?"

Laci regarded Ephraim for a moment, then returned his gaze to Zita. "Where did you meet him?" he asked.

Zita sighed and forced herself to smile. She recognized this phase. Her grandfather's short-term memory sometimes vanished. Getting angry wouldn't help. She just had to answer his questions, again and again, with as much patience and humor as she could manage.

"In the Labyrinth. He cast a spell in Latin," she said, trying to derail her grandfather's questions with more information.

"Oh, that's right," he said. They'd reached the hotel. The doorman opened the doors for them. In the lobby, the concierge smiled and waved at Zita, obviously happy that she'd found her grandfather.

"Did it work? Did the spell work?" her grandfather asked in a voice so loud that Zita was certain his words carried to every person there.

"Yes, it did," Zita whispered. "The binding spell worked. It slowed the demons down, both in the Labyrinth and at Heroes' Square."

"Maybe it will work," Laci said as they walked into the elevator.

"What will work?" Zita asked.

"Where did you meet him?"

Zita watched her grandfather swaying with the movement of the bus. He'd insisted on standing, even though there were plenty of empty seats. Ephraim had chosen to stand as well, so they both hung over her, like two bodyguards.

On their way to the stop, her grandfather had pushed both of them into the doorway of a building, to get out of the way of the bombs. Then he'd started calling her Judit. He'd been quiet since they'd boarded the bus. Zita worried about him, but she didn't know what to do. Stealing the plaque, battling demons, seemed easy in comparison to fighting her grandfather's decline.

None of them spoke on their short walk from the bus stop on Castle Hill to the street where the entrance to the Labyrinth stood. When they rounded the corner, they found barricades across the road with a crowd on one side, police on the other.

Zita saw all the uniforms and took a step back. She couldn't help but remember the night before, the glowing eye staring from the center of the cop's hat. Ephraim did the same.

Laci also stopped, but he didn't retreat. He said over his shoulder, "We need to find out what happened." He nodded to himself and bent his head forward.

Joy filled Zita's heart as Laci came alive. His face grew animated. He drew his shoulders back and stood upright, looking again like the man she'd always known and loved. He was taller than Ephraim, something she never would have realized with her grandfather in his reduced state.

Laci approached the edge of the crowd, spoke with a couple of people, then pushed his way forward. He wormed his way to the policemen standing next to the barricade. After rummaging for a moment, he pulled a pack of cigarettes from his bag. Where had he gotten those? He didn't smoke. He offered one to the policeman. Within seconds, Zita saw the subtle bribe work. Soon, Laci laughed and joked with the cop. Zita didn't know how her grandfather did it, but he could charm anyone.

After a short while, Laci thanked the man and came

back to Ephraim and Zita. Lead filled his eyes. His features slumped. He had shrunk again.

"They stole the plaque, early this morning, right after they opened. They killed the desk clerk."

Waves of guilt rolled over Zita. They should have come sooner. She inspected the people closest to them. Were the demons still there? Her legs trembled. What were they going to do now? That poor clerk. She hoped it hadn't been one of the two women they'd met the day before.

She peered at her grandfather, then turned away. The guilt she felt was magnified ten times on his face. His eyes spoke of the sacrifice he was prepared to make—his life, so no others would be taken.

"Maybe we could steal the plaque back," she said. "From the demons." She swayed, fear souring her mouth. She didn't want to get any closer to those, those, *things* that had attacked her and Ephraim. She didn't want to go into another cave. Memories of her nightmares rose up, trapping her in motionless terror.

Her grandfather grunted, captured her elbow, and turned them back down the street. "Hush, *édes*," he said when she tried to continue her train of thought.

He led them to a street café, then to a table away from everyone else. Zita sat, grateful she no longer had to stand on her weakened legs.

"Tejeskávé?" her grandfather asked.

"Please," Zita said, grateful all over again. Though she could conduct her own way around this foreign city, it felt good to rely on someone else, even for just a little while.

Laci turned to Ephraim.

"I'm game," Ephraim said with a shrug. He obviously had no idea what her grandfather proposed, but was willing to try.

Zita had a momentary flashback of Peter negotiating all their food whenever they tried a new restaurant. How could she have let him control everything that way? It wasn't that he was unwilling to try new things: it always had to be on his strict terms.

Her grandfather ordered more than just coffee when the waitress came. Zita didn't know for certain, but she could swear he flirted with the girl. Regret needled Zita. At any other time, she would have loved coming to Budapest with her grandfather, letting him play native guide, touring all the grand buildings. He would have bought her flowers every day.

The waitress returned with a silver tray loaded with dishes. Only after they'd eaten their pastries and second cups of coffee had been served did Laci allow them to talk about the task at hand.

Zita couldn't allow herself to think about the poor clerk. How it could be have been them, either in the Labyrinth, or at Heroes' Square, if Ephraim hadn't read the spell.

"We know where the thing lives," she started, ticking off points on her fingers. "We know it can't move until it breaks the last plaque."

Ephraim interrupted. "Don't you think it's already broken the plaque? I mean, now that it has it?"

Zita sat back, horror choking her throat. Were they already too late? Her grandfather had speculated on possible historical events associated with the breaking of each plaque: the 1848 Hungarian War of Independence, both World Wars, the Russians in 1956. What would happen when the last plaque broke? Would the horror stay in Eastern Europe, or would it spill out over the world?

"No," her grandfather said. "It'll wait until the first night of the new moon."

Was that this evening? Zita didn't know. They'd have to check. Maybe they did have more time. She doubted it. But it did explain why the demons had let the exhibit with the plaque open, if only for a day. "Do you still remember the incantation?" Zita asked.

Ephraim shuddered and nodded.

A plan blossomed in Zita's mind. She held up her hand, letting it come to fruition. She saw two problems: resources, and creating a distraction. The latter, she realized with a sinking feeling, she must solve herself. Despair and panic threatened to choke off her words. She forced herself to speak anyway.

"We have the binding spell. Why don't we just re-bind Bélusz? Do we have to destroy it?"

Laci shook his head. "It will never work."

"Yes, it will. We can bind it before it breaks the plaque. Then we'll have some time to figure out how to destroy it." *Without destroying you,* she didn't add. "First, Ephraim needs to write out the binding spell. We need to find a Latin-English dictionary for the parts you don't know in English," Zita paused, frustrated.

"I'm sure we'll find one in that fancy bookstore downtown," Ephraim said.

A knot loosened in Zita's stomach. Of course.

"Next," she said, ticking off the second point on her finger, "we need to find a lead sheet, plus some way to write on it."

"Why lead?" her grandfather asked.

"That's what the original plaques were written on," she explained.

Ephraim jumped in. "Originally, the Romans used lead because it was ubiquitous, a very common material. It wasn't until later that the lead was actually mentioned as part of the spell."

Zita turned to Ephraim, surprised. How had he suddenly become an expert on Roman curse tablets?

He smiled at her. "While you two washed up this morning, I popped by the Internet café and did some research."

Laci nodded and said, "I'll find something we can write the curse on."

Zita bit her lip. She didn't want her grandfather going off by himself. She wasn't convinced he'd find them again, that he wouldn't get lost in the past someplace. The demons were real, but so was her grandfather's forgetfulness. She couldn't trust that this good cycle would last. Maybe they could go together.

As if replying to her thoughts, Laci turned to Zita

and said, "If you don't let me go by myself to find the materials, I won't tell you where the demon's cave is."

Zita opened her mouth, then shut it again. She didn't acquiesce to his demand, but she didn't disagree either. They could argue about it later.

"Now, the third part," she started, then stopped. "You said there was an open area about the main part of the cave—"

"A dry gallery," her grandfather said.

"Only the eagle sat there, right? The demons weren't there?"

"Yes," he said, drawing out the "s."

"Okay. Then." Zita stopped and took a deep breath. This part of the plan scared her the most. But she had to do it. They all had their part. This must be hers.

"I'll go into the cave, in the lower part, and distract Bélusz and his minions. While they're occupied, Ephraim can read the curse from the gallery and re-bind Bélusz. His reading will slow down the rest of the demons as well. They won't be able to reach him, at least for a while. Then you can come and rescue me," Zita said, forcing herself to smile as she faced her grandfather.

She didn't want to be some damsel in distress, but someone had to cause a distraction. It would be better if no one walked into harm's way.

"János will be there," Laci said.

"Then I'll distract him too."

Laci shook his head. "No, *édes*, you're not the one to divert the demon's attention. What's to stop it from killing you instantly? Nothing. János is very powerful. Bélusz would want to gloat over me. And it has to be careful how it kills me, or it risks killing itself. No. I must be the distraction. You must rescue me."

He opened his mouth as if to say more, then shut it and smiled at her, his dark eyes filling with remembered light. "Besides, if I'm the distraction, that means I must stay alive, and not die right away. That's important, yes?"

Zita bit her lip to keep tears from spilling over.

"Your young man is powerful. He'll be able to rebind the demon," Laci said, obviously trying to reassure her.

Her grandfather's doubt rose so strongly from him Zita swore she could smell it.

She didn't say anything though. He reached over and squeezed her hand. Zita covered his hand with hers and held it tightly. She wanted to be glad that he'd finally said he didn't have to die. Yet even letting him go in the cave felt like sending him to his death.

Zita couldn't believe how well everything had fallen into place. Ephraim had agreed to write the curse. Laci had suggested that Ephraim do it five times, one for each of the original curse tablets. Zita had disagreed—wouldn't once be enough? Her grandfather had pointed out that the demon had five eyes, so it probably wasn't coincidence that the original magician had created five tablets.

They didn't know where they'd find one lead tablet, let alone five, so they decided that if they had problems, just using one tablet would be fine. The tablets had been separated and scattered to keep the demon bound, not as part of the magic. The group had debated for a while before they decided to cast the curse twice in Latin, once in Hungarian, once in Hebrew, and once in English. They'd easily found the dictionaries they'd needed, both the English-Latin and English-Hebrew.

Laci had also grown stubborn about going by himself to hunt for the lead on which to write the curse. When Zita and her grandfather had reached the stone-silent staring point, Ephraim had stepped in.

Her grandfather had agreed to go only for an hour, and had also agreed to wear Ephraim's watch, with an alarm set as a reminder. The formality with which they'd done the transfer had first bemused, then repelled Zita. It was as if they enacted a ceremony, their movements precise and ritualistic. They both looked so solemn. It occurred to her that the handing of a talisman from one magician to another was serious. She looked away. She didn't want to inadvertently see anything unnatural, abnormal. It disturbed her that something of Ephraim's might have power, or that her grandfather could use that power.

No matter how cute or charming Ephraim might seem, he wasn't normal, and neither was her grandfather. A part of Zita longed to return to her old, mundane world, where magicians and demons were just in dreams or nightmares and her grandfather was harmless, not covered in blue lights of power and knowledgeable of the ways of demons.

While Zita went out, Ephraim and her grandfather would work on the Hungarian version. Zita hoped Ephraim would talk her grandfather into letting him go along to look for the materials on which to write the curse. She knew she couldn't.

She still worried about her grandfather wandering alone in the city, looking for a lead tablet, even though he seemed to be in one of his "there" phases, more so since they'd come up with a workable plan. He'd stopped repeating himself, and even seemed to remember Ephraim's name.

Zita needed to find a statue sitting on a chair, all in one piece, as mentioned in the curse. As well as spend another hour doing research on the Internet, finding out the exact time of the moonrise and learning anything else she could about curses, demons, and caves.

She shook her head as she walked down the strand, thinking about that afternoon. Everyone had contributed ideas, then volunteered for their "jobs." It was the way meetings were supposed to run.

A sudden thought struck her. It was the way her boss, Frank, ran meetings.

Zita stopped as the realization soaked through her skin, into her bones, like a wave of cold water. Zita had merely directed things. She hadn't been at the one extreme of "in control"; nor had she let chaos rule. A minute line ran between the two. The middle ground was difficult to find, let alone walk along.

Her boss did it though. Not all the time. Frank tended to be disorganized, while Zita had to admit to herself that her meetings were too organized, with only one viewpoint—hers—allowed.

A surge of respect toward her boss filled Zita. He *could* do his job. A second revelation socked her. His job was worse than hers. He only dealt with people. All the time. He had to be more giving, more flexible.

Maybe she didn't want his position.

Only when someone bumped into her from behind did Zita realize she stood, dead still, in the middle of the strand. She shook herself and started forward again. She needed time to think about all these things. Time she didn't have.

She walked toward the market stalls arranged in the square just north of her hotel. Originally, she'd thought to find a toy store for figures and chairs. Now she had a new idea.

Next to the knife stand—had it really been only yesterday that she'd seen it for the first time—stood a booth selling chess sets. In the onyx set, a man seated on a throne represented the king. What could be more appropriate? She bought three of the chess sets, not trying to negotiate the price, then headed toward the Internet café.

On the way, she passed two bright red phone booths. She glanced at her watch, suddenly feeling guilty. She hadn't called Peter since early morning the day before. He'd be worried. It was about four p.m. her time, which made it ten a.m. his time. He worked afternoons that week and so was probably awake.

She walked into the first booth. The phone had no dial tone. A businessman occupied the next booth. Zita paused, debating whether to wait or not. What would she say to Peter? She didn't want to break up with him on the phone.

The man in the next booth finished his call and

exited before she turned away. Zita compelled herself
to go into the booth. The receiver felt warm against
her ear. She tried to ignore the sour sweat smell coming from the speaker. She decided to make a collect
call, as she'd end up paying for it in the long run.
She scolded herself for the uncharitable thought, even
though it was the truth.

A large yellow card hung above the phone, giving
instructions in five languages for how to make a call:
English, German, French, Japanese, and Hungarian.
Dialing was easy. The international operator spoke
English with a slight accent.

The answering service picked up at home, which
meant Peter was on the phone. The service only
picked up when the machine couldn't. Zita hung up,
feeling guilty over her relief. She made her way down
the crowded street to the Internet café.

Zita decided to send Peter a short e-mail as soon
as she signed on. What should she say though? "Hi
there. Having a wonderful time. Being chased by
demons. Am going to stop a war tonight. Wish you
were here." Finally, she decided the shorter, the better, and so sent him a single line.

*Hey, Peter—just tried to call—phone's busy—talk
with you later—Z.*

She spent a little time looking through her other e-
mail: a couple of jokes she'd heard before, Susan and
Kate asking for news of her trip, spam from a mortgage company. After she'd deleted most of it and re-
freshed her screen, she saw she'd received e-mail from
Peter. It took her a moment to make herself open it.
She didn't want to face him.

A pop-up window displayed when she clicked on
the message. Anger drove out Zita's guilt, as well as
any soft feelings she might have momentarily had for
Peter. The sender wanted confirmation that the message had been received. She'd done this type of thing
herself when sending *work* e-mail, to make sure a col-
league got an important message. She'd been re-

quested to do the same a few times herself. She'd
never been offended before. Now she saw it as part
of Peter's perpetual need for control.

Damn him if she would play that game. She clicked
Cancel and didn't send it.

Call me now was his entire message.

Zita sighed, thinking it through. She and Peter had
only one phone line coming into the apartment. Even
though she hadn't sent the confirmation, Peter would
wait only five minutes, then get off the Internet and
sit next to the phone, anticipating her call, growing
more impatient every minute. It wouldn't matter to
him if she had other things to do. He'd commanded.
She must obey.

Damn him. She called up a search engine, but
couldn't make herself type in a query. What exactly
was she looking for? A way into the caves. A way out
of her relationship. She couldn't focus. She needed to
settle this now. Her research loomed—Peter was just
a distraction. But he felt like a more real problem
than the demons.

Zita got up and paid for fifteen minutes of Internet
connection time, even though she'd been on for only
five. Then she walked back up the street to the phones.
Of course, three giggling Japanese teenage girls now
filled the one booth that worked. They still read the
instructions, one pointing to the words on the yellow
sign. Who knew how many people they'd try to call?

Where else had Zita seen a phone? She didn't want
to go to her hotel room to make the call. Ephraim
worked there. It would be uncomfortable. It shouldn't
be, but it would be.

A memory tugged at her—someplace with a lot of
noise. It came to her after a moment. A wall of tele-
phone booths stood opposite the ticket booth in the
metro station. They weren't enclosed. They'd be noisy.
Serve Peter right if he couldn't hear her. At least she'd
be able to say she'd tried.

She returned to the street, her anger building.
Damn Peter for trying to control her, as well as the

situation. Some things were impossible to subjugate. Would he understand that? She doubted it. The only important problems were his own. And how could she tell him of her life now? Of the magic she struggled with, the demons they had to stop, her fears about her grandfather?

How long had she bent herself to Peter's will? Wrapped herself around his strength, instead of standing on her own? No matter. She didn't know how to disentangle herself from him, but she would. She must. Maybe she would break up with him on the phone.

The metro station echoed as loudly as she remembered it. It made her smile. She walked up to the first available phone. The instructions showed her how to jack up the volume on the dial tone. She did, then placed her call, this time charging it against her credit card.

Peter picked up after the second ring. "Hello?"

"*Hálló, Péter. Hogy vagy?*" Zita said, lowering her voice, doing her best Hungarian imitation.

"Hello? Who is this?" Peter asked.

"It's me," Zita said.

"Oh. What were you doing?"

"I just said hello in Hungarian."

"You know I don't speak Hungarian. Why did you do that?"

Zita sighed. "Why not?" she said, steeling herself for what she would have to say next.

As if Peter somehow knew what she had in mind, he went into a rant about his job, the rally he'd been at the night before, the stupid trial he'd read about in the paper that morning. He talked on and on, not letting her speak a single word.

Zita noticed something and wondered why she'd never seen it before. Peter talked only about things external to himself. When was the last time he'd said anything personal, about how *he* was?

Eventually, when Peter seemed to run out of steam, Zita interrupted. "I'm fine. Thank you for asking. I found Grandpa."

"When are you coming home?"

"My return ticket is for two weeks from now," she said. If they could rebind Bélusz, maybe she could spend some time in Budapest with her grandfather, have a real vacation. If they couldn't rebind the demon, she wasn't sure what would happen.

"I miss you," Peter said.

Zita jerked her head back. Peter so rarely responded emotionally. Before this trip, Zita would have melted with just that one line. Now suspicion tripped along her spine. Did he really miss her? Or did he just say that because he knew he should?

"What have you been doing?" he asked.

Zita could see him, stretched out on her chair in front of the computer. She wondered if he'd actually listen to her, or if he'd bring up a game of solitaire and play that while she talked.

"After that horrible car ride, I, ah, went to the caves. First to the ones in the hills. Then to one in the castle district." She didn't want to tell him about the attack in the Labyrinth. She still had problems believing it herself. "I cut my hair," she said, trying to think of things she could tell him. Should she break up with him now?

"You what?" he asked.

She had his attention now.

"Why would you do that? It was lovely, the way it hung down."

The way it covered me, hid me. Her grandfather had told her how beautiful she looked now, and so had Ephraim—not in words, but with his eyes, his expression. This stranger thought she looked beautiful.

"I suppose you've been out drinking every night as well," Peter added.

Zita didn't know how to respond. "I've got to go," she said. She shouldn't have called him. She had more important things to do than argue with her old boyfriend, her old life.

"I'm just kidding," Peter said.

"No, you're not," Zita said, her anger making her speak the truth. "You don't approve. You don't want me to drink wine, or go dancing, or have a good time."

"Zita, there was a point in your life when you had too good a time," Peter said in his strict headmaster voice.

Zita found herself reaching up toward her head, to pull on her hair. As her hand passed her forehead, the remembered warmth of her grandfather's kiss stopped her.

Yes, she'd partied and she'd failed some classes, been forced to drop out of college for a while. But she'd gone back, graduated. She hadn't failed her life. Her grandfather was proud of her. Why couldn't Peter be?

"I was younger then, more prone to, well, extremes." She paused again. She tried to share her recent revelations. "There's a middle ground, a middle way. That's the path I need to follow," she said, the realization about her job ringing through the rest of the parts of her life, like a plucked harp string echoing through an empty hall. That center path. Not the excesses of her old life, nor Peter's sharp esthetic.

"You still there?" Peter asked after a moment.

Zita nodded, then said, "Yes."

"I'll love you"—Peter paused—"whatever path you follow."

Zita stood still, frozen with shock. He'd just lied to her. If she'd been in the same room with him, she'd smell it on him.

He wouldn't love her on her current path. He'd forced those words out. Why did he think he could fool her? He wanted her to follow his direction, and no other way.

"Good-bye, Peter," she said. The finality in her voice both scared and pleased her. She hung up before he could respond. She couldn't stand to hear another lie.

Zita didn't just want to break up with him. She wanted to be free of him. Free to stand on her own, like a stalagmite in the center of a cave, pushing through the ground, growing centimeter by slow centimeter, rising toward the empty spaces above her.

Chapter 14

Ephraim

It had taken ten minutes for the trio to get the dictionaries Ephraim needed. It took more than an hour for Laci and Ephraim to put together the Hungarian version of the curse. First, Ephraim had to relax enough, almost put himself into a trance, before he could remember the Latin. Then the phrases rolled off his tongue too quickly, dispersing into the air like spider thread. He had trouble stopping himself to write the English translation. Plus, he didn't recognize all the Latin words. They just came to him, as part of the whole. For example, what did *gena* translate to? It wasn't in his dictionary. It occurred in the listing of face parts, between nose—*nasium*—and lips—*labia*—so he assumed it meant cheeks, but he didn't know for certain.

Once they had the English translation, Laci spilled out the Hungarian effortlessly. When he finished, he read it aloud. To Ephraim's ears, it sounded as melodious and flowing as the Latin. He wished he could spend more time with the old man, learning this beautiful, difficult language. Because Hungarian didn't have an Indo-European base, Ephraim didn't recognize any of the words in Laci's version. At the same time, because Hungarian is phonetic, even Ephraim could sound out the version once Laci had written it down.

Ephraim wanted to delay Laci. He shared Zita's worry about her grandfather and hoped that if he delayed, Zita would return and would be able to go with him.

"Did you grow up in Budapest?" he asked. Maybe

if he got the old man talking about his childhood, he'd stay.

"No, Miskolc. It's north of here. Where is your family from?"

Ephraim paused before he answered. Every once in a while he couldn't see Laci clearly. When they'd been introduced and Ephraim had shaken the other man's hand, he'd frozen, overwhelmed by brief images of weird, symmetrical clouds that had blossomed around Laci, then dissolved into ashes that fell like gray snow. His question had stirred the vision, roused the powdered pieces, as if the old man stood in the center of a snow globe that had just been shaken. Ephraim wondered if the dust was some kind of manifestation of the old man's confusion.

"My grandfather came from here, from Hungary," Ephraim replied. "He left as a young man, with his family."

"In 1956?" Laci asked, frowning, his disapproval apparent.

What was wrong with escaping from the Communists? Hadn't Laci done that?

"No, in 1944," Ephraim said. "My grandfather and his wife escaped from the countryside, in the north, to Budapest. Even though the city was 'safe' at that time for Jews, they knew what was coming. They came here, gathered the rest of the family, and took off. Eventually they made their way to the coast of Slovenia and got passage to America."

"I'm glad they escaped," Laci said. He paused, frozen.

Ephraim wondered what memories the old man relived. Finding the Jewish families in the cave? Or his own escape from Hungary? Ephraim felt he must distract Laci.

"How . . . important . . . is tonight? Do we all have to go? Does Zita?" Ephraim didn't know if he could somehow protect her from the evening's activities. Maybe he and Laci could take care of the demons on their own.

The ash around Laci thickened in response to the question. "We aren't saving my soul tonight."

"What do you mean?" Ephraim asked, confused.

"Bélusz, it would destroy Budapest if it succeeded in freeing itself. But all it craves is sunshine and warmth. János, though, craves power. He'd destroy the world."

The strange top-heavy clouds sprang up again, occluding the dust for a moment. As they fell back, their import crashed down on Ephraim.

Bizarre *mushroom-shaped* clouds. The ashes of the dead covering the globe.

Terror struck Ephraim in the chest, choking off his air. Sweat started trickling down his sides. His heart sounded loud in his ears.

He didn't want to believe it. Maybe Laci just projected those images. Maybe they only represented the old man's fears.

His own reaction told him the truth. These visions would come to pass if they didn't stop the demons.

Ephraim had been willing to go along with Zita, to protect her from the demons, to help her save the grandfather she loved so dearly. He hadn't really thought they'd be able to steal the plaque. He'd hoped that once they got to the Labyrinth he'd be able to talk her out of the actual deed.

Now they must follow through on their task. Or die trying.

"Where did you meet Zita?" Laci asked.

Ephraim bit his lip to hide his smile. Now the old man was trying to distract him. Or possibly he'd forgotten that Zita had already told him.

"I saw her first at the caves, over in Buda. I didn't really meet her until the attack in the Labyrinth."

"What's your interest in the caves?"

The old man's attitude reminded him of an overprotective father, ensuring that his daughter would be home from the dance on time. He half expected Laci's next question to be, "What are your intentions toward my granddaughter?"

"It's kind of silly," Ephraim said.

Laci stared hard at him. A man claiming a nonserious goal didn't make a proper suitor.

Ephraim pushed on. "My grandfather told me our people had left gold behind in the caves of Buda." Ephraim watched guilt shade Laci's eyes. Ephraim pushed on. "I didn't come here so much to find the gold, as to do something unexpected. To break my habits, change my life."

Laci nodded, looking off into the distance, and said, "I understand about changing your routine. That's why I must look for the material we'll write the curse on by myself."

Ephraim blinked, not knowing what to say. What rut was Zita's grandfather trying to break out of? Ephraim felt certain even Zita didn't know.

"Have you 'struck' gold?" the old man asked briskly, redirecting the conversation away from himself.

"I think so," Ephraim hedged. He loved the traveling he'd done, the unexpected turns that had come. Had he been here only three days? His old life beckoned from so far away, more like three centuries ago. His habits no longer defined him. He'd broken his curse. The rituals were different, real now, not binding. They didn't obsess him as much as intrigue him.

The other gold he'd found would be in Zita's hair, the way it shone in the spring sunlight, brighter than the water on the Danube. Softer than any metal, such a fine frame for her beautiful face and figure. . . .

"She is a treasure," Laci said, as if reading Ephraim's mind. "And she should be cherished, not like real gold, which is hoarded."

Ephraim blinked, considering. Zita had her passions, as Janet had. No valley could contain those flames. Not that Ephraim would want to. Zita didn't flare like wildfire, first here, then there; instead, she burned steady, strong, and hot, feet planted, unswerving. "Absolutely," he replied.

Laci grunted, then paused and stuck out his hand. "Take good care of her, won't you?"

As Ephraim shook the old man's hand, accepting his duty, the swirling dust dissipated. He held on to the old man's hand for a moment, troubled by the finality of his phrasing as much as by the look in his eyes.

Ferenc, Ephraim's grandfather, had worn a similar expression just before he'd died.

As Laci got up to go, Ephraim suggested, "Since this is mostly done, why don't I go with you?"

The old man just shook his head and walked out the door.

Ephraim wondered if he should follow. He respected the other man's desire to get out of a rut. What routines did Zita's grandfather have that he needed to change?

Spreading both hands wide, Ephraim made a blessing gesture toward the door. Then he curved his hands and returned them to his chest, unsure if the ritual would work, if it would help bring Laci back. Though he now knew the habitual gesturing was based in magic, he still had trouble distinguishing what was obsessive custom and what was real.

Ephraim put aside the image of the old man ducking for cover under clear, empty skies, and returned to his translations. The English to Hebrew version went slowly, not just because of the grammar, but because of the lettering as well. He felt as if he wrote a real magic spell, if for no other reason than because the words were so different and the writing was, well, backward from English, going from right to left instead of from left to right.

He envisioned what the final curse tablet would look like: first the Latin, angular and majestic. Then the rolling Hungarian, with accent marks flying above the letters. The Hebrew centered it, the letters elegant and mysterious. Plain old English under that, the familiar repetition of the phrases hammering the curse into something greater than just the words. Then another time in Latin, to make it whole.

Ephraim realized he just stared into space, and had

been for a while. He'd stopped translating. Words and phrases flew in the air above his head. He couldn't wrestle them to the paper before him. He felt as if his head also floated above his body. He needed something that would force him back to the ground.

Zita's earthy frame was beyond him. He spent a moment remembering how good it had felt with his arm around her, how wonderfully she smelled, how soft and round her figure was. Ephraim sighed heavily. Thinking about Zita was also just a distraction. He needed something to help him focus.

He couldn't declare his intentions toward Zita, as he'd felt her grandfather had wanted him to do. Not because he felt he wasn't worthy; no, he'd settled that when he'd remembered all the parts of his first love with Janet, not just the bad times but the good times too. Zita worried too much about her grandfather, and their perilous plan to save the world, to need any more complications. Ephraim grinned wryly. They did have demons to fight after all. He wished he could call his own grandfather and talk with him about being in Budapest. The old man would have been so happy that his grandson visited there. Ephraim rubbed the scar on his left arm.

When Ephraim was ten, his father had left. Though Ephraim had tried once, after college, he'd never found his father, or figured out why he'd gone. He'd just walked out of their lives and never returned. Ephraim's mother moved to Tucson, not for work, but for the free child care offered by her father while she went back to school. But Ferenc agreed to look after the boy only if he got to teach Ephraim Hebrew and everything else Ephraim needed to learn in order to have a proper Bar Mitzvah.

So, while the other boys who lived in their apartment complex played in the pool or hunted snakes and rabbits in the wash behind the buildings, Ephraim sat sweating at the kitchen table, learning Hebrew and memorizing prayers. His grandfather had been horrified to hear his grandson knew Latin, the "Church language" as he called it. To counterbalance its effects, he made Ephraim memorize not only the Torah and haftarah tropes that he needed to learn for his Bar Mitzvah, but also learn the Hebrew language itself.

It wasn't all torture. His grandfather also told great stories, funny ones about Rabbi Chabad, who always tricked the scholars. Or folk tales about tiny men who made shoes or horses that had human hands. Sometimes he talked about his life in Hungary, about the gold or the caves or walking through the mountains to the coast to make their escape.

Looking back, Ephraim realized how precious that time had been. His grandfater had died a few months after Ephraim's Bar Mitzvah. Ferenc had had cancer, something that slowly ate away his gut. He'd known his death approached him the last time Ephraim saw him. It had shown in his dark eyes, like it had shown in Laci's.

As a child, Ephraim had felt put upon, tortured with lessons. So one afternoon, he'd lied to his grandfather, saying he needed to go back to school for something. He'd gone bike riding through the wash behind their building instead. It had been so long since he'd gone out and played just on his own.

Of course, he'd fallen. A buried iron pole with a jagged edge waited for him just below the sand. He'd gashed his left arm open, from wrist to elbow. Scared he'd be punished for lying, he hadn't told anyone about his accident. He'd done a ritual to take the pain away and to heal his arm, or so he'd thought.

His mother didn't find out about his accident until two days later, when Ephraim lay in bed with a fever from the infection. She'd rushed him to the hospital, where they'd used more than forty stitches to bind his arm together. He'd been lucky he hadn't lost it.

Thinking about the accident now, Ephraim wondered if that was when he started planning everything, checking everything, doing ineffective rituals. Maybe that first fall had started the second, the fall into his rut.

Sitting in Budapest, rubbing the long scar, Ephraim knew what he had to do. He couldn't talk to his grandfather. But he could call Janet.

And let go.

Completely leave his old life. Though Janet had divorced him, he was still bonded to her, cursed to continue his useless habits until he moved her into his past and gave himself a new, different future. Even if they died tonight, or the world came to an end, he still needed to do this.

He used his credit card to make the call. He didn't want to charge it to Zita's room. Too many sitcoms were based on just that type of misunderstanding.

Janet picked up on the second ring.

"Hi, Janet."

"Ephraim. How are you? Where are you?"

"I'm still in Budapest," he said, unsure where to begin. "It's been kind of crazy here." He picked his pen up off the desk and tapped it against the pad of paper containing the rough drafts of the curses.

"You okay?"

"Yeah. I just called to . . . I don't know. Tell you to take care." How could he tell her he'd called to say good-bye? They'd done that years ago when they'd gotten divorced. If only he could tell her in person, maybe she'd see it in his eyes and he wouldn't have to say anything. This felt so awkward. He shouldn't have called.

"Eph . . . what's wrong? Aren't you coming back?"

"Nothing's wrong. It's just, well, I wanted you to know, I, ah, I've met someone."

Dead silence greeted him from the other end.

"Hello? Janet? You still there?"

"I'm here." She sighed with exasperation. "You called me just to say that? Really, Ephraim. You've been free to date other women for a long time. What's the matter with you?"

Ephraim shook his head. He didn't know if Janet was angry at him or at herself. He stood up, wishing he could pace.

"Believe it or not, Janet, I didn't call to start an argument with you. I don't want to fight with you any more. I just want to be friends."

As the words came out of Ephraim's mouth he realized he'd spoken his heart. To be friends with his ex-wife. Someone he called, maybe on birthdays and holidays. And nothing more. He didn't need her anymore, to prove his value or lack of it. He was worthy of love, of life, of everything he could imagine. The magic could be real.

"I don't know, Eph. Haven't we always fought?"

The wry cheer in her voice made Ephraim smile.

"Do you remember our third date? In the park?"

"Before or after the protest?" Janet quipped.

Now Ephraim sighed with exasperation. "We didn't go to a protest. It was just us. I made a picnic lunch. It was the first time you'd ever had aged cheese. I served it to you with Granny Smith apples. Remember?"

"Yeah," Janet said, in a noncommittal way.

"We didn't fight that day. And you told me later that it had been the most relaxing afternoon you'd ever had."

"Ephraim," Janet said, then paused. "Life isn't always a romantic dream, a summer picnic. We're privileged, and we have to recognize that privilege because we *can* have those times."

"Yes, but you don't have to feel guilty every time you enjoy the sunshine. You can have an afternoon picnic or an evening in front of the fireplace. Life is hard enough. You don't have to spend all your time on the battleground to prove it."

Ephraim paused. He didn't know where his point lay. This unseen path unnerved him more than playing bridge with a novice partner, one who didn't even know how to count tricks. Yet he knew he followed the right track.

"There has to middle ground, Janet, between flogging yourself for the problems of the world and ignoring them for your own pleasures. Yes, the pollution in Budapest is astonishing. Black soot from the leaded gas covers the first four to five feet of the buildings. Beggars stand in wait at almost every metro station. At the same time, the architecture is amazing. The caves are like a whole new world, just waiting to be explored. I've never seen any place so magical."

The golden Latin binding curse beckoned. Would he ever forget the magic that flowed from him? Did he want to? It wasn't the same as the rituals that bound him. His gesturing had set him apart. He'd always felt he had to hide it, hide his difference. That wasn't to say that he wanted to proclaim his newfound abilities to the world, but they made him feel a part of something, something bigger than himself and his petty attempts at controlling everything.

The only thing that countered the magic was the sunlight in Zita's hair, her solid form, her very human beauty.

"You called to say good-bye, didn't you."

Janet's flat statement caught Ephraim by surprise.

"Yeah, I guess I did. Not because I don't want to know you, Janet. I just don't want to continue how we have been."

"What's her name?"

"Zita."

"You know, Eph, I always told myself that I'd be the one to move on first. Because I always did. I moved away from you, from our marriage. Now you're the one going forward. I wish you luck."

Ephraim didn't know how to respond to the envy in his ex-wife's voice.

She really was his ex now.

"Good-bye," he said.

"Good-bye."

Ephraim hung up the phone. He swayed for a moment, but stayed standing. He'd really done it. He'd really broken with Janet this time. Humpty Dumpty had fallen, and no magic would meld the pieces back together. He didn't want to put the pieces back together. However, he couldn't help but feel sad.

Ephraim took a deep breath, sensing the floor beneath him, as if he were growing from the ground, rising from the earth, rooted, solid in himself, as eternal as a stalagmite.

After an unknown time, he sat back down, ready to work on the binding curse, on his future, once again.

Chapter 15

Laci

Three businessmen rode down in the elevator with Laci, wearing somber suits with lapels so sharply pressed they could have severed limbs. Laci watched them suspiciously, but no demons directed their actions, or at least none Laci could see. They got off at the floor above the lobby, going to the conference rooms there.

Laci pushed himself forward when the elevator doors opened. At least he hadn't forgotten what he needed to do. Yet. He needed to find a lead tablet, or something similar, to write the curse on. He had to prove that he wasn't a coward, that he wouldn't run away again. Though he couldn't remember if it was Tuesday or Thursday, or which day came before which, he did remember the demons. What they had done. What they threatened to do. Why he couldn't run away this time.

He hadn't told Zita about János' threats and plans. About how Bélusz would transfer its power to János. He had meant to. More than once. Shame had kept him silent. He didn't want to admit that he'd agreed to help, fallen back into his old habit of not doing what needed to be done.

He *had* told Zita and her young man—what was his name?—that János would be there. Zita's young man could handle János, with or without Bélusz' powers. Magic flowed through him more strongly than he knew. He would save Zita. Laci would take care of Bélusz and die in the process. There had to be a balancing, Laci's life and Bélusz', János and those Jewish families. That was the way it would be.

Just outside the door of the hotel Laci lost his momentum, not sure where to go next. His panic rose with his confusion. He tried to calm himself, convince himself that he would figure it out. He had to keep moving as if he knew where to go.

The small foreign cars parked in the U-shaped driveway in front of the hotel reminded him that he was no longer in America. He didn't know any neighborhood hardware store he could go to, where the clerks knew his name and could help him search for what he needed, particularly if he'd written it down. Or who would tell him to go home if he'd already bought that item three times that week. Not that he listened to them when they did that. It made him angry, and he usually stormed out.

Maybe he could find one of those huge hardware stores, the ones that took over entire blocks. They would certainly have some kind of lead there.

Laci started walking. He couldn't take the metro. He knew the noise and confusion would overwhelm him. He needed to remember where and when he was. The day was slipping into one of his bad ones. It had started out well enough, with finding Zita and all. He'd been a little confused at first, seeing her here, in Budapest. Hadn't he told her to stay in America? Hadn't she promised she would?

He wasn't angry with her though. No matter what Zita said, how she accounted for her actions, Laci understood the ways of demons. They'd made her come, thinking to twist him into an unnatural fate. But the plan hadn't worked. By bringing his granddaughter here, he was more determined than ever to stop János, to kill Bélusz. To die. The binding would work.

If only the *csoda szarvas* could help them. . . . Grandmother Zita whispered that it would.

Laci turned to his left, toward the busy downtown. Many stores lined the streets—maybe he'd find a hardware store there. The noise flowing from the pedestrian mall made him hesitate, but he plunged forward. Disco blasted from a shop with windows full of headless mannequins wearing baggy beige clothing. Well-dressed men and women formed an obstacle course Laci swerved around, determination pushing him forward.

Embroidered items, like those his mother used to make, hung in windows for all to see. Didn't these shopkeepers understand that those sheets and blouses were only for special occasions? Beautiful tablecloths should be shown only to guests. A man wearing a plaque and handing out lilac-colored flyers stood unmoving in the center of the street like a stalagmite, causing everyone to flow by him.

Laci didn't recognize these foreign people, this foreign place. This wasn't the Budapest he remembered.

He stopped, confused.

Tins of Russian caviar filled the storefront before him. Those damn Communists. He remembered them. They'd shot Judit, his sweet wife. Where was she? Where was Margit, their little girl? Was he on his way to pick her up from school? Or was he going somewhere else?

When Laci looked back the way he came, he saw a man in a blue pin-striped suit staring at him. A shadow, almost like an extra head, sat on the man's shoulders. A minion.

Laci pushed his way through the crowd again. He couldn't let the demons or the Communists catch him.

Without warning, Laci was transported.

He no longer stood in the smartly paved pedestrian mall. The street he walked along now had torn-up rail tracks on one side, a dead tank on the other. None of the windows in the shop in front of him had survived. A heavy weight on his left arm pulled at him. He didn't remember stealing someone's watch, but he must have, as one now hung on his wrist.

He had to hide. If the AVO—the secret police— found out about his theft they'd put him in the basement in that awful building near the bridge and torture him for no reason other than that they could. All the horror stories Laci had heard strained his belief. He'd never known anyone personally, or met anyone himself, who had been "treated" there. Some of the tales had to be exaggerated. On the other hand, too many of them had the exact same details for them all to be false.

Laci didn't want to find out for himself. Turning to his left, Laci made his way to the Duna. Through the buildings, he caught sight of the hills of Buda. The greenery loosened his chest. He remembered to breathe. The hills sent out their invitation to him, so reassuring. His mother's special sewing chair, the one they'd had to sell when they'd left Miskolc, had that same color, warming quickly to the touch as you relaxed, sinking into it.

A beeping noise startled Laci. It took him a moment to realize it came from the watch he wore, the one that Ephraim had loaned him. It brought him back to the present.

Laci looked around, the wind from the Danube cutting through the remaining fog in his head. No demons chased him. The beautiful sight of the water struck his heart with its purity. How could anything awful happen in such a light?

Then he remembered the corrupted gold pouring from János' eyes. The demons existed and would be coming after him soon. He needed to do something about them. Something to do with Zita's new young man, some poem he had. Something ubiquitous. Something permanent.

What was all around and yet permanent? Nothing lasted forever, not even the lovely hills filling his eyes with peace. Everything changed, which made it hard to remember. Nothing existed everywhere. Except maybe the ground he walked on, worked with, built on when he'd been working as an engineer. He had a sudden memory of kneeling next to a barrel cactus, rounding out a hole for a knife-edged agave. How could he write a lasting curse in the dirt?

Laci regarded the green hills across the river with

longing. He had an urge to climb into them, hide in them, just for a while. Just until he could think straight again, until the world took its normal shape and color. He needed to figure everything out. Where he was. When he was. He could puzzle it out, if he had enough time and a space to do it in.

Bridges connecting Pest to Buda stretched across the water to either side of him. Which would be better? Lánc híd? Or Erzsébet híd? Laci chose the chain bridge, the one to his right. None of the bridges had survived the war: as the Germans had left, they'd blown them all up. The bridges weren't permanent.

He remembered how he'd despised all the soldiers, first the Germans, then the Russians. Now he didn't want to hate. He wanted to see another dawn. He wanted Judit to live in the flesh, not just the simulacrum he saw every time he looked at Margit, his too-practical "American" daughter, who had disdained her Hungarian heritage until it became popular to be "ethnic." He wanted his granddaughter, the real child of his heart, to be free. She represented his grandmother incarnate, the true heir of all his knowledge, his powers.

No feelings lasted forever. Man passed away. Yet every generation expressed the same feelings. Love. Fear. Hate. Devotion. Laci fought to make his way through the labyrinth in his head. You could write with emotion, but on what?

Laci began walking again. Moving helped lessen his confusion and panic. He had control over what he did. His destiny didn't pull all the strings.

As Laci drew close to the bridge, a man bumped into him. Then another. Laci moved to the side, trying to stay out of the way of the youths, tourists, and businessmen who suddenly filled the korzó. He kept his sight firmly locked on the hills to his right. Yet another jostled Laci, forcing him to look away. The demon sitting on the man's shoulder took a playful swipe at Laci's nose, maybe because it had none itself. Laci recoiled. The man didn't notice anything, didn't pause in his conversation, his cell phone pressed tightly to his ear.

Laci gazed at the crowd finally. Demons blocked his path forward. One pointed to a bus making its way across the bridge. In his mind's eye, Laci saw fire blossoming across the top of the vehicle. He examined the woman who didn't notice the dark shape controlling her. How could people be so unaware of the influences shaping their decisions?

The demon clearly warned Laci not to cross the bridge by bus. And walking, well, it would be too easy for him to slip, fall, or be pushed. The river didn't frighten him. He could swim. But demons might be in the water, there to hold him down. He couldn't take the risk.

Laci glowered at the hills, the lovely, taunting green, so far away. They'd always been out of his reach. Only the richest people lived there. He and his mother, then later, he and his wife, had lived on the Pest side. As a child, his room had faced a smelly courtyard, full of broken glass and building rubbish, no proper playing place for a boy with dreams of playing soccer for a big league someday.

The cold of those days struck him: the gray, the wretched bread crusts, watered-down soup, and desperate poverty; never knowing if there would be enough food for more than a few days; living on jam and promises.

Laci began moving again, trying to run away from those memories. There had been good times too. The quiet of the nights when the Allies didn't bomb the city. The soft kiss of the wind from the hills. The night he'd climbed to the roof of their apartment building to watch the snow drift down.

White descended before Laci's eyes, and he was transported.

The dark city lay before him, the air full of the smell of burning wood. Wind cut through his thin jacket, chilling his very marrow. Laci didn't remember how long he'd been sitting there, but he decided it had been long enough. He scooted over to the edge of the roof, swung his legs over the side and onto the ladder. The icy metal rungs bit into his unprotected hands, freezing them into claws.

Laci got to their apartment door just as János arrived. His classmate carried a sled, an extra overcoat, and boots.

"Let's go," he said.

Laci ignored the overcoat and boots. He took the sled from János and led the way out of the building.

They rode a bus over to the Buda side and climbed the first hill. The snow hushed all the extra sounds. The boys didn't talk. They didn't want to intrude on the quiet.

János had gone down first. He owned the sled, after all. Laci stood in the sifting silence, stamping his feet to chase away the chill creeping up his legs while his excitement built. Wind blew ridges into the snow, making it look like a sand dune. Laci couldn't wait to glide across it. Icy blue shadows stretched across the hill, breaking the solid white surface into bands and borders to be crossed. The anticipated freedom of the ride filled his head with images of flying.

Laci's turn finally came. He lay down on the sled, controlling the way it turned with his bare hands. He didn't want to sit up, like a peasant in a cart. Every bump threw him into the air, like a ship tossed by waves. He went faster than any train. The cold bored icy nails into his cheeks and slapped his chest as he gained speed. His knuckles froze. Laci wondered if he'd ever be able to unclench his hands.

He hadn't worried about running into anything or being dumped in the snow. He had a child's immortality that night, the perfect crisp lines of good and bad, no corrupted friends, no running away, no time for regret.

As he reached the bottom of the hill, Laci slid back into the present. The soft wind from the Duna chased away the cold of his memories. Weight and age returned to his limbs. Rage overcrowded Laci, until he realized he didn't know if he was angrier at losing that childhood place or for having gotten lost there.

He slowed down, straightened his course. He'd been racing around the other people on the strand, treating them like obstacles on a slalom course. He panted as if he'd been running for a while. Maybe he had been. He stopped to breathe for a moment, leaning against the glass of a shop.

Slowly the words next to his shoulder resolved. *AKCIO! FOR SALE!* The shop window contained a winter scene, with white paper snowflakes hanging from the top of the case, twisting slightly. A neon orange plastic toboggan with blue racing stripes going down the center of it hung there also.

"Aki keres, talál." One who seeks, finds.

Laci's mouth dropped open. A plastic sled.

Perfect for writing a curse.

It didn't look the same as the sleds he remembered from his childhood. Wood and metal sleds probably only existed in museums now. It wasn't permanent, though it would be difficult to break or rip. It symbolized something permanent and ubiquitous though—children lived everywhere. They all played, and hoped, and dreamed. And he had to keep the children safe, didn't he?

Besides, using something from his stolen childhood to rebind Bélusz, well, somehow, it just fit.

Part IV

Siphon, Subterranean Stream

"What part did you like best?" Judit asked Laci as they walked along the *körút*.

"Being with you," Laci said, taking his wife's hand and tucking it into his elbow.

"I'm serious," she said, batting at him with her purse.

"So am I," he said, putting his other hand on hers.

Judit smiled up at Laci with so much love he nearly choked. How could he be so lucky? He really hadn't watched the play. He couldn't pay attention to the artificial lines or unrealistic relationships. He'd spent the evening watching his wife, reveling in her delight, enjoying how the lights from the stage highlighted her long lashes and dark eyes. Her smile reflected all the beauty and goodness in the world.

They passed a vendor selling flowers. Laci stopped at the stand, over Judit's protests. He tried one rose, then another, holding them next to her cheek, seeing if he could find a flower that matched the perfection of her skin. Laci bought a pale pink rose eventually, giving the seller a generous tip.

Judit whispered to Laci as they walked away, "You know we can't afford this."

Laci waved away her objections. "You heard who my company just hired? Kovacs Miklos. I went to university with him until they accused him of being a landowner."

"Really?" Judit asked, her eyes wide. "I remember you talking about him. The political officer has allowed such a 'decadent' influence into your office?"

Laci grinned with his wife. "Yes. And I've heard they've been interviewing other engineers. Good men. *Qualified* men."

Judit bit her lip and nodded, her expression faraway and misty. She understood, having heard her husband complain about how management had hired men with the proper political leanings over the ones who could actually do the work. How his boss didn't know a square measure from a ruler.

"And the protests are still going on," Laci added. "The students have been at the university for at least a week. The Russians haven't stopped them. So maybe we can afford more flowers for you."

Judit turned back to her husband, her eyes shining with tears.

"Don't cry," Laci said, reaching out his hand and caressing her cheek.

"It's just that we've dreamed of these days for so long. Freedom for our dear country. It's so close."

Laci nodded, tears threatening his own eyes. They stood for a moment, the soft October air swirling the leaves around their feet. The streetlights blazed above them with an amber glow, banishing the shadows of the past years, the shortages, the official truths, the actual lies.

"Can you imagine what it will be like? In four years, it will be 1960. Can you imagine what our country might be like?" Judit asked.

Wind buffeted against Laci's legs, stronger but still warm. Laci took his wife's hand again and said, "It will be wonderful, no matter what happens, because you'll be there."

The couple started walking again, warm in their dreams.

"Have you—" Laci started.

"Laci!" a voice interrupted him.

Judit and Laci stopped and looked around.

"Over here, old friend," came a cultured voice from the sidewalk café to their left.

Memories of that voice shook Laci's core. He forced himself to see where it came from.

János, his former classmate, beckoned to them.

Laci couldn't stop the shudder that ran through him, or the chill that raced across his shoulders and down his back.

"Come, come," János said, gesturing broadly.

Laci took a deep quaking breath. His wife tugged on his arm. He'd never told her of János, how Bélusz had corrupted his friend, or how his own death was linked to the death of a demon. How could he tell of these things? Of dark caves and magic? She was a creature of the light. Besides, she wouldn't have believed him.

Slowly, Laci let Judit lead him to where János sat. The remains of a fine meal and more than one bottle of wine covered the table in front of his former classmate. Just one bottle would have cost Laci a month's salary.

Judit nudged him. Laci realized he stared at János. Even though Bélusz had taken Laci's special sight, he still could see that something was wrong with János. The human side of his old classmate had weathered the war and its aftermath well: he wore a hand-tailored somber suit made of Italian silk; the nails on his hands shone, as though they'd been buffed; his face radiated sleek health. The demon encased him tighter than his clothes. Laci had an image of shadows that both supported and restricted his old friend. Soon he would lose all his own muscles and wouldn't be able to stand alone.

"May I introduce my wife, Judit," Laci said. He refused to give János her full name. He didn't want to give either János or Bélusz any power over her.

"I am extremely honored to meet you," János said, rising and extending his hand. He took Judit's hand and kissed the back of it.

Laci held himself back from grabbing his wife's hand and rubbing it clean.

"Please, join me," János said, pulling out the chair next to him for Judit.

"I'm afraid we can't," Laci said stiffly.

"Yes," Judit added. "We've been away from our daughter long enough."

Laci's jaw clenched. Unfailingly polite, Judit had just given János the perfect excuse for why the couple couldn't stay. However, she shouldn't have mentioned their daughter. Not to János.

"You have a daughter, old friend? Wonderful! How old is she?"

"She's five," Laci said through gritted teeth.

"She attends the Young Pioneers' preschool, doesn't she? I thought I saw her there when I picked up my cousin."

Laci found he couldn't take a breath. János had been watching Margit? They must enroll her in a new school. Would that be enough though?

"You take care of her. I see she's already a beauty. And someday, who knows? I might need a wife."

Laci's mouth opened in astonishment. He didn't know what to say. Judit just smiled in amusement, taking János' joking at face value. She couldn't understand the awfulness of János' suggestion. His daughter married to this minion of Bélusz?

She looked from one man to the other, finally breaking the silence by asking, "What are you celebrating?"

"A very special friend, an archaeologist, has made a new discovery," János said, rolling his shoulders slightly.

"Really?" Judit asked. "What is it?"

Laci didn't listen to János' lies. He knew what they had unearthed. They'd found the fourth plaque. A single plaque remained hidden. Only one plaque still bound the demon to its throne.

"We have to be going," Laci said, interrupting János.

"Well, do be careful, old friend. You never know what kind of chaos will suddenly erupt in the streets. Students protesting—who knows what will happen next? You might want to stay home when it does. And keep your lovely wife and daughter at home too, eh?" János stood and bowed slightly.

Laci took Judit's hand, turned abruptly, and left. He hurried through the streets, the wind now blowing cold against his back. He didn't respond to Judit's questions about who that had been, what he had meant, why Laci was so upset. What could he tell her?

Though Laci made them walk home as fast as they could go, he still couldn't rid himself of the chill János' words had given him.

Chapter 16

Zita

"It's not what we planned," Zita said again. How could they not understand?

"It's perfect. I don't see what you're complaining about," her grandfather argued. "I got exactly what you asked for." He folded his arms across his chest and glared at Zita. "I did it. I did it right this time."

Zita blinked back tears of frustration and fear. Her grandfather had always been stubborn. She'd never thought of him as unreasonable before. It frightened her how far he'd slipped away from her.

Laci relented for a moment. He held up one of the pens he'd bought, that he thought they should use on the sled. "See, look at these," he said, a pleading tone creeping into his voice. " 'Magic Marker.' It says it right there. Says that it's magic. Why won't these work?"

Ephraim spoke up. "Romans used lead because it was ubiquitous. Plastic is everywhere in our age. This could work."

Zita shook her head. The plan had been to use lead and to somehow chisel words into it. It didn't matter if no one could read the words—that would just make it more authentic. The pictures of the Roman curse tablets Zita had found on the Internet were illegible.

Using a child's plastic sled struck Zita as, well, irreverent. Particularly using a neon-orange toboggan with blue racing stripes down the center. She picked it up and held it at arm's length, looking it up and down. It had been curled up for so long it wouldn't even hang straight.

However, her grandfather hadn't given them any time to look for a real lead plaque. It was after six. He should have been back by four. Most of the stores had closed. Why had she let him go on his own? She should have followed him or something. Worry had nagged at her while she'd waited for his return. She'd wandered out of the Internet café more than once and walked along the streets, looking for him, afraid that he'd disappear again, maybe try to go and fight Bélusz on his own.

Her grandfather's appearance, when he did finally show up, hadn't made her feel better. His hair was disheveled, his hands shook, and he stank of sweat, as if he'd been running from the demons. Maybe he had been. He wouldn't tell them about it. Zita suspected that he didn't remember what he'd done for most of the afternoon.

They needed to get to the cave before Bélusz broke the last plaque. Ephraim had thought the ceremony would occur at midnight, but Zita, after her time on the Internet that afternoon, thought it was just as likely the demons would do it at moonrise, about nine thirty. Laci had agreed with Zita.

"The plan . . ." Zita started.

"What about 'The Plan'?" Ephraim asked, interrupting her.

Zita jerked her head back, as if Ephraim had slapped her.

Was it the plan that was important? Or her control of it?

Zita realized her mouth was open. She shut it, took a deep breath in, then let go of everything as she breathed out: her need for extremes, Peter's voice inside her head, her own doubts and failures. She drew herself up straighter. She'd been hunched over, weighted down with the need to arrange everything to the last detail. She caught an image of herself as a bull, lowering its horns and pushing through its life with brute force. She didn't have to do that anymore. Yes, it was good to have plans. Gliding through life without making conscience decisions left her without choices, left her staying in places like the Water Hell Hotel. On the other hand, she didn't need to be bound to every plan, like Sisyphus to his rock. She could step to the side, let the rock roll down the hill. Find a new plan.

Choose again.

"Okay." Zita made herself smile, then felt the smile grow naturally larger as she relaxed further. "Let's use this. It'll be fine."

Her grandfather nodded sagely. *"Ha ló nincs, jó a szamár is."*

Zita looked at him enquiringly.

"No horse, use a donkey."

Zita smiled. Her old grandfather had returned, the one she knew.

She reached out and stroked one of his hands. His skin seemed paper thin. It felt soft under her fingertips, as if the years had worn it smooth.

Zita bit her lip, refusing to cry. She would *not* lose him.

Ephraim took the sled from Zita. He held it, weighed it in his hands, then glanced over his shoulder at the desk, clearly weighing his options. After a moment's consideration, Ephraim shrugged and knelt on the floor, spreading the sled out. It wouldn't stay flat.

"Laci, could you hold the top there, please?" Ephraim asked. Laci complied. Ephraim stood up, got his notes, then knelt again, holding down the bottom of the sled with his knees.

The blue light that Zita had seen before flared. It surrounded Ephraim, flowed out from him, and lapped at her grandfather, whose own light didn't shine as steadily.

Zita let the light in, flooding her vision. It soothed her nerves, something she'd never imagined magic could do. The image of a monk-scribe kneeling before a nameless god superimposed itself on Zita's eyes. His hair flowed out over his collar, curling slightly and soft as an angel's. His off-white shirt and olive-green khakis transformed into robes. She could just make out the twisted gold rope tightened around his waist. For an instant, she smelled cloying incense.

Her grandfather sat with his eyes closed, lips moving, hands spread wide to hold down the curling edges of their parchment. He looked like a petitioner, supplicating himself before an altar.

Or maybe, preparing himself as a sacrifice.

Ephraim's light continued to wash over her grandfather, cover him, and subsume him. The words he wrote had their own golden radiance, weaving around both men, binding them to a single purpose.

As the vision disappeared, Zita choked down on her revulsion. Yes, she'd just seen more than a normal person would. But the voice in her head telling her it was wrong sounded more like Peter's than her own.

Zita spent the entire bus trip up the hill trying to talk her grandfather into letting her go into the cave first, to act as the distraction.

"They don't know me. They won't realize anything is going on if they see me," she said.

"They know you. János knows you. He's been watching you. He saw you at the airport." Laci hesitated, as if about to say something. He said nothing though, and just reached out to stroke Zita's short hair. He'd told her how much he'd loved her new look. He'd also told her how much he liked Ephraim, even if he couldn't recall her friend's name half the time.

"Didn't they attack you at Hösök Tér?" he continued. "The demons know you. They won't spare you if they meet you again. Me, Bélusz will want to gloat over. So you'll have time to rescue me. Please."

Zita didn't like this plan. As they came closer to their destination, more and more anxiety piled on her. What if it didn't work? She didn't want to sacrifice her grandfather. What would she do without him? She wished she'd spent more time with him these last few years, gone over to his house more often, had accepted more of his invitations to dinners in his garden. Why had she wasted her days with Peter?

"*Édes*, you've lived your life as best you could. You must keep living it." Her grandfather hesitated, then continued. "I've lived my life as well."

Zita wanted to stop the bus right then and turn it around. She wanted to spend another night with her grandfather, walking along the Danube arm in arm, listening to street musicians, drinking wine under the stars.

She didn't have another night.

She had to move forward. She looked across her grandfather to Ephraim, who gave her an encouraging smile. At least she didn't face either the demons or her grandfather's decline completely alone.

Though not many streetlights lined the road, Laci knew where to get off. A simple stone shelter marked the stop. After the bus took off, the quiet of the night descended upon them. No cars were on the road. The faint windlike noise of Budapest's traffic sounded in the distance. The moon hadn't risen yet. The ruddy glow of the city lights outshone any stars that might have come out.

Laci directed them to a dirt path that went across a small meadow. Zita stopped before she stepped off the sidewalk and onto the trail. Dread lined her stomach. She didn't want to continue. What if they failed? They didn't have another plan. They had to stop Bélusz tonight, or else. Ephraim might be able to get them out by repeatedly reading the curse, but what then? What if another war broke out? What if the demons destroyed everything?

Her grandfather leaned over and kissed her hair. "It will be all right, *édes*. Everything is going to be fine." He put his arm around her and nudged her forward.

Zita bowed her head and took the first step, feeling as though it led irrevocably to her, as well as her grandfather's, last.

They strolled across the meadow and into the trees.

The city beneath them shone vibrant and fairylike. Under different circumstances, Zita would have loved going on a night outing up above Pest with her grandfather, the smell of mulch, the talkative wind, and the soft air brushing against her cheeks.

The path was wide enough for the three of them to walk abreast, Laci and Ephraim on the outside, Zita in the middle. She stumbled on an unseen rock. Both men reached out to catch her. She tucked her hand into the crook of Laci's elbow and kept hold of Ephraim's hand as well.

He'd been such a good friend these past few days, not taking, not asking for more than she could give. He'd committed himself to their cause unhesitatingly. She loved his scent—spicy—even without cologne. He'd even smelled that way in the morning, soft and sweet, not overpowering, like Peter.

Zita slowed down, pulling against the men on either side of her. She told herself it was because she didn't want to trip again, but in reality, it was so she could think about what lay ahead. Not about their task. She could do without their life-or-death situation. She didn't want to say good-bye to her grandfather. Her fear had grown while she hadn't been looking, leaving her slightly nauseous and unable to take deep breaths. She didn't want to put him into a situation where she had to rescue him.

She also wanted to explore the feelings she had for Ephraim. The unfairness of it struck her. He was such a nice guy, even if he was a magician. Why couldn't she have met him under ordinary circumstances, when she didn't have to fear him? Yet she didn't have the same nervousness now as she had earlier that day. He did remind her of her grandfather. If she could accept her family's power, she could accept Ephraim's as well.

Far too soon, the woods around them changed. The twisted trees told Zita they neared their goal. The trunks didn't glow with bilious color, but Zita could easily imagine them doing so. Coiled branches lurched across the path. Zita found herself ducking her head as she walked under them, to protect herself from goo or spiders or whatever might drop from them. Large white mushrooms sprouted near the roots. Laci had served her "tree ear" mushrooms more than once. These, though, didn't make her hungry. They looked bloated and poisonous, unnaturally white and bulbous.

Zita couldn't stop herself from shuddering once they left the diseased trees. Silently the trio marched across the field. Zita felt like Dorothy with her faithful companions going to face the wicked witch. Though she'd always thought of her grandfather as leonine, now she realized he should play the scarecrow, scrounging for his brain. And Ephraim? The tin man, she decided, searching for his heart. Where was Toto? She giggled, then realized hysteria tinged her laugh.

The gate surrounding the cave was only closed, not locked. Ephraim looked at Zita and shrugged as he pushed it open, as if to say "Whoever goes through finds what they deserve." The demons didn't need to lock it.

Or maybe they'd left it open on purpose. What if the demons expected them? Zita turned to walk away.

Her grandfather stood in her path, his arms open.

Zita settled into his hug, then tightened it. How could she send him into the lion's den alone? She continued their argument, as if they'd never stopped.

"You're too precious to risk. You can't go."

Her grandfather hugged her tighter. "I have to go. I can't run away again. Besides, if I'm so precious, you'll be sure to rescue me, right?"

He pushed himself back and kissed Zita's forehead. Tears started down her cheeks.

"I trust you," he whispered against her face. "You've always made me proud. You're the true daughter of my heart." He pulled back for a moment. "Now you must let me do what I need to do. You have to let me go first, *édes*."

Zita pulled her grandfather close one more time, breathing his scent in, that dusty old-man scent layered with medicine smells, with hints of the vigorous young man, deep musk, still lurking at the bottom. She couldn't control him. She couldn't stop whatever ate his mind, stealing him from her.

She had to let him go.

"*Isten veled,*" he said, letting his arms fall and turning away.

"No, no, *Nagyapa. Viszontlátásra.* I *will* see you again. Soon," Zita said, fervently wishing it to be true. She would make it true. She couldn't control him, but she could take charge of her own destiny.

Ropes lay waiting for them, already strung through the large metal loop bolted to the ground next to the entrance. They would have company, as her grandfather had warned they would.

Laci began to lower himself down. "*Isten veled, édes,*" he called out. Then he disappeared down the hole.

"God be with you too," Zita replied softly. She turned away and looked back at the diseased wood. She tried to convince herself that they did the right thing, that someone needed to stop the demons that night, that it must be them.

She counted to ten, as slowly as she could, using "Mississippi elephant apartment" as the phrase between the numbers to force her pace to be leisurely. The plan had been that Zita and Ephraim would give Laci a ten-minute head start so he could distract Bélusz and János. Laci would go to the main cavern, while Zita and Ephraim, when they followed, would take the high path to the dry gallery, so they could be above the demons, out of harm's way. Ephraim would read the binding spell, immobilize everything in the chamber below them, then Zita would rescue her grandfather.

Zita turned to Ephraim. He was still setting the timer on his watch.

"Let's go," she said.

"What?" he asked. "I thought we'd agreed to give Laci ten minutes before we followed him."

"It doesn't have to be that long," Zita said. "We

should go now." She smiled, hearing herself throw away a plan—The Plan—they had all agreed on.

"Your grandfather isn't expecting us yet. What if he isn't ready?" Ephraim said.

"Grandpa isn't expecting anything tonight," Zita said. She couldn't say the rest of her sentence aloud. *Except to die.* "We need to go now. We shouldn't have sent him down by himself. What if he gets lost?"

"Then maybe we should give him time enough to find himself," Ephraim said. "It'll be okay."

"No." Zita said emphatically. "We have to go now."

Ephraim sighed and rolled his head. Finally he said, "What about 'The Plan'?"

Even in the dark, Zita saw the width of Ephraim's grin. How could he tease her at a time like this? Didn't he know how serious this was?

Ephraim reached across the frosty space between them and took Zita's hand. "Okay. Let's go now," he said.

A lump formed in Zita's throat. He'd only been trying to lighten the situation, to make her feel better.

She squeezed his hand and said, "Thanks." She couldn't manage to say anything more. She wanted to thank him for being there, for trying to make things better, for trying to help. For supporting her and her family's crazy quest.

The words would have to wait until later. If a "later" came.

Zita went down the hole first. The thin, modern ropes had no stretch in them. They weren't like the one she remembered from elementary school gym class, dull brown, thick, and prickly. She had difficulty maintaining a grip, and wished knots had been tied in the lines. Ephraim stood at the top and shone a light against the wall, illuminating spots where she could put her feet. Then Zita did the same for Ephraim.

Only one path led away from the sinkhole. Zita couldn't see anything through the blackness. This cave didn't have the feel of the ones Zita had taken tours of. Here, the dark actively pressed in on her. A dank smell tickled the bottom of her throat. She didn't want to brush against the walls for fear the mold growing there would somehow get a foothold in her lungs.

Zita forced herself forward, into the unlit passage. The thick blackness made her feel as though she walked underwater. She kept her light in a small beam, focused on the floor, watching where she placed her feet. There was nothing to see when she shone it higher, only flowing rock that too easily metamorphosed in her mind's eye into demon faces.

Ephraim stumbled behind her. She turned around and shone her light on her hand, reaching out to him. He gave her his hand, and she placed it on the small of her back. He understood and tucked his fingers into her waistband. Now they were connected and wouldn't get separated. Zita immediately felt better with Ephraim's tenuous touch, though fear still dried her mouth and made her heart pound.

More than once, Zita hesitated over minor paths leading up and away from the main one. None of them seemed wide enough though. She worried that they'd made an incorrect assumption. Since people had obviously done work in the cave, maybe they had blocked off the path to the upper gallery.

And they had. A wide path broke off to her left. A large pile of rocks and rubble stretched across it, about knee-high. The height of the rubble caught Zita's eye before she walked past it. The barrier was obviously artificial. She paused and shone her light in that direction. Another barrier, a wall made of loose stones, stood behind the first. A large gaping hole lay sandwiched between the top of the wall and the ceiling. Was this the way to the upper gallery? She hesitated. She didn't want to get lost, not down here. She hoped they wouldn't have to leave in a hurry. Those slick ropes wouldn't be any easier climbing out. And what were the demons doing to her grandfather while she dithered? She gulped.

Ephraim leaned over and whispered in her ear, "Yes. That's the right way."

Zita nodded, aware that Ephraim would feel the movement. She leaned back against him for a second, feeling the warmth of his chest against her back. She briefly wished that they could stay that way for a year or so, with him resting his chin against her hair, his breath whispering by her ear, and his heartbeat echoing through her skin. The slight physical contact comforted her.

They had to move on. She pulled away from Ephraim, stepped over the barrier, and walked up to the wall. Up closer, she saw bird droppings at the top of it. Turul, the great eagle, had come this way more than once. It had to be the right direction.

A few protruding rocks stuck out of the wall, not too many. It didn't look impossible to climb, but it didn't look easy either. Zita turned to hand the flashlight to Ephraim. He shook his head and continued to make full sweeping motions with his hands, as if conducting a symphony. He ended with pushing gestures, first to the left side of the wall, then the right, then the center.

"Try it," he whispered.

"Try what?"

"Squeezing past the wall. There might be room now."

Zita bit down on the revulsion that rose from her gut. She didn't want to believe that this wonderful, cute guy had just cast a magic spell. It made him too similar to the demons.

It also made him similar to her grandfather. Who she loved.

Zita went up to the right side of the wall and shone the flashlight on it, trying to see if a space had opened up between the edge of the wall and the tunnel. She didn't see one. She tried the other side, but didn't see anything there either. She looked at Ephraim.

He shrugged. "It was worth a try."

Zita bit her lip. No, it hadn't been. Not if they wasted their time.

She handed the flashlight to Ephraim without a

word and reached out to touch one of the protruding rocks.

She had to stretch her arm farther than she thought she would before she actually touched the wall. It took her a moment to figure out what had happened.

The protruding rocks were *behind* the others.

A gap ran up the middle of the wall, hidden by a tricky arrangement of rocks woven together. The clever optical illusion couldn't be spoiled even by close observation.

Zita turned to Ephraim in wonder. Had he made this? He shrugged. He didn't know.

Zita pushed her way through the gap in the wall, first with one shoulder, scraping her ear as she searched for an opening big enough for her head, bruising her breasts as she pulled them through. She made a futile attempt to brush herself off, then turned to offer Ephraim a hand.

Her arm froze halfway up its arc. The wall seemed to flex for Ephraim, as if *he* was real and *it* wasn't. He didn't have any of the difficulty she'd had as he walked through.

She gulped, spun away from the display of his freakish power, and resolutely started back up the tunnel.

Ephraim stopped her. "The net?"

Zita considered. She shone her flashlight on the path. It climbed quickly, twisting as it did so. She shook her head. They didn't have any room to maneuver, to capture Turul in their net if the great eagle chose to attack. They didn't need to get it out until later.

Zita started back up the trail. The tunnel narrowed, and Zita had to bend over, far enough to touch her toes, more than once.

She heard the demons before she saw them, great catcalls and jeers, like an angry mob. The distorted sound made her wonder how many partied there. She rushed as fast as she could, banging her head in the process.

The last hairpin turn in the path opened onto a hole

that light streamed through. She couldn't see anything beyond the glare: Zita's eyes had grown accustomed to the dark. She paused and blinked.

"Wait—" Ephraim said.

Zita ignored him and pushed forward. The net wouldn't help them here either. And she didn't want to see him do any more magic.

Pale squishy material streaked with puce and olive swirls covered the ground. The smell told Zita where it came from. Did that many bats live in the gallery? To produce that much guano?

Zita took a deep breath, wishing she could hold it forever; then she forced herself down to her hands and knees. She couldn't stop herself from gagging as she crawled forward. She hoped the noise from the crowd hid the slight sound.

Zita peered over the edge of the dry gallery into the main cavern below. She searched for her grandfather. The light in the cavern came mostly from several large flashlights stuck into the ground. A motor caused a few of them to circle, like searchlights at a movie premier. In addition, every stalagmite in the cave had been leveled off and had a lit candle placed on it.

Laci stood with his head bowed before another man. Zita peered at him, not able to make out his features. He seemed covered by a great shadow.

"János," Ephraim said beside her, the word filled with dread determination.

Zita nodded. Her grandfather had warned them that his old classmate would be here.

A large cut across her grandfather's forehead bled into his eyes. He swayed as if blown by a strong wind. She couldn't hear him, but she thought he moaned. She wondered if they'd drugged him. Beside her grandfather stood a magnificent stag statue. Behind János the Traitor hulked a large rock formation.

At least half a dozen youths cavorted in tight circles. They all wore the kind of bulky camo that the boys she'd seen at her apartment had worn. She wondered what kind of desecration they'd do here in the cave. Their bodies jerked and they stamped their feet to some unheard music.

A pair of young men ran full speed at one another, smashing their chests together, then fell back, onto one of the motors. The light swept all around the room as it fell, momentarily blinding Zita. She blinked hard, trying to chase away the purple afterimages.

Then she saw . . . something.

Shadows. Dancing with the young men. She blinked again. Too many shadows stirred down there. The extra darkness had the same otherworldly quality to it as the blue light she'd seen around Ephraim. Zita stared harder at the spaces between the light, seeing long purple fingers that ended in claws, ears that dripped mucus, and long verdant tongues.

She shook her head and closed her eyes. She didn't want to see, or believe. Something in her still rebelled at the idea that all this truly existed. Yes, she and Ephraim knelt in the gallery and her grandfather stood below along with his former classmate, but she didn't want the demons to have life. She wanted them to just be in her grandfather's head. She and Ephraim hadn't really seen anything that night they'd been attacked. He couldn't have just made a magic hole in the wall.

Yet . . .

Something was down there.

She opened her eyes and stared at the rock formation in front of her grandfather. Did the lights trick her? Or did that thing seem to have a horrible face? With a hollow for a nose, broken stalactites for a mouth, and those three knobs across its forehead that had the appearance of extra eyes?

She turned away, then looked back. Had one of the piles of rocks, which could be mistaken for an arm, moved? She tried peering at it out of the corner of her eye, like she'd done in the Labyrinth. She couldn't

see the figure clearly, but she now saw the shadows
that stretched from it, crept up János' back, and
formed the cloak she perceived around him.

Zita closed her eyes and counted to five. When she
opened them again, all she could see were the youths,
János, and her grandfather.

One of the youths danced up to her grandfather
and struck him across the shoulders. He barely seemed
to notice the blow, though his shirt tore. Zita couldn't
watch another minute.

She turned to Ephraim. His face looked ghostly. Or
maybe he'd just turned pale from the sights below.
She crawled behind him, grimacing at the white material supporting her knees. Something crunched. She
held her breath and leaned down to see. A little pile
of bones and fur sat next to her knee.

They didn't kneel in bat guano. All this came from
an owl. Or an eagle. Turul maybe. Only a sick bird
befouled its own nest this way. Zita recalled the stories
her grandfather had told her, of how the great eagle
lived at the top of the Tree of Life and escorted souls
to heaven. It, too, had been corrupted, like the forest
above them.

Zita pulled the sled out of the pack Ephraim wore
and unrolled it, checking to make sure that none of
the lettering had smudged. It hadn't. The Magic Mark-
ers had dried beautifully.

She got out the five little kings and placed them in
a semicircle in front of Ephraim. As she reached
across her friend, she noticed he didn't move or look
at her. His attention never left the scene below.

Something down there had trapped him.

Zita held up the sled, blocking his vision of the
things below them. Ephraim blinked and seemed to
see Zita again. He brushed his hand across his eyes,
moving as if wet concrete filled the air. What had he
been watching? Could he see more than she could?

Ephraim stared at Zita, as if noticing her for the
first time. Color crawled back into his cheeks.

What had he seen? Zita wanted to ask him, but her questions would have to wait; she didn't want to make any noise that might attract the attention of those things below them. She wished she could ease the haunted look Ephraim's face still wore. Maybe Ephraim could do magic, maybe he could make things easier in his life, but he paid a price for it. It made him seem more human. Made her own sight not as threatening. Maybe being able to do magic wasn't all bad.

When Ephraim opened his eyes, she handed him the rolled-up sled with both hands, formally. The image of Ephraim as a priest from ancient times came back to her. As an acolyte she handed the priest a magic scroll. The blue light around him flickered, then solidified.

And blackened.

Words rolled from Ephraim. They formed a golden light, which first flowed out and away from him, but then swept back, encased his heart, burning that organ and cramming it with ashes.

Zita shook her head. The image disappeared.

Ephraim unrolled the sled. He held it before him with both hands, like a town crier reading an announcement. The image of the reader turning into stone stayed with Zita, even after she turned away.

Zita positioned herself so she could look over Ephraim's shoulder at the crowd below. The hollering had grown several notches. János suddenly slapped her grandfather across the face. His head bobbed, and he started to arch his back, as if he balanced something precious on his chest that he couldn't risk dropping.

Fear filled Zita as her grandfather stretched his arms out, taking a sacrificial posture. János poked at her grandfather's chest. For a moment, she thought he used a knife.

János would kill her grandfather, then find them and kill them too. Zita found she couldn't swallow, couldn't move, and could barely breathe. Her remembered fear from her nightmares amplified the echoing fright she felt now. She bit down hard, willing herself not to scream as the dread overtook her.

Ephraim started reading aloud. Marvelous Latin chanting loaded the air. The revelers grew silent. The words floated down on them, like snow sifting through the clouds, laying a hushed blanket on everything it touched. The spell flowed out from the dry gallery, diminishing the shadows as it descended, white and pure.

The words and the light thawed Zita a little, allowing her to lean forward, lightly touching Ephraim's shoulder. The youths stood motionless, their mouths open, frozen in space. Zita saw the demons more clearly now, terrible and immobile. The scent of the guano rushed over her, choking her.

Zita tried to pretend the repulsive creatures below were statues, not real, not alive. She tried not to see the rotten cloth covering decaying bones, the wisps of hair pushing out of blue-green mottled skin, the internal organs, still pulsing, though no blood circulated. More than one demon had a nose, or ears, or lips, missing. The dread she'd felt remained, a solid core in the center of her being, with only a shadow of humanity wrapped around it.

Yet everyone stood still. Even her grandfather. Even János. They all stared up at the gallery.

She glanced at the rock formation and wished she hadn't. She saw Bélusz now, its hideous features laid bare in the binding. She wished she couldn't. Its corrupt stone face would fill her nightmares for the rest of her life.

It, too, sat frozen.

Maybe the spell was working. Maybe they could rebind the demon, save her grandfather, leave the cave and all its horrors behind. Maybe they could go back up into the fresh air and sunshine, forget all the magic and insanity, and lead normal lives again.

Zita couldn't stop herself from smiling as her hope buoyed up.

Chapter 17

Ephraim

All the creatures whirled to gaze at them. Ephraim knew if he closed his eyes, he'd still see them: the elongated skulls, muzzles twisted and grinning, that mocked human form; the random animal parts, like beaks, webbing, or wings, attached to bodies in unnatural ways; claws that dripped ichor, mouths that drooled black sap, and rotten fur not adequate to cover bones. He'd never be able to forget these corruptions, no matter how many years he lived, how much he drank, or how many cleansing rituals he went through.

Ephraim wondered at the gray stone fountain now blossoming on Laci's chest. János had made it rise after Laci had arched his back. The fountain was shaped like a three-tiered wedding cake, with lion heads spouting water. Ephraim didn't know how he knew this, but somehow, the fount was connected to Laci's soul. János had spun straws out of shadows, stuck them into Laci's chest, and had sipped at one until Ephraim had started reading the curse. Laci looked like a mutant porcupine, the straws bobbing slightly as he breathed.

That the demons had stopped heartened Ephraim. Some, however, continued swaying. Maybe when he finished reading the curse five times they would be as still as stone.

Ephraim let the glorious words take him again, spewing golden light with each syllable. Echoes of the cantor from his synagogue chimed through his memory, the high clear notes of prayer. The soaring tones he heard in his head weren't appropriate here, but their purity was. Ephraim's soul resonated with perfect clarity.

A piercing screech broke Ephraim's concentration, like a dark cloud obscuring the sun.

The eagle Turul had arrived.

And the net they had to restrain it still sat in their backpack. In their haste, they'd forgotten to retrieve it.

The eagle dove at Ephraim, striking at the sled with its sharp claws. The strength of its blow pushed Ephraim back, forced him off his knees and onto his butt. Zita screamed. One claw broke through the tough plastic, a single rent on the left side. The eagle didn't gain purchase though. It veered off and circled around.

Ephraim held the sled out in front of him like a shield. He braced himself for the next round. "Stay there!" he ordered Zita when he heard her scrambling to get up. He didn't know how he could shelter her from the fury of Turul's talons. All he could think of at that moment was to protect her, even at the cost of his own life.

"Stop!" sang out a deep, smooth voice.

Turul screamed, but didn't dive again. Instead, it landed on a broken column, not far from the upper gallery, and glared at them.

Ephraim took a deep breath, about to start reading the curse from the beginning again. He didn't remember where he'd stopped. He figured it was best for each recitation of the curse to be whole.

"If you continue, my old friend dies," a smooth voice with a British accent now called out.

Zita gasped.

Ephraim leaned forward and peered over the edge. János held a serrated knife against Laci's exposed neck. The old man moaned and swayed slightly in his classmate's grasp.

Ephraim had no doubt that János meant what he'd said. He'd kill Laci the instant Ephraim continued.

The problem was that though Ephraim didn't hold the knife to Laci's throat, it would be the same as if he did. *He* would be the one to kill the grandfather of the woman fast becoming the most important thing in his world. Could he live with blood like that on his hands? Would she be able to abide him if he did?

Could he not continue, and live with the bloodshed to come?

Laci suddenly screamed. "Do it!"

Ephraim didn't know if the old man directed his comment to János or to him.

"I'm dead anyway," Laci continued.

Ephraim shuddered at the fatality in Laci's voice. Still, he hesitated. He'd never killed a man. Ephraim had been raised in a time of peace. Janet had railed at the idea of acceptable sacrifices, insisting that every casualty hurt, rather than helped, a cause. Did Ephraim believe that? Was he really a pacifist? Or was it just a label he'd accepted from Janet?

He didn't know how he'd live with his shame and guilt if he acted. Yet, somehow, other people did, war heroes, soldiers and generals. Ephraim would just have to sacrifice himself, as they did.

He had to follow the plan, complete the ritual.

Ephraim started reading again. The golden words took him into the light, away from the putrefied pelts and unnatural monsters below.

Darkness descended over his eyes before he completed the first stanza. For a second, Ephraim thought the demons tricked him. Then he realized Zita had put her hands over his eyes. He could have continued from memory, but her touch, light though it was, distracted him more than the hordes below could have.

"I can't let you do this," she said. "I can't let you turn your soul to ashes."

Ephraim hung his head. She spoke the truth, as always. He'd never be able to live with himself if he actively killed her grandfather. He didn't know if he could live with himself had he passively killed the old man either. He didn't see a way out of their dilemma.

He'd stopped for too long. Now they didn't have another choice.

The demons spilled into the gallery, their rotted smell overpowering the guano. They grabbed Ephraim first, then Zita, binding their arms. Ephraim was surprised that something made only of bone and flapping bark felt harder than cement.

The demons hurried them down the path, taking a shortcut into the large room. They forced Ephraim down on his knees with rough hands. The pain as he hit the stone floor made him cry out. Zita whimpered. Ephraim braced himself, afraid that the demons would stick things in his chest as well.

Zita knelt next to him, on his left, while Laci stood to the far side of her. Bruises blossomed on the old man's forehead, below his eye, and on his chin. Blood flowed across his forehead and into his eyes. A thin red streak dribbled down his neck from where János had nicked him. His clothes were torn and dirty from being rolled on the ground.

The gray stone fountain had sunk back into Laci's chest, pulling the demon straws with it. Ephraim had an impression of a stylized lion's head, peppered with tiny darts that wouldn't shake off, spread across Laci's shirt.

Ephraim turned forward. For the first time, he saw where the deep voice came from. Though he'd seen the other demons, he'd mistaken the one in front of him, Bélusz, for a rock formation.

It had human features—a recognizable head, torso, limbs—yet it existed as the most inhuman of all the creatures there. Ephraim had never imagined that stone could be corrupted. Mold and lichen ate at its arms and torso. Bélusz' skin bubbled like cave pearls, yet most of the round formations were broken, leaving jagged spines, damaged and unnatural. The semiluminescent quality of the rock made Bélusz' skin seem radioactive.

The demon laughed, sending its minions into howling fits. It moved its arms in a sweeping motion.

Seeing Bélusz was bad enough. Seeing it move made the nightmare come alive. Ephraim couldn't stop the shudder that went through him.

As the cacophony died down, Ephraim heard Laci moaning and chanting. The old man spoke in Hungarian. A poem? A prayer? Something with a lilting, rhyming quality to it.

Ephraim leaned toward Zita. That's when he noticed the demons hadn't bound Laci's arms. He stood without restraint. Should Ephraim tell him to run? Maybe Ephraim and Zita could provide a distraction, and Laci could go get help. . . .

No. The old man was too far gone. Laci moved his head as if he named and cursed each demon he saw. His gaze stopped places where Ephraim saw only shadow. To Ephraim, many of the demons had an unreal quality. Some of the demons he could barely see, as if through a dark veil. What did Laci see?

Laci said over his shoulder to Zita, "*Annyian vagy olyan sokan vannak, mint az oroszok.*"

"English, *Nagyapa*?"

"Too many, too many of them. As many as Russians," Laci replied, faltering.

Bélusz gestured again for silence. Now Ephraim heard English words mingled with Laci's Hungarian. "Broken wings . . . Be gone . . . fleshless fiends . . . I command you . . ."

"So nice to have an audience," Bélusz said, his buttery voice sliding through the chamber. Even Laci fell quiet. "More magicians," it sneered, staring at Ephraim. "How loudly will you sing when I crush the dust of your bones?"

Ephraim's mouth dried in fear. He should have kept reading the binding curse.

Bélusz turned away and called out, "Bring the false plaque!"

Two demons—tree men reduced to bare branches crawling with worms—came forward, clutching the sled between them in their twiglike fingers.

"Watch carefully, Magician. Soon this will happen

to you," Bélusz said. The eye in the center of its forehead slowly opened. An elongated pupil sat in a yellow-brown iris. Bloodred lines ran through the white of the eye. It pulsed in its socket, throbbing with an unnatural beat.

A sickly flaxen light spilled from the eye and shone on the sled. The toboggan crackled like frozen cellophane. Starting from the spot where the demon stared, the neon orange color faded and died. The gray crawled from that spot in streaks of vibrating infection. The lines spread, grew thicker, and eventually covered the whole of the sled.

Bélusz had turned their "plaque" to stone.

The weight made the demons holding it sag. They still had enough strength to turn in a circle, displaying their master's work.

With great solemnity, the demons raised the now-stone toboggan over their heads. They hesitated for a moment, then hurled it down. The sled broke into hundreds of pieces, the words of the binding spell shattered.

Ephraim hung his head. They'd tried. It was too late now. The demons not only had Laci, but Zita as well. The Latin seared across the backs of Ephraim's eyes, but he couldn't risk repeating them. He couldn't place either of the people beside him in more peril.

He glanced at Zita. Her stare fixed on Bélusz and wouldn't let go, as if it, too, were made of stone. He could practically see the wheels turning in her head. Could they rebind Bélusz before it turned on them? How could they get away from its followers? How could she keep her grandfather alive? Her plans didn't help her.

Nothing would.

"Now, magicians . . ." Bélusz started; then his voice tailed off.

Ephraim lifted his gaze to the demon, determined to meet his death with as much bravery as he could muster.

"Watch," the demon commanded.

Ephraim couldn't stop feeling relief at his brief reprieve.

A single being trundled forward, carrying the dull lead tablet in its hand. More shadows covered this minion than most of the rest of the beings Ephraim saw. Ephraim stared hard at the thing, before he finally came to the conclusion that the creature had been a man once. Most of its flesh had rotted off and dull yellow bone showed through. A decaying blue velvet cap covered its ears. Only its eyes cut through the darkness: bright blue fanatical eyes.

"Ah, my lovely bringer. He brought me the first plaque, then broke it, thinking that would grant him power over me. Now he shall break the last, proving my power over him."

Was it Ephraim's imagination, or did something in the creature still fight Bélusz' control? The set of its bony shoulders showed defiance even as it complied with the demon's orders. It raised its right hand over its head, while cradling the tablet in the other. Ancient words spilled out of the hole it used for a mouth, harsh and guttural. It gestured toward the tablet, toward the stag, toward Bélusz.

The ancient magician placed the lead tablet on the ground at its feet and now raised both hands. A dark cloud gathered between its palms. Streaks of verdant green and gold flashed through the cloud. When the ball coalesced, it hesitated. It looked up at Bélusz.

"Do it. You must. I command you."

The creature struggled for a moment and cocked its arms back slightly, as if to throw the ball into Bélusz' face. Something—habit, or knowledge of the futility of not doing so—made it obey. It threw the blackness between its palms down onto the tablet. A sizzling sound filled the cavern as the plaque melted into the ground.

A loud crack, like thunder at the start of a storm, echoed through the chamber. Bélusz slid forward on its chair, making a sound like boulders shoved together. It gripped the arms of its throne and pushed itself to a standing position. The rest of the demons in the room froze. The bony thing that had broken the curse turned and looked with fresh pity at Ephraim.

The demon stood still for a moment before calling out, "I'm free!"

It kicked at the throne that had held it for so long. A sifting sound poured into the cavern, like sand through a giant sieve. The chair toppled and crumbled. The minions took this as their sign to start the celebration.

Bélusz stretched its arms out to its side slowly, as if testing every muscle in order. It raised its arms above its head, then abruptly brought its hands together, causing a loud cracking sound, like a thunderclap. It walked away from where it had been imprisoned, over to one of the large searchlights, warming its hands over it for a moment.

Ephraim couldn't bear to watch Bélusz. Not only was the demon's freedom a reminder of their failure, it sickened him to watch rock move in a way it shouldn't, the way the ground undulated during an earthquake.

János didn't pay any attention to Bélusz or its minions. He leaned over and whispered in Laci's ear. Zita strained forward as if trying to hear what they said.

No one watched Ephraim. Maybe he could get away. But what good would that do? Bélusz had its freedom. Mushroom clouds loomed on the horizon. Swirling ash would cover them all.

He didn't want to spend his last days deep underground. He wanted to get away before Bélusz remembered him and fulfilled its threats.

Ephraim flexed his hands behind his back. A breaking ritual blossomed in his mind, an up and down motion, requiring the full use of both his hands. He couldn't move how he envisioned. The ropes cut into his wrists too tightly.

He didn't think he could free himself. He couldn't see the ties that held him.

But he could see Zita's.

Maybe if he concentrated on how the ritual felt, rather than actually doing it, he could at least free her hands. He had to concentrate on the nuances of the motion, how the energy built from his center and flowed into his fingers, how it left behind a red residue, only to be overwashed with blue power again.

Ephraim closed his eyes, breathed deeply, and began the ritual, moving his hands in tiny increments. He watched the charge trickle out from his palms and gather itself into a ball. Then a thread of it crept away, around Ephraim, toward Zita.

Ephraim opened his eyes. A thin blue snake of power inched its way toward Zita's bonds. If it could wrap itself around the rope, it could follow the knots and loosen them. Ephraim concentrated on the ritual, pushing out bit by bit, continuing to pool his force with cool, untangled thoughts.

Ephraim saw János' foot come down, the heel of his boot cutting through the line of power, before Ephraim felt the sharp pain it brought. He gasped, shaken, his hands hurt, as if needles had been driven through both his palms.

"So, little man, you thought you would be her rescuer?" János bent down and hissed in Ephraim's face. "I think not. She will look only to *me*."

Ephraim sat back, blinking in surprise. He opened his mouth and shut it again. János wanted Zita? Why?

"Such children she will bear."

Had János really said that? He wanted Zita's children? Of course. They would be powerful magicians. She had so much magic herself, brimming with it. The luminance that came from her almost blinded Ephraim.

Her power came in a different form than his. She couldn't do rituals like he could. But she *saw* things, the true heart of any situation, any person. And something else, some kind of flame above her forehead—

János interrupted Ephraim's thought by saying, "Why not?" He held out his hand. Zita's bonds crawled away from her wrists. She pulled her hands in front of her and rubbed them. János put one hand on her head, tangled his fingers in her hair, and forced her to look up at him.

Ephraim stiffened at the bolt of amber light that shot from János' eyes into Zita's. What had János just done to her? What kind of spell had he just put her under?

"Soon," János said, patting her head. She nodded and sat back, complacent.

Bélusz' smooth voice broke through Ephraim's worry. "Let the transference begin!"

János walked up to the demon and knelt before it. What kind of trick was the old man up to now?

Bélusz put its hands above János' head and began a chant in a language Ephraim didn't understand. It sounded older than the ancient Hebrew he'd had to learn to satisfy his grandfather. It was also powerful, as if every word had magical roots. Slowly the demon lowered its hands. Static electricity made János' hair stand on end, reaching for the demon. Now the waving hair encased the rock fingers, a bed of seaweed covering a school of fish.

The demon's words grew louder. Flickers of yellow light shot out from its palms. János jerked slightly as they touched him, though he obviously tried to control himself.

The demon's hands moved down, inexorably, like continents moving together.

"Wait!" Laci called out, his voice a sudden roar through the cavern.

Bélusz stopped chanting. The echoes of the magic danced around the chamber, like the afterimages of a bright flash of light. Ephraim found he'd been holding his breath, waiting to see what would happen next.

"János is going to betray you. He plans to ruin the transference, so that when I die, you'll die."

The demon chuckled, a sound that sent chills down Ephraim's back. Zita continued to sit motionless. He wished he could see her face, see if the demon's chant had somehow broken János' spell.

"You thought I didn't know this?" Bélusz chuckled again. "His screams will drown yours."

János struggled to say something, "Bélusz, I—never—why would you believe—"

Bélusz reached down and put a finger over János' lips, a parody of gentleness. "Of course I knew. It amused me to let you have your plans. But you cannot stop this. You don't know what you thought you did."

"But, Father, I would never—"

The demon dismissed János with a wave of its hand. "No matter," it said, interrupting him.

Bélusz reached one hand up to its forehead and dug its fingers into its own skull, causing a rasping sound like a great file rubbed across stone. After more grinding, the demon removed its hand. A gaping fist-sized hole now brooded in the center of its forehead, where one of its eyes had sat, the one that had turned the sled to stone.

"Here," Bélusz said. With no additional ceremony, the demon smashed the eye into János' forehead.

János screamed. Blood poured down from the wound, overflowing his eyes and streaming down his cheeks like tears. The demon paid no attention to his struggles. It calmly put one hand behind the human's head and continued pushing with the other until it was satisfied.

"Very pretty. Now show your prize," it commanded.

János stood. His head wobbled, as if it were now too heavy for his neck. The blood had dried around the wound, as if heat from the demon's eye had cauterized the hole. The eye, about the size of a cue ball, shone wan and unsound. It blinked and gazed wildly around, independent of where János looked. Obviously, János did not control it.

"All the power you wanted. All yours. Enjoy it while you can. After you die, I will take it all back."

The demon turned away from János. "You know what happens next," it said to Laci.

Laci turned to Zita, who continued to gaze at János.

He sighed and nodded. With a hand, he gestured at the stag. "Here? Please?" he asked.

An unexpected tone rang through Laci's voice. Almost as if two people spoke at the same time. Ephraim watched the old man carefully. As he turned back toward the demon, he noticed Zita looking up at her grandfather. Ephraim could have sworn the briefest flicker of light passed between them. But it couldn't have been enough. Zita's gaze turned back away, toward János again. She was lost.

As were they all.

"Always honest, aren't you, little magician? I will grant you your wish, to be sacrificed on your great stag."

Laci nodded. Then, without another word, he climbed up onto the stag. He laid on his back, his arms spread, the perfect sacrifice. The fount of his life rose without bidding, the lion heads more fierce this time.

The demon walked up to Laci, the rock stretching and gaining height until it could look down easily on the old man. It reached out with one hand to touch Laci's fount, then hesitated.

"Human, you almost distracted me enough to kill you with my own hands. But that will not be. János," it called.

The augmented man, dazed, turned toward the sound of the voice. Ephraim wondered what else he saw with his new appendage. It seemed to overpower his normal vision. He walked like a blind man toward the demon, sensing where it stood with something other than his eyes.

The demon picked up the knife János had held to Laci's neck earlier. Then it put its hands around János' waist and raised him up level with Laci.

Without hesitation, János slashed at his old friend, severing his neck, stabbing his chest. The fount on Laci's chest suddenly spit blood. A great cyan light sprang from Laci as his power streamed out and wrapped around his prone body, trying to protect him. The light quickly faded. His life fount crumbled. Soon only an ordinary old man lay on the stag, dead. The blood that flowed from his wounds stained the back of the statue, turning the stone to the color of a living deer.

Bélusz lowered János. Then, casually, without preamble, it hit János' head hard, snapping his neck. It dropped the body on the ground and turned to the stag.

"Finally, I can destroy this beast," it said, its oily voice spreading over the statue and the room. "I've had to stare at it for so many centuries."

Then Bélusz turned to Ephraim. "Then you, *Magician*," it sneered.

The demon advanced on the stag. Zita sat immobile, staring at the statue. Ephraim didn't know what thoughts she had in her head. He didn't care what happened to him. He freed his own hands, a sudden twist of power, and crawled over to Zita, his knees reporting every rock they found.

Very carefully, he reached out to her. She stiffened when his hands touched her. Tears streamed down her face. Ephraim wished he could comfort for her, draw her into his arms and hide the scene before her eyes. He could only provide the simplest of touches and hope it would be enough, unsure if she wanted even that.

He looked over her shoulder at the stag. A lump formed in his throat, making it difficult to swallow or breathe. He'd never seen such a magnificent statue before. The blood spilled down its side seemed more like an accent, highlighting its vitality. No wonder so many poems and songs had been written about this stag.

Ephraim wanted to look away. He didn't want to see such beauty desecrated. It was all his fault. János had killed Laci. Ephraim made himself watch the upcoming desecration, made himself follow the demon's hand as it pulled back, made himself not turn away at the first blow.

Rock flew everywhere. A dust cloud rose. The demon

laughed. "My minions could never harm you. Now, finally, I can!" It reached out farther and struck again on the stag's side. Bélusz' fist sunk into the stone, as if Laci's blood had softened it.

Nothing happened for a moment; then Laci's body tumbled off the back of the stag. A sheet of rock dropped down, burying it. Zita drew in a slight breath, then let it out with a soft sigh. Ephraim placed his hand on her shoulder. She shook it off.

Ephraim returned his attention to the defilement, trying to distract himself from his breaking heart. He examined the stag and wondered if the rock had been porous, if Laci's blood had soaked in deeply, because underneath the layers of stone that Bélusz had dropped remained another layer, brown and smooth.

Bélusz screamed its displeasure. "Die!" it called out. It struck the neck of the stag with its other hand.

Zita suddenly stood up and went to the stag. Ephraim reached out a hand to her, then let it fall. Zita didn't go to the demon, to try to stop it. Instead, she struck the stag with her fists.

János had corrupted her.

Ephraim's world grew cold. Ash filtered into his heart as dust filled the cavern. No reason existed for him to try to escape now. No reason to live, as the demon had captured the true heart of his heart.

"Ephraim. Ephraim!"

He forced himself to look up. Zita had hooked her fingers under a layer of stone and pulled at it.

"Come help!"

She peeled off some of the cold gray rock on top, exposing more of the living brown layer.

Ephraim stood up. He understood what she did, why she attacked the stone of the statue.

Under the rock stood the Great Stag itself. Laci's blood had soaked through the stone and awoken the beast. His sacrifice hadn't been for nothing. How had he known? What else had the old man seen?

Now Bélusz and Zita had just freed it.

The demon screamed in pure terror as it backed up.

The golden light of the stag's eyes caught Bélusz, held it paralyzed. Daintily, the stag stepped beyond its stone prison.

Ephraim couldn't believe how powerful the stag looked. It moved with exquisite grace. Fully exposed to the air, it grew until it was twice the size the statue had represented. Ephraim had seen elk once when he'd visited relatives in Michigan. The stag made them seem like fawns.

The stag lowered its head and touched Bélusz' chest with the tip of one of its mighty antlers. The demon froze for a moment, its face distorted in a painful grimace. A shiver went through its body; then its arms crumbled and fell, like aged stone. Its head lolled from one side to the other, before it tumbled down to the ground. Pieces of rock flew from the demon's legs until they collapsed. Finally, the torso submitted to the pressure from the stag and disintegrated.

A sigh went up from the chorus of minions. Many of them clattered and fell, as bones held together by the demon's power disconnected one from another.

A great screeching filled the cavern as Turul the eagle came down from its perch. Ephraim caught his breath when it flew through one of the lights. He couldn't believe the change that had taken place. All of the ragged feathers had been replaced with fresh ones. Its great hooked beak shone adamant and black. Its talons no longer held a sickly gray color: now they looked white and sharp as knives. The eagle pounced on the collection of small rocks that had once been Bélusz, tore at them with its feet, and pecked at them with its beak. In a moment, it had dug down to what it wanted.

With a loud shriek, it announced its victory and pulled up an eye-shaped boulder in its claws. If Ephraim stared hard, he could see a man-shaped shadow surrounding the rock, as if the rock sat at its heart. With another loud caterwaul, the eagle took off, flying farther into the cave. Ephraim didn't know where the eagle went with Bélusz' soul, but he hoped

Turul would drop it down the deepest, darkest hole it could find.

The stag had taken only a few steps beyond the rock pile before Turul popped back into the cave. This time, with much more care, it pecked at and rolled the rocks away from the body of Laci. With its great talons, it gripped the old man's body. Zita had moved back from the rubble. Tears poured down her face. Slowly the eagle rose. A Laci-shaped shadow went with it. Suggestions of other forms—the corrupted minions possibly—streamed after the eagle as well. This time Turul flew straight up, through the cavern ceiling. Direct to heaven, Ephraim hoped, not only for Laci, but for all the souls of all the men corrupted by the demon.

The stag made a slow tour of the room, its golden eyes illuminating everything it saw. It gently stepped over piles of bones, heaps of broken stone, mounds of garbage. Its light snagged at the corrupt and broken cave pearls covering the walls.

In the far corner, something reflected the light back. Gold lay there, in the shape of platters, goblets, picture frames. Was this the treasure Ephraim's grandfather had told him about?

Ephraim gasped. The stag turned its head toward the sound, the light from its eyes blinding Ephraim. Ephraim stared as the glare grew brighter and brighter, overcoming everything else. The scent of rotten fur and false flesh fell away, borne on spring winds, gentle and balmy, carrying desert warmth and dryness.

Ephraim saw an image of himself running through washes like a wild thing, the sand and dirt beneath him sparkling like a path of diamonds. He veered and zigzagged without thought or concern, trusting his feet to take him where he needed to go. He realized the stag hadn't given him a vision as much as a memory from when he'd been a child. How could he have been so carefree?

He relived his bicycle accident, the pain of his fall.

He'd gained the long scar down his left arm and lost his freedom. Was the stag giving that back to him? A soft sigh fluttered onto his heart, cocooning it with warmth, giving it the strength to run free again, full of magic, worth, and love.

Ephraim withstood the stag's gaze pouring into him for as long as he could; then he had to close his eyes.

When he opened them, he found himself still blinded, only the light no longer shone golden. It was white, artificial, from the flashlight of a rescue worker. Ephraim didn't kneel in the center of a large cavern. He rested against the edge of a tunnel. Zita lay beside him, head twisted to the side.

"Zita!" Ephraim cried out. He couldn't lose her.

She opened her eyes slowly. The light of the rescuers illuminated her hair—the only gold Ephraim really needed. He smiled at her.

The man held out his hand to Zita, then to Ephraim, helping them to stand. Ephraim reached out and held Zita. He looked beyond her shoulder and stiffened involuntarily.

Laci lay there, covered with dirt and blood. Zita cried out and rushed to his side.

The man said something in Hungarian. Ephraim shook his head and asked, "English?"

"Nothing we can do. He's dead."

Ephraim nodded. Of course. He glanced around the cave. He didn't see János' body. Had the stag not brought it out? Or had some of János' men already spirited it away?

"Why are you here?" the man asked.

"To save him," Ephraim said, pointing at Laci with his chin. He paused. "He saved all of us instead."

Epilogue

Zita

Zita stood next to Ephraim, not saying anything. They stood on Fisherman's Bastion, on Castle Hill, overlooking Pest. They weren't too far from the Labyrinth, where they'd first met.

It seemed too bright, too cheery, for a funeral. An impossible blue stretched across the sky. A few white puffy clouds floated by in contrast. The Danube shone a glassy green, no wind chopping it up or setting the waves dancing. The Parliament stood across the river and just to the left of them, its dusty red dome and bright white spires lending it an air of majesty. Trees, verdant and lush, stood on this side of the river, while saffron, turquoise, and gray buildings marched into the horizon on the other.

Grandpa would have loved a day like this. If they'd been vacationing, they would have spent the morning wandering through the city and the afternoon in some street café, drinking red wine and solving the problems of the world.

Zita paused for a moment, her grief sucking away the brightness of the day. She'd cried so much already and knew that she'd mourn her grandfather for the rest of her life. She would always miss him, even if he had died stopping the demons so they could have bright blue skies. She wanted to believe her dreamtime vision of Turul carrying her grandfather's soul to heaven.

She couldn't stay much longer in Budapest. The city held too many things that she'd regret not sharing with her grandfather. She would have to come back after her grief had aged, to place snapdragons on his grave.

It had been surprisingly easy to get her grandfather buried here in his beloved Budapest. She wondered if his friend János had had anything to do with how easy it had been to get through all the red tape, if he still had some sort of power structure in place to take care of such things. She knew Bélusz had killed him, though his body had never been found. After a single sleepless night, she decided she didn't care. Her grandfather had come home. That was all that mattered.

Ephraim shifted and sighed. Zita glanced over at him. He leaned on his elbows looking over the edge. He held his hands together tightly, as if holding on to something. Zita had the impression of patience and waiting, as if he disciplined himself to it.

What could he be waiting for? She glanced at her watch. It had been several hours since the internment. She swallowed. Her throat was dried and parched, and her chin ached from clenching her teeth together, holding back the constant tears. It had also been several hours since she'd said a word. Maybe that was what he waited for.

She smiled. Ephraim had been so considerate, just following her around, being supportive, never intrusive. She'd relied on him a lot, then treated him without consideration.

She leaned over and bumped him with her shoulder. He glanced at her, a small smile touching his lips, filling his eyes.

"Hey," she said.

"Hey," he replied.

Silence ensued. He *was* waiting for her.

"Did I tell you what they marked down as the official cause of Grandpa's death?" she asked. It had infuriated her, but before she could do anything about it, the paperwork for the internment had gone through, and she'd had to bury the body. She'd never had any official paperwork cleared up so quickly; she suspected János' minions.

"No, what did they say?" Ephraim asked.

"Radiation poisoning. That's the official explanation

for everything, by the way. If we told anyone about seeing something down in the cave, they would tell us it was due to the toxic waste. The doctors would say we were having hallucinations. They've closed the cave and are applying for funds to clean it up."

Ephraim looked down at his hands for a moment before he drew himself up and faced Zita.

"Do you believe them?" he asked.

"What do you mean?"

"What do you think happened?"

Zita leaned against the balustrade and thought. She knew what she'd seen. She knew that it had all actually happened—Bélusz, the Miraculous Stag, the Great Eagle.

"I wonder," Zita said. Knowing it had happened, and accepting it, were two different things. It meant accepting that the man beside her could do magic. It meant acknowledging that she could see things now, such as when a person lied. It meant changing her definition of herself, a revisioning, a new interpretation. Going along with the official report would certainly be easier than loving a man who did magic like her grandfather, who possibly saw more than a normal person could, like she could.

"What do you think happened?" she asked Ephraim.

He laughed. "We'll never be able to prove anything. Everything we saw is gone. The only thing we can do is decide how to go on from here. Do we act as if nothing happened"—Ephraim paused and looked out over the city—"as if everything is unchanged?" He swung his gaze back and stared at Zita. "Or as if everything happened?"

The full import of his words struck Zita. She'd received an e-mail, if not apologetic, at least contrite, from Peter. She could return to her safe, comfortable life, so tightly strung together. She could return to her ex-boyfriend, her rock.

But Peter would bury her, weigh her down. He'd never encourage her to fly. He wouldn't understand that she didn't want to return to her precollege days, with the endless parties and drunken nights. She didn't want extremes. A new middle way had opened for her, the path she wanted to follow.

Zita took Ephraim's hand.

"I couldn't go back," she said. She pulled Ephraim down toward her. This particular direction, the one she chose now, may not last forever, but it was the trail she wanted to explore, at least for a while. She placed a whisper of a kiss on Ephraim's lips.

Doors to all the paths swung open at her choice. Endless places to go.

Zita couldn't wait to begin.

Bibliography

This is not a complete bibliography of all the research sources I used for this novel, but it is a good starting point for readers interested in Hungary and the other elements that make up this novel.

Nonfiction

Doernberg, Myrna. *Stolen Mind: The Slow Disappearance of Ray Doernberg*. Chapel Hill, NC: Algonquin Books of Chapel Hill, 1989.

Gager, John, ed. *Curse Tables and Binding Spells from the Ancient World*. New York: Oxford University Press, 1992.

Gadney, Reg. *Cry Hungary: Uprising 1956*. New York: MacMillan, 1986.

Gerö, András. *Heroes' Square Budapest: Hungary's History in Stone and Bronze*. Budapest, Hungary: Corvina, 1990.

Lukacs, John. *Budapest 1900: A Historical Portrait of a City and Its Culture*. New York: Grove Press, 1988.

Mace, Nancy L. and Peter V. Rabins, M.D. *The 36-Hour Day: A Family Guide to Caring for Persons with Alzheimer Disease, Related Dementing Illness, and Memory Loss in Later Life*. Baltimore: The Johns Hopkins University Press, 1982.

McClurg, David R. *Adventure of Caving*. Carlsbad, NM: D&J Press, 1996.

Middleton, John, and Tony Waltham. *The Underground*

Atlas: A Gazetteer of the World's Cave Regions. London: The Promotional Reprint Company, 1992.

Rapport, Judith L., M.D. *The Boy Who Couldn't Stop Washing: The Experience and Treatment of Obsessive Compulsive Disorder.* New York: Plume, 1989.

Memoir and Poetry

Denes, Magda. *Castles Burning: A Child's Life in War.* New York: W.W. Norton & Company, 1997.

Makkai, Adam, ed. *In Quest of the Miracle Stag: The Poetry of Hungary.* Champaign, IL: University of Illinois Press, 1996.

Michener, James A. *The Bridge at Andau.* New York: Random House, 1957.

Nyiri, János. Translated by William Brandon. *Battlefields and Playgrounds.* New York: Farrar, Straus and Giroux, 1995.

Polcz, Alaine. *A Wartime Memoir: Hungary 1944–1945.* Budapest, Hungary: Corvina, 1998.

Teglas, Csaba. *Budapest Exit: A Memoir of Fascism, Communism, and Freedom.* College Street, TX: Texas A&M University Press, 1998.

Myth

Ausubel, Nathan, ed. *A Treasury of Jewish Folklore.* New York: Crown Publishers, 1949.

Palkó, Zsuzsanna. Edited by Linda Dégh. Translated by Vera Kalm. *Hungarian Folktales: The Art of Zsuzsanna Palkó.* Jackson: University Press of Mississippi, 1995.

Petuchowski, Jakob J., ed. *Our Masters Taught: Rabbinic Stories and Sayings.* New York: Crossroad Publishing Company, 1982.

Róheim, Géza. *Hungarian and Vogul Mythology.* Seattle: University of Washington Press, 1966.

Weinreich, Beatrice Silverman, ed. *Yiddish Folktales.* New York: Pantheon Books, 1988.

Web Sources

Web sites come and go faster than waves on the Danube, but when last I checked (September 2003) all these sites were available.

Corvinus Library—virtual library of Hungarian history texts:
www.hungary.com/corvinus/
General index of Hungarian information:
www2.4dcomm.com/millenia/
A Hungarian language course:
www.people.fas.harvard.edu/~arubin/hungarian.html
General information about Hungary and Hungarian culture:
www.hungariansoup.com/
Online English to Hungarian and Hungarian to English dictionary:
www.freedict.com/onldict/hun.html
All about alchemy:
www.levity.com/alchemy/home.html
Traditions of magic in late antiquity:
www.lib.umich.edu/pap/magic/
Historical text archive:
http://historicaltextarchive.com/
A gallery of demons:
www.deliriumsrealm.com/delirium/mythology/demons.asp

Now Available in Paperback

Roc Science Fiction & Fantasy
COMING IN MAY 2004

CHOICE OF THE CAT
by E. E. Knight
0-451-45973-3

In Book Two of *The Vampire Earth*, David Valentine, a member of the human resistance, is sent on his first mission—to investigate a new force under the alien Reaper's control.

COVENANTS: *A Borderlands Novel*
by Lorna Freeman
0-451-45980-6

This exciting new series features Rabbit, a trooper with the Border Guards. But this trooper is different than the others—he is the son of nobility and a mage who doesn't know his own power.

NIGHTSEER
by Laurell K. Hamilton
0-451-45143-0

New York Times bestselling author Laurell K. Hamilton's spellbinding debut novel—a tale of a woman known as sorcerer, prophet and enchantress.

Three novels in one volume!

Dennis L. McKiernan's

THE IRON TOWER
0-451-45810-9

The diabolical Modru is sending forth his
sorceress Shadowlight to cloak the lands
in darkness. Against ravaging hoards,
men, elves, and dwarfs must stand united
to withstand the baleful influence of the
Shadowlight. This omnibus contains the
first three *Mithgar* novels:

The Dark Tide
Shadows of Doom
The Darkest Day

R406

SHADOWS AND LIGHT

by
Anne Bishop

SECOND IN THE TIR ALAINN TRILOGY

"Plenty of thrills, faerie magic, human nastiness,
and romance." —*Locus*

An encroaching evil threatens the lives of every witch,
woman, and Fae in the realm. And only the Bard,
the Muse, and the Gatherer of Souls possess the
power to stop the bloodshed.

0-451-45899-0

**Praise for *Pillars of the World*, Book I in the
Tir Alainn Trilogy:**
"Bishop only adds luster to her reputation for fine fantasy."
—*Booklist*
"Reads like a beautiful ballad involving two humans who
believe love is the ultimate magical force in the universe...Fans
of romance and fantasy will delight in this engaging tale."
—*Book Browser*

Available wherever books are sold, or
to order call: 1-800-788-6262

R421

$$\begin{array}{r} {}^{61}2\,6 \\ 1\,7 \\ \hline {}^{9}\quad 9 \end{array}$$